Madeleine Orrick was born in Hampshire and has lived there all her life. She has a close-knit family of one son, two daughters, six grandchildren and five great-grandchildren. She has been a widow for eight years and since then has lived alone enjoying many other pastimes as well as writing, which include spending time with her young granddaughter, walking with the family and their dogs, gardening, home improvement and craft work.

ANDERS FULL CIRCLE

By the same author

Anders Folly
Vanguard Press (2009)
ISBN: 978 1 84386 426 3

Anders Heritage
Vanguard Press (2011)
ISBN: 978 184386 653 4

Madeleine Orrick

ANDERS FULL CIRCLE

Vanguard Press

VANGUARD PAPERBACK

© Copyright 2013
Madeleine Orrick

A CIP catalogue record for this title is
available from the British Library.

ISBN 978 1 84386 751 7

Vanguard Press is an imprint of
Pegasus Elliot MacKenzie Publishers Ltd.
www.pegasuspublishers.com

First Published in 2013

Vanguard Press
Sheraton House Castle Park
Cambridge England

Printed & Bound in Great Britain

To my son Steven x
God bless

Acknowledgement

My thanks to Robert Judkins at Pegasus Elliot MacKenzie Publishers for his patient attention to detail and kindly guidance. A gentleman. Very reassuring to work with. My idea of a perfect editor. Thank you Robert.

List of characters

Gerald Anders – owner of Anders Folly.
Darren Anders – Gerald's grandson.
Samantha and Timothy – Darren's twin children
Mellisa – wife of Darren. Jack – their son
Francesca – Darren's half-sister
Adam Wesley – Francesca's husband.
Robert, James, William, Philipa and Celine – their children.
Charles and Felicity – Gerald's half brother and his wife.
Sophie and Matthew – daughter and son-in-law to Charles and Felicity.
Abigail – family nurse maid,
Lorna and George – housekeeper and manservant to Gerald.
Maisie, Dora and Mary – Lorna's nieces – daily help. Daveth – handyman.
Sol and Ella – stable manager and his wife.
Bryn – Samantha's college days' sweetheart
Jocelyn – Bryn's fellow student.
Meg – personal assistant to Samantha.
Luke Hathaway – an American businessman.
Kellie – wife to Luke. Kimberley– their daughter.
William Jessop – owner of London clinic.
Ann Murry – sister to William Jessop, old friends of Pamela Anders.
Colin Murry – Alexander's partner in Anders Folly.
Mike and Nicole Jennings – friends of Fran and Adam, living in America
Chas Cartwright – Luke's boyhood friend and business helper.
William Spencer – managing director of Anders Motors.
Monica Spencer, alias Monique Langloise alias Barbara Hayle – his wife.
Peter Chambers – William's nephew and top salesman at Anders Motors.
Lindsey Chambers – Peter's wife and Monica's daughter.
Wendy Parker – private secretary to William Spencer
Amy Bishop – successor to Wendy.
Simon Hall – retired manager of Anders Motors.
Emanuel Lorenzo – property dealer in Tenerife. Pablo – his son.
Yana – sister to Emanuel Lorenzo.

CHAPTER ONE

MARCH 2008

The ice blue sports car sped along the Cornish coast road, slowing down as the turning into the narrow, private lane dropped gently away and the rambling, stone built house came into view. Sprawling comfortably in its surrounding acres with the sea sparkling in the background, it wore an unfamiliar, shuttered look.

A sob caught in Samantha's throat at the sight of the drawn blinds. Why had she allowed herself to think it could be otherwise? Nothing could ever be the same again. She pulled onto the verge and stopped the sports car's powerful engine as tears blinded her. It was the first time she had returned to Anders Folly since that dreadful day when Grandfather had been laid to rest beside other family members, most of whom she had never known. Just a few, short months ago, she had never wanted to see her childhood home ever again, but drastic changes had brought her hurrying back to the one place where she felt safe; her childhood home where love and loyalty filled her life. There had been times when she had foolishly felt smothered and desperate to get away. Now it was a much needed haven, the only place she wanted to be; sure in her own mind that just to sit in Grandfather's chair and feel his presence would help her come to terms with the undreamt of events that had turned her young life upside down.

*

Many changes had taken place in the two years leading up to the death of Gerald Anders. Matthew and Sophie had filled the house with music and dreams of even better things to come, while Gerald watched, content with the apparent, longed for, safe future of his beloved home.

Charlotte had been there enjoying her twilight years, which had gone from being the quiet, lonely existence in Hampshire to a veritable luxurious whirl of cosseting and attention from a loving family. Her bright, intelligent observations and the fact that she never missed a chance to learn more of the family history seemed to unite them around her. Stories were unearthed that would never have been told and the younger members were enthralled to hear about Alexander's exploits, which seemed to vary according to the teller. Abigail, his staunch defender would skirt around his shortcomings while Charles and Gerald looked on sceptically, accepting that perhaps it was for the best if the worst of his misdemeanours were kept from young ears. James in particular was very curious about the yacht parties and thought it would be a great idea to anchor a boat in the bay again, with a sign on the gangplank saying, no one over sixteen allowed onboard. At twelve years old he was sympathetic towards Alexander's distain for authority; and his ideas on how to live were, 'dead cool', he told his brother Robert.

Going about his duties George overheard and gave a shiver, remembering Alexander's sly, wilful ways and the trouble he had caused his family; recognising all too well the tell tale signs in his present day clone, because the likeness didn't stop there; James had the same well built frame, curly auburn hair and slate grey eyes.

"If 'e didn' 'ave that mop o red 'air, we'd see three sixes on the back of 'is neck – I reckon," he would confide to Lorna.

Lorna would always smile and give her usual reply. "You reckon?" unconvinced that any child could be as bad as Alexander.

Charlotte's passing, just after her one hundred and fourth birthday, brought much sadness but as Charles said, when he thanked them all in his final tribute to her, "We must be glad we were able to make her last years the happiest she had ever known."

Less than a year later, disaster struck, when Matthew was found to have leukaemia. In a state of shock, he and Sophie decided the best treatment would be available in America; and within a short space of time, they returned to their family, leaving Felicity and Charles to cancel bookings and attend to any other details.

Matthew had suggested passing the management of the musical retreat over to a fellow musician but Gerald would not hear of it.

"I couldn't have strangers running the place. It wouldn't be the same and in any case you will be back when you have completed your treatment," Gerald had claimed optimistically, endeavouring to convince himself that, that would surely be the case.

Two months went by without news but the treatment was lengthy and complicated and according to the consultant, there were many avenues to go down; they must be patient. It was then that Felicity and Charles decided they must go to America and stay as long as it took; Sophie was in bits and needed them. Gerald was devastated and although he sent them on their way with his blessing, he sunk into a deep depression, his hopes dashed yet again in his seemingly never-ending struggle to secure the future of his home, plus the loneliness of only Abigail and himself to share the long evenings.

In desperation, Charles contacted Samantha. "We have faced this situation before," he told her. "He needs a new direction; one that will give him hope and you are possibly the only one who can satisfy that need. It could also be a wonderful career for you," he added, optimistically ignoring his misgivings about Gerald's ambitious plans for her, in an effort to make up for not being there himself, to see Gerald through this bad patch.

Afraid of losing her grandfather, in his present state of depression, Samantha turned down the place she had recently secured in the London University and agreed to join the family firm. She had the satisfaction of seeing his spirits lift and George reported daily that he was sleeping better. Going to Southampton straight away meant giving up the holidays she had been looking forward to, but Bob and Marcia offered her a home with them, so that she wouldn't be amongst total strangers; and the biggest plus there, of course, was that she could ride in the evenings.

Things went ahead without any problems; she settled into the routine of the Southampton offices and travelled home at the weekends when she would spend Saturday evenings with Gerald in his study. He never tired of hearing about the new methods introduced since his day, even though he disagreed with most of them, which led to lively discussions. At the end of the evening she would leave the study and exchange a little smile with George as he held the front door open for her.

"'E'll sleep tanight Miss."

"That's the plan George."

Although not her chosen career, she enjoyed life in a big city. There were young people in the vast office block, and in time, she hoped to get to know some of them, although her exalted position of, having her own office and the title of 'trainee manager' did have its drawbacks.

Peter Chambers, the top sales representative appeared to have no problem with her being the big boss's great-granddaughter. He was very attentive, and free with advice, which he considered the key to his success.

"Look sincere and enthusiastic – convince the customers that you have their best interests at heart," he explained, teasing her about toughening up and learning a few tricks of the trade for when she became the big boss.

"Plenty of time for that," she had answered as they stood together in her office one day.

He had looked at her intently. "Maybe you're right. I like you as you are."

She blushed and her stomach somersaulted as he moved closer but a knock on the door saved her from discovering what his intention was, as Wendy the managing director's personal assistant entered with a folder.

"Your signature is needed on these documents, Miss Anders. I will leave them on your desk. Are you ready for your coffee yet?"

"Yes, thank you, Wendy," she replied briskly, returning to her desk.

Wendy left the door open and returned instantly with a tray; placing it on the desk, she turned to Peter. "Mr Spencer was asking for you ten minutes ago Mr Chambers."

He was gone in an instant with a hasty goodbye.

"Mr Chambers knows to say how high when Mr Spencer says jump," she said with an unreadable expression, reminding Samantha of Miss Jean Brodie without the Scottish accent.

"How clever," Samantha murmured opening the folder. Pen poised she scanned the sheets of paper and gave a small frown.

"These would appear to need the assistant manager's attention Wendy, not mine."

"That's right, Miss Anders." Wendy retrieved the folder and turning as she reached the door, smiled broadly. "These are only copies. Well done!"

"Just testing," Samantha said through pursed lips as the door closed. How often had granddad tested her in similar ways? "I can see it isn't only my ability that is going to be well and truly tested but my patience as well," she said aloud to the framed photograph of her grandfather, on her desk.

As he had done many times before, Gerald bounced back and over the next three months, it became evident to Samantha that she was being speedily groomed by Wendy to take over, but why the rush, she asked him one evening.

"The quicker the better; by the time you are twenty-one I want you fully capable of taking over the family business; that way you won't have time to get bored and opt for another career like my eldest son. *You* are going to be the one who *won't* disappoint me."

After that statement, the need to live up to his expectations drove her on. Of course, her father was the rightful successor but he had made it very clear that he would prefer not to have the responsibility.

On the one occasion when he had spoken up in her defence, he had backed down quickly when it was suggested that he should take her place.

"Just go easy on her; she is only eighteen," he had ended feebly.

Gerald had been scathing. "At eighteen she's got more business sense than any of the male Anders; your sister Francesca is the only other capable one and she is too wrapped up in that family of hers to be of help.

"Perhaps she is just content to be a wonderful mother," Darren, defended hotly.

"Perhaps you are right," Gerald had relented seeing his miserable expression.

"Don't upset yourself; I will only ask what I know Samantha is capable of."

It had been left like that and true to his word, Gerald paved the way and put opportunities in her way without realising how she would turn them to the firm's advantage. Trips abroad, to introduce her to buyers for the export market were combined with visits to top fashion houses and as Sir Gerald Anders' granddaughter, she attracted a lot of attention. Her picture appeared in glossy magazines, wearing fabulous outfits from top designers, which she was allowed to keep – and she always made sure the name Anders Motors was in evidence. Gerald's confidence in her soared and in a short space of time she was known as Samantha Anders, and shortly after that just, 'Samantha'. She was cosseted and dined and although friendly to everyone, never went out alone. Her personal assistant, for these trips, was a no-nonsense woman in her mid thirties, chosen by Wendy. Two fashion houses offered Samantha modelling jobs at astounding salaries, but she turned them down, knowing the life wasn't for her; she much preferred life at Bob and Marcia's, joining in the horse jumping practice and promising herself that in the spring she would saddle one of the horses and ride through the forest. Solitary rides with only Nocturn and the dogs for company were what she missed most, except for Bryn, her constant companion through their college days together.

Sitting on the window seat in her bedroom one evening, she watched the rain falling steadily on the driveway and smiled to herself, picturing Bryn's lopsided grin and serious brown eyes that crinkled at the corners when he smiled. Bryn was studying to be a doctor; they kept in touch but couldn't be sure when their paths would cross because he was in London, a hundred miles away. All through college, he had understood her reluctance to take their friendship further. They were both still very young with ambitious careers ahead of them; that had always been her excuse but he knew about her ordeal when she was fourteen and the scars it had left and was content to just have her company until the time was right. He had won her trust as no other boy could have.

They wrote to each other frequently about their new lives and Bryn wrote that he hoped Samantha's sophisticated lifestyle wouldn't change her. He found it hard to believe that the glamorous image, in the magazines on sale in the newsagents, was the girl he had gone to college with only months ago, and his friends were well impressed; but he worried, aware that no matter how worldly she looked, she was still apprehensive in male company.

For her part, Samantha was not sure how she felt about Bryn's new friends. He was obviously enjoying the life and had made a particular friend of a fellow medical student.

He wrote: *'Jo is good fun and we are planning a trip to France at half term with another four students. We also have seasonal jobs lined up for Christmas. None of us has ever waited at table before, but the money will help. It means I won't be coming home to Cornwall until the summer holidays after all, as Easter is already booked for a tour of London, so hope you will be home sometime during July and August when we can get together.'*

She wrote back suggesting perhaps she could arrange to be in France at the same time, and was disappointed by his reply that they would be back-packing and couldn't be sure of being in a particular area.

Assuming that he would have jumped at the chance to see her, her next letter was short and accusing; consequently, Bryn's reply was several weeks in coming; and when it did, she was taken aback by his remarks.

'Dear Sam, You know I value our friendship above almost everything, but our lives are oceans apart now. Yours is full of meeting glamorous people and sharing the excitement of big business with them. At the same time, you are secure in the protection of your family. It is a great chance for you and I wish you every happiness and success. Mine on the other hand has the pressure of study and exams which I am enjoying, but the need to relax and unwind is important and I am lucky enough to have found good companions who share my needs; please don't begrudge me this as I was really disappointed by your decision not to come to university. I will always remain your true friend, no matter how many others come into my life. Love as always, Bryn.'

She had written back immediately, apologising for her selfishness but it brought home to her even more, how privilege can separate.

They continued to write although less frequently and in the meantime, life held many changes for her. Peter now popped in daily, as a matter of course and occasionally they ate lunch together. It was flattering to have his full attention when other girls and women were doing their best to catch his eye. His dark good looks and challenging light grey eyes made him a great favourite with the female staff. He always behaved impeccably towards her when people were around, but when they were alone he would flirt outrageously, making no effort to hide his desire. And the more she kept him at arm's length the more interested he became, because in his experience, women didn't stiffen up and move away when he made a pass – quite the opposite in fact; so it was just a matter of finding the right approach, he consoled himself. This in mind, he invited her to dinner and took her to a nightclub.

"I thought you said we were going to eat," she said in an accusing voice, overcome with panic as she saw couples moving together on a postage stamp, sized dance floor.

"We are, but this way we can enjoy a shuffle between courses," he said placing a familiar hand on her hip.

"I don't dance," she said removing his hand.

"Anybody can dance with me," he teased.

"I didn't say I couldn't, I said I don't." Her voice was shrill even to her own ears, and as she turned to leave, he caught her arm.

"What's the matter? I'm not bothered about dancing I assumed it would please you. Don't go; we can just eat if that's what you want."

His grey eyes pleaded with her and she took a deep breath, forcing herself to relax. He had obviously planned the evening to please her and wasn't to know about her bad memories of dancing, so she nodded and walked towards a small, round table, away from the dance floor.

The evening went quickly; he seemed to have an endless repertoire of funny stories and jokes which he told well, messing the punch line up on purpose sometimes to make her laugh even more. The food was mediocre and she suspected it looked better in the dimness of their surroundings than it would have done otherwise, but she enjoyed herself and just ignored his surprised expression when she refused wine. He ordered a bottle of House Red and asked her, was she sure when pouring his own.

"Very sure thank you," she said in a voice that he was quickly learning to accept without question.

Mmm, no dancing, no drinking. What next? he asked himself, studying her guardedly in the candlelight. This could be a tough one. He had watched as she purposely chose a seat with her back to the dance floor, leaving him without hope and hiding his disappointment as he watched other smooching couples. If he could only hold her, he knew he could make her relax. He had met girls who needed a bit of persuasion but never one quite as cool as this one. Time will tell though, he assured himself, relishing the challenge.

At half past eleven, he said, "Better get you home before twelve, Cinderella; we've got an early start in the morning. We must do this on a weekend next time."

"I go home on the weekends." She smiled apologetically.

"Can't you make an exception – just for me?" He looked deep into her green eyes as she stared back, reluctantly half persuaded by his half teasing, half serious pleading.

"Perhaps," she faltered.

They parted in the car park. He had suggested leaving early, in the hope that they would sit in his car for a while and get to know one another better, but she said she wanted to get back before lights out at 'The Vintage'.

"Back to boarding school eh?" he joked.

She flushed in the darkness, sensitive to the jibe and he realised his mistake as she quickly got into her car with an abrupt, "Thank you for a nice evening; see you in the morning."

Pulling away as he stood there, she dwelt on his remark, questioning in her own mind, whether living at the Equestrian Centre gave her a bad image.

In her position most girls would have their own flat she supposed; after all, she would be nineteen soon.

CHAPTER TWO

Darren settled back on the well-filled feather cushions of the settee and watched Jack playing with a dumper truck. It was his favourite toy in spite of Darren's efforts to introduce him to aeroplanes.

He and Melly had enjoyed living in the cottage for the last two years but he couldn't see it as a place where he wanted to spend the rest of his life.

He and Melly had talked of moving to America; but that was before Matthew had been diagnosed with cancer. It was impossible to leave Grandfather, now that Charles and Felicity had also gone, and Sam needed them here as well he thought dolefully; so when would he ever be free to live his own life? Anders Folly seemed to have a strangle hold on him he reflected, not for the first time sympathising with his father Robert; understanding more and more his reasons for breaking away to follow his own dream. It was hard to imagine his mild mannered father standing up to Grandfather – must have been pretty serious to make him leave and change his name though, and they would probably never know the whole truth.

When he first arrived at Anders Folly, Fran told him how she and the children came to be there and that Grandfather had forbidden any mention of the subject; it was to be left that Robert was her father; and they agreed never to talk about it again.

The air delivery business had taken all of his attention after that and he hadn't wanted to know about more family skeletons. Finding out he had family other than Fran and the children had been shock enough. Melly didn't know Alexander was Fran's father; maybe he should tell her sometime. Adam obviously knew. Charles and Felicity had never broached the subject and he would certainly never ask them. It was best left in the past; bad enough to have an uncle like Alexander without his decadent ways being bandied about by all and sundry, if the likes of James ever got to know—

Melly interrupted his thoughts: noting his morose expression as she sat down beside him.

"Cheer up it can't be that bad."

He smiled, drawing her into the circle of his arm.

"We'll get there when the time is right," she said guessing his thoughts. Resting her head against his shoulder, they watched Jack crashing his truck against the armchair, laughing gleefully when the bricks shot out.

"Little thug," Darren said fondly as Melly laughed and got up saying:

"Come along little one, bath-time."

Jack got up and ran to the stairs. Bath-time was his very favourite game.

Darren watched them disappear, Melly counting the stairs as they went up. She was such a wonderful wife and mother, he should just be content with the life they had. He thought about his father again. Had he ever regretted his decision to break away from his family? There certainly wasn't any sign if he had. They had been a close family, content with their full life. People from all walks of life had frequented the spacious bookshop, with its shelves stacked from floor to ceiling and quiet corners to read in. He himself had not appreciated it at the time; his only interest had been in flying but Fran had loved the whole scene, he remembered. She took after Dad, never happier than when taking stock or filling shelves. What a blow it must have been to her to have to give it up when their parents died – and yet she had never complained, had always been there for him, even to comforting and caring for the twins after their mother died. He dwelt again on his father not being Fran's. What a well kept secret it was in this complex family; and what a pity, in some ways that it had ever been revealed; good job it was never talked about now; Sam and Tim didn't know and he didn't want them to. Even Charlotte's probing had never brought that secret out.

'Oh what a tangled web we weave', he murmured.

Splashes and tears of indignation broke into his thoughts and he knew bath-time was over. He pushed himself out of the chair and started up the stairs calling, "I'm coming to get you." There was a moment of whispering before Jack went whizzing past the top of the stairs, his little body still dripping with bath water as giggling and shouting he raced around the bedroom and went to hide in the same place as always. Fran stayed to tidy the bathroom and Darren, taking the big towel she passed him proceeded to catch and dry his squirming son. Half an hour later, an exhausted Jack was asleep and they returned downstairs, where Darren poured them a glass of wine and turned on the television.

"If this is as bad as it gets until we can start a new life, it isn't too hard to bear is it?" Melly saw he had resumed the downcast expression and gave a sympathetic smile.

"I have just got this horrible feeling that if I don't get away soon I will end up taking on the whole blessed lot, forever."

"Not now, you won't. Sam is being trained to take over."

"You mean because she has sacrificed her dream to appease Grandfather?"

"Don't be so hard on him. She made the decision and she is going to end up a very wealthy young woman."

"That's not the point. Grandfather always wins one way or another."

"Is that what is really bugging you?" Melly looked annoyed.

"No, well, yes. There was only one person who ever stood up to him and won, and even then, Grandfather turned the tables after Dad died; and now he is driving Sam to do the very thing Dad refused to."

Melly shook her head in confusion. "You are going to drive yourself mad if you go on thinking like this."

For the rest of the evening she refused to talk about it and Darren sat in dejected silence.

The following morning after Darren had left for work, Melly dressed Jack, put him in the car and headed for the coast road.

As usual, Fran's house was a hive of activity with Mary the daily help vacuuming the sitting room and Fran knee deep in washing and ironing.

"You look as if something's up; I'll make coffee," Fran greeted her switching the iron off.

Melly lifted Jack over the baby gate into the playroom where he went off happily to play with the twins. "Don't let me stop you."

"Oh please do," Fran said thankfully.

Over coffee, Melly unburdened her worries and only realised she had put her foot in it when Fran asked in a quiet voice, "So – when did you and Darren think you might mention this great plan of yours?"

"It isn't a plan, it's just something we talked about because Darren's got it in his head that he will never get away from under his grandfather's thumb unless we go a long way away, and that isn't possible because we can't leave Sam."

Tears rolled down Melly's lovely face and Fran, realising how difficult and defeatist her brother could be when he was frustrated, bit back angry words.

"Don't cry. I will speak to Darren. I'm glad he at least understands that Sam needs you around for now."

Melly looked pleadingly at her and she rolled her eyes.

"Oh don't worry, I won't let on that you told me about going to America. Come to dinner on Saturday evening and we'll bring it up in conversation."

Melly hesitated. "Sam will be home, but she always spends the evening with Grandfather anyway."

"I'll invite them as well; it will give the poor girl a break from talking shop. Does she know about this plan?" Fran poured more coffee in to their cups as Melly shook her head.

"I know Grandfather can be relentless but what if he and his father hadn't cared enough to provide a wonderful family home? It must be pretty awful to have it all thrown back in his face by two sons, and now Darren, who it has to be said wouldn't be as comfortably set up as he is, without Grandfather's help. Even Tim has everything his little heart desires without lifting a finger – bless him – to go off wherever he wants without a care in the world; study any darn thing he wants without earning a penny, knowing he never has to worry about where his next meal will come from or who will pay the bills. Can you blame Grandfather for latching onto the only member of the family who, not only has the ability but also actually takes an interest? She has my undying gratitude and admiration."

It was a long speech and, Melly sat glued to the spot, before saying faintly:

"I didn't realise you felt so strongly. I never thought of it like that."

"Why would you when no one else does? I'm as bad; Grandfather has tried to get me involved many times but Adam and I want our family to come first. It must seem to him though, that the family doesn't want what he has spent a life time building for them."

Melly was silent. She had come for help in what now seemed like a minor problem compared to the larger picture. "Poor man," she said at last, feeling that she had just had a lesson in growing up which she shouldn't have needed.

"Darren has been saying for a long time now that he should be responsible for his own children. Well talk is cheap. It's time to put his money where his mouth is and pay for the cottage where he lives rent free, and for Tim's expenses, if he is so convinced that he wants to be independent."

Fran hadn't meant to be so outspoken but she was hurt that Darren could want to go to live in America and hadn't even mentioned it. It hurt her to say those things about her brother but it was time he recognised, how much had been done for him and stop whinging about the compromises he had to make.

Melly was looking wide-eyed. She had never heard Fran say a single bad word against her brother and she suddenly saw their position in a different light.

Fran regretted her outburst instantly, after all, it wasn't fair that Melly was getting the rough edge of her tongue; she should have pointed these things out to

Darren a long time ago, when he first started feeling sorry for himself and blaming life at Anders Folly for everything that went wrong.

"Sorry," she murmured. "That wasn't fair."

"But you're right." Melly had stopped crying. "Being an Anders is all we have to do to receive his generosity. What a burden to take on yourself."

"He doesn't see it like that," Fran assured her.

"That makes it even worse." Melly rose from the table. "Thanks. As always, you've put things in perspective. I shall tell Darren what you have said, in my own words and trust he will see that running away to America isn't the answer."

Melly suddenly sounded positive and reassured as she went to gather a screaming Jack from the playroom and feeling a little shamefaced Fran suggested leaving him to play with the girls while Melly did her shopping.

"Are you sure? That would be good," Melly, said gratefully, quickly putting her small son back over the safety gate, whereupon he promptly stopped yelling and ran back to the indoor slide. Melly and Fran exchanged resigned smiles and Fran invited her to stop for lunch when she came back to pick Jack up.

Melly hugged her. "You are a sister-in-law in a million, do you know?"

"So are you," Fran returned. "Now off you go or I will never get finished."

Left alone, Fran thought about her brother. She had known for a long time he didn't want the responsibility of Anders Folly but was he actually so scared that he would run away to America? Grandfather would be devastated.

Saturday arrived and when they had finished the Salmon and Prawn fish pie, topped with mash potato, served with Anders Folly fresh vegetables, Darren cleared his throat and said hesitantly:

"Melly says she has told you Fran and I don't know if you have said anything to Grandfather or Sam but I thought I should clear the air."

Fran nodded approval and assured him that she hadn't said anything.

"It's something we have talked about, that's all," he assured them earnestly. "It's not something I would keep to myself if plans had been made. I want you to believe that."

"I take it you are talking about going to America," Gerald said calmly as Samantha gave a cry of dismay.

"You knew?" Fran was flabbergasted.

"Darren has been thinking about it, since the first time he flew Matthew over to sort his family out," Gerald answered complacently, nodding absently to Adam who was offering him more wine.

"I thought you would be gone by now but I have to say I'm glad you are still here m'boy; we would all miss you both and little Jack. Can we hope that you have changed your mind?"

"Please say you have Daddy; Mamma, say you don't want to go."

"It's just something Daddy wants to try one day, Sam, but certainly not while you still need us."

"I'll always need you," Sam said woefully. "America is so far away."

"You can forget it for the foreseeable future Princess," Darren assured her, his courage failing him at the look on her face.

Fran and Adam exchanged glances, glad that the need for her to bring the subject up had been avoided. Melly, catching the look, smiled and got up to help clear the dinner plates, saying, "We mustn't, spoil this lovely dinner, with all this doom and gloom," as Fran placed a huge Pavlova on the table, to a chorus of oohs and the conversation took a more cheerful turn.

Noting Darren's downcast expression, Gerald knew that the subject of America was only shelved for the time being, to placate Samantha. Just as long as nothing interrupted *her* progress in the firm though, he could live with Darren's rejection.

"This is as good as Marie's," he complimented Fran.

"Praise indeed; thank you Grandfather," Fran said flushing with pleasure.

"Yes," he nodded.

It always pleased her that he enjoyed a meal in their home, which was so totally different to what he was accustomed to; there were no servants or elegant dining room, just the homely atmosphere of the kitchen. Albeit, it was always tidied for the occasion and looked quite different from normal, earning remarks like, 'have I come to the wrong house?' or 'Sir Gerald must be coming', from Adam.

As if reading her thoughts Gerald said, "It always reminds me of Marie, when I come to you. We ate in the kitchen most of the time, before Grandma agreed to have help. That was when Lorna joined us – and then Maisie came," he reminisced his eyes glazing over.

"The good old days Gerald," Adam said nostalgically, rising and refilling his wine glass again.

"Yes, we had good times around that table and you will have the same, God willing." Gerald raised his glass. "To the future, whatever it holds and may you always share good fortune with the ones you love."

CHAPTER THREE

Christmas was the quietest one Anders Folly had known in many years. Only Fran and Darren's families came for the two days and stayed just for Christmas night. Timothy had remained in Egypt where he and Nigel had just joined a new 'Dig', having decided that as he would be coming home for a month in the summer he wouldn't be missed, which of course upset Darren and Samantha but Gerald once again was strangely unmoved.

"He is a young man; and men have to do what men have to do," he quoted to their long faces.

"So if I decide to shoot off, that will be alright will it, Granddad?" Samantha spoke hastily in her disappointment and regretted it immediately when she saw the alarm on Gerald's face.

"It's alright, I'm not going to," she added more softly watching his expression turn to one of relief.

"And if I want to go to America?" Darren challenged.

"I think you already know my view on that." Gerald frowned, glancing quickly at Samantha, knowing the remark would upset her, but she was staring out of the window, her attention caught by Sol, leading four ponies with children on their backs down to the cove.

"I must go. Sol could do with a hand…" She dropped a kiss on Gerald's cheek. "See you later Daddy," she called on her way out of the door.

Winter wore on, with January and February cold and misty, then March brought the proverbial winds followed by slightly warmer April days and then suddenly it was summer and Samantha was arranging two weeks' holiday in August, to be in Cornwall for Bryn's summer break. She could hardly contain her excitement at the thought of seeing him again, having realized how much she missed him, wanting to strengthen the bond between them.

For their nineteenth birthday in July, Gerald opened generous bank accounts for both of them, and he also gave her a seat on the board. Now she felt much more a part of the business and did her best to understand the procedures. There were times though when she suspected they were being made unnecessarily complicated to confuse her. The executives were politely patronising she thought and William Spencer, the managing director was downright dismissive, making it clear that in his opinion she was far too young to be given a voice or taken seriously.

Wendy Parker was watchful as ever, rescuing her from embarrassing situations; loyal to Gerald's wishes as always; but then suddenly, Wendy wasn't there any more.

At fifty-eight Wendy was close to retirement and considered herself one of the old-school, having been with the Anders family business for thirty-nine years; longer than any of the present board members she often reminded herself with a satisfied smile. Simon Hall had been the manager when she had started work just after her seventeenth birthday and she had watched the firm grow and expand under him until he retired. It hadn't been easy working under new people with new ideas, but she had taken it all in her stride. She had always been Gerald's eyes and ears after his accident and was still excellent at her job, having moved with the times by learning the necessary skills to work the new office equipment; and keeping up with younger staff, who, although inclined to laugh at her meticulous ways, nevertheless, respected her abilities.

There was one girl however, who considered she would be better at Wendy's job and constantly watched for her early retirement.

Amy Bishop was always immaculate with long, dark hair neatly caught up in a clip and a crisp white blouse under a smart business suit. She was good at her job, and always kept herself to herself, so it came as a jolt to Wendy when Amy first started offering to do things for her. In a loud, patronizing voice she would say things like, 'let me do that, it's too heavy for you.' At the same time, relieving Wendy of a bulky file she was carrying. Then when Wendy was taking Samantha's coffee up to her, she would say, 'you shouldn't be running up and down stairs at your age; I'll do it my legs are younger than yours.' Always in the hearing of other staff, always with a sympathetic smile.

At first, Wendy was at a loss to know how to deal with the constant references to her age, aware that the remarks were having their intended effect on the girls under her, until one evening, as they were closing down their computers, she said loudly enough for them all to hear:

"I'm not past it yet Amy, and I don't intend to retire for another eight years."

Smiling around at the surprised faces, she went briskly into her office, closed the door behind her and lent against it, picturing Amy's dull-red face as she picked up her handbag and marched out of the office with:

"Well that's the last time I offer to help her," as the other girls sniggered.

But, Wendy had made an enemy, and was completely unprepared for her next move.

Memos started going astray, invoices were wrong, and three letters, privately addressed to William Spencer, turned up, already opened, on Samantha's desk. This was bad for Wendy because she was the only one to handle his private mail, which on his strictest orders was to be left, unopened on his desk. No other staff entered his domain in his absence, so only Wendy was responsible for his post going astray. She received a severe warning, but when the same thing happened again, and yet more faults caused complaints from customers, Wendy was suspended.

Samantha had read the letters on both occasions before realising they were private and now with time on her hands, began to question what all the fuss had been about. With Wendy gone, she felt she had lost her only ally; even more so when a certain Amy Bishop took over. She definitely had an attitude problem.

From the very day Amy took charge, Samantha noticed the difference. She missed Wendy's cheerful little visits, with coffee laid out nicely on a tray; now a cup was placed impatiently on her desk and there were no notes in her diary to keep her in touch with daily programmes, as there had been. She missed an executive meeting because she wasn't informed of a last minute change and when asked why, Amy replied, Mr Spencer said it wasn't necessary for her to be there. Time hung heavy, and to relieve her boredom she scrolled through her computer, to find she had no access to the programs; passwords had been changed. She pressed the buzzer for Amy and after waiting ten minutes, went in search of her to ask for the spreadsheets.

Amy looked blank and continued working at her computer.

"It's a perfectly simple request; now go and fetch them and bring them to my office immediately," Samantha demanded.

"I'll have to ask."

"If you want to keep your job you will just go and get them," Samantha warned beginning to get annoyed.

Amy disappeared and came back five minutes later without the paperwork.

"Mr Spencer would like to speak to you in his office Miss."

Samantha rose, strode round her desk and stared into Amy's dark brown, heavily made up eyes, golden flecks flashing in her own.

"That will be, *Miss Anders*; and where are the papers I asked you for?"

"That's what Mr Spencer wants to speak to you about; if you would like to follow me."

31

William Spencer greeted her looking distracted and Samantha wondered why such a simple request as wanting to see the spreadsheets warranted a summons from him.

"I am very busy Samantha I can only give you five minutes."

"Well what did you want to see me about then, Mr Spencer? Couldn't it have waited?"

"I need you to attend a show in Earls Court for the next three weeks, starting this coming weekend. It means going up on Friday, so take the rest of the week off."

He looked at her impatiently when she didn't reply straight away and frowned when she shook her head.

"I'm sorry Mr Spencer; my annual leave starts in two weeks' time."

"That's fine, go for the two weeks, I'm sure Peter will manage on his own for the last one. Ask Amy for the details: hotels, venues etcetera. Now I really must dash, I'm late already."

"And the spreadsheets?" Samantha reminded him.

His look was cool as he replied. "You will have them when they are ready. Why do you want them?"

"I've nothing to do since Wendy left; familiarising myself with company policy will fill my time."

"Wendy is a great loss to all of us but you will get plenty of entertainment next week and you must realize that your position is quite unusual my dear, we can't just put you to work with the other girls."

"I don't see why not; I'm here to learn, not to be entertained, Mr Spencer."

"Well your grandfather would not approve; now I really must go. Just do what you do best my dear; look pretty, sell cars but leave the business to us."

She was ushered out of the well-furbished office and left to make her own way back through the maze of corridors to her own office. Within twenty minutes, there was a knock at the door and Peter's head appeared.

"Care to join me for lunch? I hear you're coming to the London show next week."

"It would seem so; news travels quickly."

"What's up, aren't you pleased? It'll be fun."

"I would have liked more notice."

"Not always possible old girl." He grinned. "But it's good to live dangerously sometimes."

His cheerfulness was contagious so she picked up her bag.

"Where is that lunch then? I doubt they will even notice I'm gone."

"Good. I'll make it a long one then," he said with a twinkle in his eye.

That evening she telephoned home to say that she had to go away for two weeks. Darren said he would fetch her and fly her to London on the Friday.

"That would be great, Daddy, and would you mind if I have dinner with Granddad tomorrow; I won't see him for two weeks."

"'Course not Princess; I'll tell him to expect you."

The next day was Wednesday and she was home by late morning to pack ready for London on the Friday.

Her unexpected appearance delighted Gerald and when they had retired to the study after dinner she asked about the spreadsheets, anticipating that he would receive them regularly. He showed them to her, but they weren't up to date and she wasn't able to judge if anything was wrong anyway. Gerald's reluctance to discuss them made her suspect he didn't understand them either, but her questions did make him curious.

"If something is worrying you, you must tell me," he said watching her keenly.

"Not worrying exactly; something just doesn't feel right." She told him about the letters mentioning the transfer of shares, and the patronising treatment she had received from William Spencer.

Gerald gave a guarded smile. "People very often need to sell their shares. I will have a word though to put your mind at rest."

"No, don't do that; I'm already in his bad books for reading his mail."

Shortly afterwards Gerald pleaded tiredness and rang for George.

"I'm feeling very tired George. Bring me a nightcap will you? I think I'll have an early night."

Both George and Samantha were surprised. The one night he always wanted to stay up late was when Samantha came but she kissed him goodnight and left. As soon as the door closed behind her, Gerald sat up straight, making George ask curiously, "Ev'rythin oright sir?"

"I hope so George. I hope so. I'll have that nightcap, though."

George left and Gerald immediately picked up the phone, dialled a number he hadn't called for a long time and when a voice answered said, "Hello Simon, I need you to look into something for me."

"Certainly Sir Gerald."

Gerald explained that he didn't want to arouse any suspicions yet and Simon agreed to travel down and go through the spreadsheets with him the next day.

Gerald put the phone down and cursed that he had never mastered the computer. Charles had mastered it, of course – but Charles wasn't here any more. He thumped the padded arm of his wheelchair and winced as pain shot up his arm. If Simon found anything untoward, Adam would look into it but he didn't want to make it known to the family that he wasn't on top of things unless it became absolutely necessary. He was finding it hard these days. All this new fangled way of doing things didn't sit right with him; give him a set of books and he would still do a better job than any machine. He sat staring at the papers on the desk, morose thoughts darkening his mood. William Spencer had been with them for ten years and had always been trustworthy; everything would be alright, he convinced himself. He was sorry now that he had caused Samantha to go home early. Picking up his glass, he finished his brandy and rang for George.

"I think I'll have another, George," he declared with forced cheerfulness and drummed the arm of his chair while George poured the golden liquid into his glass.

"Funny goins on tanight," George said returning to his seat beside Lorna, who was watching television in their sitting room.

"You reckon?" Lorna said engrossed in 'Coronation Street'.

"Yea I reckon."

"Ee the things they get up to up north." Lorna's eyes widened as she clapped her hand over her mouth, while George smiled indulgently. Anywhere above Cornwall was north, to Lorna.

CHAPTER FOUR

Following Gerald's urgent request, Simon Hall arrived at Anders Folly on the Thursday. A chauffer driven car picked him up from his home in the New Forest at six am and he was sitting in Gerald's study with him by ten o'clock. A table had been placed beside the French doors, and the walnut filing cabinet had been wheeled from the alcove. Simon eyed it appreciatively, admiring the patina on the antique piece of furniture, and the fact that it was in a good light. The years of paper work had taken their toll on his eyesight; only for Gerald, would he have allowed himself to be dragged out of retirement. Gardening was his life these days and he and Joyce were very happy in their two-up-two-down cottage on the edge of Lyndhurst. The years had been kind to him and he didn't look his seventy-five years, Gerald noticed as they sat drinking coffee and exchanging pleasantries leading up to the serious subject on Gerald's mind.

"Well now," Gerald said in a suitable pause. "I'm sorry to bring you all this way for what may be just a false alarm."

"Best clear up any doubts," Simon reassured him, glancing at Gerald's long, blue veined fingers drumming the arm of his chair. Apparently relaxed, it was the only sign that ever gave away his true feelings Simon remembered from old.

"What exactly is it that makes your granddaughter suspect something is not right?"

"William Spencer's seemingly extreme agitation, to several letters being left on her desk by mistake, referring to the transfer of shares; plus his manner toward her when she asked to see the spreadsheets; and the fact that Wendy Parker has been suspended due to said letters being on Samantha's desk in the first place. It does seem a minor error, to warrant suspending her after her years of service to the firm."

"Now *that* is suspicious. Wendy is an extremely efficient secretary," Simon said indignantly.

"I suppose we have to consider that we are all getting older and the memory does slip occasionally," Gerald said reluctantly.

"It's a possibility; I think I might get in touch with her and hear her version though. She was always meticulous over details."

Simon rose and went over to the filing cabinet, quickly finding the relevant paperwork and spreading it on the table. An hour later, during which time Gerald sat on the terrace gazing out to sea with a jaded expression, Simon joined him with a set of figures.

"I don't find anything obviously amiss, Sir Gerald."

"I would prefer that our suspicions were not revealed until I have more to go on but I would appreciate you having a word with Wendy and depending on the outcome I will have a word with William about reinstating her; she must be very upset."

George knocked the door and entered to announce lunch was ready and after lunch, although the offer was there to stay the night, Simon opted to go home.

"I think I might get in touch with Wendy tomorrow or even this evening."

"Thank you Simon, I can always depend on you."

"Leave it with me sir and I will be in touch as soon as possible." Gerald's thoughts were nostalgic as they shook hands at the top of the broad front steps. The chauffeur was waiting by the open car door and he watched it disappear out of the drive, remembering other times when Simon had been there for him, never wavering in his loyalty or discretion as he had proved frequently in Alexander's time.

Sitting in the back seat of the luxurious limousine Simon's thoughts were also of the past, when he had worked for both Sir Gerald and David Anders. They were both true gentlemen; what if there was something amiss, now that Gerald was unable to keep a sharp eye on things himself. He had heard about the granddaughter; a chip off the old block some said, but at nineteen was she capable of standing up to men like William Spencer and his nephew? She had obviously picked up on something to make her mention it to her grandfather, he thought drowsily. His eyes closed; it had been an early start and the excellent lunch of freshly cooked gammon, new potatoes and fresh salad from the garden, followed by apple pie with plenty of cinnamon and homemade custard had made him sleepy. The soft hum of the engine and the warm day did the rest and soon he was dozing comfortably.

*

"Hello Wendy."

"Hello Simon," she answered, recognising his voice immediately.

"Joyce and I were wondering if you would like to join us for lunch tomorrow; there is something I would like to discuss with you but not over the phone."

"I would be happy to, just let me make sure nothing else is happening."

Pages rustled as she checked her diary. "Yes, that would be fine; what time would you like me to come?"

"I thought about eleven thirty and then we can sit in the garden and talk before we eat."

"I'll look forward to that Simon; thank Joyce for me."

"So will we; bye then." Simon hung up and Wendy stood for a few seconds staring at the receiver, wondering what could be important enough to warrant the invitation at such short notice.

It was pleasant sitting in the Halls' garden. The colourful tablecloth was set for lunch, with a matching umbrella throwing welcome shade and Wendy and Joyce were sitting in comfortable garden chairs, watching Simon, coming towards them with a tray of drinks.

"Your garden is looking beautiful," Wendy said admiring the colourful cottage-garden borders, as he placed a glass of white wine in front of each of them and helped himself to a lager.

"That's Joyce's department; I stick to the vegetables," he said glancing happily at his wife.

"You work hard," she said, turning to Joyce.

"It doesn't seem like work when you enjoy it."

"Speaking of work," Simon chipped in. "I was sorry to hear of your retirement, I always assumed you would carry on until you had to leave."

Wendy was silent for a moment. "It's hardly voluntary; I've been suspended and offered early retirement." Her eyes glistened with unshed tears and she blinked hard avoiding his gaze.

"What happened lass?"

"I'm going to leave you two to talk and get on with lunch," Joyce said getting to her feet and picking up her glass of wine.

They watched her go. Wendy and Joyce were old friends. Simon had introduced them when Joyce had suffered a miscarriage and learnt she would never have children. At the same time, Wendy was left to care for three-year-old daughter Ann when her husband deserted them. It was a devastating time for all of them but Joyce and Simon became doting aunt and uncle to Ann, while Wendy worked. It had been a 'godsend' to the three of them

"What a treasure she is," Wendy said now.

"Yes, I'm a lucky man," Simon said contentedly.

"And Joyce is a lucky woman," she answered emotionally reaching across and patting his hand. He gripped her fingers looking at her earnestly.

"Before you say anything, I spoke to Sir Gerald yesterday. He is very upset by your leaving and there are a few things he wants cleared up."

Wendy looked horrified.

"Neither of us believe you were negligent," he hastened to reassure her, "but we would like to hear your side of it."

She gulped and took a deep breath. "I can't explain; an office girl remembers seeing me with them in my hand when I left my desk and I know I put the letters on Spencer's desk."

"How can this girl be so sure they were the same letters?" Simon asked sharply.

"She sorted the mail and remembered a bright blue envelope that day. I did go to Miss Samantha's office first, but I distinctly remember going to Spencer's office afterwards and placing them on his pad."

"Could you have left the wrong ones?" he asked, looking for an explanation.

She shook her head adamantly, and continued. "Then the memos I put on the notice board went missing, and several important appointments were missed."

She looked about to cry but shook her head again as Simon said:

"Surely one bad day didn't warrant such dire reaction?"

"That was the problem, it happened, a number of times, memos and appointments kept disappearing and they were always found in my desk and it was inferred that the job was too much for me at my age. I was offered a lower position and when I refused…" Overcome with confusion and embarrassment, the tears finally flowed.

"There, there lass, Sir Gerald is wondering if there is more to this than meets the eye. Did you read the letters left on Samantha's desk?"

"Good heavens no, but that was something else, the envelopes were also found in my drawer; they were marked private so there was no way I would have opened them. No, I believe someone wanted me out."

"Mmm." Simon's eyes narrowed thoughtfully.

"Miss Samantha did read the letters and what she understood from them, was that a lot of shares were being cashed in, and she asked her grandfather why."

"The shares have been doing well for some time now; that might explain why people are cashing them in." She pursed her lips questioningly.

"Did you ever think anything suspicious was going on?" he asked tensely.

"Not really, but then I was always told to take an early lunch when his foreign golfing buddies arrived." She gave a gasp. "A take over?"

He gave a worried frown. "Just examining all possibilities at the moment, but something has made Sir Gerald suspicious or he wouldn't have sent for me in such a hurry."

"Mr Hughes hasn't been around to keep an eye on things for a while and Sir Gerald doesn't understand the new systems," Wendy replied.

"I suppose William Spencer could have got ambitious, thinking that he does all the work and runs the company; Sir Gerald has been hardly more than a figurehead for a while now."

"That will be why he is desperate for Samantha to take over so quickly; I wondered why it was so urgent. I'm not sure if it is realistic; she is a very bright young woman but there are limits to her abilities at nineteen and she is dealing with experienced men."

They began to see things in a new light and what had seemed improbable suddenly seemed possible.

"We need proof," Simon said decisively

"If Sir Gerald is up to calling a board meeting, perhaps you could go along and ask questions about the shares; you will know by his reaction if Spencer has anything to hide."

"Do you think anyone else is involved?"

"If the lunchtime meetings are significant then, John Denzel in finance could be involved I suppose."

"Phew, Denzel has been with Anders a long time; I worked with him." Simon looked strained. When William Spencer had taken over from him ten years ago, he had come with excellent qualifications, having worked his way up through the trade. Gerald had employed him without hesitation. It would be a bitter blow to him if his judgment proved wrong.

"Well if we're right, he is afraid Samantha will find out something he doesn't want known."

They sat in silence each with their own uncertain thoughts until Joyce called from the kitchen to say lunch was ready and Wendy went to help her carry the food to the table.

Simon stared unseeingly at the tall silver birch tree where a wonderful variety of birds vied for the plentiful supply of food he put out daily, then coming to a decision he got up and went indoors to telephone Gerald, just as Joyce put his dinner in front of him.

"Why do men always do that?" she asked calmly.

CHAPTER FIVE

William Spencer glowered at Peter. "Don't get any ideas about the Anders girl; she is off limits to you. Just keep her busy for the next two weeks in London, so she doesn't ask any more fool questions; at least she's out of my way for the rest of this week."

In his late fifties, William was looking his age. The last two years had taken their toll of him and it irked him to see Peter looking relaxed and ten years younger than his forty-two years. He went to the tray of drinks in the corner of his luxurious office and poured whisky into a tumbler.

"What's the problem?" Peter asked nonchalantly.

"She has started poking about. Just keep her out of my hair for the next two weeks," he repeated harshly.

"Okay, okay. She shall have my undivided attention."

"Mm, that's what I'm worried about – just don't go over the top," William said sarcastically, looking worried as he eyed his nephew up and down impatiently.

"Leave it to me," Peter answered seriously, picking up his briefcase.

"You can rely on me Uncle; just don't let Lindsey get wind of me being in London with a good looking woman or I'll never hear the end of it."

"She should be used to it by now," William said caustically.

"The words, pot and kettle spring to mind," Peter grinned.

"Well just remember it's my step-daughter you will be cheating on."

"I will." He spoke offhandedly, confident of William's discretion, since discovering he had had an illicit relationship with a family friend.

Once outside the office Peter gave a devil may care glance back at the door, thinking of two whole weeks in London, getting to know the delectable Miss Samantha Anders.

*

The hotel was crowded and noisy and the whole place seemed to be full of raised voices speaking every language except English.

Surely they could have found somewhere quieter than this for you." Darren followed Samantha to the reception desk, staring around with undisguised disapproval at the busy foyer as they joined a queue waiting to be booked in.

"It really doesn't matter Daddy, I will hardly be here, other than to sleep. All of the Anders team are staying here. Don't worry."

"That's how you see yourself, is it; one of the team?"

"That's *what* I am," she answered quietly.

"I could no more do this than fly to the moon."

"That's *why I* am," she answered firmly.

"Is that the only reason?" he asked sharply.

"Another reason is because granddad needs me, but it isn't all self sacrifice. I am actually enjoying the experience." She smiled up at him. "Don't worry, everything will turn out for the best."

He shrugged. "You can say no, you know."

The conversation came to an abrupt end as she gave her name to the desk clerk and ten minutes later, they were standing in her room on the first floor. It was small but adequate, with an en suite shower and a side street view.

"Good job you haven't brought a cat to swing," Darren said morosely. He hated the idea of leaving her in this place and a few minutes later Peter gave him further cause for worry, by walking in without knocking, stopping in his tracks when he saw Darren.

"Oh sorry, didn't think you were here yet." He glanced curiously at Darren before Samantha introduced them.

"My apologies sir; I thought you must be one of the team."

"I hope you aren't going to make a habit of walking into my daughter's bedroom uninvited, Mr Chambers."

"No sir, of course not, I just came along to check that Miss Anders' room had everything, but I can see she is in good hands. We will all be meeting across the road to talk tactics, in about an hour; you would be welcome to join us sir, if you wish." He left and silence followed while Samantha started to unpack.

"I don't like his type," Darren said at last.

"Which is?" Samantha began to think it had been a mistake to let her father bring her.

"Too fast talking and slick for my liking."

She laughed with genuine amusement. "He is the top salesman, Daddy. What do you expect?"

"That he doesn't become too familiar with you; promise me you will keep your distance."

"I promise," she assured him, disappearing for a moment to leave her toilet bag in the tiny bathroom before returning to hug him.

"Please leave now Daddy before you get upset."

"I'm already upset; I hate this idea."

"You've got to trust me."

He looked at her thinking how beautiful she was. "I do; it's the types you are mixing with that I don't. I don't know what your grandfather is thinking of."

He started to get angry again and suddenly she snapped.

"Don't start blaming Grandfather again, or I shall get angry. Please go Daddy before we say things we will regret."

"I should have known you would stand up for him; you always do. I sometimes think you love him more than you do me."

She hated it when he got all peevish and child like.

"Listen to yourself. Please don't do this now. You know I love you to bits, but please go and let me concentrate on getting ready."

She hugged him and kissed his cheek, he turned to go, feeling that same helplessness he had felt when she was fourteen, and he hadn't been there to protect her. At the door he turned.

"I could stay and take care of you."

"I don't need taking care of Daddy; I'm nearly nineteen. Now please go and let me get changed."

On his way down in the lift, four youngsters crowded in and he cringed at their colourful language.

"Every other word was a swear word. I couldn't bear it if Sam got like that," he said miserably to Melly, later that evening.

"You're not giving her enough credit," she answered sympathetically.

Darren's moods seemed to be getting worse again and she knew he was still brooding about getting away, even though he had let everyone think that the idea had been forgotten.

In her hotel room, Samantha flopped on to the bed and closed her eyes with a sigh of relief. Her nerves were taut with the strangeness of everything because although she had travelled before, it had been in Europe, and she had never been left to her own devices. Wendy Parker had always arranged a personal assistant to accompany her, who also acted as a companion and shared an adjoining room, by express orders from her grandfather. Not for the first time she realized how much she had taken Wendy for granted. Little niceties generating respect for her as Sir Gerald's granddaughter were missing; she was as she had told her father, – one of the team. A tap on the door interrupted her thoughts, and she rose, straightened her pencil slim skirt and went to answer it. Peter stood there wearing a sheepish grin.

"I watched him leave. Sorry if I put my foot in it."

"All dads are the same I suspect."

She still had her hand on the door and he asked if he could come in and talk for a few minutes.

"I would but I really need to shower and change."

"Isn't the shower big enough for two?" he asked with a teasing smile.

She coloured furiously and he apologised promptly adding:

"I'll see you downstairs in the foyer and show you where the pub is in half an hour. The others will all be there and I can introduce you." He turned on his heel and surprised her by stopping at the neighbouring door.

"You see, I'm not far away if you need me," and with that same teasing smile, he slid the card into the door and disappeared inside.

Samantha's stomach was churning as she closed her door; she hadn't expected to be so close to him. Without more ado, she rang down to reception and asked if she could change her room.

The receptionist sounded harassed. "You are in the Anders party and they are all on that floor; seven single rooms were booked and they are all the same."

"Do you have a larger room on another floor then?"

There was the sound of pages being turned. "The only other one available is a double on the same floor at twice the price, and I would have to get permission from your firm to give you that one." She was sounding slightly impatient by now.

"That will be no problem. Perhaps you would send someone up with the key straight away."

Her hand trembled as she replaced the receiver, wondering what Peter's reaction would be. By the time the key arrived, she had quickly repacked her things and was waiting by the open door. The young man in a chocolate coloured uniform picked up her case and led the way past closely-knit rooms to a wider landing where small tables with vases of fresh flowers stood between the rooms. A lift took them up to the fourth floor and she waited while he opened the door and placed her two, cream leather suitcases inside; his eyes lit up as she placed five pounds in his hand.

"Thanks Miss."

"Thank you, and my name is Miss Anders."

"I'm Tim and if you ever need anything done, you just send for me – Miss Anders." He touched his cap.

Left alone she looked around and was immediately glad of her decision. This was far more like the rooms she was used to occupying. Two armchairs and a round table, stood in front of doors leading onto a small balcony overlooking a park – 'and room to swing the cat Daddy', she laughed; then remembering that the desk clerk had said the room was on the same floor, she decided to make sure there hadn't been a mistake before unpacking.

The receptionist used a very different tone this time.

"Yes Miss Anders, how can I help you?"

"I'm wondering if I have the right room; you said it would be on the same floor."

"Your grandfather said you were to have the best room available and anything else you require. I do hope you are comfortable."

"You spoke to my grandfather?"

"He telephoned the manager apparently, shortly before you asked for another room; I understand it was a request from your father."

"Oh, thank you." Samantha thought she realized what had happened but in actual fact, Darren had rung Gerald demanding that Sam was taken off the team and brought home immediately, saying he hadn't realized the kind of people she would be working with and he was appalled at the lack of security for a young woman on her own. Gerald had told him to calm down but had then realised with a sense of shock that in Wendy's absence, his explicit instructions for Samantha's well being were not in place.

An urgent call to William Spencer's office quickly put him in the picture, when William said she had been booked in with the rest of the team by his personal assistant, who must have thought that as Miss Anders was part of the team she should be treated the same. Gerald wasn't quite sure whether William was voicing the assistant's thoughts or his own – so he quickly put him in the picture.

"It seems your assistant needs lessons from Wendy Parker. As the future owner of 'Anders', my granddaughter will never be just one of the team. Who has taken over from Wendy, anyway?"

"I thought it time we had some new, young blood; her name is Amy Bishop and she has been with the firm three years."

"Well tell her if she wants to make it to four, she is to show my granddaughter the respect due to her, and that goes for anyone else who has a problem with that; young blood – or old."

Gerald's hackles were up. He was picking up an undertone in William's voice as if he wanted to say something but didn't dare.

And while we are on the subject, I offered to reinstate Wendy Parker." He heard a gasp from William.

"I really must object Sir Gerald. Miss Bishop is quicker and far more up to speed. She actually corrected Miss Parker's mistakes and saved us from further embarrassment. I am very satisfied with her as a personal assistant."

"Yes I'm sure you are," Gerald, answered with heavy sarcasm. "Well you needn't get het up, Miss Parker hastily declined the offer, which brings me to my next point: she is to be extremely well compensated for her years of loyal service. I am not happy with the way she has been treated. Goodbye William."

He put the phone down and leant back in his chair, breathing hard. Simon's advice to call a board meeting as soon as possible was sound; he hadn't intended to be so forthright with William but his attitude, plus the way Darren had just spoken to him rankled. With Wendy gone and Charles not at the wheel, he was without an ally if William Spencer wasn't to be trusted. If only Charles was still here, they would stand together as they always had in times of trouble. For the first time he considered whether he was expecting too much from Samantha, but without question, she was the only lifeline for 'Anders'.

*

"Goodbye Sir Gerald."

Wendy replaced her receiver and gazed unseeingly in the oval shaped mirror above the hall table. A phone call from Sir Gerald himself? He must be very anxious. There was plenty of time to phone for a taxi and catch the four thirty train. Starting up the stairs, she changed her mind and returned to the telephone, dialled and waited for Simon to answer.

"Hello Simon. I've just had a phone call from Sir Gerald asking me to go to London tonight and assist Samantha; he seems to be worried that she's without a chaperone. Would you be free to take me to the station? I need to run a few questions by you."

After agreeing a time, she went upstairs to pack and change into suitable clothes. She had been planning a quiet weekend and the idea of tripping off to London for two weeks was much more exciting, but there was a worrying side to being responsible for a teenager in London, especially Sir Gerald's great granddaughter. He had explained it was a last minute decision because the usual companion was on holiday.

Simon arrived and she was ready and waiting with her packed case, in the small hallway of her neat semi-detached house. Simon had spoken to Gerald after she called and on the way to the station, he passed on a message, to just follow Sir Gerald's usual orders and use her own judgment.

"This arrangement is nothing to do with the team and you aren't answerable to William Spencer's nephew, where Samantha's comfort and well being are concerned."

It was one of the things that had been on Wendy's own mind and she was grateful to Simon for making her position clear. Simon smiled to himself as he saw her sit up straight and take a deep breath; this would restore some of her bruised confidence.

*

Peter greeted Samantha as she joined him in the foyer. "I knocked your door but you weren't there."

She met his surprised look calmly. "I'm in a different room."

His face dropped. "You didn't tell me."

"You know now," she said with a disarming smile, as they walked towards the entrance.

"What number are you in then? Have you swapped with someone?"

She was saved from answering by a girl who came up and introduced herself as Sandra.

"Everyone is in the pub, down there," she said to Peter, pointing to a small side road."

"What's up with the usual one?" Peter frowned, not liking his decision changed.

"Standing room only," Sandra replied cheerfully falling into step and leading them to a spacious bar where the other four members were already seated at a round table.

Peter introduced her to Carol, Sue, John and Trevor and it was all very friendly and relaxed as Peter outlined his plan for the following day, while they waited for the drinks and nibbles to arrive.

They worked in couples and Peter said she would be working with him and Sandra. It occurred to her that she wasn't actually needed and Peter pointed out that she was needed, if only to sit on the bonnets of cars, show a lot of leg and look sexy.

"You will fit the bill very nicely," he whispered, looking her up and down with a sly grin.

47

She blushed, looking around to make sure the others hadn't heard, but they were all busy planning what to do that evening.

"It's four o'clock; why don't we go back to the hotel, rest up and meet in the hotel restaurant at seven," Peter suggested nonchalantly.

At that moment, a mobile phone rang and realizing it was hers, Samantha quickly unzipped her bag, apologising for the interruption.

It was her father checking that she was all right and after a brief reassurance, she said goodbye, hoping he wasn't going to embarrass her by constantly phoning at awkward moments.

Replacing her phone in her open shoulder bag, she saw Peter gazing at her room key.

"How come you've got a key? We've all got cards."

"No idea."

"Why did you move? I was looking forward to having you next door."

"My grandfather arranged for me to have a double room. It's no big deal; apparently Daddy went back and said how small the room was."

"Lucky ole you; a double eh?" his eyes twinkled at her. "Very useful."

She turned away, stomach churning and followed the others who were on their way back to the hotel. Peter was obviously expecting to join her in her room; how was she going to stop him without pulling rank she wondered as they walked through the revolving doors and entered the foyer. As if in answer, she saw her father waiting for her.

She walked up to him with a huge smile and the anxious look on his face disappeared. He had worried she would be upset with him for being there.

"Thought I would just check you are happy, before going home." He nodded to Peter. "All set to sell a nice lot of cars then?"

Peter's hopes of going back to Samantha's room crashed.

"Hope so sir."

"I'll just come up and see your new room, before I go, shall I?"

Peter's hopes rose, but Samantha tucked her arm through Darren's, saying, "Absolutely Daddy; it's really nice, and you don't have to rush away do you?" Turning to Peter, she added, "See, you at seven o'clock, Peter."

"Yes of course," Peter said faintly, his hopes completely crushed.

Watching his expression, Darren guessed what had been on his mind and seethed with anger. "Over my dead body," he muttered, prepared to sit outside her door all night if he had to.

"What was that Daddy?"

"Nothing sweetheart, just thinking aloud."

He had tried hard to book the adjoining room to Samantha's, but there was no persuading the receptionist.

"Sorry sir it's more than my job is worth to let that room go."

He had tried every 'but' and 'what if', without success and now as he tried the door between the rooms and found it locked he had to be content with sticking a chair under the handle.

"Daddy what on earth are you doing?"

"I don't trust that Chambers bloke, one inch."

Samantha giggled, "You are funny; but Auntie Fran says the word no is the safest thing."

"I'm sure she is right; she always is; but just in case." He went to the French doors and looked out. They were five floors up – but even so, he locked the doors.

"Don't you think you are being just a wee bit over the top?" she asked curiously, as he methodically checked the bathroom window, which didn't open at all.

"Maybe, but I don't want you to be nervous."

"You're doing a pretty good job of making me," she said seriously.

"Sorry Princess," he said, contritely, realising at last how he was behaving.

"Why don't I make you a nice cup of tea or coffee?" she offered.

"To be honest I could do with a stiff whisky," he admitted.

"There is a mini bar, I believe." She found the small fridge and drinks cabinet and watching his hand shake as he helped himself, blamed herself for the stress she was causing him.

"Daddy I'm alright, really I am. Please go home to Mamma and if it really means so much to you, go to America. I will cope."

The mention of America brightened him, and finally she realized just how much of a burden, Anders Folly and everything it represented, was to him; Granddad, Tim, herself, he loved them all but couldn't cope with the responsibility that should, by rights, be his.

"Please go home Daddy. I love you dearly, but I don't want you to spend your life being afraid for me. What happened in the past, happened because I was too innocent; it will never happen again."

Little did she know how she would be forced to eat her words in the year to come.

They sat in the armchairs watching the sun go down, whiling away the time before Samantha would go down to dinner and Darren would take a taxi back to the airfield and fly home. In hindsight, it was the closest they had ever been or would be again.

At seven o'clock, Darren said, "I think I need to eat, perhaps I will join you for dinner before I head back."

"That sounds good sense to me," Samantha agreed.

They arrived in the dining room before the rest of the team, and Samantha chose a table for two.

"Won't you be expected to sit with them?" Darren asked.

"I want to sit with my father," she said fondly, watching the team as they sat at a table on the other side of the large restaurant. When they had finished Darren got up reluctantly. It was eight o'clock; time to make his way home.

"I could sleep on your floor," he said in a last desperate bid as they were saying goodbye in the foyer; and for the second time that day, it seemed fate took a hand as Wendy's voice floated across to them. "Hello there."

Samantha turned, quite overcome with relief; she had been wondering how long it would be before Peter knocked at her door and now she knew her worries were over. Wendy had arrived whilst they were having dinner and was already comfortably settled in the adjoining room Darren had been unable to book, even at twice the price.

"More than my job's worth," the receptionist had assured him and now he understood why. Was there anywhere that Grandfather's word didn't carry weight he thought, gritting his teeth, but went away with a peaceful mind and had to agree that it had served its purpose well, this time.

Later while sharing a bedtime drink and dainty sandwiches ordered from room service, Samantha and Wendy exchanged news.

"I can only gather that your grandfather wasn't satisfied with the arrangements made for you."

"It's not the same since you left," Samantha admitted, smiling sheepishly. "I realise now how much you spoiled me. I expect Amy thought she was doing me a favour, including me in the team."

"I wouldn't be too sure of that," Wendy said bitterly.

"Why do you say that?"

"That girl has a mean spirit; she wanted my job and didn't care how she went about getting it."

"You think she caused the trouble?" Samantha gasped.

"I can't prove anything, but William Spencer never liked the fact that I was loyal to Sir Gerald; he had been looking for a reason to get rid of me for ages. He and Amy Bishop will make a good pair."

Samantha hated her defeated look.

"Grandfather thinks the world of you – and with very good reason," she said softly and was rewarded with a sad smile.

Dusk had fallen and the warm July night was closing in as Wendy rose and closed the French doors.

"Best keep the midges out," she advised, just as there was a tap at the door.

"It's probably the waiter to clear the supper things; I'll answer it."

Samantha went into the bathroom and heard Wendy ask primly:

"Isn't this rather late to be calling Mr Chambers? Miss Samantha has retired. It *is* ten thirty," she said glancing at her wristwatch.

"How come you are here Wendy?" Peter Chambers' annoyed voice reached Samantha through the open bathroom door and she listened for Wendy's reply.

"A personal request from Sir Gerald; he was not satisfied with the arrangements made for his granddaughter. Is there anything *I* can do for you?"

"I shouldn't imagine so, for one minute, Miss Parker," Peter replied caustically, before turning on his heel and stomping back to the lift.

"I think the phrase 'tail between his legs', would be appropriate," Wendy said as Samantha popped her head round the door grinning broadly.

For the next two weeks, Wendy thwarted his every attempt to get Samantha alone and by the time Darren arrived to pick them both up, Peter, was thoroughly disgruntled.

"See you in two weeks then," he said in an injured voice, as she was saying goodbye to the team and thanking them for their help and advice.

With two weeks' holiday to look forward to she could hardly wait to get home. She pictured riding Nocturn every morning and spending time with Sol and the dogs; but best of all, Bryn would be there. She had to let him know how much she had missed him and realised now that she had been in love with him for a long time. She also wanted to let him know that she was over her fear of being touched by him. He had always been so understanding in spite of her not being able to return his feelings, but things were different now.

CHAPTER SIX

Samantha replaced the receiver, struggling to smother her disappointment. She had been expecting to meet Bryn from the train later in the day, but his mother had telephoned, to say he wouldn't be home for another four days and he had a lift all the way. She sounded flustered and there had been no time for questions, so Samantha was left guessing as to why travel arrangements had changed. He usually only managed to get a lift for part of the journey.

With time to kill, she asked Melly if she fancied going shopping.

"As long as I'm back for half three, to pick Jack up from nursery," Melly said, pleased to be asked.

"I'm sure we can squeeze some serious retail therapy into four hours. Can I drive?" Samantha called, on her way upstairs to collect her bag.

"Are you sure you should? We haven't sent out a warning to other drivers."

"Ha, ha, my test is next week and I'm going to pass first time; you see if I don't."

"I would be most surprised if you didn't, wearing a skirt that short," Melly teased, as she returned downstairs.

It's the fashion, in case you have completely forgotten what that is."

"As a matter of fact, I have. No call for an up-to-date wardrobe now; jeans are best for picking Jack up and running the house."

"We mustn't let that happen; Daddy must treat you," Samantha said, frowning.

"He's having a few problems at the moment, so don't let's mention clothes."

"Money?" Samantha asked with raised eyebrows, never having known that particular problem.

"Amongst other things; nothing for you to worry about though."

"Granddad will sort it," Samantha said confidently, sliding into the driving seat.

And there lies the problem, Melly thought, absently pointing out that Sam hadn't looked in her mirror before starting off.

"Mamma, we are still in the drive."

"It's a habit you must get into."

They went to a small, upmarket boutique and Samantha insisted on treating Melly to two short, linen skirts.

"I can't have my glamorous Mamma, in last year's fashions, and I can afford it," she said when Melly demurred. "It's rather fun too; I'm usually on the receiving end."

Melly gave in graciously, realising that Samantha was enjoying her new independence, and it was certainly a new experience for her, to be the one taking advice. She made a mental note: 'mustn't let myself go'.

Samantha wished that she had arranged her holiday later now; by the time Bryn arrived, one week would be almost over and she had wanted to spend the whole fortnight with him.

She whiled the days away by riding Nocturn, playing on the beach with Jack and spending time at Anders Folly. They were things that she had, had all the time in the world for before, but it was different now and she wanted to make every moment count. The day of Bryn's homecoming finally arrived and she waited eagerly for his phone call. She had kept her mobile phone switched on permanently and had tried to contact him every day, without success.

"Probably can't find anywhere to recharge it, if he is moving about," Melly said, seeing her disappointment.

"Yes that must be it," Samantha answered cheering up.

"You are really looking forward to seeing him; is there something you haven't told us?" Melly gave a teasing smile.

Samantha smiled happily. "Maybe, but I must tell Bryn first."

They were sitting at the breakfast bar, having a mid morning cup of coffee while Sam painted her nails pale pink; unusually, she was wearing a cornflower blue dress, instead of stable clothes and her mobile phone was beside her.

Melly gave an enlightened "Ahh!"

By lunchtime, she was on tenterhooks and kept looking at her small, gold wristwatch; a present from Bryn when they finished college and were planning to go to university together. She also checked her mobile constantly to make sure it was working and by two o'clock, in desperation, rang his home number.

His mother answered sounding busy and there was a babble of voices in the background. Sam's spirits rose; he must be home. There was a pause and then Bryn came on the line. "Hello Sam, I was going to phone you, after we finished lunch."

She was bubbling over with excitement. "I thought you would never get here; I can't wait to see you; I have something really important I need to tell you. When can we meet?"

There was a pause, quite a long one this time. "Perhaps we can meet tomorrow, the family are having a get together today and actually I have something really important to tell you, as well."

Her senses swam with joy. "I thought we would definitely see each other today; can't you slip away for a little while?" She knew she sounded desperate. "I'll die, if I have to wait another day."

"I'll see what I can do." He hesitated. "Hold on a minute." She could hear muted voices and waited. He would come; she knew he would. She was trying to picture how he would react, when she told him how she felt, as he came back on the line.

"I'll meet you on The Point, in half an hour. Bye for now."

He hung up before she could say anything and she turned to Melly, eyes shining. "Do I look alright? Perhaps I should wear the green instead."

"You look fine; really beautiful in fact." Melly gave a whimsical smile, remembering that wonderful feeling, well.

"Would you give me a lift to The Point, please?"

"Not riding Nocturn?" Melly teased.

Samantha hesitated briefly. "It's too hot for him and anyway I want to look good."

"Bryn will think you look wonderful, however you are dressed," Melly assured her.

They arrived at The Point first, and Melly drove off, leaving her waiting on the grassy cliff.

Samantha was surprised when a car pulled up and Bryn got out of the passenger seat; she had assumed he would cycle. She ran to him as he strode towards her but stopped, embarrassed as another figure emerged from the car. He frowned reproachfully at a plump girl, indicating that she should have stayed in the car. Samantha read hostility in the girl's dark brown eyes.

"Sam, this is Jocelyn," he said miserably. "This isn't how I intended to tell you, but we are getting married in a few weeks' time. I'm sorry."

"What are you sorry about?" Jocelyn demanded.

Samantha was speechless and stood rooted to the spot, trying to take in that Jo was short for Jocelyn; she had assumed that Bryn was hers. How could this have happened? She turned and stumbled away.

"Sam, talk to me; we can't leave it like this. Get into the car Jo; I will be with you in a few minutes."

Jocelyn got back into the car reluctantly and Bryn caught up with Samantha as she walked back along the cliff.

"Don't let's fall out; I will always want you as my dearest friend," Bryn pleaded.

"I was ready for more than that," Samantha confessed. "That was what I wanted to tell you today." Numb with shock, she gazed at him, her eyes brimming with tears.

"I thought you would only ever want friendship, Sam. Jo is the only girl I have been remotely close to because you were the only one I ever wanted, but even you have to admit that our worlds are miles apart; as a mere doctor, how could I ever give 'Granddad's Princess' the home she is used to?"

"Any kind of home with you would have been enough."

"But how was I supposed to know that? You wouldn't even let me touch you."

Suddenly she was crying, realizing how blind she had been. Bryn had been there for her and she had thought it was just a case of whenever she was ready.

"Well that has taught me a lesson." She turned on him angrily, heedless of what she was saying. "Don't worry about me. Go; go to your fat little Jo. See if I care."

She started to storm off and his voice stopped her in her tracks.

"She isn't fat, she's pregnant."

Without turning round, she managed, "I hope you will be very happy," before striding on along the cliff, back towards the cottage.

"Back already," Melly said anxiously, having seen Samantha climbing the path up from the back road, looking quite different to when she had left her less than an hour ago.

"Yes, things didn't quite work out as planned," Samantha said coldly.

"Do you want to talk about it?" Melly asked, not liking her look.

"Not really," she replied on her way upstairs.

Ten minutes later, she reappeared in her stable clothes, left the cottage, and disappeared down the path leading to Anders Folly.

Ella watched as Samantha walked Nocturn out of his stable and Sol started to object that it was too hot to ride him.

Without a word, Samantha walked him back in and closed the door.

"What's the matter lass?"

"Nothing. It was thoughtless of me. I'll come back later." She started walking back to the house.

"Hi Sam, I've just made some tea; come and share a cup." Ella walked out onto the veranda carrying a tray.

Sam hesitated. She wanted to be alone and yet she needed to be with someone. She didn't actually know what she wanted, so she just nodded.

"We thought we would take all of the horses to the cove this evening, when it gets cool; why don't you come," Ella said casually, receiving a surprised look from Sol as she gave him a warning look. It was the first he had heard of it. Ella always had her reasons though he reminded himself and something had certainly changed since yesterday, when Sam had been practically jumping for joy all day.

They sat companionably together on the veranda; there was always something peaceful about having sleeping dogs beside them and hearing the occasional whinny from the horses in the big field, where the resplendent, horse chestnut trees, gave them plenty of shelter from the sun.

"Even the birds are quiet." Sol broke the silence, stretching contentedly, before settling down and closing his eyes." Just ten minutes," he murmured.

Ella smiled, and looked across at Sam, noting her far-away, unhappy look. Not ready to talk yet she judged, narrowing her eyes. She had been badly hurt again. Ella's eyes were troubled. What a deeply complex life this young woman had ahead of her. An older man was going to play a large part, but he wasn't to be trusted. She closed her eyes trying to blot out the images. She wanted to protect Sam but could see vulnerable situations that would be beyond her. A vivid picture burst into her head and she looked across at Samantha giving a quiet gasp of dismay. Sam had fallen asleep. 'Sleep well little one', she murmured sadly. Knowing the future didn't always mean you could alter it.

For the rest of the holiday, Samantha was very quiet. She went for solitary rides on Nocturn early in the mornings and played with the four dogs on the beach, spent some time with Jack and visited Fran, who, worried because she was bottling things up, wanted to help. She refused to talk about Bryn and both Fran and Melly, had to draw their own conclusions. At night, her light was on until well past midnight, but when Darren tried her door, he found it locked and her faint voice reached him, insisting that she wanted to be left alone.

Eventually, Melly heard from village gossip that a French girl was pregnant by Bryn.

"It must have been awful for you, why didn't you say?" Melly reproached sympathetically.

"Nothing you could do," Samantha said in a brittle voice. "I just don't want to talk about it. If he wants some French tart, that's up to him."

Melly was shocked into silence.

"It's going to take a long time for her to get over this," she told Darren later that night.

"It's her birthday in two days' time; perhaps that will cheer her up. Hope she likes her present."

"She will love it." Melly got out of bed, went to her dressing-table drawer and returned with a leather case; opening it, she took out a gold charm bracelet with letters, circled by horseshoes, spelling out Nocturn. They looked at each other and smiled, pleased with their choice.

Samantha's birthday fell on the Saturday before she was due to go back to Southampton on the Monday and she was actually looking forward to going, because after visiting the shops in town and seeing Bryn and Jocelyn in the distance, she had stayed away, hating the idea of bumping into them. The only other time she had seen them was the day she took her driving test, when she actually lost concentration because they were waiting by the crossing and she had to stop for them. Jocelyn didn't see her, but Bryn stared long and hard and she stared back, earning a sharp reminder from the examiner, to drive on because she was holding up the traffic. She passed with flying colours, spurred on by sheer anger.

Saturday dawned and for the first time ever, she and Timothy would spend their birthday apart. She shed a few tears over that before leaving her bedroom and wondered why Jack wasn't being his usual noisy self. The kitchen door was closed and the whole house was unusually silent, until she opened the door and a sudden burst of 'happy birthday' greeted her as Jack ran to her with a big card, shouting that he had painted tractors for her. While she was twirling him around, she noticed the table, set with her favourite breakfast foods and balloons tied to the back of her chair. Melly and Darren stood together and presented her with the leather case and there was no doubting her pleasure when she opened it. There was another quite large parcel by her plate, wrapped in pale blue, shiny paper and the card simply said: *Love from Granddad*. She opened it smiling happily. Melly looked eagerly over her shoulder, but Darren stood back, trying to hide his resentment. Wrapped in a layer of blue tissue paper was a pair of pale blue leather gloves and below that were layers and layers of more tissue paper until eventually, an ice blue, velvet bag was revealed. By now, even Darren couldn't hide his curiosity. She felt inside the bag; it was something very hard and turned out to be a leather case. Darren turned away in disgust; it was jewellery, camouflaged in a big box to create suspense. Why did Grandfather always have to go one better? It was sure to be more expensive than their present. A sudden squeal of delight came from Samantha and Melly said in an awestruck voice:

"Come and look at this, Darren."

Darren turned back to see Samantha holding up a set of keys and gazing at a picture of a Mercedes Cabriolet SL6oo.

They were staring at it as the sound of a car, pulling onto the drive and tooting its horn, took them to the door in time to see an ice blue sports car, complete with balloons and George, sitting at the wheel. Climbing out of the passenger seat was a vaguely familiar figure that came towards them calling, "Happy birthday Sam."

At the sound of his voice, Samantha threw herself at him. "Tim. Happy birthday, this is the best present ever."

With his face and arms deeply tanned and loose, unfamiliar clothing, he could have passed for an Arab.

"Not better than the car surely?"

"Even better than that," she said crying and laughing at the same time.

"I must just try out the driving seat though," she said releasing him. George opened the door, grinning widely and they all inspected it, while she tried the various knobs and handles. Seeing her father's downcast face, she said, "I shall need help Daddy; I've only just passed my test." She smiled straight at him and his world brightened.

George said he must get back and with a mischievous smile Samantha offered to drive him.

"No offence Miss, but I reckon I'll take the path."

She pulled a face and they all went back into the cottage laughing.

Over breakfast, Timothy told them of his travels and all the wonderful things he had done and seen.

"So are you home to stay?" Sam asked eagerly.

He shook his head. "Not possible Sis; you wouldn't believe the excitement that exists on these new sites, when discoveries, thousands of years old are found. I just can't imagine living any other way now."

She gave a sad but understanding nod. "Well you just make sure to come home often; do you hear?"

"I need to sleep," Tim said, visibly drooping now that the first excitement had died down. I've been travelling for three days and Grandfather is expecting us all to dinner tonight. Where can I go?"

"Use my room," Samantha offered, seeing Melly panic.

"I can put a bed up in Jack's room," Melly said, talking to herself, as she busily started to clear away.

"How long are you planning to stay, son?" Darren asked, hoping that his visit would keep Sam at home for longer as well.

"Nearly two weeks."

It was a lovely evening; Fran, Adam and the boys joined them and even James behaved; too fascinated by Tim's stories to think up new ways to upset George. Gerald was in his element, having the twins sitting in their customary place either side of him again.

CHAPTER SEVEN

Amy Bishop put a neat pile of papers in front of William Spencer.

"These are ready for you to sign, sir."

Leaning back in his comfortable office chair, he eyed her speculatively, wondering just how far he could trust her. So far, they had flirted and he had brushed up against her, accidentally on purpose; she seemed to enjoy it, but he had to be careful. It was a long time since he had a secretary as lissom as this one.

More importantly, he wanted the granddaughter occupied. Amy clearly resented her and found it belittling to take orders from a teenager, so that could be his opening gambit.

"Coffee in five minutes, and I will have these ready for you. Bring a cup for yourself; I need to have a word." He picked up a pen and taking it as dismissal, Amy left, wondering what was coming. He obviously fancied her and if she played her cards right, she could get everything she wanted from this job; double salary – for a start.

Returning five minutes later, she placed the coffee on the desk and sat in a chair facing him, making sure to hitch her skirt and cross her shapely legs, to afford him the full benefit of slim thighs.

William avoided looking straight at her and cleared his throat; she hid a smile as his eyes kept flickering downwards.

"I need your cooperation Miss Bishop."

"That is what I am here for sir," she said calmly.

"But I need to know I can completely trust you."

"With your life, sir, I promise you."

He cleared his throat again. "I need you to keep Miss Anders busy."

Was that all, Amy groaned inwardly, trying to look interested.

"How would you like me to do that sir? It isn't easy with her limited knowledge of how we do things."

He coughed nervously. "Precisely; think of something to keep her out of her office – so that she doesn't get bored," he added quickly.

60

Beginning to get the picture, Amy was emboldened to say quietly, "Are you saying you don't want her – examining – things and running back to her grandfather sir?" She raised her eyebrows innocently and he started to deny the suggestion.

"No, no, of course not, all I mean—"

"Because if you were, I would have to—" she hesitated and saw panic in his eyes, "suggest that we put her on the shop floor and let her sell cars, which is what she is best at, after all."

He slumped back with relief. "That is a very good suggestion – exactly what I had in mind. Well I think that will be all Miss Bishop."

He had lost interest in her legs she noticed and was perspiring freely.

"My goodness sir, you look all hot and bothered; can I do anything for you?"

She moved forward and reached across him for the box of tissues, allowing her cleavage to come in contact briefly, before drawing back and holding the box out to him. At the same time, she perched on the desk so that her legs were within easy reach.

"Tell me sir, am I to understand, that you want me to be in charge of her daily schedule?"

He drummed the arm of the chair and stared intently into her dark brown, heavily pencilled eyes. "Perhaps we understand each other."

She leant forward and whispered in his ear, "You only have to say – sir."

He was sweating even more, as he laid a trembling hand on her thigh, just as the door opened after a brief knock and Peter strode in, giving a surprised, "Well, well, well," as Amy slid casually of the desk, collected the coffee cups and left, completely ignoring his smirk.

"She's a cool one," he commented as the door closed.

"What do you want? Haven't you heard of knocking?" William demanded.

"Sorry if I interrupted – something," Peter grinned.

"If you must know, I was trying to find out if I could trust her; she understood alright and took over, now I'm worried because I don't know what I've let myself in for."

Peter laughed loudly. "You didn't look too worried to me when I walked in. Good job it was nobody else; it would be round the building by lunchtime."

"Laugh if you must, but don't forget I'm thinking of our future; don't forget you aren't totally innocent."

"I just sell cars," Peter said, his smile disappearing.

"Oh, and what about all of the backhanders you take?"

"Just gifts from grateful clients," Peter said guardedly.

William stared, realising how easily his nephew could cover his own tracks and how dangerously close to the wind, he himself was sailing.

"Well the best thing you can do is help keep that girl busy; see that she doesn't poke around. Amy Bishop will set up the schedule. I rely on you to do the rest."

"Suddenly I can do whatever I want?"

"Do whatever you have to; just do it, and get out of my sight."

"Yes Uncle." Peter stood to attention and saluted. "Whatever you say Uncle."

Peter clicked his heels, turned smartly and left, leaving William muttering, "I could seriously go off that boy."

*

Samantha was in her office, scrolling through records and figures. Wendy had explained, but it was hopeless without knowing exactly what to look for; there were just pages and pages of seemingly endless columns of figures and the very fact that she was allowed to see them, more or less told her they weren't important.

Amy kept popping in over the next two days, with lame excuses and Peter took her to lunch. She went because she had to eat and he was quite good company – when he didn't keep making suggestive remarks. To Peter though she had become a challenge he couldn't resist.

Sitting in the local wine bar together, his thoughts turned to Amy Bishop. Uncle William was right to be suspicious; girls like her were only ever after one thing from an old man; a sugar daddy. She could do worse he supposed. Uncle wasn't short of a bob or two with a wealthy wife like Monica providing a luxurious life style. What would she have to say about Amy Bishop, he wondered, with a sardonic smile.

Over lunch, he asked Samantha if she fancied staying in town for the weekend, and going to a show.

"My brother is home; it's his last weekend before he returns to Africa next week. I'm going home Thursday evening and I won't be back until Tuesday."

"Alright for some," he joked. "Oh well, I'll have to find someone else to keep me happy."

"That's the usual thing to do, I believe," she snapped.

He shot her a curious look. "Have you been dumped?"

"Not strictly speaking," she answered coldly.

"You have." He looked more closely. "Maybe I stand a chance now; I knew there had to be something or someone holding you back."

"Because you are so irresistible of course," she said caustically.

"Ouch!"

"I'm sorry, that was mean," she said, touching his arm.

"I forgive you," he smiled, "But only because I really fancy you rotten and if you give me a chance, I could make you forget him; how about it?"

She gave a non-committal laugh. "You are incorrigible."

"Well, just let me show you where we could be alone," he suggested seriously.

It was impossible not to be flattered when her ego had taken such a battering.

"Maybe."

"Is that a definite maybe?"

She looked uncertain. "I'll think about it."

"I'll hold you to that; it's good to live dangerously sometimes." His light grey eyes challenged her and she felt an unfamiliar rush of – what?

On returning to the huge Anders building, Peter pointed upwards. "That is where we can be alone; no one will know except us."

Samantha looked up and frowned.

"Hospitality apartments, on the top floor?" he said, tutting as she shook her head.

"I shall familiarise myself with the whole building this very afternoon. It will give me something to do."

"Steady on; I can show you the important bits." He suddenly remembered this was what his Uncle was trying to avoid.

"I rather think, that your idea of important and mine will be quite different," she said with a knowing look. "But thanks for pointing out my next step. Bye for now."

Peter kicked himself, realizing he had walked right into that one and headed straight for William Spencer's office.

Amy was just leaving and the atmosphere was charged.

"Is it my imagination or are her skirts getting shorter?" Peter joked, having watched her swaying departure with some amusement.

"What's the problem?" William asked affably, his manner changing as Peter told him Samantha intended exploring all of the floors, leaving out his own idea for one of the hospitality apartments, of course, but William, somehow guessed that he had put her up to it.

"Just how stupid can you get?"

"Well, it was only a matter of time; don't underestimate her; she might be young but she's not stupid."

William scowled. "What are you saying?"

"She is like her great-grandfather and the only reason you have been able to pull the wool over his eyes is because he is an invalid, out of touch with modern methods; you would never have been able to do it, a few years back."

"Well do your best not to make any more stupid suggestions and stop her," William snapped giving him a withering look, pressing the buzzer for Amy.

"Get the girl downstairs in the showroom and make sure she stays there for the next two weeks," he barked at her. "And you, get yourself down there and do what you are paid to do," he barked at Peter.

Amy hurried out and hastily arranged a sales promotion, to keep Samantha busy over the next month, thoroughly enjoying the importance of being in charge, on William Spencer's specific orders.

She met Samantha coming out of her office, armed with a plan of the building, which she had just down loaded.

"Leave whatever you are doing and get down to the front showroom. Here is your schedule for the next month." She pushed a folder at Samantha, who just ignored it and raised her eyebrows. Realizing she had overstepped herself, Amy explained, "Mr Spencer's orders."

Samantha looked haughty. "I would hope he didn't intend them to be delivered in that fashion."

Amy flushed and turned to go, saying, "No Miss."

"Oh, and Amy, I hope I won't have to remind you again. I take it, you do like working here?"

Amy couldn't bring herself to turn round. "Yes, Miss Anders."

Samantha watched her go back to her desk, remembering Wendy's suspicions about her. Definitely one to watch she decided; glad at least to have been given something positive to do. Bryn was never far from her thoughts and the ache of knowing he would soon be married refused to go away. Why was the thought of being in his arms all she could think of now, when she had waited so long, afraid of feeling emotion?

She was walking through the showroom, looking slightly bewildered and Peter, mistaking the reason, called to her.

"All a bit strange, but you'll soon feel at home."

"Yes, yes of course." She pulled herself together with an effort and smiled.

"Thought you were going to cry for a minute," he joked, not realizing how near the truth he was.

She gave a false laugh and looked away.

The next two days passed quickly and Darren arrived to pick her up early on the Thursday. Spending time with Tim took her mind off Bryn and it was only when she went to bed that tears came.

She spent time with Gerald on the Saturday when Darren took Tim flying with him and it was then she learnt about the apartments and their purpose.

"Years ago we thought it a good solution to provide reasonable accommodation for travellers. The scheme paid for itself in the past but the apartments aren't used these days." He studied her, made a steeple of his long thin fingers and said abruptly, "Don't think of staying there, will you?"

She laughed. "No worries, I like it with Bob and Marcia. I might take a peep though. I should at least know what is on each floor. I'm being kept pretty busy at the moment; a last minute sales promotion has been organized and I'm hardly in my office, so if you want to contact me ring my mobile."

Gerald nodded. "Well it is all part of learning the business I suppose."

After she had gone back to the cottage and Gerald was alone he stared unseeingly at the wall opposite, with narrowed eyes, steepling the tips of his fingers together. Perhaps he was being impatient, but if he had been there, she would be spending her time learning the financial side; all she was doing at the moment was what they paid sales teams to do. He must have another word with Spencer.

At eight thirty in the morning, he telephoned, to speak to William. "I will get him to ring you as soon as he arrives, sir," Amy informed him in a businesslike voice.

Replacing the receiver, she dialled a number and said:

"Best get down to your office."

CHAPTER EIGHT

Samantha leant back in the luxurious, pale blue leather chair that had been waiting in her office for her that morning, unconsciously copying Gerald's habit by making a steeple of her fingers. The chair, a birthday present from Tim, tearfully reminded her of his departure back to Egypt earlier that morning. Picking up her mobile phone, she sent a text. *Wonderful surprise. Wonderful chair. Missing you already. love n hugs. x*

He would get it when he got off the plane, she thought reaching in the top drawer for a tissue. As she did so, her attention was caught by the plan of the building she had printed off, on the day the sales promotion started.

She glanced at her wristwatch; it was still only eight o'clock; she wasn't normally in the office this early, but she had wanted to see Tim off. Darren had flown them to the airport then dropped her off on the way back. Everywhere was quiet and with time on her hands, it was a perfect opportunity to explore. Picking up the plan, she left the office and went along the corridor to the lifts. The apartments were on the top floor and as she stepped out a young woman was coming towards her.

"Hi there, hold the lift, will you?"

Sam obliged saying, "I didn't expect to see anyone this early; do you stay here?"

"Now and then." She gave a conspiratorial smile and held out her hand. "I'm Cherie."

Samantha took the outstretched hand. "Samantha. Are the apartments occupied then?"

"Oh yes, they are very popular, but then they would be."

"Really?"

Cherie laughed. "You wait and see; real five star."

"Really?" Samantha repeated.

"Luxury, with a capital L. Must dash, might see you around again."

The lift doors closed and Samantha stared along a beige carpeted corridor. It stretched to the right, where Cherie had come from. The sound of a cistern flushing made her realise, that this might not be such a good idea after all; she hurried back to the lifts and returned to her office, full of questions. It was still only eight twenty and no other staff would arrive until nine. Perhaps she could find where they made tea in this maze. The typing pool would be the most likely place to start looking, she imagined. At least she knew where to find that.

On her way past Amy Bishop's desk, she saw her memo pad open and out of curiosity, looked. In the top right hand corner of the page, encircled with red ink was, 'keep G busy, he, he.' On the next page, the same thing appeared and the next and the next; even when no other entries had been made; it was on every page. Obviously something personal that amused Amy.

The tea making facilities turned out to be at the far end of the office behind a tall screen. While she waited for the kettle to boil she found a mug and a teabag and discovered a small amount of milk in an otherwise empty fridge. Carrying her tea carefully she was unaware of Amy standing with her back to her, until the telephone rang; she carried on walking, intending to make her presence known, and heard Amy say, "Mr Spencer hasn't arrived yet but I will get him to ring you the moment he arrives, sir."

Before she reached her, Amy dialled a number and said quietly, "Best get down here."

As she replaced the receiver, Samantha said, "Good morning Miss Bishop."

Amy spun round, guiltily and stuttered.

"Wh – what are you doing? Why are you sp – spying on me?"

Recoiling at her reaction, Samantha, managed to say coolly, "I'm sorry if I startled you, but I do have every right to be here and as for spying on you – have you got something to hide?"

"No, no of course not, you made me jump – that's all; I didn't think anyone else was here yet."

"I was making myself a cup of tea to kill time."

"Why *are* you here so early?" Amy asked impertinently.

"I could ask the same question of you. I shall come more often, though; it's a good time to get the feel of the place – providing that's alright with you, of course, and doesn't interfere with your private plans?"

Samantha's sarcasm took Amy unawares and lost for words, she hurried away towards the lifts.

Samantha wandered after her and watched the lift travel straight to the top floor.

"Curious," she murmured wondering who the phone call was to. With the question still in mind, she retraced her steps, pressed redial and sat at Amy's desk, waiting for her to return.

It was ten to nine before she reappeared, looking calmer until she saw Samantha waiting for her.

"I need to get to my desk – Miss Anders."

Samantha rose, glanced at the memo pad and pointed to the right hand corner. "Interesting little memo; not hard to work out; I used to do things like that at junior school, about teachers."

Amy looked as if she was about to lash out, but brushed past and sat at the desk looking sulky.

Samantha decided not to question her about the phone call to apartment two, but to just check on exactly what the apartments were used for. She rang Wendy and asked whose job it would be to deal with the rooms. Wendy said to try Sandra Williams in finance.

"They were closed years ago. The reps prefer to go to a hotel now. Mr Spencer has the keys," Sandra Williams told her in a singsong, Welsh accent.

Samantha tried unsuccessfully to see William Spencer three times that morning and decided in the end to telephone her grandfather.

Gerald was alarmed. "Why are you so interested, Princess? I don't like you wandering about an empty floor by yourself; it could be dangerous."

"I just want to have a look Granddad; perhaps we could put them to use if they are refurbished."

"Well, they did pay their way at one time, before expenses improved; now I'm told everyone wants hotel accommodation."

"Then perhaps we can let them as franchises," Samantha suggested.

Gerald gave a loud laugh. "By golly I knew I was right. You are going to make a first rate business woman."

"So now can I have a look?"

"I'll talk to Spencer," Gerald said still laughing gleefully.

"Today please?"

"Of course."

She waited until five o'clock but there was no word and eventually she rang Peter's mobile.

"How about this apartment you were going to show me? I'm free after work."

"I can be there in half an hour," he answered sounding eager.

"Fine."

He was there in twenty minutes and she greeted him gaily. "That was quick."

"Didn't want you to change your mind."

"We are only going to look at apartments."

His eyes twinkled at her as he held open the door of her office. She walked swiftly to the lift and he followed in happy anticipation.

He had never seen her in this mood and he liked it.

The cream painted door, with a brass number one, swung open and she was taken unawares by a well-furnished room. Fresh linen covered a king size bed and immaculate, pale gold carpets and curtains, met her gaze before she wandered through into the small, well-equipped bathroom, where fluffy white towels and dressing gowns hung on chrome rails. Beyond that was a small, but luxuriously fitted kitchen alcove, with top of the range equipment. Obviously, no expense had been spared.

She looked at him with a puzzled frown. "I don't understand; I thought the rooms were run down and unused."

"So did I; this one must be kept for a special customer." Peter was looking at the big bed longingly.

"Don't you just want to try it?" he tried to tempt her.

"I just can't get over it. I was expecting to find a project I could work on."

With a sickening jolt, Peter realised he had probably dropped his uncle right in it. This had to be the lucrative sideline he had going. If he had only told him – probably thought he would want a share, he thought resentfully. He felt sick; William was going to kill him if he found out that he had brought Sam up here.

"I think we should go," he said, his ardour suddenly dampened.

"Can't I see the rest of the flats?" Samantha pleaded.

"I only brought the one key." It had been the only one in his uncle's desk drawer.

Seeing his discomfit, Samantha decided to let it drop, promising herself that first thing tomorrow morning, she would tackle William Spencer in his office.

The following morning she waited, but when he hadn't shown up by ten o'clock she gave up, went back to her desk and called Amy on the intercom to ask where Mr Spencer was.

"He is attending an all day conference."

Samantha could hear the smirk in her voice, so she said, "I will have my coffee now," and flicked the switch off.

Fifteen minutes went by and Samantha went to see where the coffee was; she found Amy on the telephone and raised her eyebrows questioningly.

Amy quickly replaced the receiver. "That was Mr Spencer. He won't be in again tomorrow."

"I see." She turned away and spoke to a girl at a nearby filing cabinet. "Would you bring me a cup of coffee, served on a tray like Mrs Parker used to and bring it to my office please?"

The girls face lit up. "Oh, yes Miss Anders, happy to."

"Meg is filing, I will get your coffee, now I'm not busy," Amy bridled.

"Oh, I would hate to interrupt your busy schedule; cream and sugar please Meg," Samantha called over her shoulder, as she returned to her office.

When the coffee arrived, it was laid out on a tray with cream, sugar and biscuits. "Thank you Meg, that's just how Wendy did it."

"Any time Miss Anders; you only have to say. Mrs Parker always did things nicely. I really miss her."

"So do I. By the way do you know anyone called Cherie?"

"Can't say I do Miss Anders, is she employed here?"

"Well, I assume so; she was on the top floor very early this morning when I spoke to her."

"We could look her up." Meg turned the computer on and went down the employees list. It was long and she eventually said, "Perhaps it isn't her real name. There is no one with that first name."

"That's disappointing; there are several questions I would like to ask her."

"Perhaps she was just visiting, in which case she would have to sign the visitors' book at the entrance lobby."

Samantha looked at her admiringly. "You really are a star."

"Do you want me to fetch it for you?"

"Can you?"

"If I say I'm doing an errand for you." She gave an impish smile and Samantha, became aware of how attractive she was. Short, dark curly hair, dark brown eyes and olive skin, topped a slim, almost boyish figure. She moved agilely, left the room and returned ten minutes later, carrying a narrow ledger.

"I'll have to take it straight back before it's missed," she said laying it on the desk in front of Samantha. They went down the page, for the day before and that morning, because Meg said Cherie would have needed to sign in – and out, but no one had signed the book at all, which was strange because there had been other occupants – of that Samantha was absolutely sure.

"We've drawn a blank I'm afraid; any more ideas?"

"Not right now, but I'll have a think." Meg picked the book up and left the office again, leaving Samantha thinking what a good P.A. she would make.

When Meg got back to her filing, Amy asked her where she had been.

"I ran an errand for Miss Anders."

70

"What sort of an errand?" Amy demanded.

Just a small one; she wanted to know if someone by the name of Cherie visited yesterday, so I fetched the visitors' book, but it wasn't in there; do you know of anyone by that name?"

Amy paled. "You aren't paid to run silly errands; get back to filing those applications."

"Yes Miss."

"Yes Miss Bishop," Amy snapped.

Meg turned to the filing cabinet, rolling her eyes.

Samantha sent a text to Peter asking if they could look at another flat and received no answer, but having got the bit between her teeth, she decided to go and look for the keys herself.

It was nearly five o'clock, so she gathered her things and told Amy she was going home, making as if to leave. Once out of sight she found her way to William Spencer's office, praying that the door would be unlocked. Luck was with her; a plumber was fixing a leak in the private bathroom with just a junior office boy guarding the door and of course, he knew her by sight. She sat at the desk, looking through a folder, left lying on top, trying not to appear to be rifling as she glanced into the drawers. In the top one, there was a single key, it looked like the one Peter had used, but she couldn't be sure; she would have to take a chance.

The plumber came out of the bathroom carrying his bag of tools and the office boy walked towards her holding out a key asking if she would lock up after herself.

"Oh I'm quite finished; you can lock up safely. Good bye."

Making sure that Amy had gone home, she went through the corridors and took the lift to the top floor, but on arriving, a raised voice reached her ears and she recognised it. Amy was on the telephone and it was coming from the slightly open door of apartment two.

"She is suspicious, I tell you. I *can't* do this on my own," she insisted loudly.

Holding her breath, Samantha crept to the third door and inserted the key. It turned and the door opened. What an amazing bit of luck. The room was a replica of room one. Very gently, she closed the door and moved on to the next one; to be greeted with yet another identical room. She decided it must be a skeleton key and just to be sure, tried a third door, much further along the hallway. This time she heard running water as the door swung inwards; someone was taking a shower. Rooted to the spot, she heard the water stop and guessed that any minute, the occupant would appear. Galvanised into action, she took a quick glance around, noting a man's jacket on a pine stand and an expensive looking bottle of aftershave, next to various other toiletries on the dressing table. The bathroom door started to open and she stepped quickly back, pulling the door shut and slipping the key out of the lock. It made quite a loud click and she held her breath as a man's voice asked, "Is that you Cherie?"

The door opened and a heavily set, grey-haired figure appeared with a towel fastened around his middle. With no time to move, Samantha said nervously, "Sorry I must have the wrong room."

"Which one you looking for, honey?" the man asked in a broad American accent.

"Number one," she said, thinking quickly.

He looked her up and down admiringly. "That'll be back by the lift, honey. But if you ever get lost again, you come and see me." His blue eyes crinkled in a wide grin as she backed away thanking him. Arms akimbo he watched her hurry back down the landing. At number one she turned and waved to him, pretending to press the bell; the man waved back, then disappeared and she quickly stepped into the waiting lift, pressing the button, just as the other lift opened and she caught a glimpse of Cherie, stepping out, before her own door closed.

As the lift descended, she gave a great, whew! Then eyes shining with nervous excitement she took a quick look at the visitors' book as she passed the security desk. There were no new entries, and she returned to Bob and Marcia's, in a thoughtful mood.

Riding alone through the forest that evening she came to several decisions, one of which she put into action as soon as Amy was at her desk the following morning.

"I require an assistant for the day, Miss Bishop; send Meg to my office straight away."

"She can't be spared for a full day; she has a work schedule arranged."

"Then you will have to rearrange. I shall expect to see her in five minutes. Oh, and I won't be helping with the promotion; I can keep myself busy today, thank you."

Amy got up and headed for the staff room and Samantha returned to her office, feeling almost sorry for her until she reminded herself that Amy had been responsible for Wendy's dismissal.

Meg arrived, bearing note pad, pencil and a tray of coffee and they set to work on the computer, learning which department did what and familiarising Samantha with key names. Meg had excellent computer skills and by mid afternoon, memos had been sent to all departments inviting managers and under managers to attend Miss Anders' office, the following Monday morning at nine o'clock, sharp.

When they had finished, they looked at each other, half apprehensively.

"That will stir things up," Meg said, her brown eyes dancing.

"That is the intention; they need to know that they can't mess with me, just because I'm nineteen and a woman."

Meg slumped back in her chair, looking satisfied and Samantha told her to take the rest of the afternoon off because they had missed lunch.

Later when Samantha left her office to go home, Meg was still working and she went over to her.

"I thought I said you could go home."

"She had to stay and finish her work," Amy's voice answered from behind the screen.

"I expect my wishes to be followed. And have the courtesy to stop hiding behind that screen when you speak to me," Samantha said coldly.

Amy poked her head round.

"Mr Spencer left me in charge. I have to get the work done."

Samantha turned to Meg and spoke firmly.

"Go home; starting Monday, come straight to my office; from now on you are my personal assistant."

Meg's face broke into a broad smile. "Oh, thank you. I won't let you down."

"I know you won't; off you go now, while I have a word with our Miss Bishop."

Amy came from behind the screen. "She still has work to do Miss Anders."

"Starting Monday morning, Meg will be my permanent, personal assistant, so make alternative arrangements. Goodnight Miss Bishop."

"Mr Spencer won't agree to that," Amy called after her. "He wants you in the show room."

"Then he will have the opportunity to tell me himself at the meeting on Monday morning, because we wouldn't want to interfere with his all day conference on the golf course, tomorrow, would we?"

Amy's mouth dropped open. "Mr Spencer is the Managing Director; you can't give him orders."

"But I can and you would do well not to forget it." Samantha's head went up and she walked out leaving Amy looking flummoxed.

On arriving back at 'The Vintage', she rang her father.

"Can you spare time to pick me up Daddy?"

"What's up, Princess? You don't usually come home on a Thursday."

"Something I need to talk over with Granddad. I'll tell you on the way home; tomorrow morning will do if you can't make it tonight."

"I'll be there in half an hour; I'm delivering in Surrey."

"Wonderful! Thanks Daddy."

CHAPTER NINE

Darren touched down just after six o'clock. It was a clear, still evening and Samantha could barely wait to change and take Nocturn out.

"Aren't you going to eat something," Melly called, as Samantha ran past the kitchen door on the way to the path.

"Won't be long; need to unwind, before I see Granddad."

Melly watched her from the window, glad to see her looking happier.

Bryn was still at his parents' home and she had heard that the wedding would be in two weeks' time. Thank goodness, it was to be in France. Apparently, the baby was due in September. Sam must be feeling awful, but she had obviously got a bee in her bonnet about something to come home this early, she mused, starting to prepare the evening meal.

Nocturn galloped along the cliff top toward 'The Point', exhilarated at the unexpected outing. Hair streaming in the breeze, Samantha thrilled as always to the strength of the huge stallion beneath her. This was their next favourite place when the tide was in and the cove was flooded. They moved as one and just a softly spoken word was all that was needed for him to drop down to a trot and then a walk as they reached the end of the half-mile run. Only then did she see and recognise the lone figure sitting by the roadside. Bryn stared and hesitated, not knowing how she would react and she stared back. For a moment, she shook with anger but his obvious dismay tugged at her heart as she remembered how precious their friendship had been; slipping off Nocturn's back, she ran to him. He caught her to him and they embraced as they never had before; and then they were kissing and she thought she would die with happiness. They sank to the ground, and long suppressed needs took over. She was wearing very little under her favourite, old blue dress and his fingers trembled as they undid the small pearl buttons, to reveal her full breasts. Engulfed in rapturous abandonment under the darkening evening sky, time stood still. It was dusk before they drew apart and lay on their backs looking wondrously at each other.

"I knew you would come back to me," she whispered.

"I came up here to be by myself and think. I had no idea you would be here." He raised himself onto his elbow. "But Jocelyn is still having my child."

"You can't marry her, now we know we love each other," Sam protested.

"I wish it were that easy." He sat up, resting his elbows on his knees, burying his head in his hands. "*All, because, of one, silly, New Year's Eve.*"

"What happened?" Sam heard herself asking dully.

"We finished our shift, long past midnight after working our socks off all evening. The six of us, Kate, Terry, Joanne, Jon, Jo and I, decided to stay at Kate's, because she lived closest and a taxi would have cost the earth on New Year's Eve. We had to sleep on the floor because there was only one bed. We had several drinks before we settled down." He looked at her apologetically, before continuing. "I woke in the morning, to find Jo in my sleeping bag with me."

"Do you love her?" Sam asked sadly.

"I love you and I was prepared to wait forever if necessary; I must have got carried away."

"Don't you remember?"

"I was deathly tired; there was wine; everyone was feeling more than a little merry and I remember us kissing under the mistletoe."

"Can we meet here again tomorrow?" Sam asked wistfully.

"I didn't think you would want any more to do with me," Bryn said laying down again and burying his face in her neck.

They made love again and promised to see each other the next evening.

"I don't see how I can marry Jocelyn, after tonight," Bryn said softly as they parted.

Melly and Darren looked at her curiously when she arrived home, noting the crumpled dress and dreamy look.

"Aren't you hungry?" Melly asked with concern.

"Not really. Do you mind if I go straight to bed? It has been a long day."

"What happened about the urgent need to see Granddad?" Darren asked in a puzzled voice, having heard most of the story on their journey home.

Jerked back to earth, Samantha remembered her reason for coming home.

"Oh gosh, it's too late now. I'll have to see him first thing in the morning."

How could she have forgotten so completely? Lying in bed half an hour later though, her only thoughts were of Bryn, as she relived their moments together.

First thing in the morning she ran lightly down the cliff path, and joined Gerald, who was about to have breakfast. Helping herself to the array of grilled

76

food from the sideboard, she sat down next to him and buttered a slice of toast, talking animatedly about her discoveries.

"I've called a meeting in my office for Monday morning; I'm not sure how many will come, but what I would like to happen…"

She went on to explain what she had in mind.

CHAPTER TEN

"You have been gone ages; where were you? I tried your mobile."

Jocelyn screamed frantically. "The baby is coming."

Bryn stared at her. "We must get you to the hospital. Dad will drive us. Where is mother?"

"Your aunt has been taken ill; they left soon after you went out. Where have you been? I've been so frightened."

"Have you telephoned Mum?"

"I don't know the number, do I? Do something," she screeched at him, closing her eyes in pain.

The ambulance arrived fifteen minutes later and rushed them to hospital, where she gave birth to a ten-pound baby boy, twelve hours later.

The next day went by in a haze for Bryn as he comforted Jocelyn and held his newborn son. Exhausted by the difficult, forceps birth, Jocelyn had to remain in hospital for a full week and Bryn stayed by her bedside, torn by guilt. He made a quick call to Samantha and heard the sadness in her voice when she asked how long it would be before they could be together. Since then, between attending to Jocelyn and trying not to arouse his parents' suspicion, it had been impossible to phone again. He spent two sleepless nights, lying in a single bed, waiting for Jocelyn to fall asleep, in the hope of creeping out and phoning, but somehow she would always wake as he was leaving and get hysterical. With time to dwell on his situation he came to realise, he couldn't leave her and his son. The scandal would not only destroy his parents' lives, it would also damage his career and result in him never being able to join his father's practice in this area. After considering these overwhelming facts, he wrote a brief note, saying only that he would be in touch soon.

Samantha didn't know what to think; his reticence left her on edge, waiting for a phone call but when there was no further word by Sunday evening, she had to return to 'The Vintage' and prepare herself for the meeting on Monday morning.

At eight o'clock, she and Meg were both in her office, where Meg was sending memos, transferring the meeting to the boardroom at ten o'clock sharp.

On Amy's desk there was a message telling her to inform Mr Spencer, his presence was urgently required, on an important matter.

By ten o'clock, all members had arrived except William Spencer and they were nervously watching Gerald drumming his fingers on the long table.

At a nod from Gerald, Samantha pressed a button on the intercom and William's voice answered, "Yes?"

"Maybe you didn't get my message, Mr Spencer?"

"I did but I am very busy and unable to attend."

"I need you to attend immediately."

"If this important matter is about your not wanting to do the sales promotion, we don't need a board meeting for that. And in any case you have no authority to call a board meeting."

"Nevertheless your presence is required straightaway."

There was a short silence, then, "Very well then, I will be there in half an hour." This time, his words were accompanied by an unmistakable, stifled giggle.

"What are you playing at man? Get down here now," Gerald roared.

There was a stunned silence before William gasped, "Yes, Sir Gerald; right away Sir Gerald."

Two minutes later, a red-faced William shot through the door.

"Good morning Sir Gerald, wonderful to see you. I had no idea you were well enough to travel," he blustered

"Obviously," Gerald replied, stony faced. "Just what was this busy morning you had lined up?"

"A client, Sir Gerald."

"Going by the name of Amy Bishop, I presume."

"She is my personal assistant Sir Gerald." William looked affronted.

"I am aware of that William; rather *too* personal I believe."

"I assure you Sir Gerald, you have been misled." William shot a venomous look at Samantha, as Gerald stared at him with raised eyebrows and continued.

"Moving onto the first item on the agenda, I understand the apartments are in use."

William started to sweat. "Just a project I have wanted to surprise you with Sir Gerald."

"You would seem to have achieved your aim in that direction," Gerald agreed. "When did you plan on surprising me? Quite a money spinner, I imagine."

"Oh indeed sir. If you will allow me, I will fetch the figures."

Gerald nodded and William left hastily, assuring Gerald that it would just take a few minutes.

Once out of the boardroom, William broke into a fast trot, passing Amy who was on her way from his office.

"What's the matter? You look dreadful." She turned around to follow him.

"I've got to get away."

"I'm coming with you then; you promised you would take me."

"There's no time to talk now!" he panted. He made straight for the safe on reaching his office, punching the numbers with trembling fingers at the same time as telling her to get the briefcase from under his desk.

"Just four more days; that's all I needed, four more days. That wretched girl has ruined everything."

He was practically crying as he swung the heavy door back and started to pack large bundles of notes into the briefcase.

Amy's eyes boggled and she started to laugh. "With all of that we can go abroad."

"You've been watching too much television. I've got to get out of the country first."

"Don't you mean, we?" Amy asked sharply.

He snapped the bulging briefcase shut and turned to her, looking sorrowful.

"I'll have to send for you, just don't tell them anything."

"You can't leave me; you promised we would go away together if I helped you!" she cried.

"I just needed four more days, but now I have to make a run for it – on my own." He was crying as he kissed her clumsily and ran to the door. "I'll send for you."

He disappeared and she slumped onto a chair, staring at the closing door. Five minutes passed before the intercom buzzed.

"How long does it take to pick up those papers?" Gerald asked irritably.

"Mr Spencer is on his way," she answered tonelessly and the intercom went dead. She had won him a few minutes. Slowly she returned to her own desk and tried to look normal.

In the boardroom Gerald lost patience and sent a junior to look for William. The boy returned and reported that Mr Spencer had been seen leaving the building fifteen minutes earlier.

Bedlam broke out as Simon Hall and Wendy, who had been working in the finance department, arrived with the disquieting news that it appeared the company had been defrauded of a very significant sum.

Renting the apartments had all been done in a purely private arrangement with wealthy businessmen from abroad, willing to part with large sums of money to indulge themselves.

"He needed help to do all of this," Simon said, looking around at the other board members who had been detained, his eyes resting on John Denzel from Finance.

"Don't look at me," John said fidgeting uncomfortably, frantically wondering how he was going to deny his part in this so called foolproof scheme that he had so foolishly allowed William to persuade him into; well he certainly didn't intend to be left holding the can now that William had absconded.

"You are his nephew, Mr Chambers; you must have known what was going on," Gerald accused sharply, transferring his attention to Peter.

"It's news to me," Peter answered looking miserable. "In fact I probably gave the game away by showing your granddaughter the apartment."

"That's true Grandfather," Samantha agreed.

Gerald suddenly slumped; the long journey followed by the excitement had taken its toll. George gave a concerned look.

"Ye Grandfather needs rest, Miss Samantha."

Samantha turned panic-stricken eyes to where Gerald sat breathing heavily, blaming herself for her thoughtlessness. "Let's take you up to one of the rooms Granddad. You can sleep and George will bring you food. Everything will be taken care of here. Wendy and Simon will tell me what needs to be done."

Gerald closed his eyes and she nodded at George to follow as she led the way to the lift. Uniformed policemen were already stationed at various points and she requested that Sir Anders should not be disturbed as George guided the wheelchair into one of the apartments.

"Write a list of whatever you need and I will see that it is sent up immediately," Samantha told George as he looked around with a practised eye and set to work, producing a hip flask of brandy from a leather case stowed under the wheelchair and holding a small glass to Gerald's lips.

Samantha watched helplessly as he swiftly made Gerald comfortable, thankful to see a small amount of colour returning to his pallid cheeks as she took his outstretched hand.

"Don't worry Princess; I'm alright now. You go and take care of things, while I rest."

"I shouldn't have asked you to come."

"I'm glad you did." He waved his hand dismissively. "Go and take charge for me."

She looked at George who stopped long enough to reassure her that everything was in hand and opened the door as a knock announced the arrival of the food. With a lingering backward glance through the open door, she saw George capably attending to her grandfather's needs before hurrying away, knowing he had the best possible care.

Making her way down to the first floor she passed members of staff and told them that everything was in hand and they would be informed what was happening shortly. Some kind of explanation about the police activity was obviously necessary, but Simon and Wendy would know when and how that should be made she decided making straight for the boardroom where all board members were still gathered.

Simon and Wendy looked serious. There was evidence that a huge sum of money had been transferred but just how much had not yet been confirmed.

"How could that happen?" Samantha asked, assuming that security would be in place.

John Denzel looked frightened and Peter was staring at the investigating team, dreading what they were going to discover. His own backhanders were minute – in comparison to the figure he had heard whispered, but even so it was still fraud; what on earth had Uncle William been up to? More than letting flats, that was for sure.

"Someone has hacked into the system," Wendy explained eventually. "It had to be someone with inside knowledge, to override the security check, like William Spencer or or ..." she looked questioningly at John Denzel who went white with fear.

"I swear I know nothing about that; all I did was to cover up the refurbishment costs. Mr Spencer gave his word he would return the money before the year was up."

He was taken away for questioning by the police.

Peter suddenly volunteered: "Uncle William can only just about manage to log on; he couldn't have done it."

"So where is he and why has he run away?" Simon asked, looking at him askance.

"Frightened I suppose. Have you tried his house?"

A detective entered at that moment, went straight to Simon and after a few quietly spoken words, Simon turned to Peter. "It would appear that his house is displaying a sold sign; any other suggestions?"

Peter's mouth dropped open. "I was only there two weeks ago and there was no mention of moving then."

"The sale was completed two weeks ago according to the estate agent and there is no forwarding address."

Peter's eyes were wide with shock.

"Mrs Spencer booked two plane tickets for next Friday, but it turns out they were one way tickets; two more were bought, very late last Friday night by two women matching the description of your wife and her mother," Wendy said, adding quietly as they all watched for his reaction, "The tickets were all for Switzerland."

Amy had been sitting in a far corner and tears sprung to her eyes as her dream of luxury crashed.

Peter slumped in his chair with glazed eyes. "He never said a word."

An independent computer expert had been brought in and the mind-boggling figure showing on the screen danced crazily in front of Samantha; eleven followed by six noughts. The money had gone out over the weekend. It had been transferred to a Swiss bank account, Friday night. Further bad news was that the money had been withdrawn again and the account closed this very morning, while they had been investigating. It then came to light that the whole system had crashed overnight on Friday and it had taken all day Saturday and Sunday to rectify.

"My grandfather must not know about this, his heart won't take it."

She looked at Wendy and Simon and they nodded.

"I'll ask George to take him home straight away and then I will call Uncle Charles; hopefully he will know how to deal with the situation."

Wendy and Simon looked relieved. Gerald agreed to go home, after Samantha promised to let him know of any further development and she waved him off, with a heavy heart, wishing she had asked Charles to deal with it in the first place.

Charles was on the next plane and brought the good news that Matthew was in remission, which made his own absence less worrying for the family.

He stayed in a nearby hotel and dealt diplomatically with the situation of the apartments. Six tenants, each unwittingly having paid a second year's rent in advance that very weekend, understandably objected to being asked to leave, but were more cooperative once the police became involved in a big way. The fact that the businessmen and their guests were allowed to enter and leave without security checks, made it harder to whittle down further suspects. It also negated insurance cover. William Spencer had created far more problems than even he could have foreseen.

Samantha spent the days helping where she could and yearning for Bryn to contact her. It was a long week and she was glad when the weekend arrived.

Darren picked her up and she went straight to see Gerald. He looked frail and was having difficulty in breathing, but wanted to know what was happening.

They are still searching for William Spencer so we know very little more yet," she said cautiously.

"He can't run forever. Have they questioned his wife?"

"Apparently they have been unable to contact her, but police are watching the house."

Gerald gave a satisfied sigh. "Well at least nothing has been released to the press; I asked that it should be suppressed."

She avoided telling him that trading had ceased and a police guard had taken over. The staff were all under investigation, but so far there was nothing to go on. Amy was questioned closely but still convinced that William would keep his promise she said nothing, continued sending text messages to his mobile and optimistically prepared to leave at a minute's notice, while feigning innocence by spending time at the job centre.

CHAPTER ELEVEN

William sat in his maroon Daimler, hidden from view in the woods opposite his substantial home. He had spent the night there and was cold, hungry and in need of a shave and shower. A police car stood in the drive and he wondered what his wife Monica was doing. He hadn't been home for the weekend and last night no lights had shown in any part of the house. Perhaps she had gone to stay with Lindsey rather than spend the weekend alone and hadn't returned yet. He cursed himself for staying in the flat over the weekend with Amy, but it was to have been their last weekend and he couldn't resist the temptation. Pity he had to let Amy down, but Monica was the important one.

He watched as the police guards were replaced, realizing then that getting into his home was out of the question. He rang Lindsey his stepdaughter but there was no reply either at home or on her mobile; where the devil was Monica when he needed her? Frustration seized him, before sanity returned and he realised that she couldn't know of recent events if she had been away from home.

About to turn the engine on he changed his mind and let the hand-break off, allowing the car to roll slowly backwards down the incline to a narrow lane before switching on the engine. Within twenty minutes he was in view of Peter and Lindsey's modern, four-bedroom detached house – a wedding present from Monica to Lindsey. It made him shudder to think what it had cost. Driving slowly, he saw Peter's car in the drive. He wouldn't be in this mess if it wasn't for him he fumed, as Peter appeared, dressed ready for work, apparently going about his normal routine. William pulled up opposite and catching sight of him, Peter hurried across.

"What are you doing here? The police are looking for you. Nice mess you left me in."

"I need a shower and fresh clothes."

"Well don't look at me for help; I arrived home last night with a police escort. They searched the house and grounds; heaven only knows what for but apparently they found nothing. They want to speak to Lindsey but there's no note and I traced her mobile phone to the kitchen bin when I phoned it. I just don't understand what is going on?"

"I don't know, do I?" William snapped impatiently, sounding frightened. "The police are guarding the house."

"Are you surprised? You've bankrupted Anders." Peter looked peeved. "You could have let me in on what you were doing – come to think of it though, I don't want to know."

"I was afraid you would let something slip; I was going to send for you when we were settled. What do you mean, practically bankrupted them? They will hardly miss a million, with all of their money."

"Eleven million more like," Peter said, hotly.

"What are you talking about?" William demanded.

"That's what I overheard. Money went missing last Friday night; and you were staying at the flat on the weekend; don't try and deny it. I told them that you couldn't have done it, because you wouldn't know how." He gave a disgusted sneer.

William's mouth dropped open and he leant his head back, shutting his eyes.

"Go to my house and see what is going on. Lindsey must have gone home to her mother," he said urgently, hoping to spur Peter on.

"So why don't they answer the phones?"

Nagging doubt began to dawn on William. "Just find out what is going on, for both of us," he urged Peter desperately.

Overwrought with his own situation, Peter recalled the conversation that had taken place in the boardroom.

"Your house has been sold, you must have known about that." he accused.

William looked uncomfortable. "I was going to tell you but there wasn't time; that interfering granddaughter messed everything up. I told you to keep her busy," he ended angrily.

"Oh so now it's all my fault."

William realised he needed Peter's help and tried to make amends. "No of course not, but we need to stick together and find out just where Lindsey and her mother are; that's why you have to go to the house."

"No point, they aren't there; they went to Switzerland. I heard that yesterday morning."

William slumped against the steering wheel.

"So that's where she is," he said in a tight voice.

"So, have they just gone on holiday?"

"Yes. No. I don't know. I'm sure Monica will be in touch when things calm down; then we will join them. She obviously heard something, couldn't reach me and decided it was safer not to wait."

"Wait, what for? You aren't making sense."

William looked at him sharply. "You didn't mention Amy to Lindsey did you?"

"No of course not," Peter said, going red as he remembered joking mildly about Uncle William's dolly bird secretary at a dinner party; but luckily, William was distracted by a passing car.

"Even so, that wouldn't explain why Lindsey has gone off," Peter said half to himself.

William sat up straight wracking his brain for answers. It was no secret that Lindsey was unhappy with Peter's philandering ways and had been for some time; but it didn't stop her from being completely besotted with him and he would trust Monica with his life; she wouldn't betray him, she adored him. She would get in touch in a few days and say where to meet her, he decided confidently. In the meantime though, he had to hide. He had the money from the safe, so no need to use his card, which was always a dead giveaway according to television films.

"What are you thinking?" Peter asked, breaking into his thoughts.

"I'm wondering where to go, until I can get out of the country. Monica will get in touch in a few days and she'll have something planned," he said confidently.

"How can you be so sure?" Peter asked curiously.

"Because the whole thing was her idea; she planned it from the start. She must have gone in and hacked into the account without me." He grinned suddenly. "She is a real whiz on the computer. I can't believe she went for eleven million though."

Peter looked gloomy. "So Lindsey's gone with her?"

"Not much doubt. They will be sitting comfortably in Switzerland as we speak." He gave a decisive nod, desperately hoping he was right.

"Surely that means Lindsey is involved and neither of them will ever be able to return home?"

"Don't worry, no one will suspect Monica of stealing all that money; she will have covered herself and she'll be in touch soon."

He spoke confidently, hoping to stop Peter from panicking, because for all his worldliness, Peter was very insecure when things went wrong and would speak without thinking. William had provided for him since he was eight years old, when his mother died; and marrying him to Lindsey was the best thing he had ever done.

"Keep it in the family," he had convinced Monica. "Any other man will divorce her and walk away with half of your money."

"Why don't you stay on the yacht?" Peter said, breaking into his thoughts, referring to the luxurious, thirty-two foot *Westerley*, belonging to William and Monica.

William looked surprised. "Of course, why didn't I think of that?"

Peter looked pleased with himself. "Where is it anchored now?"

"If you don't know, you can't let it slip." With a parting shot of: "I'll keep in touch." William put his foot down on the accelerator and drove off, sending grit flying all over Peter.

"Thanks Uncle," he said ruefully, brushing down his freshly, dry-cleaned suit and viewing his newly polished shoes, now covered in dust.

With a grunt, he returned to the house, regretting spending the weekend at a Beer Festival in Germany. Now he came to think of it, Lindsey had been a bit quiet when he left on Friday afternoon; there had been no mention of a holiday though. The more he thought about it, the more doubtful he became. If things had gone wrong with the plan and she couldn't contact William, Monica had probably panicked and taken off. He just couldn't imagine Lindsey being a part of it though; she didn't care about having pots of money, she was a quiet homemaker; her biggest ambition was to have children. Thinking now about their relationship, he realised he needed their comfortable life together. He would make a real effort to settle down when she came back. Full of self pity he sat head in hands, struggling with thoughts that kept going off at a tangent. He wasn't sure how long he sat there but a cheerful voice calling, "Anyone home?" roused him as footsteps came towards the lounge and their next door neighbour Joanne appeared, carrying her one-year-old daughter Poppy and a large bag of toys. Joanne was a bubbly personality and her expressive features broke into a smile as she greeted him with a surprised, "Hi Peter, didn't expect to see you."

"Hi Joanne," he answered distractedly.

"Sorry, is this a bad time?"

"No, no of course not."

His face fell as she said, "Lindsey is looking after Poppy this morning while I go and make myself glamorous." She struck a pose by sweeping her long, mousy brown hair on top of her head.

"She must have forgotten," he said gloomily. "It would seem she has gone on holiday with her mother and forgot to mention that as well."

Joanne laughed, thinking he was joking, but quickly saw that he wasn't.

"I've been away since Friday. Did she mention anything to you?" he asked.

"No it must have been a very sudden decision; I only saw her on Thursday. Didn't she leave a note?"

He shook his head.

"Let me make coffee; you look as if you need one. Have you eaten?"

He shook his head again, following her as she made for the kitchen, where he sat at the table looking dejected, watching Poppy play happily on the floor whilst Joanne made coffee and toast.

Joanne and her husband Terry lived next door and they had all moved in at the same time, ten years ago. Lindsey and he were Poppy's godparents and Lindsey often looked after her. It wasn't something she would have forgotten he assured himself; but then with Monica in one of her forceful moods, Lindsey wouldn't have stood a chance. Yes, that was about it he decided. He had always held a grudging admiration for his mother-in-law, but never in his wildest dreams had he imagined her capable of fraud on this scale. He was frightened. Lindsey was no match for her mother and her mother didn't like him…

*

William drove carefully, taking the back roads to where his yacht was moored. Viewing the peaceful scene from the small stone bridge spanning the River Hamble, confirmed his thought that there would be little activity at this time in the morning. A slight mist hung over the secluded harbour and the owners of the yachts were only just stirring. An appetizing aroma of freshly baked bread emanating from the nearby bakery, reminding him he hadn't eaten made him long to stay and relax as he and Monica had so often done. But today he must find an even more secluded hideaway for his pride and joy, *The Lady Monica*.

Turning onto a dirt track road, he brought the car to a standstill at a row of private garages standing back from the water's edge, before taking a key from the glove compartment and easing himself out of the driving seat. The up and over door glided easily and he nodded with satisfaction, knowing that the maroon Mercedes would be safe until he could collect it. Pulling the door down and switching on an overhead light he took the precaution of removing the personalised number plates and replacing them with the original ones. Then collecting his briefcase and laptop from the back seat, he left the garage and made his way down to where the boat was moored, looking about nervously, expecting any minute to hear a voice challenging him to stop. But he reached the short jetty and jumped aboard, nearly falling over with the weight of the briefcase and laptop as he landed.

Recovering unsteadily, he went into the cabin, removed his jacket and tie and leant against the open door sweating and panting, his heart pounding with fear. A decanter of whisky stood on the highly polished, wooden shelf and he poured himself a good measure, relaxing as the liquid burned his throat.

So far so good, he told himself but he wasn't out of the woods yet; he had to get going; what if any of their friends let slip about the yacht? No one knew where it was actually moored, but it wouldn't take the police long to find out.

Thank goodness he had insisted on keeping it as their 'Retreat'.

Within half an hour he was steering along the River Hamble, hugging the bank until he came to a backwater where willow trees afforded shelter from prying eyes. He nosed the prow in, making sure it was completely hidden before tying up to a tree, then went down to the cabin to pour himself another whisky. Trembling and distraught he told himself that he had never expected to be on his own. Monica was the instigator; she should be here. Where the devil was she? Why had she gone without him and taken Lindsey? Lindsey wasn't even supposed to know about the plan; he and Monica were supposed to be arriving in Switzerland, three days from now. What had made her change the plan? Snatching up his mobile phone he rang Monica's number and his nerves jolted as a voice said: 'this number is no longer in use'.

She must have got rid of her old one so that she couldn't be traced. Yes of course, that was it; she would phone him soon with the new number. He would just have to wait; in the meantime he would put the mobile on charge, to be on the safe side and get himself something to eat while he was waiting.

There was plenty of tinned food in the cupboards; he could last out. She would get in touch he consoled himself, because – why wouldn't she? By teatime, he was beside himself, worrying if she had been in a plane crash. What could be keeping her? She would be busy of course – but doing what? According to Peter, they had taken the night flight on Friday; it was Tuesday today; surely, she could have phoned or sent a text, by now. His laptop was on the seat beside him and he plugged it in. Waiting for it to boot up he took some papers out of his briefcase and selected an envelope. Perhaps he could get in touch with her through the hotel they were booked into in Switzerland.

Half an hour later, he was staring into space, with a dazed expression. His email had been returned promptly, stating that Mrs Monica Spencer and daughter had checked out early on Monday morning to catch a flight to South America.

Slowly as in a dream, he picked up his mobile phone and rang Peter.

"South America?" Peter shouted hoarsely down the phone, making William flinch.

"That is what the hotel in Switzerland said."

"They must have made a mistake. Lindsey just wouldn't up and leave me like this."

"I'll give Monica another twenty-four hours. I'm sure she will get in touch by then. We planned this together."

Peter could hear that he wasn't sounding quite so sure now.

"In the meantime, I need your help. Can you get into my house and get me some clothes?"

"No chance. It's guarded day and night."

"Then I will have to have new. Casual stuff to travel in; can you do that and bring them to me at the 'Robin Hood' pub?"

"I suppose so, but I don't want to get into this mess any further than I am. You were doing all right, why did you have to get greedy? Old Man Anders was a good boss and you've ruined him."

"So you don't want to know when Monica gets in touch then?" William asked sarcastically.

"No, I don't actually. All I want is my old life back. I just can't imagine how that wife of yours persuaded Lindsey to get involved."

"She is her mother," William reminded him, still in the same sarcastic tone.

"Then she should have known better," Peter, retorted hotly.

"Well, some children are loyal to their family."

"Don't talk of loyalty; may I remind you that in the grand scheme of things, I would have known nothing until after you and Monica had disappeared with your ill gotten gains; did Lindsey know?"

"Of course not; it was never meant to be like this. We were going to send for you both."

"And pigs might fly."

"Well believe it or not; see if I care." William suddenly lost his temper and switched the mobile off, then realised immediately it was a stupid thing to do because now he would have to ring back and apologise. "Aaargh."

The number rang but there was no reply. He waited a few minutes and tried again; this time he was informed by an exchange that the mobile he was trying to reach was switched off. William broke out into a sweat. Peter was sulking and when Peter sulked, it could go on for days. He tried several more times, always with the same result and by the evening, had decided to take a chance and slip out to get the clothes himself. He would wait until it was dark and go to one of the late night stores.

A narrow towpath led all the way back to the small harbour and with the aid of a torch he eventually found his way along it and skirted the area, keeping a sharp eye open until he reached the garage. The car started easily and he began to back out, halting and holding his breath as a car drove past on its way to the dirt track road flashing its lights as a thank you.

Having accomplished his shopping, he looked longingly at the food hall where cooked chicken and spare ribs were displayed temptingly, but just as he was about to approach the counter, he noticed a store detective standing in the way that all policemen and servicemen stand, very upright and alert, head tilted slightly up, eyes travelling and missing nothing. Without a second glance at the food he hurried out of the store and back to the car, parked well away from the brightly lit area. Feeling pleased with himself he drove the few miles back to the harbour and was about to go over the stone bridge, when by craning his neck, he glimpsed a police car parked beside the row of garages.

His first instinct was to put his foot down and drive off fast, but common sense prevailed and he pulled gently away, the purr of the expensive engine hardly audible on the night air, amidst the activity below.

Denied the safe, comfortable haven of the yacht, he faced the prospect of spending the night in the car. How had the police found him so quickly? With a sickening jolt, he realised he had left his laptop on board but consoled himself that the yacht was well hidden and wouldn't be found easily; he would return at dawn and sail across The Solent. There were many small inlets on the Isle of Wight, where he could hide and wait for Monica to contact him.

During the long night, parked in a lonely wooded area he was glad of the blankets and cushions that Monica always kept in the spacious boot of the car also the small, well-stocked drinks bar that provided him with his favourite whisky. Comfortable enough, he thought longingly of the cooked chicken then looked at his watch; it was twelve o'clock, if only he could contact Monica and work out how he was going to join her. By four o'clock, he decided to make a move; having worked out on the map that he could pick the towpath up from the other direction and get to the yacht without being seen. He would have to leave the car; a pity but with all the money they had now – he smiled broadly, thinking of the awaiting luxury.

He pulled in beside a five bar gate and decided to check his mobile before getting out of the car. There were three texts from Amy that he hadn't bothered to answer but still nothing from Monica. Slipping the phone in his pocket, he opened the gate and started across the field to where the towpath was just visible. As soon as he was safely across The Solent, he would shower and change his clothes he promised himself, trudging disconsolately through the wet grass, feeling the water seeping into his shoes and up his trouser legs. With only twenty yards to go to the towpath, he saw movement on the river and nearly collapsed at the sight of *The Lady Monica*, a uniformed figure at the wheel, disappearing down river. Crouching low, legs trembling, threatening to give way any moment, he stumbled back to the car, managed to open the door with fingers that had lost all control and drove off heedless of direction. After what seemed like an age he pulled into a lay-by, where a mobile van advertised breakfast. Approaching warily, he ordered bacon sandwiches and coffee, in answer to the owner's gruff, "What can I get yer?" While he stood waiting for the bacon to cook, William sipped the coffee and looked about nervously. It was barely light and a slight drizzle had begun to fall, making the prospect of not having the yacht even more depressing. Another, more serious thought struck him; the police would have his laptop. All of his private transactions were on it, including the name of the hotel where Monica was staying. Thank goodness, Monica had moved on; she must have anticipated trouble in her capable way. He pictured her tall, slim figure and blonde hair. Always well groomed, she was a fantastic looking woman as well as an immense driving force in his life, but sometimes, in fact quite often, he felt undermined by her dominance. That was why he needed someone like Amy, sometimes.

The van owner interrupted his thoughts. "Three pound, guv," he said placing the greaseproof wrapped sandwich on the counter; looking up as a large lorry drove in to the lay-by.

"I should move yer car, these guys are non-too patient this time in the mornin'."

William threw a five-pound-note down, picked up the sandwich and quickly, took his advice, casting an anxious eye at the lorry driver, tooting his horn because the car was blocking his way.

"You forgot your change, guv."

William raised his hand, continuing on his way as the owner saluted and pocketed the two pounds, his face breaking into a smile for the first time that morning.

After driving a short distance, he came upon a roadside picnic area where public toilets gave him the opportunity to change his clothes and have a quick wash, but first he ate the chunky sandwich, still warm and very satisfying with its three thick rashers cooked crispy, just as he liked it. Feeling slightly better humoured he took out his mobile phone, desperately hoping for a text from Monica, but there were still just the three from Amy, telling him to contact her.

He sat pondering as a possible solution came to him – but only as a last resort.

*

Monica slid out of the king sized bed, stretched luxuriously and strolled to the open balcony doors, slipping into a bikini as she stood looking down through the glass roof into the depths of the indoor swimming pool. In the early morning light, the crystal-clear water shimmered invitingly, its pale green tiled depths, creating a pleasing sense of calm to the luxurious chalet in the mountains.

Lindsey appeared on the neighbouring balcony, looking drawn and unhappy.

"Coming for a swim? It looks heavenly." Monica spoke brightly, hiding her impatience. Here they were, far away from their dull lives in England, and all she had done so far, was mope after that philandering husband of hers. Well I certainly don't intend to waste time missing William, she vowed. For the last two years, she and William had been planning to go to South America, to live in absolute luxury. All they needed was that extra million to buy the house of their dreams and it had been within reach; just one week to go, when she heard him promise his secretary that it would be the two of *them* going away together.

William had told her he would be staying in the hotel where the conference was being held and not to expect him home until Monday teatime – like a fool she had believed him, she recalled bitterly.

On the Friday night, she had arrived at the rear entrance of Anders, intending to let herself in and take the lift up to the accounts department on the third floor, when the night guard was on his rounds at eleven thirty. She had taken William's spare set of office keys from the safe in his den, intending to do a practice run for the following Friday, when she intended transferring the money. Out of habit, she pressed the wrong button and went straight to the top floor. Refurbishing the apartments had been her idea and going up and down was something she had done frequently in the past year. About to press the button to go down a floor, William's voice reached her. She remembered shrinking into the corner of the lift as he walked by with his arm around his young secretary, laughing and making promises to take her away to a life of luxury. Transfixed, she watched him open a door and allow the girl to enter first, following her with hungry eyes. That was when blinding rage took over and the plan was changed. She couldn't believe how smoothly it had all gone, except that in her anger she had pressed the key twice; one million became eleven million and temptation to leave it proved too much. When she had finished she installed a virus so that when the system was next switched on, the whole thing would crash and technical support officers would hopefully take until Sunday to restore it.

Lindsey had been crying for weeks about Peter and the amount of time he spent away from home, so on completing her mission, Monica drove straight to Lindsey's house and got her out of bed, insisting that she should accompany her on a week's holiday that very night. She took a fair amount of persuading but Monica pointed out that Peter wouldn't be home for several days, so why be lonely when she could be having a lovely trip to Switzerland and still be back before Peter.

"He might appreciate you more if you weren't at his beck and call all the time," Monica ended waspishly, unknowingly repeating a chance remark Lindsey had overheard from friends.

It was all done in a rush, and unbeknown to Lindsey, the note she left on the kitchen table was somewhere in an airport rubbish bin, disposed of by Monica, after dropping Lindsey's mobile phone in their kitchen waste bin.

"It must be in your bag or luggage. Don't worry, I've got mine," Monica lied, hurrying her out of the house and into the car.

After going back to her own house and throwing things into a suitcase, they caught an overnight flight to Zurich and booked into the same hotel suite reserved for her and William. The following morning, without telling Lindsey, Monica booked tickets to South America and informed hotel reception they would be leaving that morning. At the same time, she rented this house in the mountains and hired a car. Used to her taking charge, Lindsey followed obediently, too absorbed with her own problems to question her mother's irrational behaviour.

Studying Lindsey now, Monica, debated when to explain why they could never return to Britain, but at this very moment she wanted a swim in that luxurious pool followed by breakfast on the terrace.

"For goodness sake cheer up and enjoy this wonderful place," she said sharply. "Peter isn't worth all this unhappiness."

"I love him Mother; I don't want to lose him." Lindsey went and got back into bed, pulled the clothes over her head and sobbed.

Monica sighed and called, "Please don't spoil today, I really need to relax and think."

"Sorry, I'll join you soon, when I've found a swimsuit." She sounded so forlorn that Monica despaired. Why on earth would Peter want other women, when he had the best already? But then the same could be said of William, she preened, allowing herself to remember the good times together, at home and on the yacht. Their marriage had worked well; she had always known he liked other women; but it was regarded as normal today.

Anger filled her as she pictured him on the 'Lady Monica'; would he dare take that woman on her namesake: their love nest? The thought stayed with her whilst she swam vigorously up and down the pool working off her anger until, exhausted, she lay on her back floating, calmly coming to a decision. Waiting until after breakfast when Lindsey was lazing by the pool, she made one phone call lasting less than a minute, then white with emotion, joined Lindsey.

CHAPTER TWELVE

From her office window, Samantha gazed down at the scene below. Wet roads and pavements glistened in the glare of headlights as muffled figures hurried along, fighting against the high wind threatening to rob them of their hats and scarves. She watched a man grab frantically for his newspaper blowing wildly along the pavement before wrapping itself around a tree, likening his doomed efforts to her own situation. Everything was slipping through her fingers; she was never going to be able to fulfil Grandfather's dream; not that he would ever know that, because Uncle Charles had decided it was best to protect him from the full extent of William Spencer's betrayal.

Simon and Wendy agreed with the decision and were doing everything in their power to support him in closing down the business. It was hard to believe that a short time ago everything was thriving. It had never occurred to her that things could happen so quickly.

She closed the vertical blind, blotting out the darkening afternoon, sighing as she pictured her grandfather, desperately trying to rally himself and maintain his pride, in the face of disloyalty. What a hateful man William Spencer was. A steely determination filled her and she vowed that somehow he would pay for his treachery.

She wondered miserably what was happening to Bryn; his letter had said he couldn't leave Jo at this time, but he would be in touch soon and hopefully they could meet. That had been four weeks ago and she was aching to see him.

A light knock brought her back to earth and she called, "Come in."

Simon held the door open for Wendy and Meg who followed bearing a tray of coffee and biscuits.

"We need to talk," Wendy said. Her tone was gently concerned.

"If you are going to say, go home, the answer is no. I would be letting Grandfather down." Samantha leant back in her blue leather chair, elbows resting on the arms, the tips of her fingers together, glancing from one to the other of them.

Simon smiled in spite of himself, picturing Gerald sitting in just the same pose.

"I think your grandfather would be glad to see you right now," Wendy said finding difficulty in holding back the tears.

"Do you know something I don't?" Samantha asked sharply, sensing they were trying to break something gently.

"Mr Hughes telephoned a short while ago; he doesn't want to alarm you but a visit would greatly cheer your grandfather." Simon nodded encouragingly.

Galvanised into action, Samantha rose quickly. "Ring my father and ask him to pick me up, Meg."

"He is already on his way, Miss Anders. He will call from the airfield."

Samantha sat down again, feeling her strength draining away.

"What aren't you telling me?" she whispered.

"We were only told that your grandfather wished to see you," Wendy assured her.

Half an hour later the call came, to say that Darren would be landing in ten minutes and Simon drove her to the airfield.

On that cold, blustery afternoon, the flight home to Anders Folly was bumpy and both Darren and Samantha were glad to see the runway lights. Fifteen minutes later, Samantha was standing at Gerald's bedside, smilingly reassuring him that everything was going well and business would soon be back to normal.

There were tears in his eyes as he shook his head.

"I heard on the radio that we've gone under. It's entirely my fault; I'm so sorry, Princess."

Samantha could see there was no point in denying it any longer.

"No one could have imagined William Spencer capable of such deception, Grandfather."

"You were suspicious from the start," he pointed out, gasping painfully.

"At first I thought his attitude was because I was a girl, but when Wendy said she was sure Amy Bishop was responsible for her losing her job it made me wonder. Then a memo in Amy's diary, saying she had to keep me busy made me suspicious there was something he didn't want me to see. But at the same time, I arrived early on the morning Daddy took Tim to the airport, and quite by chance discovered that Amy and William were more than just boss and P. A.; and I thought that was what he was trying to hide. However, the penny finally dropped when I saw the hospitality apartments. Poor Peter. His uncle will disown him, I imagine. He was never a part of the fraud you know," she said with a mischievous smile.

"That's as may be, but just why *did* Chambers take you up to the apartments?" Gerald asked, frowning ferociously. "What was he up to?"

"Let's just say he was mistaken in more ways than one," she assured him, patting his hand as it laid in hers.

Gerald grunted. "I'm glad the place is closing. Your father was right; no place for a nice young woman; not like in my day," he whispered sadly.

"I'm not finished; I plan to start up again." She looked at him eagerly.

"No, I want it to die with me. Let it remain David and Gerald Anders' dream. Make one of your own, Princess."

"Don't say that," she cried. "Don't talk about dying; I won't let you."

She threw herself across him and he held her, stroking her hair until her sobs subsided.

"That wonderful auburn hair, so like your great grandmother's. You are like her in so many ways; headstrong and impetuous, full of life and yet so loyal to those you love."

Samantha raised a tearstained face. "I think you have just described yourself, Granddad."

He smiled happily and closed his eyes. "Have a good life, my lovely Princess."

George had been hovering and seemed to know that it was the right moment to take over.

"Let 'im sleep now, Miss; talk agen later."

She looked at Gerald's still face, then anxiously at George.

"'E's on'y sleepin'," he reassured her. "I'll make the fire up and you rest in the chair." He went to the big fireplace and placed several logs in the dog, sending sparks flying up the chimney and creating a cheerful blaze, before replacing the fireguard; then he set the big wing chair at an angle so that she could see Gerald and placed the footstool in front of it.

"I'll fetch ya a nice cuppa tea an' a bit a Lorna's lemon drizzle cake," he comforted her, glad that she had come home in time to see Gerald; because the time had come to say goodbye and now that he had seen his Princess, he would die happy.

"Thank you George, what would we do without you?"

Gerald slept peacefully; the huge, four-poster bed he and Pamela had shared had been adapted for his needs when he had returned to their room. For years after Pamela died, he had been so angry he had slept in his parents' room, not wanting any reminders of her, but now she came to him every night and death had no fears for him.

George looked in at regular intervals bringing Samantha, dinner and a light snack at suppertime. On his last visit at twelve o'clock, he found Samantha curled up on the bed, her warm dressing gown wrapped tightly around her slim figure, sound asleep beside her grandfather. Fetching a spare blanket from the ottoman, he covered her, allowing the tears, held back when they were awake, to fall. Neither of them stirred when he replenished the fire and turned the lights out, leaving the room dancing in firelight. During the night, Gerald woke briefly, saw a mass of red hair on the snowy white pillow beside his own, smiled and went back to sleep with Pamela's name on his lips.

Waking in the morning the space beside him was empty, but his heart was full.

Miraculously Gerald rallied briefly; he slept a lot and was greatly comforted to have Samantha there. She read to him and played his favourite classical music; never leaving his side, and when he was feeling well enough, George took him down for dinner and he would spend a little while in the sitting room in the evening.

Samantha continued to live in hope of hearing from Bryn, wondering why his mobile was always switched off and what was taking so long, until one evening when Felicity was reading the local paper she suddenly said:

"The Banns are being read for the doctor's son." She carried on reading, unaware of the bombshell she had dropped. Everyone continued watching the television and Samantha blinked stinging tears back, pretending to be engrossed in the television, but as soon as possible she escaped and slipped over to see Sol and Ella.

"Am I disturbing you?" she asked anxiously as Ella opened the door.

"Not a bit, come in." Ella led the way and Sol greeted her with a wide smile.

He was sitting with his feet up watching a programme on bird life.

"I'll put the kettle on." Ella smiled; she missed Samantha's company.

Sol turned down the sound on the television as Ella disappeared into the kitchen.

"Something wrong, lass?"

"No, no I'm fine, just thought it would be nice to get out of the house for a while. Tim has gone to a local history talk in the village and the oldies are watching gardening." She pulled a face.

"I expect you're missing the city life, although I must say it's lovely to have you back and you've put new life into your granddad."

"He has perked up, hasn't he?" she agreed eagerly.

"He certainly has and it's all down to you," Ella said, popping in at that moment with a tin of biscuits and leaving again.

Sol smiled fondly. "She's right lass."

"Do you think so?" The tears that had been threatening brimmed.

"No, I know so. Now don't take on lass or you'll have me at it."

Ella returned carrying the tea tray and shot a piercing look at Samantha.

"What's new then?" she asked chattily.

"Not much; just wishing Tim would stay home; I miss him." She looked forlorn and Ella shot her a searching look, putting her fingers over her lips, in silent dismay.

An hour later, Samantha said she must get back to Granddad, and when she had gone, Sol said, "I know that look, please don't tell me you're getting visions again."

"Not visions, no. I'll tell you when I'm sure," and from there she refused to be drawn.

CHAPTER THIRTEEN

Cold November winds buffeted the house, sending out puffs of smoke from the fireplaces, where huge fires were kept burning, causing Gerald to comment that it was time to get the chimneys swept again.

George informed Charles that they were swept quite recently and no soot was falling.

"Just the direction of the wind," Charles reassured Gerald. "Don't worry, between us all, Anders Folly is in good hands."

Samantha went to sit on the footstool beside him.

"George will be in with your brandy, soon."

Gerald nodded and smiled at her. "What a comfort you are." He relaxed and she covered his blue veined hand with her small soft one.

"I think I shall bring Nocturn to see you tomorrow, he told me he hasn't seen you for a long time." Green eyes met amused, dark ones and he nodded, playing the childish game they had always played, pretending the big horse was half-human.

"It's too cold on the terrace, so we may have to chat in here, or even your bedroom," she said seriously.

"You would bring him up in the lift, I suppose?" Gerald said showing no surprise.

"If I must."

Charles and Felicity were laughing by now; they had heard this game played often when Samantha was younger, when her imagination had run to even greater fantasies.

George came in carrying Gerald's supper and was cheered to see them all enjoying themselves.

"I am expecting a visitor tomorrow George."

"Indeed, sir. Can I ask oo?"

"Nocturn; and he will be coming up in the lift with Miss Samantha. See that he is given every comfort will you?"

"Certainly, sir, I'll get Lorna to make some oat cakes with molasses. Will that be all, sir?" George entered into the nonsense with a serious face and Samantha added:

"Perhaps you could make up the spare room, in case he wants to bed down for the night?"

"Enough, enough, you will have him inviting his friends next." Gerald gave a tired smile.

"What a wonderful idea, Granddad."

George handed Gerald his glass of brandy. "It's a long time since ye played that game," he laughed as he left the room.

"There are some things you never get too old for," Charles said looking at Gerald's peaceful smile.

Samantha got up. "Let's watch 'Who wants to be a Millionaire', it's Granddad's favourite." She switched the television on and returned to the footstool, taking Gerald's hand in hers again. The programme had already started and someone was winning two hundred and fifty thousand pounds. Samantha expected Gerald to say well done as he usually did and when there was no sound, she thought he must have fallen asleep, until Charles got up and laid his hand over theirs. Eyes wide, she stared up at him.

"He's gone, sweetheart." Felicity was crying softly. And so it was on that cold November night, Gerald went to join Pamela, at last.

The following hours were unreal; everything seemed to be happening in a dream and Samantha sat dry-eyed in Gerald's room long into the night after George had laid him out. Her eyes were burning; why couldn't she cry when every part of her wanted to? Her heart felt as if it had stopped beating and a dreadful numbness filled her mind and body, blotting out all thought, except that her Grandfather would never be there for her again. At long last she fell asleep and George, who had been keeping watch, crept in, covered her with a blanket and withdrew.

Lorna was waiting for him, two mugs of steaming cocoa, sitting on the kitchen table like any other night; except that it wasn't like any other night because their whole world had crashed. Lorna's whole life had been built around the Anders family; she had come to them at the age of twenty-seven, serving past and present members with fierce love and loyalty. George had dedicated the last twenty years to taking care of Mr Gerald's every need and had been treated more as a friend than his manservant; neither of them could imagine life without their beloved employer.

They sat opposite one another united in grief, each wondering what further changes were to come, because there had been many changes over the years – some bad – but mostly good. Through them all though, Mr Gerald had always been there to take charge.

"Who will take charge now?" Lorna dabbed her eyes.

"Your guess is as good as mine lass. Mr Darren by rights, but 'e don't wannit."

"What about Mr Charles?"

"'E won't wanna' stay, not now 'is families all in America."

"That only leaves Miss Samantha, poor lamb." Lorna dabbed her eyes again.

"And Master Timothy," she added as an afterthought.

"No good relyin on 'im; 'e's on'y intrestid in them deadens. Na I reckon it's Miss Samantha or none." George gave a tremulous sigh.

Charles made all of the arrangements for the funeral and Lorna, Felicity and Fran organized the food. With nothing to do and no idea of what was expected, Samantha sought comfort in the nursery, lying on her old bed, dry-eyed, staring up at the sloping ceiling. Abigail kept an eye on her and Darren came every day, pleading with her to come home to the cottage. Her only reply was, "I like it here." Then she would turn her face to the wall and close her eyes.

Fran and Melly tried to persuade her to leave the nursery, but after three days of not eating, Melly got in touch with Bryn.

"This is just between you and me because I think she might listen to you. We are all very worried and I know she is unhappy about not seeing you. Will you phone her?"

Bryn called Samantha's mobile and her heart gave a lurch as she saw it was Bryn. "Hello," she said in a breathless little voice.

"Sam? It's Bryn. Are you all right?"

"I really need to see you."

"I'll come to the cottage this afternoon. What time? Be quick."

Samantha thought frantically. "Two o'clock."

"I'll be there; got to go. Bye."

She heard Jocelyn's voice in the background, asking who he was talking to, and then the phone went dead.

The big nursery clock showed half past twelve. She must get over to the cottage. Melly would go out shopping before picking Jack up from school. They could be, alone.

Lorna insisted on getting her food and realising it would be quicker to eat than argue, she sat in the warm kitchen and ate chicken omelette, agreeing afterwards that she felt much better, to Lorna's anxious question.

"You always know best, Lorna." She kissed her cheek, noting how sad she looked and then put her arms around her and rocked her gently, while Lorna wept softly.

The wind was blowing wildly and the sea was crashing against the rocks; a day when even the most intrepid seagulls were taking shelter on their rocky perches, high up on the cliffs

Picking her way up the path, she stopped and looked back at Anders Folly; it was something she always did and Grandfather was always at one of the windows waiting to wave to her. A movement caught her eye and she waved back unthinkingly, before walking on a couple of steps and turning again; had that really been a hand waving? There was nothing now. She continued on up, bracing herself against the force of the wind, fighting her way to the front door. Melly called out from the kitchen.

"Saw you coming; just made a cup of tea; let's go in the sitting room it's warmer." She appeared carrying a tray and led the way, smiling brightly.

"You're looking very pleased with yourself," Samantha said as they sat down together.

"Am I? It must be the thought of not having to cook this evening. Daddy is away picking up the family from America and Auntie Fran has asked us to dinner; I'm sure she wouldn't mind if you came as well."

"Thanks all the same, I feel like being on my own for a while. Give my love to Auntie Fran though." Sitting on the edge of the settee, fidgeting with the fringe on her pashmina, Samantha looked anxious.

"I'm going out in about twenty minutes, will you be alright? Jack is sleeping over for the night, so I won't be home early."

"Yes, of course." Samantha relaxed visibly and Melly hid a smile. Bryn had phoned her back to say what time he would come.

"It will be pretty busy at the big house tomorrow; Daddy has gone to fetch David, Caitlin, Laurie, Una, Ellie, Simon and the two children back with him." She ticked them off on her fingers. "That will be eight of them."

Samantha was hardly listening; she just wished Melly would leave. Bryn would be here soon.

"Will you come home while they are staying?" Melly chatted on, pretending not to notice Samantha looking surreptitiously at her watch.

Just when she thought she couldn't bear it any longer, Melly looked at the mantle clock.

"I must dash; need to do a bit of shopping before I pick Jack up."

Samantha felt guilty. "Sorry I'm not much company. I'd love to come home, while Uncle Charles's family are staying. It will be lovely to be with you."

Melly gave her a long hug then hurried from the room, not trusting herself to speak just thankful that she was not still shutting herself away. Samantha could hear her putting her outdoor clothes on and willed her to hurry, hoping she wouldn't meet Bryn on his way up.

Minutes after Melly left, Bryn arrived. They stood looking at each other, speechless with longing, before he took her in his arms and held her in a long embrace before leading her upstairs.

Samantha felt she was drowning with love as their bodies melted together in her king sized bed, oblivious to the howling wind, the thunder of the waves breaking against the cliff and the darkening day outside.

Hours later, she reluctantly roused herself when Bryn sat on the edge of the bed and said, "I must go."

"I don't want you to go."

"Melly will be home soon and we don't want her to find me here do we?"

Samantha smiled softly. "Would it matter if we are going to be together anyway?"

Bryn was silent.

"We are going to be together aren't we?"

"I can't Sam; you know I can't. I'm getting married in a few weeks."

"But I thought this meant you *wanted me*," she said urgently.

"And I do; you know I do." He bent and kissed her lips, wishing with all his heart that he could stay longer and comfort her, but Jo and his parents would be waiting and there would be explaining to do when he got home, as it was.

CHAPTER FOURTEEN

The funeral two days later was an impressive affair; even Charles hadn't fully realised how far Gerald's business ventures reached, until he recognised the big names congregated in the church.

The family were there en masse and Samantha stood, dry-eyed beside an emotional Timothy, feeling that her own life was ebbing away as the coffin was lowered into the ground. Gerald was laid to rest beside his parents David and Marie, his wife Pamela and his son, Alexander. Her great, great grandparents, great grandmother and great uncle; all of whom she had never known. To her it felt as if she had lost her beloved grandfather to a load of strangers. She wanted to run away from the mournful scene and never see the grave again.

"He should have been buried somewhere on Anders Folly. What were you all thinking?" she accused the family hysterically when everyone else had gone.

They all looked devastated, thinking that it could have been possible, until Charles said emotionally, "He would have wished to be buried with his family. Let there be no more talk of it. You are upsetting everyone Samantha."

Samantha turned and fled.

"The worst thing is; she is right," Charles said regretfully to Felicity, later that night. "Why weren't they *all* buried at Anders Folly? It would seem in hindsight, the natural thing to do and it might have been possible."

"There's no point in agonising now; what's done is done."

Felicity looked at him anxiously, knowing his grief would be very deep but it would also be very private.

The following morning panic broke out. Samantha was missing. Her clothes had gone and so had her blue sports car.

"She must have told you, Tim," Darren said, bewildered that his daughter had just taken off.

"Not a word." Timothy was equally puzzled. "I spoke to her before I went to bed and told her I would have to leave tomorrow. She seemed to take it alright; upset, but I thought that was because of the funeral."

"I'll give Bob and Marcia a ring," Fran volunteered.

"They were going to stay in a hotel overnight," Caitlin remembered when Fran came off the phone saying she had left a message on the answer phone.

"I only know, because at the funeral I asked who was looking after the horses and they said some reliable stable lads and the head man. I expect that is where she will make for, though."

There was a sigh of relief all round, at the likely explanation.

"I shouldn't have spoken sharply to her, she was very overwrought," Charles said regretfully.

"And she shouldn't be driving that car, in the state she was in," Darren said angrily. "It's far too fast for her."

"She handles it well, Dad," Timothy said quietly.

"Let's hope you're right," Darren snapped.

Timothy left the sitting room, went to the library, shut the door after him and took his mobile from his pocket. He had already tried to call Sam but tried again and this time, although she didn't pick up, she sent a text back.

I'm okay. Will be in touch soon. Needed to get away for a while. Love you.

He sent back. *Take care. Let the family know where you are. Worried. Love you. x*

Samantha started the car again. She had pulled over when the mobile buzzed relieved to see that it was Tim. She wanted to switch it off, but was afraid she would miss Bryn's call.

Now, as she drove, she contemplated what the future held for her. She was never going back to Anders Folly; there were too many painful memories.

She turned off the road and drove through an avenue of overhanging trees. It was just getting light; the clock on the dashboard read 7.30 a.m. Bob and Marcia will have been up for hours, she comforted herself as the welcoming sight of the 'The Vintage' came in view with its imposing front entrance and numerous, mullioned windows. Surprisingly there was no sign of life, but guessing they would be in the stables, she left the car and made her way round the side of the house, fondly comparing, as she always did, how similar the huge mansion was to Anders Folly.

On reaching the stables, she found three of the regular hands attending to the horses.

Jim, the head man greeted her with a surprised, "Good morning Miss, didn't expect you back yet. Bob and Mrs Johnson are away, still."

Samantha's face fell. She had completely forgotten they were at the funeral and wouldn't have set out on the journey home until this morning; probably still in bed, enjoying the rare luxury of a lie in.

"I'll just go into the house and make a cup of tea, while I wait for them," she said.

"The house is all locked up, Miss, unless you've got a key," Jim said hopefully.

Samantha's face fell again. "I've never needed one," she said, suddenly feeling abandoned. All she wanted was to take a cup of tea to her room and fall into bed; it had been a long, overnight drive up from Cornwall; starting out at two o'clock, when everyone was sleeping.

"I'll get one of the lads to make some tea. It's warm in the tack room. Go and make yourself comfy Miss." He touched his cap and called to a lad, who was sweeping out a stable.

"Make some tea, Ed, and wash your hands first, Miss Samantha's here." He turned and gave her a cheerful grin. "Won't be, long."

Samantha walked along the stable doors, until she came to the one with 'Midnight' painted above it. A soft whinny greeted her as the big black mare left her food and trotted over.

"Hello Girl, Nocturn sent his love." She buried her face in Midnight's soft muzzle, tears running unchecked down her cheeks – the first tears.

Ed came towards her carrying a steaming mug of tea and she brushed them away, accepting the tea gratefully. "Thanks Ed."

"You're welcome Miss." With a self-conscious gesture, he touched his cap as Jim had shown him.

She sat beside Midnight in the clean hay, sipping the scalding liquid, but there was no solace in the familiar surroundings; they reminded her too much of Anders Folly.

After finishing her tea, she said goodbye and got back into her car. Without any idea of where she was heading, she drove the blue sports car, along the frost covered, New Forest road heading in a westerly direction. At this early hour on a Saturday, there was hardly any traffic about and she stopped to admire a group of ponies grazing on the grass verge; their winter coats looked ragged and the precious little grass there was for them to feed on was frozen. She wanted to herd them all together in warm, straw-filled stables with plenty of food. How many of them would perish before the winter was over? Why didn't God do something? All the television adverts of starving children and wild animals being cruelly treated; what was God doing about any of it? Why was everything so awful and sad? She started sobbing, great wracking sobs that shook her whole body with waves of uncontrollable misery as she thought of never seeing her grandfather again. An image of him waving to her from the window of his study brought numbing reminders and there was no telling how long she would have sat there, if her mobile phone hadn't rung and Bryn's name on the screen brought her to her senses.

CHAPTER FIFTEEN

"A finger in so many pies," Charles remarked to Adam, who was helping him to sort Gerald's papers.

"I wonder if he knew half of what he had himself," Adam replied doubtfully, casting a bemused expression at the piles of paperwork.

"Not in the last few years maybe, but he will have had his finger on every button before that; he was a marvellous bookkeeper; no computer for him; did it all with his own brain power," Charles boasted proudly.

Adam was seated at an oak table next to where Charles was working at Gerald's desk. They had been working for an hour, with all of the study lights blazing because although only mid-morning, a blanket of fog shrouded the house, making it virtually impossible to see without them. It promised to be a mammoth task.

They worked in silence until Adam asked Charles:

"What do you make of this one?"

Charles transferred his attention to Adam.

"It would appear to be some obscure oil company that went out of business," Adam said, adding thoughtfully. "Its shares have done quite well."

Charles gave his full attention, smiled reminiscently and there was admiration, mixed with amusement when he answered.

"Gerald helped out an old friend and it obviously came good. I remember advising him to leave well alone. Well, well, well." He laughed at his own joke. "The old friend ran out of money and couldn't continue drilling his oil well; Gerald must have bailed him out and by the looks of things, they sold out to a big oil company some years later, hanging on to a lot of shares – and, he is still getting an impressive return on his money. My brother could make money while the rest of us were still thinking about it," he said admiringly.

"Wonder why he didn't mention it?" Adam queried.

Charles looked at the date on the bill of sale and his face fell; it was around the time when Pamela and his father died and not long after that Gerald had his accident.

"Too much else on his mind," he said quietly, not wanting to enlarge.

Adam took in his quiet sadness and went back to sorting.

At the end of the day they were only a small way through Gerald's estate. "Perhaps things aren't as bad as they could be," Charles said hopefully. Darren was to have been his heir until quite recently when he made Samantha his main beneficiary. He knew Timothy was too engrossed with his own life and Darren made it clear he didn't want the responsibility.

"He might have been stuck in a wheelchair, but there was nothing wrong with his brain." Adam made the comment, leaning back in his chair, clutching a glass of whiskey that Charles had just poured. It had been a long, but engrossing day and it seemed that things weren't quite as bad as they might have been. The eleven million that William Spencer had stolen had certainly made a large dent in finances, but with a few major adjustments, the family should still be able to live comfortably.

Adam looked at his watch. "I must be getting home; Fran will be panicking because of the fog. See you in the morning, about the same time. Do you know if Samantha has been in touch? Fran is sure to ask."

"I think Felicity would have said. Sam really needs to be here though to get familiar with all of this." Charles waved a hand over the desk.

Felicity opened the door and popped her head round. "Wondering if you might like a cup of tea – maybe not," she added seeing the whiskey glasses.

"We were just wondering if Samantha telephoned. Adam is leaving and Fran will ask."

"About ten minutes ago, Abigail took a quick message to say that she is staying with a friend, will be in touch shortly and not to worry. Apparently her mobile battery was running low and she couldn't talk longer."

Adam gave a dubious mmm, recognising the boys' regular excuse, when they didn't want to explain.

Charles got up and shook Adam's hand. "At least she has been in touch. Thanks for your help, old chap; much appreciated. Don't let Fran worry too much; Children today are pretty independent."

"Mm, tell me." Adam gave an ironic grimace." He kissed Felicity on the cheek. "See you tomorrow. Thanks for lunch."

CHAPTER SIXTEEN

Samantha sat dry-eyed, watching the ponies foraging for food. She didn't know how long she had sat there staring at the bleak countryside, but it was long enough to get thoroughly cold. She started the engine, without any fixed idea of where to go and followed the road until she came to a crossroads in what seemed like the middle of nowhere. On one corner, set back amongst trees, coloured lights drew her attention and the thought of a cup of tea beckoned. Up closer, it was a small restaurant and the sight of a blazing log fire and the smell of food tempted her to sit at one of the small round tables set with knives and forks and tablemats with hunting scenes. Propped in a log holder was a menu which offered 'Real English food' served daily and she decided on lamb curry, wondering on whose say so, curry was considered to be 'Real English food' – certainly not Lorna – or Grandfather. An involuntary sob left her at the thought.

A waitress, armed with a pencil and notepad approached her and she ordered the curry, asking if she could have a cup of tea, while she waited. The waitress gave her a long searching look and left.

She had chosen a table beside the log fire and as she sipped the warming tea, she went over her conversation with Bryn. It had left her numb with misery, but now she viewed it coldly.

Okay, so he had decided – or his parents had – that he had no option, other than to marry the French one because the baby was sickly and he couldn't desert her. He would never forget their wonderful hours of lovemaking and wished with all his heart they could be together, but it must stop now that he was going to be married. It was the only honourable thing to do.

'And where does that leave me?' she asked herself, coldness turning to misery.

Her curry arrived and she ate hungrily, noting that the two waitresses and another young girl were watching her and talking. When she had finished, she ordered another cup of tea and sat gazing unseeingly into the fire, enjoying the warmth. The hands on her watch pointed to one thirty and she realised how long she must have sat in the car after Bryn had phoned. Looking around, she saw that most of the tables were occupied now; lost in thought she had missed the busy lunchtime trade going on around her.

The waitress came over and hovered. "Please, Miss Anders." Samantha looked up with surprise.

"Could I have your autograph, please? And Mr Murry says your meal is on the house."

Samantha stared. "You know me?"

"Oh yes, your picture is on the front of Vogue. I would know you anywhere."

The young girl's face was a picture of admiration as she clasped her hands under her chin.

Lost for words, Samantha took the magazine and signed it. It was over a year old, she noticed by the date.

The owner, came over, shook hands and introduced himself.

"Hello, I'm Murry and I knew your great grandmother." He looked at her admiringly. "You are so amazingly like her."

"Thank you. I take that as a great compliment."

"As well you should. She was a great lady and her name is well known, for her good work at 'Forest End'."

"Ah, now I understand. My great grandmother was matron there."

"Yes, before it became the Equestrian Centre. I have happy memories of the place myself."

Samantha left feeling quite overwhelmed and emotional. Her anger had evaporated and she considered making her way back to Bob and Marcia's, but even as the thought crossed her mind she knew she just wanted to be alone.

Without thinking, she took the familiar road that she had taken each morning to go to work and automatically turned the gleaming blue car into the underground car park, pulling in to the space with her nameplate still on it.

Sitting there looking at all the other empty spaces, her earlier depression returned and she felt tears streaming down her cheeks. What did life hold for her any more? Grandfather had gone. Bryn had left her. The business that she had hoped to take over had collapsed. Were they poor? William Spencer had taken so much money, would they even be able to keep Anders Folly? Filled with despair she clutched the steering wheel and sunk her head onto her hands, just as a tap on the car window, brought her upright again.

She wound the window down and Peter said, "I thought it was you. What are you doing here?"

She brushed her eyes fiercely. "Nothing, I just needed to stop for a minute and rest," she said indignantly. "Can't I even do that in peace?"

He looked at her, taking in the ravaged face and the droop of her shoulders.

"Of course you can and if you want me to leave, I will; but I don't like to leave you like this."

She leant on the steering wheel again. "I'm too tired to drive any more and I don't want to stay at Bob's. I'll just sleep here for a while."

"What about a hotel?"

"I suppose," she nodded.

"Move over; I'll drive."

He got in the car. "Are you sure this is what you want? I'll drive you home, if you would rather."

She shook her head vehemently.

He put the car in gear, drove to the exit then stopped.

"I've got a better idea; have you still got your keys to the apartments?"

She nodded, dejectedly.

"Then stay here overnight. I don't know what a decent hotel will think, if you walk in looking like you do."

She nodded again and he reversed the car back, before getting out and going round to her side.

"Come on, all you need is a shower and a good night's sleep. I'm pretty sure the apartments won't have been cleared yet."

She fumbled in her handbag, until he finally took it from her and tipped the contents out onto the driving seat. "Voila," he said, holding the keys aloft. "Now all we need to do is get you settled and I can go off to my interview."

She followed him to the private lift which took them up to the apartments. The first one they tried was unmade, but the second one was still immaculate with clean linen on the bed, snowy towels in the bathroom and a 'Welcome Pack' of tea and coffee bags and dried milk. He switched the electric heating on.

"It will be warm by the time you are ready to shower. I'll make you a cup of tea, then I've got to go. Are you *sure* you'll be alright? I've a really, really important interview, over dinner this evening. I hate leaving you like this, but I will be back in the morning to make sure you are okay."

"Go. Everybody else has. Just go." She pushed him to the door and slammed it after him.

"I'll be back," he shouted through the door.

Samantha, kicked her shoes off, sunk down onto the bed and went straight to sleep.

At ten o'clock the next morning, she was awoken from a dead sleep by Peter, banging on the door.

"Come on sleepyhead; time to get up. I've been here ages; thought you'd died," he said as she opened the door.

He was looking immaculate, as always and particularly cheerful.

"Why are you looking so cheerful?" she asked resentfully.

"Because I have been short listed."

"For what?" she frowned disconsolately.

"The job I went after yesterday; that little thing that pays the bills? The little thing – if you remember, I lost a few weeks ago? Or, perhaps not; it not being the difference to whether you eat or not."

"You never used to be sarcastic and it doesn't suit you." She sat on the bed and hugged one of the pillows.

"You haven't even showered; you look disgusting."

She hid her head in the pillow. "So would you, if you'd been through what I have."

He had decided on the way there, that sympathy wasn't going to work.

"Look Sam, I know you have lost your granddad and you are very unhappy, but he was an old man and these things have to be faced sooner or later; no one can live forever. He had a won-der-ful life." He petered off as her ravaged face appeared over the pillow. This wasn't going to work either he decided seeing her miserable look.

"Have a shower and we'll go out to breakfast," he coaxed.

She gave a tearful nod and slid off the bed; he tossed his eyes, thinking of all the times he had tried so hard to get her *into* one of these beds.

Freshly showered and dressed in a white cashmere jumper and slightly creased, grey trouser suit, she felt more able to deal with Peter's efforts to cheer her up.

"It might be a good idea to hang some of your clothes up," he said eyeing her critically. "Unless you *want* to go around looking like an unmade bed, of course."

She scowled, but started to do as he suggested. "I had to pack in a hurry," she muttered, rescuing garments from the suitcase where she had thrown them, before stealing out of the house.

"Obviously," he commented dryly, taking the coat hangers from her and hanging them neatly in the wardrobe.

"It's alright for you, all you've lost is your job but you will soon get another one." She stared at him reproachfully.

He gave a harsh laugh. "Oh yes, I'm great, except that my wife has gone off to heaven knows where and only heaven knows why without telling me or even leaving a note. I've no way of paying the bills because she has frozen the joint account; my company car will be reclaimed in a week's time if I can't find the money to buy it; oh, and guess what – the police are guarding my house, just in case my uncle, who is wanted for grand theft, tries to take refuge. Oh yes, I'm alright. And I might add, I was feeling quite cheered until I came to try and help a certain someone I felt sorry for, but she feels quite sorry enough for herself, thank you; she doesn't need my sympathy."

Samantha stared in dismay. "Why didn't you say?"

He pulled a long-suffering face. "We haven't exactly sat down and talked about me, have we?"

"Sorry," she whispered, tremulously.

He put his arm around her shoulders. "Me too; come on, let's get breakfast."

They went to the small restaurant, where they had always gone for lunch and he looked rueful as she automatically left him to pay the bill – as he always had of course, but that was when he had an expense account and Uncle William had gladly signed it to keep 'the granddaughter' out of his way. Thinking about it, he supposed she had paid for it anyway, in a roundabout way.

Sitting over a second cup of coffee, he asked her what she was going to do if she wasn't going home.

"Get a job I suppose. Grandfather wanted the firm to die with him." Tears rolled down her cheeks as she remembered the conversation. "By the sound of things there is no money to start again anyway."

Peter looked embarrassed. "I feel a bit responsible."

"You didn't know what your uncle was up to; no one did; even Amy only thought she knew."

If only *you* knew, Peter thought, remembering what William had said about Monica being the brain behind it all. He must keep quiet about that though, because Lindsey could get involved, even though he was certain she knew nothing about it.

Samantha noticed his faraway look. "Penny for them?"

"Just wondering what Lindsey is doing. Her mother is such a forceful woman; she bullies Lindsey all the time into doing what she wants. Lindsey is a simple soul; always wanting to please." He spoke affectionately and Samantha wondered if Bryn ever thought about her in that way.

Peter saw her tears. "Penny for them?"

117

She gave a watery smile and shook her head.

"You need to talk; it's too busy here. I know a quiet pub, not too far away."

It was raining as they drove through bleak country roads. The Deerhunter was in the forest and Peter said that Uncle William used to bring him when he was a child. Inside it was warm and rustic, with locals playing shove-halfpenny and dominoes. Peter nodded around as every eye followed them through the public bar into 'The Snug', at the rear. Peter guided her to a settle, beside the log fire and the landlord came and took their order, surprised by her request for an orange juice.

"Not his type," his wife commented, eyeing Samantha enviously.

"You stay away," he warned, looking disapprovingly at her low cut top.

"Yes dear," she said, glancing through the archway again.

His eyes narrowed, he was still suspicious of when he had caught them coming in from the car park together, a few months ago.

She picked up the tray before he could stop her. "I'll take them."

He watched jealously as she placed the drinks on the table, relaxing when Peter just nodded without a glance and continued his conversation.

Tossing her blonde head, she returned behind the bar and ten minutes later, after darting reproachful glances in Peter's direction, said she was going upstairs.

Unaware of her disappointment, Peter was absorbed and curious as to what kind of man would dump Samantha; and she in turn poured her heart out.

It was late afternoon when they left and having unburdened their troubles to each other, Samantha decided that Peter wasn't quite, the n'er-do-well she had thought and he, after hearing of her ordeal at the hands of the mechanic on the beach, understood her stand offish manner.

As they pulled into the underground car park, he said, "Why don't we eat together? I could pick you up at seven."

She agreed readily, not looking forward to being alone for the evening.

"See you at seven o'clock then," he said, stopping at the lift. "And wear that little black number with the halter neck; I want to see you in it."

He drove off with a cheery wave and her eyes followed the car up the ramp until it was out of sight.

Entering the apartment, the bare, unfamiliar surroundings swamped her with despair; she had never felt so alone in her life. Dull-eyed, she wandered towards the partly open wardrobe door intending to close it.

"Cheek," she exploded softly, smiling as she withdrew the black, Givenchy dress and hung it on the outside of the door.

At exactly seven o'clock, she took the lift down to the car park and Peter's car came to a halt in front of her, as she stepped out. Smiling broadly, he greeted her with, "Your carriage awaits Madam."

He looked her up and down while holding the door open, nodding approval as she swung her long legs in, that she was wearing the black dress, under the short, mink jacket.

"I've booked a table at Murry's."

She watched with a critical eye, as he walked round to the driving seat. She had never seen him looking anything other than immaculate, but tonight, she couldn't help admiring the snowy white shirt that contrasted deeply with a maroon jacket, matching bow tie and black evening trousers and felt a small thrill to have such a man of the world as an escort.

The rain was still falling steadily as they travelled along the dark country roads and she was glad when lights appeared a little way ahead.

"Is that where we are going?" she asked.

"Yes, do you know it?"

She peered through the rain-spattered windows.

"I'm not sure in the dark, but I think it might be where I stopped yesterday lunch time." Then, as they got closer, she cried, "Yes, it is; what a lovely surprise."

They were greeted warmly, shown to the seat by the log fire where she had chosen to sit the day before and given a complimentary bottle of wine.

Samantha didn't like to say she didn't drink, so she allowed them to pour her a glass.

Peter looked across the table at her. "Don't worry, they won't notice if you leave it; you look absolutely stunning. That dress was obviously made for you."

She blushed at the admiration in his eyes and said that she had modelled it in her first Paris show.

"I particularly like the way the bodice gathers into the neck," he said, referring to the soft folds of silk chiffon, cut low at the sides and gathered onto a black satin choker studded with diamante. The matching, diamante combs, holding her hair up in soft curls, revealed her creamy bare shoulders to perfection and the subtle perfume that had pervaded his car was wafting towards him again, making it hard to concentrate on the conversation.

"You say you will have to look for a job; surely you are already a model?" he forced himself to ask.

"I was offered contracts, but I would hate the life."

She spoke in an off-handed way, obviously not even prepared to consider the idea.

"Really? I thought it would be every woman's dream."

"Give me horses and dogs, any day."

She smiled as he said in a shocked voice, "I just can't imagine you doing anything so dirty and earthy; you are always so glamorous."

"You should see me when I'm mucking out the stables," she laughed.

"I'm sure you look beautiful, even with straw in your hair." His luminous grey eyes smiled into hers intensely and she looked away, but his admiration helped to restore her confidence, because as well as the heartache, being dumped – as Peter called it – had been a blow to her pride.

It was a pleasant, relaxed evening and they sat over the meal for a long time, enjoying coffee and dark mints when she really thought she couldn't eat another morsel.

At eleven thirty, Peter looked at his watch. "Time we were going home, I think."

He helped her on with her coat then went to pay the bill and, while he was away, the young waitress from the previous day came and asked her for another autograph; this time for her friend.

"I don't know; you go there once and people ask for your autograph; I've been going there for years and nobody asks for mine," Peter jokingly complained as they drove home.

"You can give me your autograph, if it makes you feel better," Samantha comforted.

"I'll settle for a kiss," he replied as they drew into the car park.

She kissed him briefly on the cheek and started rummaging for her key.

"I know it's here somewhere."

"Shall I have a look?"

She surrendered her small evening bag and he declared after a thorough search that it wasn't. "Sure you didn't leave it in the door?"

"Oh no." She gave a start, recalling shutting the door with the brass key and walking away.

"I'll come up and make sure everything is alright," Peter said getting out of the car. All the way up in the lift, she was on tenterhooks, wondering what to do if the key wasn't in the door. Her luggage and car keys were all inside. She was ready to start crying.

"Don't worry, you can come home with me and I'll get a locksmith in the morning," Peter consoled her, just as they got out of the lift and saw the key sitting in the lock.

"Whew, that was a close thing. What a shame though, I might have got a proper kiss." He laughed, in an effort to relax her, then seeing she was shaking, became serious, opened the door and put the light on. "There, nothing missing is there?"

She sunk down on the bed and shook her head.

"I'll put the kettle on before I go; a cup of tea will steady you."

He went to the small kitchen alcove and filled the kettle, concerned to see how upset she still was and wondering why her family weren't on her trail. Having switched the kettle on, he went to the bathroom and on his return, she was standing by the kettle, still wearing her coat.

"I'll do that," he said, taking her by the shoulders and easing her to one side.

"Feeling any better?"

She nodded but he could see she was trembling.

"Let me take your coat." She slipped her arms out of the soft fur and he hung it up in the wardrobe. "Mmm, real mink," he said smoothing it admiringly.

"Granddad's last ever Christmas present to me," she said bursting into tears.

With a sigh, he put his arms around her, asking himself how anyone was ever going to maintain the impossible standards that Gerald Anders had set for her. Looking over her head at the expensive cosmetics on the fitted dressing table, he gave a mental 'whew' as his eyes rested on a crystal bottle, extravagantly decorated with a dazzling white diamond. He recognised it instantly, from one he had seen in 'Harrods' of London, as, 'Clive Christian' and remembered that it was over 2000 dollars a bottle. No wonder it smells so good, he thought, lowering his head and taking a deep, mind-blowing breath. "Amazing," he murmured.

"My Christmas stocking present from Grandfather. What am I going to do without him?" she asked, raising a tearful face.

"Well."

She looked at him expectantly and he paused before continuing.

"The first thing is to stop being Granddad's little Princess, come down out of that lonely ivory tower." He paused to put his hands under her arms and lift her on to the worktop. "And join the real world."

She looked at him blankly and stiffened as he very gently leant to kiss her on the lips, then tried to lean back as he tried again but the wall stopped her. Seeing her lips firmly shut and unresponsive, he asked in a puzzled voice:

"Did this Bryn never kiss you?"

"Of course he did," she objected.

"Did he make love to you?"

She didn't answer and he drew the corners of his mouth down. "Mmm, How old is he?"

"Nineteen," she sobbed.

"You need a better teacher," he said decisively.

She stared at him, tears streaming down her face.

"What do you mean?"

For answer, he dried her eyes with a tissue, took her face in his hands and very firmly moved his lips against hers until she opened them slightly, then he kissed her properly.

"There, that wasn't so bad was it?" he asked, eventually, not sure whether she had stopped crying because she was in shock or because she enjoyed it. Bit of both he decided noting her dazed expression. Striking while the iron was hot, he left her for a brief moment to turn the dimmer switch down before returning to kiss the smooth curve of her neck below her ear and caress her shoulders and back. She was motionless and still kissing her he released his hold and gradually slid exploring fingers into the sides of her dress, but as she felt him touch her breasts, she pulled away. Instantly he put his lips against hers again and this time hers were soft and yielding. He felt her body relax against him as his fingers continued to find places he knew would excite her.

"I love you Bryn," she murmured.

He held her away indignantly but she drew him back, her eyes closed. Brushing aside his dented ego, he kissed her ardently and she responded. Aware now that she was drowning in emotion by reliving her time with Bryn, his uppermost thought was that there would never be another opportunity like this and gently undid the ornamental clasp at the back of her neck while supposedly caressing her; before removing the diamante, combs and allowing her hair and bodice to drop to her waist, together. She gave a small, murmur of protest, but senses reeling with emotion she was powerless to stop him as his lips travelled down her neck, smothering her breasts with kisses, until his mouth closed over her nipple, sending waves of uncontrollable desire coursing through her whole body until she cried out for more. Mesmerised by her beauty, Peter pulled her towards him, allowing her dress to fall over her slim hips and land in a dark, silken pool at her feet. Picking her up, he placed her on the bed and she become aware of his bare body crushing against her, sweeping aside any reservation she still had as she abandoned herself to his tantalizing powers of seduction, conquering the last vestiges of a fear she had lived with for so long.

Much later as they lay side by side, she looked drowsily across at him and whispered huskily, "Why didn't you tell me what I was missing?"

Leaning up on his elbow, he traced her nipple with his finger. "I'm not sure I knew myself. You are truly amazing, Samantha Anders. I have never met a woman like you."

"Really?" she said, squirming seductively at his touch.

"It will take a good man to keep you happy, so make sure you find one. Forget Bryn; the man's a fool."

Shafts of rosy coloured light filtering through the curtains when they finally slept heralded the dawn of a new life for Samantha. She had joined the world that Gerald had tried to keep at bay.

CHAPTER SEVENTEEN

Lindsey looked at her mother in horror. "Never go back home? How can you even suggest that? I want to go back to Peter."

"Why would you want to stay with someone who makes you so miserable?" Monica demanded impatiently. She hadn't actually told her daughter that she would be arrested if she went back to Britain; she had just said that she didn't intend to return.

"Because, I love him," Lindsey said woefully.

"You will soon forget him and Britain, when we settle somewhere in the sun."

Monica closed her eyes; the matter was, closed as far as she was concerned; the discussion had gone on long enough. They had been talking for the past hour and her daughter was being obstinate. Why couldn't she see that a far better way of life was being offered to her on a plate?

Seeing her mother's set expression, Lindsey knew that talking was pointless; she got up from the sunbed, where she had been sunning herself since breakfast, walked to the shallow end of the pool and slid into the water. Through half closed eyes, Monica watched her floating on her back, congratulating herself that her daughter had seen sense. With that, Monica closed her eyes again and settled down, comfortable in the knowledge that, as always, Lindsey would do as she was bidden.

*

Samantha awoke to find Peter making tea. "Morning," she said, stretching lazily and throwing the duvet back, to reveal long, slim legs, an incredibly tiny waist and firm breasts, as she slipped out of bed. He watched her sway slowly towards him, anticipating her warm body against his, thrilling at the desire in her eyes.

"Let's forget the tea, for a while," she murmured.

"You are insatiable," he told her, much later.

She laughed, slipping out of bed. "I'm going in the shower, after I've made that cup of tea."

He was amazed at her lack of shyness as she moved about naked. Who would have dreamt she could change so much, in such a short time?

Listening to her in the shower, he wondered how long he would be able to satisfy her youthful energy, but even as the thought struck him, a vision of her in the running water urged him out of bed.

"What are you doing?" Samantha gasped, startled as he pounced on her and started soaping her all over.

"I'm completing your education."

"There's more?"

"Oh yes, quite a lot. You haven't lived until—" he whispered in her ear and her gold flecked, green eyes, opened wide with amused wonder.

*

Lindsey waited for her mother to fall asleep as she always did after lunch then quietly went into the house. Midday always created an almost unearthly silence in the mountains, as if the whole world was sleeping and only she was awake. Padding barefoot across the hall and up the carved wooden staircase, she reached her mother's bedroom, checked from the balcony that Monica was still sleeping, then found what she was looking for tucked behind a box of tissues in the bedside cabinet.

*

Hands clasped behind her head, Samantha lay staring up at the ceiling. Peter had gone home to check if there was news from the firm who had short-listed him and said he would be back in an hour, but that was nearly two hours ago. She curled up in a ball. Supposing he didn't come back; what if he left her, as well? Bryn would be getting married in just over a week. Disjointed thoughts flicked through her mind. Would he try to see her one last time? She had told him she never wanted to see him again, but he would know that wasn't true. Resentment filled her at the thought of him with Jocelyn, resentment that turned to panic as she looked at the clock again. Two hours and ten minutes, where was Peter? She picked up her mobile phone just as she heard the lift and was at the door waiting for him as he walked towards her, laughing that she was still in her underwear until he saw she was crying.

"What's the matter? What's happened?"

"You said you would only be an hour. I thought you weren't coming back!" she sobbed.

He took hold of her shoulders. "I got held up; there was a letter to say I had got the job. I had to make a phone call; nothing to get so upset about."

He went to put his arms around her but she rushed back into the flat and threw herself on the bed.

"Sam, come on, why are you making such a big deal of this?"

She calmed down. "I thought you had left me as well," she said, sitting up and reaching for a tissue.

Peter gave her a worried look. "Sam, I can't stay with you; I am married, and when Lindsey comes back I shall go home."

She looked woebegone. "You said she'd left you, and that I was amazing. You really like making love to me, so couldn't we buy a house together; just a small one – and…"

Hearing a slightly hysterical note, he took her by the shoulders and gave her a little shake.

"Listen, Sam. I'm not sure Lindsey has left me. Yes, I do like making love to you and you are amazing, but we can't buy a house together because, in the first place we haven't got any money and secondly, you are too young to settle down," his voice dropped, "with someone of my age."

"You are just making excuses," she accused.

"I'm not. Lindsey and I have a small state of the art gym in the basement of a beautiful new, fully equipped, paid for house. Which incidentally is all by courtesy of my wealthy mother-in-law, who also happens to be the wife of my uncle, who has provided me with a well-paid job ever since I left school with no qualifications. In fact this will be the first job I have ever landed entirely on my own – I've been as spoilt as you have in many ways. I couldn't begin to support you like a princess."

"Don't call me that," she snapped. "Only Grandfather calls me that – or Daddy," she added as an afterthought.

"I shouldn't have said that." He looked sincerely sorry. "Forgiven?"

She nodded. "What am I going to do? I can't go back to all of those memories, not without him there."

"What about the rest of your family?" he asked curiously.

"They all want to leave; I'll be alone." She spread her hands.

Peter turned the corners of his mouth down, trying to think of an answer.

"Is there no one to look after you?"

"Lorna and George will still be there, if we have enough money to pay a housekeeper and a manservant, that is."

"My advice is to go home and see just how bad things are."

"You don't understand; I hate Anders Folly now Grandfather isn't there." She wept silently and he didn't know how to comfort her.

"What about this Bryn, can't he help?" he asked regretting the question immediately, when she wailed, "He's getting married," glaring at him as if it was his fault.

"Come on, you will find someone else; we've had a great time and there are plenty more fish in the sea," he said with an encouraging arm around her.

She looked at him accusingly. "I don't want a fish, I let you touch me because I thought we were going to be together and now I'm twice *dumped*, in as many days!"

"Please Sam it's not like that; you are being unreasonable; you knew I was married. I was just trying to cheer you up – and I did, didn't I?" he coaxed.

She looked at him and gave a resigned nod. "You helped me into the real world alright," she agreed, still accusingly.

"I made you happy as well, didn't I?" He looked into her eyes still swimming with tears and she put her arms around his neck.

At that moment, his mobile phone left a text, but unable to resist her he ignored it.

"Let me make you happy again," he said, with a teasing smile, slipping her narrow, blue shoulder straps off.

*

Lindsey looked at her mother anxiously. She had sent a text telling Peter where she was and asking him to come and fetch her, because her mother was talking about staying abroad for good; ending with: *'I have wonderful news, Daddy.'*

Feeling sure he would contact her that same evening she listened for the phone while they had dinner, but ten o'clock came and there was still no call.

Perhaps he had sent a text. Saying she was going to bed early, she went into her mother's room and got the mobile out of the bedside drawer again, but there was nothing. She turned around and Monica was standing in the doorway.

"What are you doing, sweetheart?"

"I ran out of tissues and came to borrow some. She quickly replaced the phone and plucked some tissues out of the box."

"I only put a fresh box in your room two days ago; surely you haven't finished them yet? I'll have a look."

"Oh I've just remembered they are in the bathroom." Lindsey escaped quickly; she was hopeless at telling lies. "Goodnight Mother."

Monica watched her leave, hating to see her so unhappy, then started to undress, wondering what Lindsey would say when she told her that she had bought a house for them. The tickets to South America had only been a red herring; she had cancelled them a day later, when they had moved into this house. False passports, changing their names to Monique and Linda Langloise, had cost her dearly, but at least the deeds of the new house were safely registered in that name now. A whole, new life with untraceable identities was waiting. Her eyes shone with excitement as she picked up her laptop and studied figures beyond her wildest dreams, before switching it off and slipping a dark blue sleeping mask over her eyes.

At seven thirty the following morning, she was woken by the mobile phone, beeping in the drawer beside her bed and she reacted quickly, whipping off her mask and fumbling for the phone so that Lindsey wouldn't hear. She had told her there was no signal here. Eyes widening in alarm, she read the message: *'Coming asap. So glad you called. X*

Monica looked at the sender's name with a sinking heart, realising then, what Lindsey had been doing in her room. White with anger she threw back the duvet and leapt out of bed.

"You silly, stupid little fool," she stormed, throwing open Lindsey's bedroom door. "You've ruined everything. How dare you go behind my back? How could you do this to me?"

Rudely awoken, Lindsey roused herself with difficulty, not having slept until four o'clock, for thinking about Peter. Now she blinked owlishly as Monica threw the mobile phone on the bed, demanding, "Haven't I given you everything you could want?"

Lindsey snatched the phone, suddenly wide-awake; and her face broke into a rapturous smile as she read the text.

"Peter's coming to fetch me. Don't be angry Mother. I've got to let him know he's going to be a daddy." She beamed at Monica, who had suddenly sat down on the edge of the bed looking shocked.

"You are going to be a grandmother," Lindsey said softly, holding out her hand.

"What have I done?" Monica whispered, taking it.

"I don't understand; aren't you thrilled?"

Coming to a quick decision, Monica answered over brightly, "Yes, yes of course I am sweetheart. You lie there and I'll fetch your breakfast. You need spoiling." She got up, rushed out of the room and Lindsey could hear a lot of activity as she lay grinning up at the oak beamed ceiling, planning how she was going to greet Peter, until Monica returned carrying a loaded tray. Surprisingly she was fully dressed in outdoor clothes.

"Aren't you going to have your swim this morning?" Lindsey asked, wide eyed.

"Not this morning, I have to go to the bank and sign some papers. The cleaning woman has arrived; she will have the hoover on, so I will close your door." She gave her daughter a lingering hug. "Take care, my darling. I'm so thrilled." She turned to go, stopping at the door with a hint of tears in her eyes. "Don't ever forget how much I love you."

"I love you too Mother," Lindsey said softly, waving goodbye with a wiggle of her fingers, ecstatic with excitement.

Monica wished she had a camera handy.

Some time later, Lindsey left her room to find the hoover switched on standing at the top of the stairs, unattended. She looked around for the elderly cleaning lady, but there was no sign, so she pulled the plug out. Silence fell and she called repeatedly, "Helga, where are you?" receiving no answer as she wandered down the stairs and into the kitchen. The previous night's dishes were still in the sink but still no sign of Helga. Thinking she might have fallen, Lindsey panicked, imagining her lying unconscious somewhere, and ran back upstairs. Starting in her mother's room, she found it empty and was leaving when she noticed doors and drawers wide-open, revealing empty spaces. She stared wide-eyed, heart beginning to thump as she realised how her mother had fooled her. The noise of the hoover and the closed door had been to hide her departure. Why, though?

Peter arrived late morning and didn't seem surprised.

"Maybe she needed to be somewhere and didn't want to pressure you, in your condition." He pulled a comical face and she was so relieved to see him that she forgot about her mother's strange behaviour; after all, the whole holiday had been strange from the start. In the excitement of arranging their passage home and talking about the baby, Peter decided to delay telling her about the police wanting her for questioning and William being in prison, until they were in the safety of their own home.

Her whole demeanour told *him* that she knew nothing of the robbery and he hoped the police would see that as well. He had often wondered how she had remained so innocently simple-minded, with a mother like Monica.

CHAPTER EIGHTEEN

When Peter found the message from Lindsey, he panicked

"Yesterday," he impressed on Samantha.

Samantha looked dismayed. "Does this mean you are leaving?" she asked in a dull voice.

"I have to; don't you see? Lindsey needs to come home. She is pregnant." He gave a satisfied smile.

Samantha twisted her face. "Another one; I'm surrounded by them," she said in the same dull voice.

"Another what?" Peter asked distractedly, looking in a phone book for British Airways number.

"Pregnant women," she answered, retrieving her handbag from the wardrobe and producing her address book. "Here's the number you need."

Peter stopped searching and stared, suddenly remembering Bryn's pregnant girlfriend.

"Oh gosh, I'm sorry." He took her in his arms and rocked her until she picked up his phone and gave it to him with a resigned:

"Your wife needs you."

He pressed the numbers and his card was refused because of insufficient funds and he became agitated again.

"I'll have to text Lindsey and ask her for the air fare," he said with an embarrassed grimace, switching off his phone.

"I can lend you the money," Samantha said simply.

"Would you? I'll pay you back as soon as I get home. I promise."

She reached into her purse and handed him her card; he started to phone the number again. "Oh, no, now the phone needs recharging." He buried his head in his hands and she calmly came to the rescue again by handing him her mobile. He took it sheepishly and managed to book and pay for his ticket successfully. In the meantime, she plugged his phone into the charger.

"You will need it on the journey."

"Thanks, you're a star."

"What time does your plane leave?" she asked.

"We've got a couple of hours before I need to go home and pack a bag, shall I go and buy croissants or do you want to go out for breakfast?"

"Croissants," she decided. "I'll make tea, while you're gone."

"As I said before, you are amazing." His kiss was long and ardent as they parted and he was loath to let her go, but his whole comfortable world depended on Lindsey.

After he had gone, she packed her things, locked up securely and drove towards Bob and Marcia's, with a heavy heart. On the way, she decided to drop in at 'Murry's', to collect her thoughts. The lunchtime rush was over and the girls had gone for their afternoon break. Murry was relaxing with a cup of coffee.

"Nice to see you again," he greeted her sociably. "What can I get you?"

"Just something from your excellent salad bar, please." She walked over to the glass covered counter, chose a fresh looking salad with king prawns and went to her usual table. A few minutes later, Murry placed the salad and a brown, crusty roll with butter, in front of her.

"Enjoy your meal, Miss Anders."

"Thank you." He obviously wanted to talk but she didn't really feel in the mood.

He moved away, commenting again on her remarkable likeness to Pamela. "Your great grandmother could easily have been a model, as well."

"I wish I had known her."

"I actually knew her son better."

"You knew Alexander, how exciting. Were you as wild as he was?" she joked, expecting a humorous answer.

"Never had the chance; I had to work for my living. I didn't have an indulgent mother and father."

Samantha thinking he sounded envious said, "Being spoilt has drawbacks."

"It certainly affects one's loyalties." Now he sounded bitter.

Her interest roused, she said, "Tell me about him; the family don't want to be reminded."

"I'm not surprised; he did some pretty awful things."

There were no other diners, so Colin poured himself a glass of wine and sat opposite, in a high backed wooden settle by the log fire.

"Alexander was a law unto himself. No deed was too dirty, nobody safe from his revenge. That's obvious though, isn't it?"

He paused and seemed to be reliving the past.

132

"Is it?" she asked quietly, holding her breath in case he stopped.

"He put paid to my dreams and tried hard to wreck his brother's life, although Robert got the best deal, in the end."

"How?" she whispered, hardly daring to interrupt.

"He got to finish his education, marry the girl he loved and live his own life. Alexander lived a decadent life, always depending on his mother to get him out of scrapes, and the name Anders, to get him what he wanted. After his mother died in that dreadful crash, he lived in his father's shadow; afraid every day that he would be disinherited. Robert didn't care about the money – he turned Alexander's treachery into freedom for himself and the girl his brother wronged."

Samantha sat transfixed, small things falling into place.

"How did he wrong her?" The naïve question surprised Murry, but he answered it bluntly.

"He raped her of course; his brother's girlfriend; and boasted about it to me. We were together you see at the time and I know he taunted Robert. I heard tell that Celine – that was the girl's name, had a baby girl soon after Pamela died, but by that time of course, Alexander had put paid to any reconciliation there might have been between Robert and his father. I loved Alexander at one time but I grew to hate him."

Murry was almost talking to himself and his expression told her that nothing had been forgotten or forgiven. No wonder Alexander was a taboo subject with the family, she thought as another truth struck her. Auntie Fran, must be that baby girl. How many more untold secrets were there?

"So you shared a flat?" she asked innocently.

Colin gave her a sharp look. "A cottage." He stared into the fire, reliving the day when Gerald Anders had sold him 'The Vintage', and how angry Alexander had been when he found out. He had taken his revenge though; and years later, Colin discovered how he had been cheated of his most prized possession: the manor house that was now the equestrian centre, just along the road.

Colin shook his head as if coming out of a dream.

"That's all in the past though. I was sorry to hear about your great grandfather; he was a real gentleman. Let me get you a cup of coffee." He minced over to the coffee stand and returned with a demitasse of Mocha coffee, apparently having forgotten his reminiscences of a moment ago.

Samantha drank her coffee, while he put logs on the fire and went outside to refill the wicker basket, returning in time to wave aside the money she proffered.

"It's a pleasure," he said. "Please come again."

"I certainly will and if you remember any more family stories, I can't wait to hear them."

"I shall look forward to our next meeting," Colin said nostalgically.

Outside in the wintry sunshine, Samantha stood and looked back at the Tudor style premises, which although attractive, must be a far cry from the plans he had for 'The Vintage'. Alexander suddenly took on a completely new personality to the high living, fun loving character she had fantasized about.

In a thoughtful mood, she drove through the avenue of trees leading up to the lovely old manor house trying to picture it as the high-class hotel.

"Not much different I don't suppose," she thought aloud, winding down the window to view the sweep of the undulating, well-kept lawn with its enormous weeping willow tree in the middle and clumps of huge azalea, hydrangea and rhododendron bushes, edging the drive.

"What isn't?" Bob's voice startled her; lost in thought she had missed his approach. She wound the window up and got out of the car.

"This." She waved a hand, encompassing the house and grounds.

"I have just been hearing some family history and Alexander doesn't come off too well."

"I wouldn't take too much notice of village rumours," Bob said disapprovingly.

"Oh this wasn't just rumour; it was firsthand knowledge. Did you know him Bob?"

"Vaguely; he was abroad mostly. It would be best if you didn't mention him in front of Marcia, though." Bob warned. "They didn't get on."

"Why was that?" Samantha persisted, her curiosity aroused further.

Bob looked uncomfortable, but realised that Samantha wasn't going to let this go.

"He led her daughter into bad ways," he said after a long pause, hoping that would suffice.

Samantha gave a sideways questioning look."

"That would be Tamara?"

"You don't want to go dragging up all these old stories; you'll only upset everyone," Bob advised with a heavy frown.

"But I must know; don't you see? I am proud of being an Anders, but have I been living in a fool's paradise, thinking that everything has been so upright and proper when it hasn't?"

Her eyes pleaded with him, in the way they did when she was a child and wanted something badly, and he knew she would keep on until he gave in, so he said firmly:

"I really can't talk about this. I would have to have Marcia's permission to tell you anyway, but if you value her invitation to just drop in and stay any time you want to, I should drop the subject."

"That bad?" she asked, shocked as Bob nodded.

He watched her open the boot and take her suitcase out, wondering what she was thinking, knowing full well, that she wouldn't let it rest. In his opinion she should be told but it wasn't his secret to tell.

After saying hello to Marcia, Samantha went to her room and perched on the window seat overlooking the forest where later on the trees would burst into a verdant green backdrop, to bluebells and primroses, pushing their way through the damp, leafy carpet. Her imagination raced at the innuendo of Bob's words as she tried to make sense of them. What could be that awful? she wondered, idly going through the small amount of mail that had been waiting for her. There was one from Fran, asking her to get in touch, another from Ella, telling her to please take care of herself, a friendly but disappointing note from Bryn, making no mention of them meeting, which she discarded with distain and another blue envelope with the senders name and address on the back: Miss M. Daly. 23, Grove House, Eastleigh. Samantha looked at it blankly for a second before recognising the name and her face lit up. Tearing open the envelope, she withdrew a sheet of blue note paper, and read:

Dear Samantha,

I was so sorry to hear about your granddad. I know how much you will be missing him.

I m currently looking for a new job and would you believe, I bumped into Peter the other day, when we both applied for positions at the same firm. He said he had seen you but didn't know where you were staying, so I am taking a chance that this will find you.

If you are staying at 'The Vintage' I would love to meet up and return your fountain pen which seems to have found its way into my organizer. It has your initials on, so I know it is yours. It would be nice to see you anyway and I am at home every evening if you want to telephone or drop in.

Love Megan.

She had enclosed her mobile number and drawn a small map of directions.

Samantha's spirits rose at the possibility of talking to the friendly assistant who had become her confidant. She reached into her handbag for her mobile phone, intending to ring her and felt an unfamiliar shape. Withdrawing it she gave a perplexed frown, seeing in her mind's eye, Peter, pocketing her phone after he had telephoned the airport; then recalled, unplugging the one on the work top and dropping it into her bag before leaving the flat that morning. There was a message waiting. *'Got your phone. Hope you have mine. See you soon. Peter. x.'*

She smiled to herself, thinking of their time together and jumped as the phone vibrated in her hand and an irate text appeared on the screen.

'Where the hell are you? Been trying to reach you, for ages. We need to meet.'

She looked at the name above and nearly dropped the phone; it was from William; and that could only mean, William Spencer. Thinking swiftly, she sent a text back.

'Been busy. See you at The Deerhunter'. She looked at her watch and added *'at seven thirty'.*

She sat very still, staring at the message, heart pounding, mind working sharply as she pressed the send button. Waiting for an answer, her stomach churned nervously, until a brief, arrogant *'don't be late'*, made her blood boil.

Bob was in the stables feeding the horses as she ran to him, white faced.

He listened while she explained what she had done. "We can catch him," she urged, as he gave a grim smile.

"*We* will leave it to the police."

He telephoned and within twenty minutes, someone came to take her statement.

Late that evening, they were informed William Spencer had been arrested and charged with grand theft. He was denying everything and blaming the accounts department for making regrettable blunders.

*

When William eventually contacted Amy, in the middle of the night, he was at his wits' end. Seeing his yacht towed away was like seeing his life support disappearing, depriving him of the means to stay clean and cook for himself. Five weeks had seemed like five months and he finally had to give in and ask for her help.

She had driven to where he was living rough, in a wooded area near Boarhunt and taken him back to where she lived, in a tall block of flats, on the outskirts of Southampton. On seeing him, in the electric light, she was appalled by his appearance. Unshaven and wearing dirty, crumpled, clothes, he looked half-starved, as if having lived in a cardboard box for those weeks.

"Why didn't you call me before?" she asked.

"I thought they would be watching you. I've got clean clothes in my suitcase," he said defensively, seeing her look of distaste.

"What a dreadful time you must have had," she sympathised, hastily. "I'll get you some food, while you clean up." Without waiting for an answer she showed him where the bathroom was and left him to unpack in her bedroom.

An hour later, showered, shaved and dressed in casual clothes bought from a supermarket, he looked a little more like his old self as they sat and ate a quickly made pasta dish.

"Sorry, it's only out of a packet," she apologised, seeing his dubious expression, but relaxed when he ate ravenously and accepted another helping.

Feeling more genial, he gave her a grateful smile and said how tasty it was.

"We won't have to worry about my cooking, when we get away," she joked.

In his effort to survive, William had forgotten about her expectations.

"I won't have the sort of money I expected; we may have to rough it for a bit," he said hastily, adding as he saw her disappointment, "but it won't be for long and then you shall have everything your heart desires."

He patted her hand resting on the table between them, relieved to see her smile return. Must keep her happy, there was no way he wanted to go back to living in the car, he thought, looking about him at the cheap, modern furnishings and minimalist décor. Even this was better than living without modern conveniences.

"A flat like this, somewhere warm, will be perfect," Amy said dreamily, mistaking his look for appreciation.

He forced a smile and gave an inward groan, comparing it to his and Monica's dream, of a ranch style, bungalow, complete with a wraparound porch, set in fifteen acres of ground in South America.

A soft, clean bed helped to raise his spirits though and in the morning he felt more optimistic; optimism quickly quenched, by the confines of the small flat and noise of adjoining neighbours.

"How do you stand it?" he asked at last, as the sound of children's television programmes blasted through the walls and little footsteps could be heard dancing to the music. "Thank God we are on the top floor."

"I'm usually at work, or out," she said with a defensive frown. "Why don't we go out for a bit of lunch?" She made the suggestion without thinking and grimaced instantly. This was really, really, not how she pictured their life together. Far from being the high-powered boss he had been, William looked old and grumpy with it.

William saw her disillusionment and made an effort. He badly needed her help to get out of the country, but he could hardly take her with him to look for Monica. That was why he had waited so long, but after five weeks he couldn't stand the discomfort any longer and she was his only hope.

"Why don't you go and buy us a couple of steaks and a bottle of wine? We'll celebrate in style tonight. I'll cook." He took his wallet out and extracted a fifty-pound note. "Buy yourself something as well."

Amy's eyes lit up and she flew to get ready, planting a kiss on his cheek as she ran past.

As soon as she had gone he phoned Peter. "Where is the boy?" he muttered viciously, when Peter's mobile was switched off yet again.

He got up and paced the room, wracking his brain for another way to buy a car, but there was nobody else he could ask; he needed Peter, because something else he didn't want Amy to find out about was his passport in the name of Havers. They had arrived by post on the very morning the robbery was discovered. One each for him and Monica, when they left Switzerland to live in South America; thankfully, his would get him out of Britain, now. He had put them in the office safe with the money he had collected that very same morning from the eight tenants. A year's rent, in cash, from each of the eight apartments, came to a tidy sum and while Amy was out, was a good time to find a hiding place for his briefcase.

He stopped pacing long enough to ring Peter's number again – it was still switched off.

Amy returned and struggling to maintain a jocular manner, he donned an apron and opened the bottle of wine to allow it to breathe. While he cooked the steak and chips and tossed a green salad, he thought nostalgically of the luxurious kitchen at home, where every conceivable spice, herb and ingredient, filled cupboards surrounded by black granite surfaces and top quality stainless steel appliances. From there his thoughts turned to Monica, blindly convincing himself that she would be waiting – anxious even. They had planned to settle in South America and she was obviously there, waiting for him.

Amy was happily setting the glass-topped table with bright red place mats, red handled cutlery, white candles in tall glass holders and a vase of red and white carnations purchased that afternoon. She was singing to a pop song on the television and discoing around the room, obviously enjoying the occasion tremendously.

A stab of guilt made him go and put his arms around her. Normally, he would suggest going to bed after supper, but that was the last thing on his mind now. After eating, she seemed happy enough, stretched out on the bright red settee, with a glass of wine, absorbed in a weepy film. It gave him the opportunity to slip off to the bathroom every now and then to ring Peter, getting more and more frustrated as the evening wore on, when there was no reply. He eventually left a text and received an answer the following afternoon, little knowing it was from Samantha.

*

Peter sent a text, asking Samantha for his phone and his grey eyes were full of reproach as he greeted her. She didn't deny his accusation.

"What would you have done in my place?" she challenged,

He thought for a while before admitting, "The same, I suppose."

"There is no suppose about it; he killed Grandfather."

"That's a bit strong."

They were sitting in her car in the underground car park, and strong feelings gripped her at the mere thought of his touch but her body language gave nothing away.

He had sworn he would not cheat on Lindsey again, but Samantha was so irresistible, especially now that she was the self-possessed young woman again, who had driven him to distraction, challenging his powers of seduction with her air of cool indifference. She sat calmly beside him now, with every appearance of being in complete control and the challenge to break through her defences again excited him.

She caught his eye and despite everything, had to fight the urge to be in his arms.

"Time to go, I think," she said firmly.

"No hurry." He took her hand, pressing it to his lips and she felt herself weakening.

"Don't let's do something we will be sorry for," she said drawing away.

"I could never be sorry for anything I did with you. Come up to the flat for five minutes," he begged.

Taking her in his arms he kissed her as if he couldn't bear to let her go and she responded with an uncontrollable need.

In the intimacy of the apartment, mesmerised by his seeking lips and caressing hands, she became helpless to resist his expert lovemaking again as overwhelming desire took over, leaving her heedless to everything until he whispered, "I can't live without you. We can meet, safely," he assured her.

She knew she should say no, but the thought of not seeing him was unbearable, and they parted promising to meet the following week.

A contented smile on his handsome face, Peter drove home, confident that the next few months were taken care of in a very satisfactory way. His home was back to normal; the police were satisfied that Lindsey knew nothing of the robbery, and he had landed a plum job, as manager of a well-known car sales firm. After Lindsey had the baby he would settle down, but in the meantime he looked forward to a very enjoyable few months.

The time with Peter had made her late for her meeting with Meg, but as she drove, Samantha was happy in the belief that Peter wanted her as desperately as she wanted him and that all in good time they would be together.

Arriving at Meg's address, she was surprised to see a modern, two-storied block of flats. She had somehow imagined her living at home with parents.

Meg was watching for her and waved as Samantha got out of the car. They greeted one another at the blue painted door of a ground floor flat and Meg's dark brown eyes lit up appreciatively as Samantha handed her a spray of flowers and a box of chocolates.

"Mm freesias; and chocolates; how lovely." She led the way into a small sitting room, where another surprise greeted Samantha.

Double-glazed patio doors filled one wall, revealing a small, crazy paved garden beyond, dotted with ornamental tubs containing bulbs. A small table and two chairs stood invitingly in one corner and a water feature filled another, but Samantha's gaze was transfixed on a pretty, dark-haired baby, well wrapped up in a fleecy, pink suit, sitting up in a pram.

Meg saw her surprise. "Didn't you know I had Lucy?"

"I had no idea." Samantha recovered enough to ask how old Lucy was, and from there the conversation was all about Meg and Lucy, with Meg confessing without bitterness:

"Just, the old, old story; girl meets boy, boy declares undying love, girl becomes pregnant, boy takes off."

"Aren't you angry? I would be." Samantha looked cross.

"Devastated, but not angry; I have Lucy." Meg got up saying it was time for Lucy's feed.

Samantha watched as she made up the formula, comparing the responsibility of looking after seven-month-old Lucy, with her own free life.

"How are you managing without a job?" she asked at last, when the baby was feeding contentedly in Meg's arms.

Meg had already told her that several interviews had demanded flexy hours, making child-care difficult.

"We manage," Meg said, looking down and colouring, making Samantha realise that she would have to be careful not to embarrass her.

The moment passed and Meg was her usual sunny self, playing with Lucy and asking Samantha if she would like to hold her.

Lucy held her arms out obligingly and sat, playing happily with Samantha's gold locket, while Meg made them a sandwich and a cup of tea for lunch.

Lucy went down for her afternoon nap and they sat talking. Meg made light of her life but reading between the lines, it was evident she was struggling. Her parents hadn't forgiven her for ruining her chances of going to university, and she had moved out to make a happier life for herself and Lucy.

"I was doing fine until 'Anders' closed; I even had a good baby minder." Her smile faded for a moment and she quickly agreed when Samantha said:

"That William Spencer has a lot to answer for."

"You said you would get him – and you did. That was pretty darn clever, Miss Anders." They exchanged triumphant smiles.

"The money is still missing, though."

"According to the papers, the police have investigated his affairs and he swears he doesn't have the money. Do you believe that?" Meg questioned, head on one side, eyebrows raised in disbelief.

"He may not have it, but he must know who has," Samantha answered shrewdly.

Later, on her way back to 'The Vintage', she stopped the car and sat staring into the tunnel of light created by the powerful headlights. An idea had come to her, but deciding it needed more thought before saying anything she drove on until 'Murry's' lights beckoned. In her present state of uncertainty, she didn't want to discuss her idea with Bob or Marcia, who would almost certainly disagree, on principle if nothing else.

A couple of early diners were sitting at a table on the opposite side of the log fire to where she usually sat, and Murry was sitting with them. He rose as she entered and she waved him back to his chair.

"I will just choose from the salad bar, please don't interrupt your meal," she assured him.

The young waitress started towards her with a wide smile, and Murry, after consulting his dinner guests, beckoned to her. The girl halted, nodded and continued towards Samantha.

"Murry says, he and his guests would be really pleased if you would join them for dinner."

Samantha looked across enquiringly, then walked towards them.

"I really can't intrude," she started to say, as the elderly couple sitting with him, sat staring as if they had seen a ghost.

"You won't, I promise; I want you to meet my family. Mother, meet Samantha, Pamela's great granddaughter. Samantha this is Ann, a great friend of Pamela's." He watched his mother's eyes became bright with tears, as she held her arms out. Samantha bent to receive a warm, wordless embrace realising it must be a very emotional moment for the elderly woman.

Next, Murry was introducing her to the man, standing now and looking at her, obviously very moved.

"And this is Uncle Bill, my mother's brother; also a very good—" he paused imperceptibly, "friend of your great grandmother."

Bill took her hand, looking quite dazed. "It is like seeing Pamela again." His smile was soft she noticed.

Murry watched gloatingly, enjoying what he assumed was apprehension on his uncle's part, but Bill didn't notice; he was reliving the past.

"Samantha is interested in anything we can tell her about her family."

Murry held a chair for her and she sat down, eager to listen.

Ann shot him a suspicious look. "How can we tell her anything she doesn't already know?" she asked with a warning stare. Ann didn't like her son's mischief-making streak.

Murry looked away. "By the way, we are celebrating my uncle's birthday, he won't thank me for saying how old he is, so suffice to say, he is five years younger than my mother, who was the same age as Pamela." Murry laughed at his own joke and Samantha wondered why he was being so waspish. This was a side to him she hadn't seen.

"Happy Birthday. May I call you Bill?" Samantha flashed a smile at him and his jaw dropped.

142

"Sorry," she said quickly, thinking she had been too familiar.

"You most certainly can, Samantha. I just never thought to see that smile again." Their eyes met softly.

"Tell me about her." She turned to Ann with a pleading look.

"Pamela used to bring Alexander to stay at our hotel. He and Colin were great friends as well."

"It's all right Mother, she knows we were together," Colin said impatiently.

"Your real name is Colin, then?" Samantha confirmed.

"Yes. Colin Murry, but just, 'Murry', sounds more upmarket for the business." He tossed his head and Bill tutted; he never could accept his nephew's gestures. It riled Colin and he retaliated.

"At least I'm up front about my affairs; not like some people." The accusation was barbed and Samantha was beginning to feel uncomfortable.

"I think I must go; I seem to be causing trouble," but as she stood up the meal arrived.

"Please don't go my dear. Colin, apologise and ask Samantha to stay." Ann reached out and took her hand.

"I'm sorry. Please stay." Colin held her chair and she sat down hesitantly, but compliments about Colin's choice of food and wine smoothed things over and more normal conversation resumed.

Ann talked about how much Pamela enjoyed London, and Bill added that she was an excellent nurse, explaining how she took over when one of the nurses had needed time off.

"I never knew. In fact, Granddad wouldn't talk about his illness and stay in the clinic."

"I wonder why?" Colin raised his eyebrows at Bill.

"It wasn't a happy experience for a proud man," Ann said quickly.

"My Uncle Charles always said that pride would be the death of him." Samantha gave a reminiscent smile.

They finished eating and Colin was pouring himself a large brandy to go with his coffee. He had been slurring his words slightly and Ann gave a worried frown.

"I think you have had enough alcohol for this evening, Colin."

"Why don't you tell her the truth?" Colin accused, ignoring his mother.

Bill stood up annoyed by his behaviour. "I suggest you go upstairs and sober up, unless you want to drive your customers away."

"I must be going," Samantha said quickly, anticipating a scene.

"I'll see you to your car," Bill offered.

She said goodnight to Ann, promising to keep in touch.

"Let's have lunch; I am staying for a week. We will talk some more about your great grandmother – in peace," she added meaningfully.

They exchanged understanding smiles and Samantha followed Bill to her car. Without hesitation, he went straight to the ice blue Mercedes.

"How did you know this was mine?" she asked curiously.

"You are Pamela's great granddaughter. Show me another car here that would be yours." He laughed and she felt a surge of warmth towards him.

As he opened the door, he was reminded of a time when he and Pamela had met, and suddenly knew he had to satisfy Samantha's need to hear about Pamela, whatever the consequences, knowing instinctively though that she wouldn't judge them. He withdrew his wallet and handed a card through the window.

"Come to London. I am the only one left, who can tell you about the London loving side of Pamela."

Agog with excitement, she gave him that brilliant smile again, making his world cartwheel with memories, even after all this time.

"Just ring and say you are on your way."

Driving home to 'The Vintage', her thoughts filled with curiosity at what she would learn, she wondered at the coincidence of her meeting with the three people who knew her great grandmother and Alexander so well; was she going to like what they could tell her?

Marcia greeted her coolly as she walked into the sitting room, asking why she hadn't let her know she wouldn't be in for dinner. Samantha apologised profusely and explained that she had completely forgotten in the excitement of meeting some old friends of the family.

"Why do you have to rake up the past? Why can't you leave well alone?"

Marcia left the sitting room hurriedly, leaving Samantha even more curious, as she wended her way slowly to her bedroom, wondering what Marcia had to do with the past, apart from being Grandfather's second wife. Perhaps Murry would know.

Getting ready for bed, she thought about her earlier idea, and decided she would go and see Meg in the morning.

An early ride on Midnight nearly changed her mind; it was going to be awful not riding either her or Nocturn. During breakfast, the atmosphere was very strained, even Bob was quiet with her and she left the table as quickly as possible, stopping to check if there was mail for her on the hall table. It was then that Bob's voice reached her.

"I don't know why you don't just tell her," he grumbled.

"Because I promised Gerald I wouldn't ever tell anyone. It isn't as if it's something she needs to know." Her voice was quiet and final and there was no answer from Bob.

Samantha stood stock-still, shocked by yet more evidence of guilty secrets.

It finally made up her mind to leave Bob and Marcia.

Bob was worried when she said she was leaving, and Marcia's expression was hard to read.

"Will you go home?" Bob asked anxiously.

"No, I shall stay with a friend, if she will have me."

"The one you were with last week?" Bob hadn't liked not being able to contact her.

She hesitated. "I will let you know by tonight; I promise." She kissed his cheek and smiled. "Don't worry, I'm a big girl now." She turned to Marcia.

"Thanks for putting up with me, Marcia."

She gave her a hug and Marcia said, "Come back if things don't work out. Your room will always be there."

"Don't forget us and Midnight," Bob called as they waved goodbye at the front door.

Watching the sleek blue car disappear down the drive Bob said, "I can't help feeling she is heading for trouble."

Marcia hid a worried frown by walking briskly back into the house. "She has to grow up some time."

CHAPTER NINETEEN

Meg gave a relieved sigh and switched her mobile off. She had just replied to an advert in the local paper shop, for two hours' housework, two days a week. It was a bit of a come down, but better than nothing. She had replied to several adverts for working at home, but the pay was poor for the many tedious hours required. Housework paid better, and best of all, she could take Lucy with her. Smiling to herself she checked on Lucy sleeping soundly in the garden, her pram turned out of the cold wind.

The doorbell rang as she was putting the kettle on for a cup of coffee and she went to answer it, not expecting to see Samantha so soon again.

"I've just put the kettle on. Come in. This is a lovely surprise."

"I hope you will still think so, when I tell you why I've come."

Meg looked worried. "What's the matter?"

Samantha followed her through to the kitchen and perched on the stool at the breakfast-bar.

"I need a favour."

"Fire away, anything."

"Can I stay with you?"

"Pull the other one. You, stay here?" Meg laughed.

"Sorry, but it would only be for a little while until I get a job and decide what to do."

Meg stared. "You're serious aren't you? I thought you were trying to help me out and I don't do handouts," she said frowning deeply.

"I'm perfectly serious, and *you* would be doing me a favour. I really need somewhere to stay. I can go to a hotel but I would rather stay with you, if you will have me. I'll pay my way, of course, so if it helps you as well all the better."

Meg's brow cleared. "When do you want to come?"

"My luggage is in the car."

Suddenly they were laughing and hugging each other and hauling Samantha's three large suitcases into the small second bedroom.

"Lucy still sleeps in with me, anyway," Meg explained. "I can't bear to part with her."

"Of course not," Samantha sympathised.

The arrangement worked well for them both. Samantha was there to look after Lucy, while Meg looked for a job; they shopped together in the car, saving Meg the long trek home laden with food and in return Samantha had the company she badly needed.

As promised, she drove to Murry's during the week for lunch. Ann was waiting for her, sitting at the table by the fire. They had a pleasant two hours and Ann had a few snapshots to show her. It was odd to see her great grandmother, without any of the familiar surroundings of Anders Folly, dressed to go out for an evening at the theatre with a handsome young Bill at her side, and compare the difference to her quite, rural life in Cornwall.

"I think Pamela was happy enough in Cornwall until she came to London. The last time she saw London, remember, it would have been war-torn, with bombed out buildings and poorly dressed people going about their deprived lives. She must have been glad then, to escape to a wonderfully peaceful place like her husband's family home – and of course, she absolutely adored Gerald. It was the boys who tore them apart, or rather Alexander."

Samantha was glad that Ann added that.

"So where does Bill fit in?"

"I'm going to leave him to tell you about that; and I hope you will understand that Pamela was a wonderfully caring woman who just needed to forget the horrors she had seen during her nursing career."

"Are you saying she was unstable?" Samantha asked.

"Not in the least, just greatly stressed. She idolised and spoilt Alexander, but he caused nothing but trouble; very serious trouble that she constantly had to rescue him from and it drove a wedge between her and your grandfather."

"All roads lead back to Alexander, sooner or later," Samantha said in a disillusioned voice.

"It would seem so." Ann suddenly looked stern. "I know he broke Colin's heart."

Samantha watched a hurt, faraway look come into Ann's eyes. Was there no end to Alexander's wrongdoings and the people he hurt?

As if reading her thoughts, Ann said, "Apparently his one redeeming feature was his loyalty to his nanny; he was greatly attached to her and she, like Pamela, idolised him."

Samantha's eyes opened wide. She hadn't thought of Abigail; she probably knew as much as anyone, more in fact – but that would mean going home; she dismissed the thought.

Colin came through with their coffee and the conversation ended.

He was obviously peeved at his mother's affection toward Samantha and showed it by fussing over her, himself.

"We must have lunch together Samantha and I will try and think of some more amusing stories for you." He touched her shoulder as he placed her coffee in front of her and handed her the cream.

"I'm beginning to think *amusing* stories of my family are in rather short supply," she answered seriously.

"My goodness, what has mother been telling you?" Colin laughed, pursing his lips and eyeing his mother questioningly.

"Only, what a lovely but sad woman Pamela was, through no fault of her own."

Busy pouring cream into her coffee, Samantha missed the meaningful look Ann gave him.

"Now, now Mother, you are a teensy weensy bit prejudiced, you know."

"Let's not apportion blame," Samantha interrupted, hearing the jibes getting personal.

Colin shrugged and minced back to the kitchen.

"Colin played a part in Pamela's unhappiness. He doesn't know that I know. Bill will tell you about that. He told me he has asked you to come to London. I hope you do. I think you should."

Samantha couldn't help but be intrigued and she made up her mind to go as soon as possible.

The afternoon ended on a sad note, when Ann said her husband Roy was in the clinic, suffering from an inoperable lung cancer.

"We only closed the hotel about eight years ago. Colin didn't want to take it over, so we sold up and gave him enough to buy this place. He loves this part of the world and harbours a dream of buying 'The Vintage' back.

"Poor Colin." Samantha couldn't help but feel sorry for him, knowing that the chances of that happening were practically non-existent.

They parted, saying they would meet again in London.

With Christmas less than two weeks away, a letter arrived from Fran asking if she was coming home, because if not, Charles and Felicity were going back to America to be with their family; however, they were prepared to stay at Anders Folly if she wanted to spend Christmas at home. The letter sounded terse and ended by saying they all obviously wanted to see her, or at least know where she was living, as Bob had said she had moved out. It reminded her that she had not kept her promise to let Bob know where she was staying and she telephoned straight away. Marcia answered sounding annoyed.

"Bob has been worried stupid. Why couldn't you just have called? You are very thoughtless Sam; the family are seriously worried and we feel to blame."

"I'm sorry Marcia, I didn't think."

"No, that's your trouble, Sam."

"I'll ring them tonight."

She rang off feeling contrite, realising in the next minute that she still hadn't said where she was living.

George answered when she rang Anders Folly and he sounded overjoyed to hear from her, but said that Mr and Mrs Charles had left for America that morning. He alone seemed to understand her reason for not coming home but begged her to, at least come for Christmas.

"I can't George," she sobbed over the phone. "That's probably the very worst time."

"There, there lass, don't go upsettin' yerself. Jus' giv'us an address, soas we can at least send yer a card."

She rang Fran next and said she would be staying with her friend and although disappointed Fran was relieved to hear she was all right.

"But please speak to your father, Sam; he is making life impossible for Melly." Fran sounded exasperated.

"Why, what is he doing?"

"Just harping on about America again, you know how he is."

"Oh why doesn't he just go?" Samantha snapped, feeling as if her feelings didn't matter at all.

"He's waiting for your blessing," Fran said quietly. "And if you don't intend to come back...?" she trailed off.

"I'll ring him." Samantha slumped as she rang off. Everyone wanted to leave her.

Meg saw her long face and put her arms about her. "Family problems?"

Meg listened as the whole story came out, including how deserted she felt. "Don't you think you are being a bit unreasonable?" she asked tentatively.

"Me?" Samantha was shocked.

"They are all waiting for you to make up your mind, before they make any plans; what about them? You obviously aren't the only one missing your grandfather and Christmas at the big house."

Samantha cried herself to sleep that night, recognising and hating the truth. Meg thought she had lost a friend.

149

In the morning, Samantha felt ill. She was running a temperature and her stomach was painful. Meg got her to eat some porridge, but she was sick shortly after. She felt better as the day wore on but the next morning she felt ill again.

"Maybe you've picked up Lucy's cold." Meg gave her paracetamol and plenty of fluids and she spent two days in bed.

Peter phoned, but when she said she had a virus, he rang off in a huff.

A few days before Christmas, she was still feeling under the weather, but they decorated the flat and filled a sack for Lucy, even though she was too young to appreciate the extravagant array of clothes Samantha bought her.

Once the rush of Christmas was over and Samantha felt better, her first thought was to visit London. She phoned Bill. He told her how to get to his home address and she set off, heart in mouth at the thought of driving in London. The last few miles actually driving *in* London were nerve-wracking but she arrived safely and Bill was waiting for her at his small terraced house in the mews. He was still an extremely attractive man; tall and distinguished looking, with a good head of silver grey hair and blue eyes that crinkled when he smiled. He was also easy company on his own. She found the house welcoming, with its compact, eclectic living space. He painted a vivid picture and hid nothing from her; to him, Pamela was still there and could walk through a door, any minute. The photograph of them both, still sat on his bedside table, Pamela's yellowing, white towelling dressing gown hung behind the bathroom door and Samantha gave a cry of recognition when she spied an unopened bottle of Clive Christian perfume on the dressing table. "It's the one Grandfather always buys me."

"It was her favourite."

"I didn't know." Tears of happiness welled, turning her eyes into shimmering, soft green pools and he caught his breath again at a fleeting memory.

They sat chatting and Bill couldn't help but reminisce, telling her how he and Pamela first met and then, how they came to spend an afternoon cruising down the River Thames.

"It was all very innocent and neither of us intended to fall in love."

His eyes misted over, remembering the first time they had made love, after going to the theatre to see 'The Mousetrap'. He showed her two tickets, still lodged in a large picture of Piccadilly Circus at the turn of the century.

He lost track for several moments, then becoming aware that she was sharing his sorrow, put his hand over hers, saying "We must go along to Ann's, shortly. She is cooking dinner for us."

He rose unsteadily. "And tomorrow I will take you both to lunch at a little bistro that Pamela loved."

Samantha's eyes shone softly. "That will be lovely."

Ann lived two doors down. "We moved here when we sold the hotel. Roy first became ill, a year ago and it's been a good arrangement," she explained, spooning vegetables into serving dishes while Bill carved roast lamb.

"An excellent arrangement," Bill agreed, popping a piece of lamb into his mouth and holding another piece out to Samantha. She took it, enjoying the homely gesture and Ann smiled at the relaxed friendship they shared already.

It was quite late when they finished the meal and sat chatting over coffee, and Samantha felt Pamela's presence very strongly as Bill filled in details, of how Alexander had turned on his mother, when Colin told him she was having an affair; threatening to tell his father if she didn't give Colin a job. He wanted to tell her that, Alexander didn't know about Colin already blackmailing Pamela for money, but out of consideration for Ann, he didn't.

"It was all brought to a tragic end with the accident, but even then the pair of them took advantage of your great-grandfather's grief, to gain control over 'The Vintage'. What they didn't foresee, was that Gerald would offer it to Colin, on a plate, so to speak, and Colin jumped at it. Couldn't blame him I suppose, but Alexander was furious apparently, so he planted a whole lot of illicit stock in the cellars and informed the authorities. Colin served two years in prison for that."

Ann had gone to the kitchen. It still upset her, remembering how hurt Colin had been by the betrayal, when he eventually found out the truth; even though she knew he was far from blameless.

Disappointingly, neither, Bill or Ann knew anything about Marcia's secret.

It was after their time.

It was a weekend of memories that Samantha would never forget. She slept overnight at 'Riverview', in the same room that Pamela had stayed in all those years ago and Bill showed her the room at the clinic, where Gerald had reluctantly spent nearly a year. They had lunch in the bistro, before cruising down the River Thames, then Ann showed her 'Harrod's', explaining how Pamela had bought the dress she was wearing in the snapshot. Little precious memories, Samantha realised.

"I can see you both loved her very much," Samantha said gratefully as they parted.

"It was all a long time ago, but this weekend has made it seem like only yesterday. Come again soon," Bill said as they waved her off.

Meg was pleased to see her back; she had seriously wondered if Samantha would decide to settle in London.

Peter telephoned every week and Samantha would meet him at a Travel Lodge. New owners had taken over 'Anders Motors', and the apartments were now securely locked. Their few snatched hours were not to her liking, but Peter was insistent that he needed to see her and that pleased her.

If Meg was curious, she never commented on Samantha's unhappy moods when she returned from seeing her nameless friend, because Samantha was obviously reluctant to confide in her.

A week later Samantha suddenly felt extremely ill, with stomach pains and Meg insisted she must see a doctor.

"You never know, it could be German measles or even chicken pox; they are both going around, although you haven't got any spots," she said peering closely at Sam.

Samantha remembered having them both as a child, but decided to go anyway and returned looking white and shocked.

A long silence followed her announcement that she was pregnant, while Meg looked puzzled.

"I thought you were seeing this woman friend, who needed your help?" Samantha flushed, ashamed of the story she had made up.

"Will he stand by you?" Meg asked, drawing from her own experience.

"I'm sure he will, but he is married," Samantha answered her voice hardly more than a whisper.

There was another long pause.

"What will you do?" Meg asked eventually; and Samantha shook her head, looking more and more frightened as her situation registered. How would she be able to face the family? And Bryn, what would he think? She had called Jocelyn a tart. She closed her eyes in dismay.

They were both very quiet that evening. The television played to itself as they each sat with their own thoughts.

"You could always have an abortion," Meg said eventually, her expression and straight back showing disapproval of the idea, relaxing visibly as Samantha shook her head.

"Not an option, apparently, even if I would consider it."

"How far are you, then?" Meg asked curiously.

"They can't be sure; my periods have never been regular, since I was fourteen, so I have got an appointment to go back for more tests." Tears streamed down her face and Meg put her arms around her.

"Did you just forget to take the pill?"

Samantha raised a tear-stained face. "What pill?"

Meg gave her a despairing look.

*

Samantha waited in her car. She had arrived early, to compose her thoughts, trying to guess what Peter's reaction would be. Proud, excited, or just pleased. Just pleased, she decided, thinking about how desperate he always was to see her. He said he didn't know what he would do without her; that she was the most important thing in his life and she must always be there for him; but he couldn't possibly leave his wife, yet.

Peter's car pulled in to the space beside her interrupting her thoughts and she sat in the car while he booked in.

Once inside the room he could hardly wait to get into bed but she was preoccupied and he quickly picked up on her lack of response.

"What's the matter?" His impatient question made her decide not to tell him just then, so she smiled and tried to put it to the back of her mind, but ten minutes later he asked again and this time she said softly:

"I've got something to tell you."

He leaned up on his elbow. "Don't like the sound of that; you haven't found a job out of the area have you?"

"No, that is right out of the question now."

He lay down again and pulled her to him, impatient to satisfy his needs.

"I'm pregnant," she said in a breathless little voice, smiling into his eyes, unprepared for his fury.

"You what?" he demanded pushing her away, pale grey eyes shocked with disbelief.

"I thought you would be pleased," she whispered, taken aback by the ugly expression on his face.

"Good God! Why would you think that?" he shouted leaping out of bed, all thoughts of making love completely and absolutely forgotten.

"You said we would be together eventually, when you leave your wife. I thought…"

She petered off, seeing the incredulity on his handsome face.

153

"Give me patience, but hurry," he said lifting his eyes to the ceiling. "You thought, you thought! Even you can't be that naïve and deluded. Did you really believe I would want a baby?"

"You said you couldn't live without me; what else was I to think?" Samantha sat up, clutching the duvet to her, her expression hurt and accusing.

Peter swore, snatched his underpants and trousers from the chair and rammed his well-toned legs into them.

"Get rid of it; that is my last word on the subject!" He yanked his zip up. "You told me you were on the pill!" By now, he was pushing his arms into his crisp white shirt and tucking it in.

"No I didn't."

He sat down on the bed to pull on designer socks and push his feet into well-polished shoes.

"You certainly did; the very first night, when we got back to the apartment," he accused.

"You only asked me about taking a pill for my headache," Samantha said defensively, reminded of her lecture from Meg.

"Give me strength!" he exploded, yanking his tie too tight and going red in the face. He loosened it. "I don't care how you do it; just get rid of it, then and only then, perhaps we can talk again." He thrust his arms into his jacket and inspected himself in the mirror, before taking out a comb and carefully arranging his hair.

Her green eyes flashing, she said, "I don't believe in abortion."

"Then take the damn pill!" he rejoined, slamming the door behind him.

Samantha lowered the duvet to smooth her slightly rounded stomach.

"Looks like, it's you and me, Little One."

CHAPTER TWENTY

"So what will you do?" Meg placed a rack of toast on the yellow Formica breakfast bar and balanced two, boiled eggs in eggcups, before sitting opposite to Samantha. Samantha scooped the last mouthful of porridge into Lucy's waiting, rosebud mouth and wiped her chubby face with a tissue before lifting her out of her high chair and leaving her to play on the floor while they ate.

"No idea yet, I was so sure he would be pleased."

"Join the club," Meg said with a sardonic laugh, her resigned expression reminding Samantha that the situation was nothing new to her.

"He didn't even ask when it was due; just ran as fast as he could."

Meg gave her a pitying glance. "Who is the father, anyway?" she asked, unable to hide her curiosity any longer.

Samantha looked down at her plate, avoiding Meg's enquiring gaze, and the silence lengthened. "You don't want to know," Samantha mumbled at last.

Meg got up to clear the dishes. "You can trust me, you know."

"And I do, but you are going to think I'm such a fool."

"I doubt that, given my circumstances. Is it the fellow from Cornwall; the one who's getting married?"

"If only it were. It's all his fault, though." Samantha gave an angry little sob and haltingly told the whole story.

Meg's heart sank as she listened. Peter Chambers of all people. "You really haven't had much to do with men, other than the nice kind, in your family have you?"

"I thought I had caught up recently. He was so exciting, and he made me feel wonderful." Her eyes softened as she remembered the few days in the apartment.

Meg tutted sternly, "He is old enough to be your father, the biggest womanizer around – and he took advantage when you were vulnerable. I'd like to give him a piece of my mind, or at least tell his wife."

"He was going to leave her." Samantha looked miserable as Meg gave a mirthless laugh.

"That's the second oldest story in the book."

Samantha gave an offended stare. "She is pregnant as well, otherwise he would have."

Meg exploded with exasperation, before saying calmly, "Well it's no good crying over spilt milk. We need to decide what you are going to do. You can stay here of course, but your family need to be told."

She waited for Samantha's reaction and wasn't surprised when she shook her head vigorously, whispering, "I can't," recalling her father's warnings about Peter the first time they met.

*

Peter was trembling with shock. If this came out, not only would his marriage be over but he would also be a laughing stock. He set the running machine faster, his racing thoughts keeping time with the rhythm. If only Uncle William was here. Perhaps he should visit him in prison. So far, he had stayed away, fearing he would be linked to the robbery. The police seemed to be satisfied that neither he nor Lindsey knew anything about it and he wanted it to stay that way. Perhaps Monica had the right idea in getting away from it all. Not concentrating, he suddenly stumbled, his feet went from under him and he landed heavily on the floor; the next thing he was aware of was excruciating pain in his left shoulder and their neighbour Joanne bending over him saying:

"Lie still, an ambulance is coming."

Over her shoulder, he saw Lindsey, eyes large with terror, obviously incapable of movement.

He winced as he tried to move and heard Joanne repeat, "Lie still," before everything went black again.

He woke in hospital, to a voice saying he had fractured his shoulder. All previous problems seemed trivial as he exaggeratedly pictured himself unable to lead a normal life ever again.

Lindsey was of little help and needed Joanne's constant support, just to cope with visiting him. Peter wished fervently that Monica would appear and take over like she always had – something he never imagined he would ever wish.

A week later, hearing through the grapevine that he was in the Bupa hospital, Meg visited him and asked what he intended to do about Samantha.

"She can't stop crying, and she won't go home to her parents, which is what I think she should do. You knew she was beside herself with grief and you took advantage. Her father will skin you alive."

Peter blanched. "It wasn't my fault; she practically begged me."

With Sir Gerald out of the way, he had felt reasonably safe but thinking about it now, his heart started banging and terrified he was having a heart attack, he pressed the bell to call a nurse, gasping to Meg that he was too ill to talk. She gave him a withering look and left.

A little while later, when he felt able to, he sent a text to Lindsey, saying she must contact her mother and say they wanted to visit her.

A text came back saying: *'No idea where mother is or how to contact her.'*

Refusing to believe that Monica had cut all ties with her daughter, he sent back: *'Don't be ridiculous. Do it.'*

Lindsey telephoned their solicitor and explained that she was having a baby and really wanted to see her mother. His father was an old family friend and Lindsey thought if anybody could help he could; but the solicitor didn't sound hopeful. Peter fumed, helplessly. She had made a really good job of disappearing. There was no doubt in his mind that she had the money but he didn't care about that; all he wanted was to disappear as well.

After spending a week at home, dreading every knock at the door, he was edgy and desperate, but then an envelope arrived by courier, containing instructions to be at an airfield in Goodwood on the following Saturday, where a private plane would be waiting to fly them to the south of France. A two-week booking, at a five star hotel had been, made in their name. It was unsigned.

Lindsey was adamant at first that she couldn't go, because she was busy decorating the nursery and flying wasn't good for the baby. He cajoled and pleaded without any success, then resorted to sulking, until she reluctantly gave in. He had assumed that Monica would be much further away than just across the Channel, so that made life easier.

"It's only a very short flight and I really need sunshine to get better." He rubbed his shoulder looking sorry for himself; and as usual, sympathetic to his needs, she gave way.

*

Sitting beside the pool in her new home, Monica had second thoughts. The police were looking further afield, but it would only take one small slip and— Perhaps meeting them in France wasn't such a good idea after all.

Coming to a sudden decision, she reached for her mobile phone; spoke for a few moments, then relaxed back with a satisfied nod.

CHAPTER TWENTY-ONE

Adam glanced at Fran. The children were in bed and he was working on his laptop, while she watched television; well, she was looking at the screen but he could see her mind was not on the programme.

Her grandfather's death had hit her hard and she was grieving inwardly. Darren had called round earlier and he too, noticing how quiet she was, had suggested a short break might do her good. The Easter holidays were coming up and if his mother could have the children and Charles would help Paul in the office, he would take her away for a week. It was some while since they had spent time alone together. His face softened as he looked at her. Jersey perhaps? They had spent their honeymoon there, or maybe somewhere they hadn't been before.

As if in answer to his thoughts, his mobile phone rang.

"I have got the offer of a super, duper place in Tenerife for three weeks. It belongs to a client, who owes me a favour; would you be interested, for the four of us?" Darren asked

"Very," Adam replied promptly. "Let me make a couple of phone calls and get back to you."

He glanced across at Fran; she hadn't even looked up, so he put his laptop aside and left the room. Charles was happy to fill in for him at the office, but disappointingly, his mother couldn't have the children, because they were going away themselves.

He rang Darren back. "No can do," he said sounding desperate as he explained the problem. "No one else will take on five children at such short notice."

"I think you mean six; we were depending on Mum and Dad as well."

There was a gloomy silence before Adam heard Melly's voice in the background.

"They must go; we don't all have to miss out and Fran really needs a break. I'll look after the children."

Adam heard the generous offer and his heart melted towards his young sister.

"Are you sure?" he heard Darren ask.

"Absolutely, I need my sister-in-law, in one piece – not in bits. Tell them to pack their bags."

"Did you get all that?" Darren asked.

"Certainly did. Tell her she is a star."

"He says you are a star."

"Takes one to know one," Melly quipped, gallantly hiding her disappointment.

"Don't worry about getting a flight. I'll drive. You've got two days to get ready."

Adam rang off. Fran was staring at him, finally roused by the excitement in his voice.

"What's going on? Was that Darren?"

"Your brilliant brother has found a holiday for us, and we go in three days' time."

"Your parents can't have the children, they are going away themselves." Fran gave a hopeless shrug and Adam tossed his eyes, thinking, now she tells me, but added:

"A-n-d, my little sister is child minding." Adam pulled her out of the chair and hugged her. "Not only has she given up her own holiday, she is going to stay here and look after all six of them."

Fran pulled a face.

"That doesn't seem fair. Why don't we go for about nine days and let them have the rest?"

"That's an even better idea." He rang Darren back and heard a squeal of delight from Melly, as the idea was relayed.

The next two days went in a whirl and their regrets at not being able to share the holiday were quickly forgotten in the excitement.

With Darren flying them, there was no last minute rush to a London airport and they left at a leisurely ten o'clock after the children had gone to school or pre-school. Melly waved as they drove out of the drive and watched until the car disappeared from sight on the coast road. She was sad not to be going but it was just what Fran needed, she told herself, wandering back into the house and pouring another cup of coffee from the percolator. Sitting at the long table, she dwelt on all the good times they had shared around it. Preparations had always been that bit more special when Gerald was coming and she realised why Fran missed him so. She missed him herself more than she could have thought possible. A whole way of life had disappeared with him, one that could never return. They must create their own more modern version to hold the family together as he had, after his mother and father died. That could be hard, when all Darren wanted was to go to America. Fran would hate them going. If only Sam would come home, it might stop Darren thinking so much about leaving. On impulse, she reached for her mobile and rang Sam's number. It rang for some while and she was about to switch off when Sam answered in a breathless voice.

"Hello Sam, it's me. Are you alright?"

There was a small silence and then, "Yes, yes, fine." Another silence followed and Melly thought she heard a stifled sob.

"Only you sound breathless."

"I ran in from the garden; I thought you were my friend Meg; I'm expecting her to call." Now she sounded nervous.

A baby cried in the background. "I need to go. I'll call you later. Bye."

And the phone went dead, leaving Melly staring at it wondering. Deep in thought she went upstairs to make the beds and after half an hour of pummelling and smoothing, decided that something wasn't right. Sam sounded frightened.

With everyone else away, she rang Bob and Marcia, who although concerned could only say she was living with a friend she had worked with. Marcia sounded cross. "She promised to let us know her address, but never has. Bob is worried. Should we go to the police?"

"Not right now; we'll wait until her father gets back tomorrow and see what he says. Thanks, Marcia, tell Bob not to worry and I'll be in touch."

She hung up and decided to go over to Anders Folly. Lorna and George might know something.

George was sitting at the table and rose as she entered the kitchen. Lorna was serving lunch and invited her to sit and share the appetizing fish pie she was dishing.

Melly said she had only come because she was worried about Sam. George laid a place for her.

"Going without lunch won't help," Lorna insisted.

"Didn' expect comp'ny? George said cheerfully.

"If you are sure there is enough?" Melly helped herself to carrots and broccoli.

"Ample. Jake caught it fresh this morning." Lorna gave a satisfied nod towards Jake who was working in the vegetable garden.

Melly smiled. "He certainly does a good job supplying us all with vegetables."

"Aye, but there are fewer of us now and he is worried about how long his job will last. That goes for Sol and Ella as well. Their job is their home."

Melly suddenly realised they were both trying to put on a brave face and couldn't any longer. "Miss Samantha needs to come home and let us all know where we stand," Lorna said quietly.

"That is what I came over to see you about. No one seems to know where she is living."

"Southampton; is all we know." George looked forlorn. "It ain't right. The lass needs 'er family round 'er."

"You're right George. I rang her this morning and I know something is wrong."

"Perhaps Ella or Sol could help. She confides in them, if anybody." Lorna put her hand to her lips. "If you will forgive me for saying so," she apologised.

"I know what you're saying Lorna, and you're right. I'll go and speak to them."

Sol and Ella had finished their lunch and were sitting on the veranda sharing a pot of tea, shielded from the wind, which in spite of the sunshine was quite chilly. Ella invited her to sit down and fetched another cup.

She told them why she had come, and Sol shook his head sadly.

"Can't understand, I thought she would at least have come back for Nocturn."

Melly noticed that they looked even more worried than Lorna and George.

"What is it Ella?"

After previous experiences, Melly was a great believer in Ella's visions.

Ella shuddered and gave her a worried look.

"Nothing clear; there is deep unhappiness and betrayal from an older man."

"That will be this William Spencer, who she blames for her grandfather's death." Melly was disappointed, she had hoped for something more definite to go on.

Sol got up. He didn't like it when Ella's visions upset her, and she had that far away look that told him she was seeing bad things.

"I need to get back to work; 'scuse me mam."

Melly said goodbye but Ella seemed unaware of him leaving; she was staring into space, with a pained look in her amber eyes.

Melly touched her gently. "What are you seeing Ella?"

"Everything is confused. A child is involved."

Melly remembered hearing a baby cry. "That might be her friends; I heard one cry while I was talking to her. Sam was looking after it, I think."

161

Ella shook her head. "Sam is sad, very sad. Someone she cares for deeply has left her."

"Grandfather?"

"Younger. A woman and a baby are in the background."

"That will be Bryn and his wife."

Ella was still puzzled by the many conflicting visions she was getting. So many people were influencing Samantha's life.

Ella's chin dropped to her chest. "So many babies," she whispered.

Melly sat trying to make sense of it all, wishing Darren were home. She couldn't dash off and look for Sam because of the children; and anyway, where would she start looking? Southampton was a big place. A thought struck her. That secretary, Wendy something or another; if the friend worked at Anders then she would know her.

She went to make another cup of tea, waiting for Ella to wake up and when she returned, Ella was staring into space, her eyes clouded with anxiety.

"Can you make any sense of any of it?"

"Not at the moment, but I thought perhaps the secretary would know where the friend lives. Grandfather must have her phone number somewhere. I'll go and look in his desk. She poured Ella a cup of tea and sat with her until she looked more in control and told Sol on her way out that she was leaving.

Lorna was still in the kitchen when she went back.

"I need a phone number from Grandfather's desk. The secretary who was with him for so many years might know where this friend lives. Ella has come up with some rather worrying visions."

"The study is locked but George will get the key. George," she called.

George appeared from the direction of their living quarters and disappeared again to fetch the key.

"Mr Charles ordered the study to be locked, because he doesn't want the paperwork disturbed."

"Stay and help me to find the number and lock up again George,"

It felt like walking on forbidden ground, going into Gerald's study; in fact the whole house felt still and eerily quiet, as if waiting for Gerald to wake and bring it back to life.

A sob escaped her and George was beside her immediately.

"It 'ud be on 'is phone menu, I expect," he said quietly.

He was right and Wendy Parker answered.

Melly explained who she was and why she was phoning and Wendy was clearly concerned. She didn't know off hand, but promised to find out the

162

address as soon as possible and ring back. Melly left her own number, realising it was time to pick Jack and the twins up. She drove off feeling more hopeful and was nicely surprised, when a call came from Wendy, an hour later, supplying Meg's telephone number and address. Melly couldn't thank her enough and wanted to dash off straight away, but had to be content with telling George and Sol. When Darren phoned later that evening, he was devastated to be missing once again when his daughter was in trouble. The following day, he phoned again to say take off was delayed because of fog and she went to Anders Folly, after seeing the children off to school, convinced by now that Samantha was in serious trouble. Meg's number only ever reached an answering machine; and Samantha's mobile was switched off again. Melly panicked, assuming the worst and Ella, not helping matters, insisted that she and Sol must go looking for Samantha because she was also convinced she was in real trouble.

"We'll travel this evening, to miss the traffic," Sol said reluctantly. It seemed crazy when her father would be home shortly, but knowing Ella's powers of prediction, he was afraid not to go.

"If only Darren was here to fly you; but he says it could be days if the fog doesn't lift." Melly, rung her hands, distractedly.

Sol was tempted to say, if Darren *was* here, there would be no need for them to go at all. Ella was his main concern; these visions had been worrying her since before Samantha ran away without a thought for any of them.

Mr Charles had said he would see they all kept their homes, but surely if no one wanted to live in the house or take responsibility for it, the house would have to be sold. If Mr Darren had taken charge, as the rightful heir should, Sir Gerald would have had no need to leave it on the shoulders of a young girl.

He felt highly incensed by the family's lack of appreciation. He would give his right arm for a wonderful place like Anders Folly.

Ungrateful bunch of— He checked his thoughts, knowing in reality he would defend any one of them to the death, especially Miss Samantha. "Turn in 'is grave 'e will, if anythin' 'appens to 'er."

George startled Sol by coming up behind him as he was sweeping the yard more vigorously than necessary.

"I wonder he doesn't send down a bolt of lightning to destroy the place. It would serve 'em all right." Sol attacked a pile of wet leaves, scooping them up with a shovel and depositing them in a bin. "I'll have a few words to say to Miss Samantha, when we do find her."

George had never heard Sol say anything against Samantha and he was worried.

163

"You oright mate?"

"'Course I'm not alright. Ella's been going out of her mind with these visions; won't say what they are; enough to drive a bloke crazy. Why can't she just come home and put all of our minds at rest.

George realised he was nearly as worried about Samantha as he was Ella.

"We all love that kid like she was our own." He leant on the broom and looked as if he was about to break down.

"Come 'n' sid dan mate." George took the broom and gestured to the seat.

Sol sank down with his head in his hands. "Ella's not well. I'm sure it's because of these voices. She can't sleep and keeps crying."

"'as she bin to the docs?"

"Says they'd put her in the loony bin if she told them about voices."

"Cud be roight," George said dolefully.

"She won't come out of it until she talks to Miss Samantha, that's why I'm taking her this evening," Sol said in a determined voice, straightening himself up.

"That's the ticket." George was relieved to see a bit of fight return. "Ja want me ta come?"

"We'll be fine; you look after Lorna."

"Yer," George agreed.

Later that afternoon, Ella was taken ill with stomach pains. The doctor was called and concerned by her anxious state and high temperature, gave her something to calm her. Sol stayed beside her until daybreak when she seemed a little better, but he still wouldn't let her travel and said that he must stay with her. She became frantic again and eventually he agreed to go alone, if she promised to rest.

It was around five o'clock in the morning when he turned out of the drive and had only gone a little way, when he saw a car on the side of the road. His heart nearly stopped when he recognised the ice blue Cabriolet, with Samantha slumped over the wheel. He stopped the Land Rover in the middle of the lane and jumped out.

As he reached the car, he saw her shoulders shaking and knew she was alive.

Wrenching the door open, he shouted as loud as he could for George, and then hooted the horn continuously. It sounded horrendous on the silent morning air and George appeared at the front door in his shirtsleeves almost immediately. Sol gestured wildly, panicking, not knowing what to do in case Samantha's neck or back were injured; then suddenly she moved and sat back. Her face was red and swollen and he assumed she had hit the steering wheel when the car ran off the road.

"Don't move; I'll get an ambulance." He reached for his mobile phone and saw George making his way up the slope, as Samantha spoke.

"I'm alright, I'm not hurt." He saw then that she was just crying and thankfully slipped his phone back into his pocket, gesturing to George to slow down.

"It's okay, take your time."

By this time Lorna and Ella had appeared in the drive and Jake and Maisie were looking out of their bedroom window, over the coach house.

Sol looked at Samantha, not knowing whether to be angry or relieved.

"What a fright you gave me," he said sternly.

George puffed up the last few yards and leant on the bonnet of the car, trying to get his breath back.

"Sorry George, I thought she'd had a crash. You could have shortened our lives by a few years," he said sharply, turning back to Samantha."

"Sorry Sol, sorry George. What are you doing out at this time in the morning?" She looked a picture of misery with her tear-stained face.

"I'm on my way to Southampton to fetch you home. We are all worried sick."

"Lucky you saw me," she said, shrinking back and screwing her face up. She had never seen Sol so angry before.

"Aargh." Sol shook his fists in the air and strode back to the Land Rover.

He had to drive on, because there was no room to turn.

"Hop in George," he said without a glance.

They drove the short distance to the crossroads and returned. Samantha's car had gone and they could see it parked in the driveway.

Chaos reigned in the kitchen. Lorna was clattering frying pans and talking nineteen to the dozen to no one in particular and Ella seemingly feeling better was laughing and crying at the same time, while she made tea. Samantha was being greeted boisterously by Tamar, Tavy, Mischief and Jonti, as they rushed in the door that Ella had inadvertently left open, barking and running around her, as she bent to cuddle them.

Sol took one look, welled up and walked out, while George calmly set about helping Lorna.

"All's well that ends well, Gal."

"You reckon?" Lorna gave him a quick hug and went back to frying sausages.

Samantha looked about her. The warm, familiar kitchen, the dear faces; how could she have ever thought she never wanted to see it all again? Her heart dropped at the thought of telling them her news, but that could wait awhile. Right now, she had to go and make her peace with Sol.

CHAPTER TWENTY-TWO

Samantha had sat opposite Meg at the breakfast bar, trying to be happy for her; she had arrived home from seeing Lucy's father, with the news that he wanted them to move to Norfolk with him, so that they could get married and be a family.

"I'm really sorry Sam, but I honestly believe you should go back to your family. Peter will never be there for you."

"When will you go?" she had asked.

"The day after tomorrow; please promise me you will go home."

Samantha avoided her eyes and nodded.

"Would you look after Lucy in the morning for me? I need to go to the council offices and give notice for the flat."

"I suppose they wouldn't let me take it over?"

"I could ask," Meg, answered without much enthusiasm. "But I honestly think you should go home?"

"I can't; I've let them all down."

"I'll ask and give you a ring before I do the rest of my errands."

That was the morning their answering machine was switched off and Melly finally managed to get through; and when Meg rang, it was to say they wouldn't allow her to jump the waiting list.

Feeling desperate, Samantha had decided to give Peter one last try and his mobile was picked up immediately. There was a moment's silence when she said his name, before he answered in a shocked voice:

"Samantha, what are you doing phoning me at home?"

"I just wanted to see you."

She heard him tut. "Have you done what I said?"

"No, I can't do that."

"Then there is nothing more to be said."

"You can't just abandon us."

"What do you mean us?" He sounded guarded.

"The baby and me."

"It's nothing to do with me any more Miss Anders. I work for another firm now." His voice was suddenly businesslike, and Samantha heard a woman's voice mentioning something to do with French francs before he said abruptly:

"Please don't call again Miss Anders; I suggest you take my previous advice. Goodbye."

Samantha had replaced the receiver and run to the bathroom to be sick. Lucy was sleeping in her pram, and she went outside to sit when she felt better; that was where Meg found her when she came in, and noticing her white face, assumed it was because of the flat.

"Sorry, I tried."

Receiving no answer, Meg had put the kettle on and returned a few minutes later to say that, perhaps it was a sign telling her to go home.

"Perhaps," Samantha agreed unhappily, her mind still on her conversation with Peter.

They went to bed early that night and at ten o'clock a text message had disturbed her restless sleep.

'Sorry it's late, just needed to tell you before you heard it from anyone else. Getting married next Saturday. Please stay friends.'

Hearing her sobbing under the bedclothes, Meg made a cup of tea and helped her to pack.

CHAPTER TWENTY-THREE

Darren landed in Tenerife at three o'clock in the afternoon, where a hired car was waiting on the private airstrip.

"It's ours for the three weeks," Darren told them as he drove to the villa, twenty minutes away.

"Door to door service," Adam remarked to Fran. "Thanks a lot Darren; you have certainly taken all the hassle out of travelling."

Fran added her thanks as Darren opened the car door for her.

"Just enjoy the break and come back smiling again – for me." He put a finger under her chin. "I miss that smile of yours."

Fran filled up with tears and he said quickly, "I'll just show you around before we eat; then I'll get some sleep, before the journey home; I'll be leaving at about one o'clock in the morning."

A daily maid service was available and Darren had ordered dinner to be set out in the Gothic style dining room, which overlooked the garden with its riot of colourful poinsettias and bougainvillea.

"What a wonderful place," Fran said, feeling the peace and tranquillity close around her as they sat enjoying the rare luxury of a peaceful meal.

Darren gave a deep satisfied sigh. For once, he had done something for his sister, instead of the other way round.

Leaving them sleeping peacefully, he took a taxi back to the airstrip, and about to board his plane, noticed a couple leaving one parked a short distance away. The woman's voice reached him, complaining as they walked to a private limousine; he thought the man seemed vaguely familiar, but in the half-light it was hard to be sure. They disappeared into the interior of the long, black vehicle and he forgot the incident.

Waiting for clearance to take off, he discovered there was a delay due to weather conditions, and made himself comfortable in the back of the plane to sleep away the time. It was nearly midday before the fog cleared enough for him to take off.

He naturally expected to find Melly and the children at Fran and Adam's house and was surprised to find the house locked and empty. It's teatime, he thought irritably looking at his watch and reaching for his phone.

Melly answered, instantly, obviously waiting for his call.

"I'm tired and hungry, where are you?" he asked wearily, changing his tone as Melly said Samantha was home and they were at Anders Folly.

"I'll be straight there." He got back into his car, not knowing whether to be happy or cross with his daughter, but she was definitely due for a piece of his mind.

When he did see her, he was just too relieved that she was home to say anything other than, "It's good to see you."

Lorna had made two huge meat pies, and there was mashed potato and loads of fresh vegetables for them to help themselves to, as they gathered round the kitchen table. Darren could hardly wait for Lorna to put his plate in front of him; he had only had a sandwich, since the previous evening's meal.

Laying his knife and fork together, with a satisfied sigh he leaned back in his chair and looked across at Samantha, noticing for the first time how drawn she was looking.

"Eat up, Princess; you look as if you need some good home-cooking."

She gave him a wan smile. "It's good to be home Daddy."

"We are staying at Auntie Fran's house for the next ten days; do you want to come with us? There's plenty of room."

"I think I'll stay here, if that's alright." She looked across at Lorna and George, who both smiled delightedly, as Lorna said:

"Abigail will be back soon, she's staying with a friend in the Scilly Isles for a few weeks. She'll be real pleased to see you." Her face shone with affection as she planned what food she would make to put the roses back in Samantha's cheeks.

Bathing in all of their affection, Samantha dreaded telling them her shameful news, and decided to put it off for a few days.

The March weather was cold and wet, so she contented herself with grooming Nocturn and spending time in the stables with him and the dogs.

Ella watched her, wondering when she would be ready to tell everyone her big secret. For now though, it was enough that she was home, where they could all look after her.

Helping Ella to remove dustsheets and light the fires in the sitting and dining rooms, George happened to comment as he opened the shutters, how nice it was to have family back in the house.

"Don't worry, you will soon be kept busy again," she answered, smiling to herself.

He threw her a puzzled look as she went about her chores singing softly, and after scratching his head, got on with lighting the fire.

As it happened fate lent a hand before Samantha got round to telling anyone.

She had been home for nearly three weeks, and thought her discomfort was due to indigestion, but on this occasion, she was in such pain she called for Lorna, who told George to send for an ambulance straight away, fearing it was something like appendicitis. It was four o'clock in the morning and the ambulance arrived quickly. Ella, appeared and asked to be the one to accompany her, and neither Lorna nor George thought it peculiar, until after the ambulance was on its way out of the drive. "Did you call her?" they asked each other, together, both shaking their heads.

The hospital staff quickly discovered that Samantha was actually in labour and she gave birth to a boy, seven hours later. He was premature and tiny and went straight into intensive care. Ella phoned Sol, who passed on the news to George and Lorna, before ringing Darren.

George when he could find his voice commented, "'Ow can ya 'ave a bairn wivout showin'?"

"I have heard of cases, but never really believed it." Lorna was equally flummoxed.

"I s'pose she did 'ave a little bit of a bump," Maisie said enviously. "It's just not fair, 'er not married like." Maisie and Jake had been trying for several years. "Why d'you think some do and some don't, Aunt Lorna?"

Lorna gave her a sympathetic look and shook her head. "I don't know, child."

*

Darren and Melly arrived at the hospital, after seeing the children off to school. Ashen faced, Darren stared down at the sleeping form of his daughter, with only one thought in his mind. Who did this to her? She looked thin and tired and he wanted to gather her up in his arms and take her home. Melly was speechless with shock; all she could do was remind herself that she had been right to think that Samantha was in trouble.

"Thank goodness, she came home when she did," she managed to say at last.

"Thanks to you." Darren squeezed her fingers hard.

Samantha opened her eyes and saw them. "Sorry," was all she said and went back to sleep again.

They went up to see the baby. He only weighed four and a half pounds and would have to stay in hospital until he gained weight.

"He will be fine," the nurse smilingly reassured them.

"How premature is he?" Melly asked.

"We think about eight weeks, but your daughter will be able tell us for sure, when she is up to answering questions. We don't have that information, as yet."

"Join the club," Darren said peevishly, earning a sharp look from Melly as the nurse diplomatically walked away.

Darren decided to return to the hospital after taking Melly home and he was pleased to find Samantha, propped up with a tray of food in front of her, but she stopped eating when she saw him and started to cry. He comforted her and gradually encouraged her to finish her meal.

"Got to keep your strength up; you've got a boy to feed."

"You've seen him?" she asked,

"Certainly have. Who is he like?"

"I haven't seen him yet." She looked downcast.

"You will soon, and then you can tell me if he is like his father."

It was a clumsy attempt, but he had to know.

"It doesn't matter Daddy; he doesn't want to know."

"Then he must be made to." Darren's voice rose and a nurse put her head round the door of the private room.

"Is everything all right, Miss Anders?"

"Yes thank you, Nurse, just deciding on names."

The nurse disappeared. "Keep it down Daddy, or they will ask you to leave."

"They wouldn't dare!"

"I promise you they would."

"So tell me who the father is," Darren demanded, looking her straight in the eyes.

"You won't like it."

"Don't play games with me, Sam."

"I'm not, Daddy; I just don't want you to do anything silly."

"That sounds as if I know him."

"You've met him."

A look of horror filled his eyes. "Not that yob that attacked you in the cove?" He stood up, fists clenched. "I'll kill him!"

"You see, this is what I mean; and no it wasn't Dean Masters." Her fingers twisted the white cotton sheet covering her and she whispered, "I wasn't attacked. I thought we loved each other."

Darren sat down with a thump, staring at her incredulously. "But you only left home after Granddad died."

"I knew him before that. He worked for Anders Motors," she explained hurriedly, not wanting her father to think she had just been picked up.

A nurse came in at that moment looking businesslike, just as Darren's mouth dropped open.

In his mind's eye he saw a dark haired, suave character in Samantha's bedroom at the London hotel and in the same instant, pictured the man at the airstrip in Tenerife. That was why he had looked familiar.

Seeing his face, Samantha winced and sat meekly while her temperature and blood pressure were checked, realizing he had guessed.

Waiting until the door closed behind the nurse, Darren turned on Samantha.

"You promised me you would stay away from that slimy creature. I warned you against him."

"I know, Daddy, but he was there when I really, really needed someone and he cared, I know he did. His wife had left him and we were going to be together; really we were." She fixed beseeching, listless, green eyes on him and Darren closed his in despair. "Sweetheart – sweetheart," he agonised.

"But his wife wanted him back, because she was pregnant. He was going to leave her after the baby was born, but when I became pregnant, he told me he didn't want to see me again until I got rid of it; but I wouldn't."

Tears were streaming down her cheeks and he reached for the tissues, aghast at what he was hearing.

"I would say you have had a lucky escape."

"What do you mean?"

"I mean you are better off without him. He was at the airstrip, leaving a private plane and I couldn't place him at the time. He was with a woman and they got into a limousine."

Samantha stopped crying. A private plane would cost a lot. She remembered him not having any money for the airfare. "Mother-in-law must be footing the bill again," she said peevishly.

"I'm just glad it isn't you," Darren said with feeling.

"Hardly, in our bankrupt state," she managed to joke.

Darren frowned. "What gave you *that* idea?"

"What idea?"

"That we are bankrupt."

"Well aren't we, after William Spencer embezzled all the money?"

"Not quite," he assured her with a smile.

"Thank goodness for that; I've been worried about keeping Anders Folly going. Peter assumed we were bankrupt – another reason he went back to his wife, I expect."

"He couldn't possibly know our financial situation," Darren said hotly.

"But I did overhear Uncle Charles talking to Uncle Adam, as well. Things sounded pretty serious."

"Uncle Charles will explain everything now you have come home. Get some rest and don't worry about a thing. I must get back and help Mamma."

After he had gone, Samantha thought again about him seeing Peter, in Tenerife – if in fact it was him. Why a private flight to Tenerife? It could be a business trip, of course, but somehow, she couldn't imagine him taking a pregnant wife with him, if that were the case. Her mind started to buzz with questions. Maybe that was where his mother-in-law was hiding; that would make sense of his wife being with him. Monica Spencer was supposed to be in South America but supposing she was actually in Tenerife.

The more she thought about it, the more convinced she became that Peter and his wife were visiting her mother. What was more natural when she was expecting her first child?

The orderly came in with her supper and looked concerned.

"Red cheeks, bright eyes; not running a temperature are you? Perhaps I should call nurse."

"Please don't, she was here a short while ago. I'm just excited about seeing my baby for the first time," Samantha assured her, with a bright smile.

"Ah!" She gave an understanding smile. "What are you going to name him?" She chatted cheerfully, while she removed the lids from the dishes, revealing a small bowl of soup, an omelette with side salad and a crème caramel for sweet, commenting on the wise choice.

"Most go for pie and chips, and expect to get their figure back in days." She laughed and Samantha was reminded of Meg. She had the same, short dark hair and slight figure.

"I haven't decided on a name; I thought I had plenty of time. By the way, would I be able to have a phone?" she asked.

"I'll get one sent in."

After supper, the nurse came with a wheelchair and took her up to intensive care, where she stayed for half an hour. She gazed in awe at her newborn son. He was so tiny and she felt a protective bond, holding his fingers.

"After a good night's rest, you will be able to spend time together," the nurse promised, returning him to his cot.

Laying in the dark, eyes shining with happiness, she knew it didn't matter if Peter abandoned them, he would be hers alone; a name popped into her head and she knew, for certain, it was right for her son. "Jacob. Jacob Gerald Anders," she said aloud, liking the sound.

Quite early the following morning, the nurse brought Jacob and laid him in her arms, saying that she would be back for him shortly. It was an unbelievably happy experience, and during the next hour she gradually slid down the bed, easing him in beside her, where they slept and spent the morning together.

She awoke to the sound of the lunchtime trolley and smiled down at Jacob still sleeping in the crook of her arm, delighted that she had been allowed to keep him for so long.

"There was an emergency," the orderly explained. "Nurse asked me to keep an eye on you and we decided you seemed happy enough." She grinned, reminding Samantha of Meg, again, as she picked Jacob up and laid him in his cot before wheeling the table over the bed and placing a tray on it.

"Is there any chance of that phone? I really need to ring a friend."

"Oh sorry, completely forgot when I went off duty." She dashed away and returned with a pay phone on wheels.

Meg answered her mobile straight away and was concerned to hear about the baby being premature.

"He is absolutely fine and we will go home soon."

There was quite a long silence before Meg said, "Are you going to tell Peter?"

Samantha didn't hesitate. "No. He is mine. Peter has chosen to abandon us."

It wasn't until later that she realized she had forgotten to tell Meg about Peter being in Tenerife, but she was too overjoyed with Jacob to think about that right then. Her eyes clouded as she remembered Bryn's last text. He would be married by now.

CHAPTER TWENTY-FOUR

Peter and Lindsey explored the palatial, five bed-roomed villa, marvelling at the beautiful furniture and furnishings.

"I didn't expect anything this grand," Lindsey whispered.

"Well why not, after all—" Peter hastily bit his tongue, thinking impatiently that it would be interesting to hear her mother's explanation. It hardly seemed credible that his wife hadn't put two and two together yet, but at least she had got over being bundled into a second plane, when Monica greeted them. It had come as a surprise to him as well.

Making their way downstairs after changing for dinner on that first evening, they stopped on the half landing to look at the view from the picture window. Tucked away in three acres of verdant countryside, the house enjoyed complete privacy at the rear. The extensive landscaped grounds contained a wealth of tropical trees and flowering shrubs, providing a colourful screen and backdrop to Monica's well-tended lawns and vibrant flower beds, where a kaleidoscope of rare plants filled the air with exotic perfumes. On the west side there was an enclosed swimming pool, connected to the villa by a garden room where orchids of every description flourished; these were Monica's pride and joy.

"Lovely, isn't it?" Monica called up to them from the spacious hall below, where cream tiles, scattered with rich terracotta and brown rugs complemented dark furniture, surrounded by huge flower arrangements consisting of bird-of-paradise blooms and exotic lilies, picked from her garden. Monica was wearing an embroidered silk, caftan in a brilliant peacock blue, and her once striking blonde hair, coloured to a deep auburn changed her appearance completely. No one would ever associate the elegant, French speaking Monique Langloise, with Monica Spencer, the English woman.

"Come and join me in the garden room for a sun-downer," she called gaily.

Peter took a deep satisfying breath, telling himself he could get used to this style of living, while Lindsey, although happy to be holidaying with her mother, could hardly wait to get back to decorating her nursery.

Over dinner, prepared by Luisa the Spanish housekeeper and served by Isabella a young Spanish girl, Monica and Lindsey talked about names for the baby, while Peter, having imbibed rather freely of the excellent wine, surreptitiously eyed the attractive young maid. His needs were reminding him of how long it had been since Samantha had been available. 'Stupid girl', he thought crossly, remembering her beautiful body and willingness. He had hardly been allowed to touch Lindsey, let alone have sex since she had become pregnant. He stared morosely into his half empty wine glass and downed it in one. Monica's voice was droning on suggesting names he would never agree to in a million years and suddenly he felt driven to clearing the air.

"I think we should stay here permanently, darling?"

Lindsey looked shocked and Monica glared at him.

"Bad timing, Peter. Let Lindsey get used to being here."

"What's to get used to; it's wonderful, isn't it darling?"

Monica signalled to him to be quiet, but he was working up to his salesman's pitch and nothing would stop him.

"Think of the advantages for the baby. No more cold winters, or nappies to wash; a maid to do all that, in fact you would have everything your heart could desire; plus, your mother and me as well. No more weekends working. What do you say?"

"What about your job?" Lindsey was not liking the idea at all. She liked her home and didn't want the sort of life her mother lived, having to get dressed for dinner every night. She wanted just her and Peter with a tray on their laps, in front of the television when they felt like it.

"I'm not worried about it if you aren't. I don't actually need a job." The wine was loosening his tongue and his imagination was running riot at the thought of eleven million pounds. He need never work again. It would all be Lindsey's one day, anyway."

"Please stop talking about it." Lindsey looked about to cry. "I want to go home at the end of our holiday."

"He is right about not being alone on the weekends," Monica pointed out, picking on the thing that made Lindsey most unhappy.

"But I won't be lonely any more. I will have the baby." Lindsey suddenly found the courage to stand up for herself, and Monica would have been wise enough to let the whole thing drop for the time being, but Peter wanted it settled. He felt as if he was living on a knife's edge; sooner or later it was going to come out about Samantha being pregnant and he didn't want to be around when it did. Monica had managed to disappear, why couldn't he?

He considered demanding they stay, but Monica, seeing the obstinate set of his jaw, said quietly:

"You look tired Lindsey; why don't you go on up to bed, dear?"

"I think I will, if you don't mind Mummy." She rose, kissed her mother, shot a reproachful look at Peter and left.

Monica gave Peter an exasperated glare; he was looking exactly like William, when he couldn't get his own way. "She just might come round if you would use common sense and take it slowly?"

"I want it settled. Things are impossible with Uncle William in prison. I have no one to turn to. I need a fresh start, where nobody knows me; where nobody holds me responsible for every stupid little thing." He sounded defensive and Monica was immediately suspicious.

"Nobody holds you responsible, or you would be in prison with him. What have you done? What are you running away from?"

"What are you talking about; there's nothing strange about not wanting to live in Britain any more, is there? You have a very nice little set up here."

He was blustering and Monica's suspicion grew.

Peter was thinking. He only had Uncle William's word for it, but if she hadn't taken the money, why change her name.

"The police are still looking for you, so are you responsible for Anders' missing money? You didn't buy all of this," he waved a hand theatrically and gave a sarcastic grin, "on Uncle William's salary."

"I left your uncle because he was unfaithful to me, with that little trollop of a secretary. He wouldn't be in the mess he is in now if he hadn't behaved like an adolescent school boy. Don't expect me to go and rescue him." She surveyed her painted nails, nonchalantly.

"You owe me; I actually need to get out of Britain, because of you."

Monica stared at him, realising it had been a mistake to bring him here. Wanting to see her daughter and thinking she could have her grandchild to live with her as well, she had given away her most guarded secret. She could see her moment of weakness costing her dearly; she would never be able to relax her guard with Peter. It might be time to move on again. She had assumed it was their joint decision to come and join her, but Lindsey it turned out, had thought she was just going to France for a week.

Peter had poured himself another glass of wine and was feeling assertive.

"I got her here for you; now it's your turn to talk her round."

"You didn't bring her here for me; you came on your own account, so don't try and pretend otherwise."

"She wanted *you*, because she is expecting your first grandchild," he insisted, trying the soft approach.

177

"Well now she wants to go home and I think you should take her."

"She needs *you*," he persisted, giving the indulgent smile that always won him the day.

Monica looked at him coldly, dismissing any last hope he had of moral blackmail working.

The smile disappeared and he gave up any pretence.

"I'm not going and that's flat. She can go if she likes, but I'm staying."

She recognised one of William's traits, when he was hiding something.

"Lindsey is expecting your child and you are not welcome to stay without her. What are you running away from?"

She knew she had guessed right when he stood up, saying, "I'm going to bed."

"I advise you to sleep in the room along the landing. Lindsey isn't happy with you and will be even more upset if you disturb her at this time of night."

He walked to the door, turned, bowed and said sarcastically, "As always, mother-in-law dear, your wish is my command."

After he had gone, Monica sat deep in thought for several minutes, then went to her study and sent a fax.

On his way along the broad, dimly lit landing, Peter met the Spanish maid leaving Monica's room, having turned down her bed. He smiled and she smiled politely.

"Buenos noches, Señor." She went to pass but he barred her way by resting one hand against the wall. Her smile faded and she tried to step back, but he pulled her towards him, kissing her full on the lips and running his hands down her slim body.

"Plis Señor," she objected.

He ignored her and pushed her towards the door at the end of the landing.

She stopped resisting and went into the room, where her attitude changed instantly. Striking an arrogant pose she rubbed her thumb and index finger together.

"Aah," he said reaching into his inside pocket.

Pulling out his wallet, he withdrew a ten-pound note, which she took and held her hand out for more. He raised his eyebrows and gave her another; whereupon, she shook her head, relieved him of his wallet and took another four, twenty-pound notes.

"I no cheap Señor," she said disdainfully.

"You can say that again. You'd better be good."

He had no complaints and went to sleep wondering how he could arrange to have separate rooms again.

Two days later, when Lindsey and Peter were lounging beside the pool, Monica strolled up and asked casually:

"Can I see you in my study, Peter? I won't keep him long dear; just a paper to sign. I must provide for my new grandchild." She smiled at Lindsey and turned away quickly to avoid questions. Peter got up, following her, anticipating a change of heart on his mother-in-law's part.

His hopes were soon dashed though, when on entering the well-equipped study, Monica shut the door firmly and turned on him.

"Of all the fool things to do; are you completely insane?"

"What particular fool thing are you talking about?" he asked, fighting to stay calm.

"Oh, there is more then?" she snapped.

His eyes narrowed.

"This particular fool thing, was getting the Anders girl pregnant," she spat at him, scornfully.

He scowled, wondering how the devil she had found out so quickly. "Who says?" he said sullenly.

"Someone by the name of Meg Daly; she worked at Anders?"

"Oh, *that* one," Peter shrugged, thinking quickly. "That explains everything; she's getting her own back because I turned her down; she tried to hook me for months. It was a silly bet they had in the office. Didn't think Samantha Anders would join in though; far too high and mighty to mix with mere salesmen."

"I have it on good authority that you were seen with her on a number of occasions."

"Yes we had lunch together and even dinner one evening. Her grandfather had just died and she was very upset. I was at a loose end. It was soon after you whipped Lindsey off to Switzerland, without so much as a note," he accused, cleverly.

"And that was all?" she asked, narrowing her eyes suspiciously.

"I swear."

"No more need be said then; pointless in upsetting Lindsey, if it's just a rumour." She watched him go, aware of the panic he was hiding.

You're good, she admitted – but I'm better.

Another fax to her solicitor brought more, apparently damning evidence the following day and she tackled him again.

"Why was your car parked in the Anders underground car park, all night from…?" She reeled off dates and he stared panic-stricken for several seconds before thinking of an answer.

"Engine trouble. Samantha let me leave it until a mechanic could come out." Monica noticed he was sweating, but it was a very hot day, she allowed. "And her car?" she asked, curiously.

"What about her car?" he asked giving himself thinking time, pretty sure what her next question was going to be.

"Why was it also parked there, on the same nights?"

"What's with all the questions? How do I know who else parked there? And who the devil says it was, anyway?"

"The night watchman thought it strange, because the whole place was shuttered by then."

"Well then let him answer the damn fool questions, I'm going for a swim."

He stomped out of the study and Monica smiled to herself. If she was honest, she didn't know if he was telling the truth or not, but she was enjoying his discomfort, and it might make him think twice before hurting Lindsey again.

The following day, she asked him how Samantha Anders came to pay for his air ticket and saw his nervous reaction to her having found out.

"I didn't have any money; you froze the accounts, remember?" He faced her with clenched fists. "She offered and before you ask I have paid her back."

She was looking through him, not able to prove her suspicions but knowing from old, how good he was at talking himself out of awkward situations, found it impossible to trust him.

He gave her an anxious look and escaped from the study.

"I can't help thinking your mother is losing the plot," he announced to Lindsey, who was sitting beside the pool reading a book on motherhood.

"Mm," she answered absently.

He scowled at her. "She's not alone, by the look of things. You aren't listening either."

She let her book drop. "When are we going home? I'm due for another check up next week."

"You can see a doctor here."

"No I can't, I need to go home and see my own doctor."

Peter stripped off his shorts and T-shirt and dived into the pool, where he swam aggressively up and down, before turning over and floating on his back.

"I thought you had a bad arm," Lindsey pointed out, placidly.

"As if you care," he pouted, peeved because she wasn't fussing as usual.

"I'm here aren't I?" she replied indifferently, giving a hostile stare.

He started to swim again, hoping to provoke a reaction, but she closed her eyes, holding her face up to the sun and after a while, he climbed out and lay on the sun bed on the other side of the pool. Watching him from lowered lids, tears rolled down her cheeks. She had gone looking for him the previous night and had seen Isabella coming out of his room at one o'clock in the morning.

That evening, at dinner, she caught sly looks passing between them and instead of going to bed early she stayed up. She could see Peter getting uptight and when her mother asked if she was going to bed, she replied that she wasn't tired.

"You should get your sleep, darling; think of the baby," Peter said solicitously.

"I've been resting all day; baby will be fine." She smiled sweetly. "You go if you want to. You must be tired after all that swimming."

"I think I'll just take a stroll round the garden and walk my dinner off."

"I'll come with you. How about you Mother?"

"I've got things to do, you two go." Monica kissed her cheek and went into the study.

"What's got into you all of a sudden? Normally you can't wait to go to bed." Peter tried to hide his frustration as Isabella entered and on seeing Lindsey, quickly asked if there was anything more she could do before going off duty.

"You won't be required any more tonight, thank you Isabella." Lindsey looked straight at her and Isabella muttered, "Buenos noches, Señora, Señor."

As the door closed, Lindsey said, "She will be glad of an early night, I saw her about at one o'clock this morning. I wonder what she finds to do at that time? It seems like slave labour. I must have a word with Mother."

"I would leave well alone; you could lose her, her job. I think perhaps I will go to bed after all." Peter went to kiss her.

"I'm ready as well." She took his hand and they went upstairs together.

"You need your rest. I'll sleep in the other bedroom," he said at their door, hoping that Isabella would be waiting.

"Let's stay together tonight; you go on, I'll just borrow Mother's lavender oil."

She walked in the direction of Monica's room but doubled back when she heard their door close. Reaching the far bedroom, she opened the door silently and stepped inside intending to confront Isabella but a small giggle came from under the bedclothes and anger took over. Creeping forward she picked up Isabella's clothes, and crept out again, locking the door on the outside. Passing a huge china vase on her way back to her bedroom, she popped the clothes and key in and wiped her hands together.

In the morning, there was uproar coming from the kitchen. Louisa was crying and talking nineteen to the dozen; Monica was the only one who could understand her.

"She says Isabella's bed wasn't slept in. Have either of you seen her?"

"We saw her last thing, when she said goodnight," Lindsey said innocently

Much later that morning, banging was heard coming from the end bedroom. The key was missing but the master key opened the door and a very distressed Isabella, wrapped in a sheet, was at a loss to explain where her clothes were.

Monica guessed straightaway what had been going on, and was prepared to sack her on the spot, but Lindsey stopped her.

"Leave it, Mother. Peter will never change," Lindsey said sadly

"You knew?" Monica looked astonished. "Why do you stay with him, sweetheart?"

Lindsey gave a hopeless shrug. "Because I love him and would sooner live with him than without him."

The heady perfume of orchids filled the air in the garden room and Lindsey knew they would always remind her of that moment in Tenerife, when she finally admitted to herself what a fool she was.

Monica buried her head in her hands. "How can I help?" she said dejectedly.

"You can fly me back to Britain, so that I can have my baby in my own home, then one day soon I will come and see you with my baby."

Monica straightened up, forcing a smile.

"I shall look forward to that. I will send you a forwarding address. It will be a box number."

They clung together and Monica wished with all her heart that she could turn back the clock, but avoiding prison was the best thing she could do for her daughter, now.

"Get your things together," she said pulling away. "Be ready in two hours; the car will take you to the airstrip. The police might question you when you get home; just carry on telling them I left Britain to punish William for cheating on me."

"I will." Lindsey's face lit up; a new bond had formed between them and for the first time she felt her mother was being completely open with her.

Peter spent the day in a bar, giving Lindsey and her mother, what he considered enough time to calm down, before returning in time for dinner; expecting trouble, but confident, as always, of Lindsey's forgiveness; so it didn't even occur to him that the villa would be completely deserted; even Isabella and her mother had gone. He gulped, stunned that Lindsey had actually left; she said she would, but he never expected her to. It was that mother of hers; she had taken her away again. He roamed around the deserted downstairs rooms undecided what to do and eventually went into the study to use the telephone. Two envelopes were propped on the desk and tearing open the one with Lindsey's handwriting on it, his fears were confirmed.

'My Dear Peter,
I have gone home to have our baby. Stay if you want to but mother has left and I will never return. I will wait to hear if you want us to stay together but if you do it will have to be on condition that, you are ready to be a good father and husband. I hope it isn't too late for us.

Lindsey.'

He sat looking at the words for a long time, then opened Monica's envelope and saw her strong, slanting handwriting.

'Peter,
The only reason I am giving you a chance is because, my daughter, for some reason that escapes me completely, thinks you are worth it. You have two days to decide and after that the house will be locked and in the hands of an agent. I made the mistake of trusting you and your uncle once; I won't be doing that again. By the time you read this I will be on my way to another continent, where William and I should be living our dream together now, tell him. If I am honest, I hope you don't go back to my daughter. She deserves better.'

It was unsigned but the message was clear. If he stayed, there would be no help from her; if on the other hand he went home, things would carry on as before. If he really wanted to be with Lindsey and the baby and have the comfort of their home for the rest of his life, he would have to go back and find a way of avoiding the Anders family. After debating with himself all night, he finally decided there was no alternative; poverty was not an option.

He telephoned Lindsey at home and begged her forgiveness, promising her anything she wanted to hear.

The following day he went to the bar and sat drinking with a few ex patriots, he had met previously and when it came time to go back to the villa, one of them, Tony Wakefield, offered him a lift. They chatted on the way and Peter invited him in for a drink.

"Thanks very much, it's a bit late; sure your wife won't mind?"

"My wife has gone home. I'm going tomorrow."

Tony admired the villa. "Is this your place, then?"

"No, it belongs to my mother-in-law, but she's selling. Do you want to buy?" Peter gave a cheeky grin. "Bit above our price range eh?"

"Just a tad. Why on earth would she want to sell a place like this?"

"She likes to move about."

"Oh well, nice if you've got the money to do it, I suppose. Where is she moving to?"

"I think she just sticks a pin in the map of the world. Wish I could; I wouldn't go back to Britain."

As they were parting, promising to meet up sometime, Tony suddenly offered him a lift to the airport.

"I'm actually booked on the same flight; had a last minute call from my boss; he wants me back pronto."

"Thanks, that's great; I hate flying on my own."

Tony arrived in plenty of time to make the fairly long journey from Icos to the airport and they sat together on the plane.

It was crowded, not at all like Monica's private jet that he and Lindsey had flown out in. He nodded off and woke, stiff from the cramped conditions and it was a relief when the trolley came round with a meal, which although not marvellous was at least piping hot, and a drink came with it.

The plane touched down at Gatwick and they sat, agreeing they could never understand why people preferred standing up and jostling with other passengers to reach luggage down, when they could just wait and walk off in comfort; finally they got up and sauntered along the now empty space between the rows of seats.

It was drizzling with rain and glancing over his shoulder Peter remarked gloomily, "Welcome back to Britain."

At the passport desk, he was asked to accompany an officer into a side room.

"I have nothing to declare officer."

The officer repeated, "If you would just follow me, sir."

Peter gave a tolerant sigh; glancing back over his shoulder to say this won't take long and realised that Tony was nowhere to be seen. Where had he gone? Suspicion reared, as he thought of stories about smugglers putting illegal goods in other people's luggage to avoid customs and he broke out in a sweat, eyeing his unlocked hand luggage, remembering Tony taking it from him and stowing it in the boot of his car. Had offering to drive him been planned? Now he thought of it, Tony's decision to travel home with him had been very sudden.

The Customs officer was holding the door open for him and he was obliged to follow.

He was searched before being told to sit down at a table; and an officer stood guard at the door, while the first one left the room.

Fingers twitching nervously, he kept telling himself he had nothing to worry about; he hadn't done anything.

It seemed an age before the door opened but in fact it was only five minutes before, a man in a suit entered, followed, to his relief, by Tony. Thank goodness, they had caught him.

The man in the suit introduced himself as Chief Inspector Desmond, before turning to Tony.

"And I believe you have met Detective Wakefield."

Peter gaped at Tony, seeing him in a different light to the casual fellow drinker who had been so prepared to listen to his troubles.

"That was pretty low," he accused.

"We have a job to do, Mr Chambers, and we believe you can help us with our enquiries. Unfortunately, our information came too late and Monica Spencer had already gone but you hadn't. Where is Monica Spencer?"

"What information? I have no idea where she is. I told you, she just sticks a pin in a map. You already know she left with my wife, while I was in a bar with you," he added with an accusing stare.

"Come now Mr Chambers, you must have some idea," Chief Inspector Desmond intervened.

Peter rested his elbows on the table and nursed his head in a helpless gesture, muttering, "Your guess is as good as mine; all she said in her note was that she was going to another continent, to live her and Uncle's dream."

Chief Inspector Desmond frowned deeply. Nothing was adding up yet. "Why did your pregnant wife travel home alone from Tenerife, after you travelled to France together?"

"We had a difference of opinion, but it's alright now and I'm going home."

185

"But how did you both get to Tenerife?"

"Lindsey's mother hired a private plane. It was a last minute surprise for us; my wife and I thought she was meeting us in France for a two-week holiday."

Inspector Desmond turned to Tony and gave a grunt. It was pretty much the same story that the daughter had told, except that she had said her mother left because her stepfather had had an affair with his secretary.

Peter was allowed to go home.

CHAPTER TWENTY-FIVE

Samantha took Jacob home to quite a celebration. Charles and Felicity had flown back the day before and Abigail arrived on the same day.

Fourteen sat down to dinner that evening and they had just finished the first course when another unexpected arrival created more excitement.

"You could have waited till Uncle got here." Tim grinned going straight to Samantha, laden with gifts.

"Just when I thought things couldn't get any better," she said emotionally. George set another place and Tim sat beside her laughing and answering endless questions from the boys, occasionally stopping to give her a searching look.

At nine o'clock, Samantha took Jacob upstairs and Tim joined her in her bedroom. He held Jacob while she settled in bed, ready to give him his ten o'clock feed and Abigail pottered making sure everything was at hand for the night then left them to talk while Jacob suckled contentedly.

"You look as if you've been doing it all your life," Tim said admiringly.

"I'm glad I helped Tamar with her pups; it's no different really." Sam smiled softly.

Tim suddenly looked serious. "What happened? Where is Jacob's father?"

"It isn't important; Jacob is mine."

"Does he know he has a son?" Tim asked curiously.

"No."

"Dad says it was someone you worked with."

"What else did he say?" she asked, not wanting Tim to think badly of her.

"Leaving out the swearwords just that his name is Peter Chambers; and he is a womaniser."

She nodded, flushing.

"Are you in love with him?"

"I don't know. I thought I was, when—"

Gradually the whole story came out, and like Darren, Tim listened with growing concern.

"We are talking of the family who stole from us, doesn't that seem a trifle disloyal to Grandfather?"

"It didn't seem like that at the time because I was, and still am, pretty certain he had nothing to do with the fraud," she said miserably.

"What makes you so certain?" Tim enquired, frowning.

"Well he didn't know where his wife was, or if she intended coming back; he was equally certain that his uncle wouldn't have the brains to plan anything that big. Apparently William's wife is the one suspected of the theft, but even that hasn't been proved." She gave a sharp intake of breath.

"Are you alright?" Tim leapt to his feet. "Shall I call Abigail?"

"No, no I'm fine, it's just that I had completely forgotten about Tenerife."

"Eh? You've lost me." Tim looked at her, wondering if she had gone crazy.

"Daddy saw Peter and his wife in Tenerife and it seemed possible to me that they had gone there to see her mother; I should have told the police, ages ago." She pulled a face. "How could I have forgotten?"

"Understandable, in the circumstances," Tim took out his mobile phone and spoke to his father, grinning as he slipped it back into his pocket.

"All in hand, he phoned them soon after he left the hospital."

Samantha gave a delighted "Really?"

"Yes and even better, Peter Chambers is being questioned."

Sam's face fell. "What about the mother?"

"No sign of her, but she had been there."

"What will happen to Peter?"

"Do you care?" Tim asked curiously.

"I suppose not," she answered uncertainly.

Tim threw his arms up and held his head. "When women complicate things, they certainly make a job of it." He kissed her on the cheek then kissed Jacob. "We'll talk again in the morning. I'm going to read about Cleopatra, she is less complicated – or was she?"

They parted smiling, but laying in the dark, Samantha couldn't help thinking of Peter, recalling the nights when he had made love to her so wonderfully. She switched the bedside light on and looked down at Jacob sleeping peacefully in his cradle and her heart overflowed with love as she thought how proud Grandfather would have been. Unable to relax, her thoughts went from one lovely memory to another until a picture of Gerald, on the morning he had surprised her with Nocturn, brought tears. Wide awake, she decided to go downstairs and make a cup of tea; it was a habit she had fallen into when living with Meg, when she couldn't sleep. Assuming everyone else was in bed, she was surprised to hear voices coming from the kitchen; George and Lorna were still up. Changing her mind, she went back upstairs and had just reached her room when Abigail appeared, wearing her scotch plaid, wool dressing gown.

"I thought I heard you about. Can't sleep? It's been a big day."

"Thought I would make myself a cup of tea, but George and Lorna are still up and I didn't want to disturb them. Sorry if I woke you."

"You didn't; I'll bring you one. You get back to bed, before you catch chill."

She returned ten minutes later with the tea and sat on the side of the bed, nursing her own cup and saucer, saying comfortably, "Nothing like a cup of tea."

"Nanny comes pretty close," Samantha said.

"Och away with ye."

"I'm serious. You are always there for us."

"The Anders family is the only one I have ever been part of and families don't come any better."

Samantha looked pensive. "What?" Abigail frowned.

"I've had reason to question that, of late; so many secrets and lies have been uncovered."

"All families have skeletons." Abigail tried to make light of what was becoming a serious talk, but Samantha pursued the subject.

"I met some people from London who knew Great Grandmother Pamela."

She watched Abigail's face change.

"Lady Pamela was a wonderful person," she bridled.

"That was what they said; they obviously knew her very well. They didn't seem to think so highly of Alexander though. Why won't Marcia have his name mentioned?"

Jacob stirred in his cradle and Abigail took the opportunity to avoid the question.

"He will be looking for another feed soon; I expect you feed him every three hours don't you?"

Samantha gave a concerned look at the clock. "Good heavens, it's twelve thirty all ready."

Abigail passed Jacob to her. "Might as well top him up now and get some sleep before the four o'clock one," she advised in her practical way, waiting until he was feeding before laying a spare nappy out and making sure they had everything before she left.

"You look as if you have been doing it for years," she smiled admiringly.

"That's what Tim said." Samantha gazed lovingly at her son, forgetting about the unanswered question. On her way back upstairs, Abigail gave serious thought to the answer she would give when it was asked again. She only had her suspicions, and it was something she would rather leave buried in the past.

CHAPTER TWENTY-SIX

Life settled into a routine, not greatly different to their previous one, except that Charles was regarded as the head of the house now.

It wasn't something he coveted and he lived for the day when Samantha could take over. On their own in the sitting room, after Samantha had gone to feed Jacob and Abigail had gone up to her room, Felicity put her knitting down and said tentatively:

"I suppose we can't really expect Samantha to take on the running of the house just yet, with Jacob to look after." It was more a hopeful question than a statement. Always sensitive to his feelings she was acutely aware of how he was suffering in silence.

"Not really. I wish Darren was of more help to her, but he hasn't the least idea of how to manage any house, let alone one this size."

"He runs the air transport business."

Charles gave a mirthless little laugh. "He has never run it; Gerald did. Darren never balanced the books or paid the bills; if he had, he would know the business has never paid its way. Gerald, rather foolishly, was happy to cover it up; and things won't change if Samantha keeps up the pretence." He gave a helpless shrug; he had never agreed with Gerald's desperate measures to keep the twins close, but it wasn't an opinion he had ever voiced, until now.

Felicity gave an anguished sigh, saying softly:

"Poor Gerald, he kept the family close, at such a high cost to himself."

In Felicity's mind, her husband's straight back had always reflected his character, but of late, his shoulders had drooped under the heavy burden he was carrying. Living in Anders Folly now, was the hardest thing he had ever had to do; every single room held memories of his and Gerald's life together. Losing David and Pamela, then Marie and finally Laurie, had been devastating, but this last, mind-numbing loss was impossible, even for him to come to terms with.

Watching him, fighting his emotions, Felicity was suddenly afraid, knowing that, at whatever cost to the rest of the family, they must get away; go back to their own home and find peace. Samantha was young; she would cope, and if not, then Darren and Melly must do their bit. Charles had always been such a tower of strength, but they must all be made to realise that even he had a breaking point.

"First thing in the morning, we will return home," she declared abruptly.

Charles was taken aback; it was unusual for her to be so – adamant – and now he came to think of it, she was acting out of character quite often, of late. He gave a brief nod, realizing how desperate she must be feeling.

"That's settled then; I'll tell everyone and we will leave immediately after breakfast."

As she spoke, she glanced nervously at his tight expression, but relaxed, feeling much happier when he smiled fondly at her.

Resting back in David's maroon wing chair, Charles felt that familiar sense of relief at not having to put his feelings into words with Felicity. How lucky he was to have her.

Samantha panicked when she heard of their decision, and thought up numerous arguments for them to stay.

"We won't be far and you can call or visit whenever you need to, but both Uncle Charles and I need to go home." Unusually Felicity was aggressively standing her ground, convinced that any sign of weakness would result in them staying.

"Why does everyone keep leaving me?" Samantha pouted, tearfully.

"We aren't leaving *you,* we are doing what is best for Uncle Charles right now."

Samantha looked stricken. "He's all right isn't he?"

Felicity fled, unable to cope. She just wanted to be alone with Charles in their own home, where they could nurse their sorrow and come to terms with their own devastating loss, which seemed to have been overlooked.

Tim had been home for six weeks and was desperate to go back to Egypt. He was receiving daily texts from Nigel Rowling, saying exciting things were happening at the dig. Nigel's role as tutor had finished, but for Gerald's peace of mind, he had agreed to stay on as a companion.

The truth was, that his salary had not been paid into his account for the second month running and he was worried about changes to the comfortable lifestyle he had enjoyed for so many years. Only by getting Timothy to return, could he justify his generous salary plus expenses, because the thought of roughing it with the rest of the team, after years of luxury in first class hotels, was not a welcome one.

"Will you be okay if I go back?" Timothy asked anxiously, rocking Jacob in his arms.

"I suppose I will have to be." Samantha gave a shrug.

They were in the study, waiting for Charles to arrive and explain the accounts to Samantha, and Tim had just shown her Nigel's latest text.

"I'll stay if you want me to," he said waiting with his heart in his mouth for her answer.

"Of course I want you to, but you would only be miserable."

"Thanks Sis. I'll come home for your first Christmas," he said, with a big smile at Jacob.

"You better had," Samantha said, scanning a column of figures, neatly set out in Gerald's hand.

Timothy watched over her shoulder, admiring her dedication, glad that the responsibility would never be his, knowing he would be bored out of his mind.

"It's a huge job; do you feel up to it?" he asked, sounding dubious.

Her smile was confident. "I have two very good reasons. One, it was Grandfather's wish and two it will be Jacob's inheritance; and yes, I do feel up to it. These," she said pointing to the page of figures, "are only simple household accounts. Uncle Charles says dealing with the investments will be more complicated." Her eyes shone at the prospect.

"Rather you than me." Timothy moved away, jogging Jacob as he began to whimper. "He needs feeding."

Samantha took over and discreetly put him to her breast, teasingly suggesting that she needed a nursemaid.

"You don't fancy the job, I suppose?"

"What's wrong with Abigail?"

"It's time we allowed Abigail to retire."

He raised his eyebrows. "Really? Don't let *her* hear you say that."

Jacob finished feeding just as Charles arrived.

"I'll put him in the pram and ask Abigail to change his nappy," Timothy offered, holding Jacob at arm's length, with a disgusted expression.

"On second thoughts, you will never make a nursemaid," Samantha laughed.

"Was that ever an option?" Charles asked with wry humour.

"No," Timothy assured him loudly, making a quick exit."

"He will be going back to Egypt very soon," Samantha said sadly, as the door closed.

"You will miss him; we all will."

"Everyone leaves sooner or later; something I have to get used to."

Charles gave a worried look and decided the best thing was get on with the delicate subject in hand; namely Timothy and Darren's expenses, which, in view of the need to cut down, they would have to take over themselves. Reluctant at first, Samantha eventually had to agree.

"Your grandfather made sure they both had generous allowances, but never imposed any expectations that they should use any of it to pay their own expenses."

"Mm, that was bad; strange when he was so meticulous about other things."

Samantha considered her own, previous lifestyle. Sharing with Meg had brought home a great many things, but the contrast in their daily lives weighed most heavily when she compared Meg's simple belongings with her own. Another thought struck her. "Didn't Daddy know he was taking advantage of Grandfather's generosity?"

"I doubt he gave it a thought. Your grandfather stopped at nothing, to keep you and Tim at Anders Folly, and setting your father up in business was his way of doing just that. He liked to feel you were all dependent on him, it helped to make up for his wheelchair existence."

Charles watched conflicting emotions cross Samantha's expressive face.

"Will I ever fully know my family?" she asked at last. "They seem to have such strong motives for keeping the past secret."

Charles wondered what had suddenly brought this on.

"Don't be too hard on him; his only real mistake was in trying to protect you all too much."

"Is that why Marcia won't let anyone talk about Alexander? What did he do that was so terrible?"

It was Charles's turn to look puzzled.

"You see, even you don't know." She repeated what she had overheard and he shook his head.

"If I ever did know, I have completely forgotten; there was a long gap in our relationship, when Grandfather married Marcia."

"There you go again; why was there a long gap?"

"Best not go down that road; it was all a long time ago."

Samantha clutched her head in both hands. "Aargh, I will go mad if I hear that again."

Charles looked startled, picked up the phone and dialled his number. When Felicity answered he said, "I need help," then replaced the receiver.

Felicity arrived fifteen minutes later looking flustered; thinking something dire had happened. She looked relieved when Charles explained the problem and met Samantha's enquiring look with a benign smile.

"I'm sure there is nothing to worry about, sweetheart; it was such a long—"

Charles interrupted her with an anxious look at Samantha.

"Yes, we know that dear, but Samantha needs answers; like Sophie did? So do you remember anything about Alexander upsetting Marcia?"

"Oh, goodness yes." She chuckled, reminiscently.

Samantha sat forward expectantly in her blue chair, which was now behind Gerald's desk in place of his brown one.

"He was like a red rag to a bull, to her." She looked at Charles for confirmation.

"And?" he encouraged.

She looked at him vaguely. "And what?"

"Was there anything specific, something really awful that Grandfather didn't want mentioned?" Samantha urged.

"No-o – not that I recall," Felicity pondered. "But then it was a long—"

"Yes, yes we know, dear," Charles interrupted again, looking apologetically at Samantha.

Felicity got up smiling happily. "I think I'll just have a coffee with Marie, while I'm here."

"Aunt Felicity, why did you and Uncle Charles fall out with Grandfather when he married Marcia?"

On her way to the door, Felicity turned, her expression blank.

"Did we, dear? Who is Marcia? I don't remember a Marcia, but then it was…" Charles ushered her out of the study.

"Well that didn't get far," Samantha said, flatly. "Uncle Charles?"

Charles was gazing at the closed door.

"We will have to continue another day; I think my wife needs me."

He gave her a dazed look and left.

When Charles first noticed Felicity, referring to Marie as if she was still alive and repeating herself a lot, he put it down to forgetfulness; even when he found dirty dishes in the fridge and food stacked neatly in the dishwasher, he just laughed and put things right, because they stood next to each other.

In hindsight though, how often now did she stare vacantly in to space, apparently lost in thought? Gerald's death, plus Samantha running off had upset everyone and Felicity's problem had gone unnoticed. Now though, Charles never left her side and Paul took over helping Samantha with her paperwork.

Sorting out finances and cutting back made Samantha appreciate the luxury they had all taken for granted in Gerald's time, and she felt good about being able to assure George and Lorna and Sol and Ella that their homes were safe.

Timothy had taken the changes in his stride by moving into less expensive accommodation and telling Nigel that a paid companion was beyond his means now he was paying his own way.

"It's the only way I can stay in Egypt, but it would be nice to stay together," he pointed out to a stunned Nigel.

Losing his plum job came as a complete and utter shock to Nigel. On hearing of Gerald Anders' death, he had assumed Darren Anders would continue paying for his son to be chaperoned; never even considering the need for the wealthy Anders family to economise at his expense. He was highly put out, but accepted Timothy's offer to share his room free, after viewing the decidedly less, attractive alternative, of going back to tutoring.

Darren on the other hand, had to face the bitter blow to his ego that not only had his business never paid for itself, but also his grandfather's death and his own unwillingness to accept responsibility for Anders Folly, had deprived him of a very secure lifestyle; and he became even more insecure and dissatisfied.

"Well it's too late now," Melly said practically. "Samantha must be having a really hard time, or she would never have asked it of you."

Without financial back up he was forced to close the business, and without a job, his thoughts turned again to America. He was so disheartened and gloomy that Samantha felt responsible, until Charles told her in exasperation, that continuing to support what could only be classed as an expensive hobby, must eventually bankrupt Anders Folly, if allowed to continue. So she gave her blessing and a farewell dinner at Anders Folly. Darren was seen to smile for the first time in weeks, as they departed, with Samantha holding back the tears as she waved them off from the airfield. Once more, the cottage was locked and its beautiful contents, carefully preserved.

Her days were busy and several weeks passed before Samantha got in touch with Meg. Waiting until Jacob was in bed, she telephoned looking forward to a long chat, but Meg didn't sound her usual bright self and after a few minutes, tried to end the call.

"Something is wrong; tell me," Samantha said firmly,

"I'm living back with my parents and my phone needs recharging, that's all."

"I'll ring the house phone; give me the number."

There was a small silence, before Meg said, "I'll ring you," before the line went dead.

She waited over an hour for her call, and eventually decided to ring again in the morning.

She phoned the following morning at eight thirty and Meg answered immediately, saying she was at the coach station.

"Where are you going?" Samantha asked urgently, hearing the stress in her voice.

"I have an aunt in Wales, who I think will let me stay until I get sorted."

"Meg, you can stay with me. Please come."

Meg started to cry. "Yes please then, just till I get sorted."

Samantha told her where to get the coach to and said she would pick her up at the terminus.

The coach was on time and Lucy was crying as Samantha met them at five thirty that evening.

"She's hungry," Meg explained, rummaging in her bag with shaking hands. It had been a long journey and Samantha could see she was at the end of her tether, as she produced a biscuit and a bottle of water for Lucy.

"We will be home in twenty minutes," she said, relieving Meg of Lucy to put her in Jacob's car seat.

Meg sank thankfully into the passenger seat and closed her eyes. They drove home in silence and Samantha took Meg straight up to Timothy's old room, which adjoined her own by a connecting bathroom. She helped her undress and get into bed; too exhausted to object, Meg's last waking thought was for Lucy.

"She is being fed and looked after; get some sleep. Don't worry about a thing."

Worried by her pallor and exhaustion, Samantha consulted Abigail, who sent for the doctor straight away. He diagnosed a chest infection and prescribed antibiotics, plenty of fluids and bed rest.

It puzzled Samantha how Meg came to be in this condition, but now wasn't the time for questions.

Lucy was playing happily on the kitchen floor, having been fed and changed by Maisie, who with numerous younger brothers and sisters was no stranger to baby care.

"She needs a bath, Aunt Lorna."

"You get on with that then, while I make the bottle. Poor little mite; they bin travellin' the whole day by all accounts. Best take her up to Miss Samantha's bathroom; everythin's at hand up there."

A large bag had arrived with Lucy, containing nappies, sleepwear, cuddly toys and numerous other bits and pieces, including bottles and formula. Lorna took out what she needed and handed the bag to Maisie, smiling at the intense pleasure on her niece's face as she gathered Lucy up in her arms and left the kitchen. Lorna could hear Maisie telling Lucy she was going in a lovely bath, and her heart went out to her.

By morning, Samantha was relieved to see Meg looking slightly better and sleeping when the cough allowed. Lorna suggested Maisie could look after Lucy, and Dora, another of her nieces would replace her in the kitchen, for the time being. It turned out to be an excellent arrangement. Maisie showed herself to be capable of looking after both Lucy and Jacob, and Abigail, after an obligatory show of reluctance, retired gratefully to her rooms. Although she had been finding it increasing hard to deal with Jacob, she would have died rather than admit it. She still had the magic touch though and enjoyed singing him to sleep at night, so Samantha left him with her only when he was ready for sleep and her feelings were saved. The time had come for a younger nursemaid. Maisie was overjoyed with her new position.

After a good rest, Meg was feeling much brighter and Samantha felt it was time for some answers, but her tentative questions were side tracked; Meg was obviously reluctant to talk about her problems, until one evening, when the babies were in bed and they were relaxing on the terrace she finally broached the subject herself.

"I owe you an explanation."

"You don't owe me anything, but I am curious. I left you looking forward to making a home with Lucy's father – and a few weeks later?" Samantha spread her hands and raised her eyebrows questioningly.

"I know; and it was all right at first, but Lucy began to get on Scott's nerves when she was teething; she cried a lot and kept us awake at night. He started going out drinking with his mates and when he came home he would want to make love, but I was too tired – that was when fists began to fly. I would have put up with it, but one night he smacked Lucy hard and the next day I ran away. I had nowhere else to go so I went back to my parents. In time I would have got another council flat but the waiting list is long."

"What went wrong at your parents?"

"They never stopped going on about what a mess I'd made of my life and how Dad's heart condition wouldn't stand all of the upset. You see, Scott kept coming to the house, demanding that I go back and when I refused, he started ringing up all hours of the day and night. I'm not going back, I'm too afraid of what he might do." She looked angry. "I hate to admit it but Mum and Dad were right; they said it would happen again the first time he hit me."

"And yet you went back?"

"I suppose I wanted the dream, you know, husband, home, babies; except there was no more mention of getting married and the home turned out to be a damp flat in a rundown area."

Samantha waited for tears, but Meg wasn't one to cry easily; life had taught her not to feel sorry for herself.

"Well, you don't have to worry about all that now; this is your home for as long as you want it."

"I can't impose on you, now I am better. I'll have to get a job and rent a flat."

"You can work here; I'm desperate for help and your computer skills would save me hours; that aside, it would be madness for you to pay rent for a couple of tiny rooms when we have got all this space doing nothing." She saw Meg waver and added persuasively, "We also have a built-in nanny for Lucy."

Meg's eyes began to shine as her last doubt was squashed.

"Okay, but I must earn my keep."

"Don't worry, I will work you like a galley slave."

Samantha relaxed, feeling happier than she had done for some while; at last someone was staying instead of leaving. Listening to the soft sigh of waves lapping against the shore she sensed her grandfather listening and nodding approval, as she sat where he had so often sat, looking proudly out to sea from his beloved home.

"An Englishman's home is his castle," she murmured.

Meg gave an enquiring look, unable to imagine the magic of growing up in a wonderful place like this, just extremely happy to be a small part of it for now.

"Something Grandfather used to say," Samantha explained.

CHAPTER TWENTY-SEVEN

Amy regarded the mountain of clothes and bits and pieces scattered around the living room. The whole flat was in complete chaos; painting was something she normally left to decorators, but present circumstances didn't permit. Working for an estate agent was not the glamorous career she had anticipated, in fact it was anything but; the basic salary was low and commission was only paid on completion of a sale, which, more often than not meant working evenings and Sundays. She only intended to stick it until she found something better.

She regarded the mess despondently and decided to make a cup of coffee before getting started. It had taken her an hour to empty the bedroom and even now, the curtains still needed taking down. Gazing at the empty room while she drank her coffee, she toyed with, if she could get away with, leaving the curtains up by pulling them to the middle of the window; and decided to chance it. Made of cheap white chipboard, the dressing table was fixed to the wall under the windowsill, and in reaching up to unhook the curtain from the end of the rail, she accidentally kicked the side panel loose. Stooping to push it back in place, she noticed small brads standing proud and the panel refused to fit back; there appeared to be something stopping it and she decided to leave it until later and get on with the painting.

When it came to bedtime, the smell of the silver grey emulsion paint was still very strong, so leaving the windows wide open she shut the bedroom door and made a bed up on the settee. During the night, she was woken by a loud thud and for a moment pictured someone breaking in, before reminding herself she was on the top floor. On investigating, she discovered that the draught from the open windows had blown the curtain, snagged it on one of the sharp brads, and pulled the loose panel away, causing it to fall. She pulled the windows to, released the curtains and went back to bed, grumbling.

The following morning, reminding her self that William would be telephoning from the prison later in the day with his weekly list of needs, she set about returning everything to the bedroom. It took longer than anticipated, because in a rash moment, she filled two black plastic bags with unwanted clothes, ready to take to the charity shop, then fussed over the purple voile curtains before kneeling to fix the panel on the dressing table; it still refused to slot back and in getting right down on the floor to see what was stopping it she spied something bulky in the space under the bottom rail. Her exploring fingers withdrew a brown, leather briefcase and excitement gripped her as she recognised it as the one from William's office. She pictured him stuffing bundles of money into it and with shaking hands pushed the clasp down, realising when it was locked that he would almost certainly have had the key on him when he was arrested; and at that moment it would be sitting amongst his personal belongings at the police station.

All that money and he had let her scrape and save to take him his little luxuries. Anger filled her, remembering the expensive malt whisky she had smuggled into him. She had stayed loyal, confident that he would take her away and they would live the good life eventually.

When the phone rang, she fought down her anger and managed to sound reassuring, as always. He was full of self-pity and she sympathised, thinking all the time of his deceit.

"Send me in some of that tinned lobster and another bottle of malt, will you?"

"I'm a bit short this month; I needed paint for the bedroom walls."

She waited hoping he would confide about the briefcase and offer to pay.

"I really can't survive in this place without *some* luxuries. Couldn't the bedroom walls have waited until I get out?"

He sounded desperate and normally she would have felt sorry for him, but she said sharply, "I'm struggling too; you will have to help me, if you want these expensive things. I don't earn what I did at Anders Motors."

She thought that might have some effect, but it didn't.

"My bank accounts are empty."

She wasn't even sure if that was true either.

"I'll see what I can do. I need to get on now." She put the phone down, sat thinking for a while, then got up and very purposefully fetched the briefcase and a tool kit.

Two weeks later, when he had been unable to contact Amy, William was panicking. Thoughts of her having a fatal accident and someone else renting her flat, made him break out in a sweat. How would he get his money? It was all he had between him and homeless. It hadn't helped talking to Peter, when he had visited briefly after being questioned. According to him, hell would freeze over before he got any help from Monica – she was home and free.

Holding his head in his hands he blamed first Monica and then Amy for his predicament, hating them one minute and in the next, wishing he could be with Monica. Peter had been distraught at being questioned again and vowed he would never look at another woman.

I would happily swear to that on a stack of bibles, William thought bitterly, reaching for his hip flask.

*

The rich American woman admired the orchids, a smile playing around her well-shaped, crimson lips, without reaching her strangely coloured turquoise eyes. Dark hair hung loosely to her shoulders framing a deeply suntanned face, while an abundance of delicate gold chains filled the low cut v of her slim fit, turquoise linen dress. A jewel encrusted ankle bracelet drew attention to long, smooth brown legs and slim feet encased in gold sandals, presenting an overall exotic image that excited the house agent almost as much as her next words.

"I've got to buy it," she drawled.

He was delighted with such a quick sale; expecting at the very least that she would haggle. He quickly produced a form and she signed it.

"When can I move in?" she asked

"As soon as your cheque is cleared, Mrs Hayle."

"Can't the formalities be waved? I want to move in straightaway."

She fitted a long cigarette into an even longer holder and lit it, fixing the Spanish agent with a sultry look, one eyebrow slightly raised.

He fingered the paper waiting for her signature, praying she wasn't going to withdraw her offer if he refused.

"I could ask the vendor," he offered, reaching for his phone.

"Do that, while I find a bathroom." Barbara Hayle strode back into the house, leaving him to make the call and when she returned, he was beaming.

"All arranged; Mrs Langloise said you can move in today, if you wish."

"I do. My luggage will arrive this evening and I need to start work immediately."

"I understand, Mrs Hayle."

"I hope you do; I am a writer, and I need complete privacy."

"You will be needing a housekeeper? I can recommend the one Mrs Langloise employed."

"That won't be necessary."

"Then I will say buenos dias, Mrs Hayle." He gave a polite nod and hurried out, anxious to convey to his employer, the good news that the extortionately over priced house had been sold at the asking price.

Barbara Hayle poured herself a glass of wine and went to sit in the garden room congratulating herself.

*

Amy stretched luxuriously, lying back on the sunbed, thinking of all the new clothes in her wardrobe. William was the last thing on her mind, but she couldn't help feeling a little sorry for him. Would he guess she had found the money?

A waiter arrived with her drink and she tipped him generously, having been advised by a well-travelled, older woman guest that it was the way to get good service. Having all of that money tucked away made her feel powerful, but what should she do with it, buy a property in Spain, perhaps? At this moment, it was sitting in a safety deposit box in the bank. That was what William should have done she thought, before remembering he had been in hiding and lucky for her, unable to. She had handed in her notice straight away and couldn't resist taking a luxury holiday before deciding what to do next. With nearly three hundred thousand pounds, she could do anything she wanted. A picture of Samantha in the pale blue sports car, flashed across her mind. She would learn to drive and buy a car; it had always irked her that she worked in a car showroom and couldn't afford a car. Well, now she could – thanks in a roundabout way to Miss Anders. Her eyes shone at the irony of it and she laughed out loud.

A passing waiter paused. "The señorita is happy; another pina colada, perhaps?"

"Why not?" she waved her arm gaily.

*

The taxi pulled up and William Spencer got out. He had been released that morning and his first port of call was Amy's flat. He paid the driver and hurried to the lift, squeezing in behind a mother with three children and a pushchair, as the doors were closing. Two of the children were pushing and arguing and he frowned when one of them bumped against him. "Be careful Jimmy, say sorry to the man," the mother cautioned, turning to William and apologising just as the lift stopped and they bundled out. He shuddered at the thought of living in

Amy's flat again, but he had nowhere else to go, and only the eighty pounds and some loose change that he had when he was arrested. The lift continued to the top floor and he stepped out, hardly able to control his impatience. Amy's door was at the end of the long passage and he half ran to it, pressing the bell urgently, three times. Getting no response, he pressed again, leaving his finger on the bell push for several seconds. This time footsteps dragged to the door and a woman poked her head round.

"Where's the fire?" she demanded roughly, obviously having been woken from a deep sleep.

"I need to speak to Amy Bishop," he said ignoring her aggression.

"Who's she?"

"She lives here."

"No she doesn't. I do; and I need to go back to bed."

"How long have you lived here?" he asked desperately as the door began to close.

"Four months." The door closed and he saw for the first time a printed notice, saying, NIGHT WORKER. DO NOT DISTURB, hanging on the letterbox. Ignoring it, he pressed the bell again and heard footsteps returning.

"What now?" the woman said in a longsuffering tone. "Can't you read?"

"I left something in the bedroom when Miss Bishop lived here and I will give you twenty pounds if you will just let me see if it is still there."

He held out a twenty pound note, which she took and opened the door wide.

He ran past her, stopping at the darkened bedroom, nearly collapsing as he saw an empty space where the dressing table used to be.

"W-where is the d-dressing t-table?" he stuttered.

"We threw it out; it was all in bits."

"And you didn't find a brown leather briefcase?"

"No, but I tell you what, if my husband comes home and finds you there will be trouble."

She led the way back to the front door and closed it firmly behind him.

Wandering about for the next hour, he dwelt on what he was going to do without a car and nowhere to live. A glimmer of hope came in wondering if his car was still where he had left it in the woods. How was he to get there though? In desperation, he took out his mobile phone and pressed Amy's number. Perhaps there was a simple explanation for her not being at the flat.

Number not in use came up.

Who might help? He rang his solicitor.

John Simms was sympathetic but couldn't see what William expected him to do.

"Help me to find a job?"

John nearly choked. "You are kidding; with your track record?"

"Well at least give me a lift to where I left my car."

"I can do that," John agreed.

Arriving at the spot, William stared in horror. His pride and joy had been stripped of every movable part; only the engineless chassis remained.

"Well what did you honestly expect?" John asked.

"Thieves, bloody thieves!" William raged.

John gave him an astounded look. "Now that really is rich coming from you."

William returned the look indignantly before having the grace to blush.

"So where is the Anders' money, if you haven't got it?"

William was silent, still hoping that in the fullness of time, Monica would regret her actions and forgive him, in spite of what Peter had said.

John pressed the point. "Is Monica responsible, or has some other clever hacker got it? I know nothing has ever actually been proved against her, but circumstantial evidence—"

William interrupted him impatiently. "Monica left me because I fooled around with my secretary. She didn't need money, her first husband left her pots of it; he was a business tycoon and she was his secretary before they married."

John's eyes narrowed. It sounded convincing; the story never varied; and without doubt, William was, absolutely without funds. He had spent long hours trying to get to the bottom of the case. Was Monica just acting out of jealous revenge, by not coming forward and clearing him? It was far-fetched, but perhaps, just far-fetched enough to actually be true. He had put up a good defence and William was only found guilty of using company property to further his own ends. He could still be tried again for the bigger crime, if new evidence was discovered.

It was almost certain that William would be under surveillance, as would Peter and his wife; anything suspicious would be thoroughly looked into.

John asked where he wanted to go and William just spread his hands.

"The nearest park bench, unless you have a better idea."

"Peter would put you up, surely?"

"I suppose it's worth a try," William said looking doubtful.

Much to his surprise, Lindsey agreed that he could stay with them until he found something permanent, but he had to admit she sounded rather distracted.

With her baby due any time, all she really wanted to think about were preparations for the birth.

With time on his hands to brood, now that the problem of where to stay had been solved, William concentrated on a way to get the law off their backs, and eventually came up with an idea that appealed to his particular sense of justice.

CHAPTER TWENTY-EIGHT

In the time that Meg had lived at Anders Folly, they had followed a routine of dealing with the mountains of paperwork, after handing Jacob and Lucy over to Maisie each morning after breakfast.

On this particular morning, Samantha was opening the mail, while Meg dealt with emails at the newly installed computer, when Samantha suddenly exploded, "Wow, what do you make of this?"

Meg pushed herself out of Gerald's brown leather chair and joined her, wondering what had caused the outburst.

Samantha was holding a sheet of paper, which had arrived in the post, in a bright red envelope and Meg gave a gasp as she read the bold, capital letters.

"Can it be true? Is it possible?"

Samantha read the message aloud:

'IF YOU WANT TO KNOW WHO TOOK YOUR MONEY, ASK AMY BISHOP'.

"Well if she did, it was pretty cool, to sit tight while the Spencers got the blame."

"And why did they run away and make themselves look guilty. Perhaps Spencer was only running from the apartment fraud, like the solicitor said," Meg added, following Samantha's train of thought.

"I'll call Wendy and see what she says; she knew Amy better than we did."

When Wendy answered, Samantha read out the anonymous message.

"Well I know she is bright enough and certainly devious enough, but—" there was a long pause before, sounding thoughtful, Wendy said:

"It could be true; either that or someone has a score to settle with Amy Bishop." Wendy laughed. "I wish I had thought of it," she joked. "Seriously though, tell the police; you can't do anything, so don't even try. Someone could get hurt."

"I had a horrible feeling you would say that; it's what Bob would say," Samantha sighed.

"Well thank goodness for Mr Johnson; ask him to contact the police for you."

"Perhaps you're right."

"I am." Wendy sounded positive.

"Shame though, we could have had some fun," Samantha joked.

"Perhaps I should contact Mr Johnson myself," Wendy said, sounding worried.

Samantha became serious. "Don't worry; we are far too busy to chase Amy. Meg has come to live with me and it's the best thing that could have ever happened, for both of us. You are always welcome to visit; you haven't seen Jacob yet, have you?"

"I'm not sure when my holidays are due. I have taken a part time job in the local library since speaking to you last, and it is so interesting."

"Perfect for you; congratulations."

Listening to the one-sided conversation, Meg smiled to herself.

"What are you grinning at?" Samantha asked curiously, replacing the receiver.

"Come one, come all?"

"It's an Anders thing."

Bob considered the note should be taken seriously and said he would pass on the information right away. Samantha returned to sorting the rest of the post, talking excitedly about the possibility of recovering the money until George arrived with their morning coffee. She joked good-humouredly with him about narrowly missing out on another sleuthing job; then had to tell an impressed Meg about George's karate heroics.

"I would love to learn karate; will you teach me, George?"

Samantha laughed. "So I can expect to see one or other of you, or both, in plaster casts?"

George went off smiling, glad to see the girls laughing.

William kept darting nervous looks at Lindsey; she looked enormous and had been fidgety and restless all evening. The baby was due in ten days, and the thought of her going into labour frightened the life out of him. Monica should be here he fretted, anger flaring yet again at the way she had deserted them. Deep in thought, he missed Lindsey's sudden gasp of pain.

"Uncle William," she called between deep breaths. "Uncle William, I need to get to the hospital." Her voice rose as the pain she had been experiencing all day became stronger. She had suffered a lot of discomfort all the way through her pregnancy, and knowing there was still ten days to go, had spent the day convincing herself that, as the doctor had told her several times already, it was the baby lying on a nerve that was causing her such discomfort.

"Uncle William, help me, I think I'm having the baby!" she cried loudly and this time he heard and panicked.

"You can't; you've got ten days yet."

"Tell baby that," she grimaced.

"What shall I do? Remind me."

She had been over and over what to do, but feeling sure Peter would be there, he had only half listened, thinking instead of what the Anders family were doing about his anonymous letter.

"Call, Joanne. The number is on the pad."

He snatched up the phone and dialled the neighbour's number but the answer phone cut in.

"Answer phone!" he said, staring at her wildly.

"Help me to the car; get me to the hospital," Lindsey groaned.

He managed to help her out of the armchair and they got as far as the hall, before another agonising pain gripped her.

"I think, whew, whew the baby is – whew – coming."

She looked at him, panting, "Ring for an ambulance," before sinking into a heap on the stairs.

Spurred into action, William rang 999 and blurted out that his daughter was having her baby and he couldn't get her into the car. The nurse calmly told him the ambulance would be with them as soon as possible.

"Leave the line open, make her comfortable and tell me how long it is between contractions."

"Right." William darted upstairs, snatched two duvets and two pillows off the spare room beds and raced back to find Lindsey groaning. He tucked the phone under his chin, then feeling and sounding slightly calmer, told the nurse it was less than five minutes between contractions.

Working swiftly he spread the duvets on the floor and eased Lindsey back against the pillows as another contraction came.

He spoke to the nurse again and she asked to speak to Lindsey.

Lindsey nodded between panting and felt a lot better hearing a trained voice advising her. She handed the phone back and started to push. William had rolled his sleeves up, ready to follow the nurse's instructions, and the baby was born just as the ambulance men arrived and took over. He accompanied mother and baby to the hospital, looking proudly at what he regarded as all his own work.

Riding along the dark roads in the ambulance, Lindsey held her hand out to him and he grasped it. Monica had always jealously guarded and spoilt her only daughter, never seeking his opinion or looking to him for financial help. She was independently wealthy after the death of her first husband and it had greatly surprised William, when she had proposed to him. Lindsey and he had never become properly acquainted because she was a teenager and away at college most of the time. It pleased him now to be needed for the first time at the most important moment in her life.

At three o'clock in the morning, he got a taxi home, after spending time with Lindsey and her baby son and trying to contact Peter; he eventually sent a text saying: *'You have a son. Come home straight away, Lindsey needs you.'*

The reply came five hours later. *'Got important interviews all morning; can't make it 'til afternoon.'*

'Forget interviews. Get home now,' William ordered back immediately.

'Not poss, in with good chance for job. Home asap.'

William was livid. Peter had had two months to find a job, although why he had given up the one he had before finding another was beyond understanding, and why London?

*

Showered and dressed, Peter made his way down to breakfast. The hotel was smaller than the ones he usually stayed in, because there was less chance of anyone recognising him, especially anyone to do with the Anders family. Whilst waiting he took out his mobile and replied to the text that William had sent at three thirty that morning, then receiving and answering one more he switched the phone off. After returning home from Tenerife, he had avoided going out for nearly a month, in case Darren Anders was waiting for him, imagining Darren capable of doing anything to revenge his daughter. It had been bad enough being cooped up with Lindsey talking continually about the baby all day, but then Uncle William had arrived out of prison and kept asking what he was doing about a job. What with the house in constant preparation for the forthcoming birth, Lindsey waddling around all day looking the size of a house and sitting smoothing her huge belly every evening – always with that maddening contented smile, it was a wonder he was still sane. But the very last straw was when Joanne organised a baby crèche one afternoon and the house was full of babies, toddlers and women; some even pregnant themselves, invading his privacy, carrying parcels, displaying Winnie The Poo and Disney wrapping paper, and talking non-stop about the various forthcoming births. He hurriedly escaped to his den to avoid the revolting elephantine sights and stayed there until the last one had left. That was when he decided to risk London.

Later that evening, when peace was restored and Lindsey was sitting knitting contentedly, he told her he intended looking for a job in London, where nobody knew of Uncle William and the Anders scandal and she should put the house on the market now, to be ready to move up there with him.

"We need to get away and make a new start; just the two of us," he had said firmly, trying to disguise his feelings, while asking himself why on earth women were so hell bent on becoming pregnant, when it made them look so hideous.

As he had expected she said, "Can't you get a job closer, so that we can stay here? I love this house and it's all prepared for the baby now."

"The baby will be happy anywhere as long as it is with you. You need to think of me," he had answered, frowning petulantly.

The set expression that she wore so often of late, along with, "Let's wait and see if you get a job before we start making useless plans," left him mumbling, "Don't worry about me I'm only the dogsbody around here, now you're having a baby." He tutted and glanced up at the ceiling.

"Sorry, I was counting, what was that?"

"I said…" He stared across the space dividing their armchairs and shuddered; she was counting stitches again, with her knitting needles resting on her large, round belly and he knew he was wasting his breath.

Jerking himself out of his chair, he left the room and went upstairs, where he packed a suitcase, carried it down the wide, pine staircase and deposited it in the middle of the hall floor, where Lindsey was sure to see it.

That had happened six weeks ago and life had been more to his liking since.

Going home for the weekends was just about bearable, although with Uncle William there, life had changed; absolutely nothing was the same any more and he hated it. Now the baby had arrived there would be even more changes, he thought dolefully. Perhaps the idea of moving house wasn't such a good idea. Perhaps he would go on commuting; that way he could enjoy the bachelor life all week and still have home comforts on the weekend. Uncle William would definitely have to find himself somewhere else to live; he couldn't expect it to compare with his old life style, but he only had himself to blame; between them he and Monica had certainly stuffed things up for them all.

The waitress brought his breakfast and he automatically looked her up and down, noticing her trim waist and firm, young breasts but before he could make any overtures, his attention was caught by a well dressed figure entering the dining room. He watched her choose a table by the window, speculating on what she was doing in this part of the world and came to the probable conclusion: exactly what he was, finding a job away from the scandal of Anders. She looked more affluent he thought, remembering Amy's rather tarty, short skirts and low v-necks. He noticed how confidently she scanned the menu and ordered. Must have fallen on her feet with a new job, he decided enviously.

Losing interest, he finished his breakfast and left the dining room. With four hours to kill before the job interview, he purchased a daily paper, walked to the park and found an empty seat. An hour later, glancing up as he turned a page he saw Amy coming in his direction, and quickly opened the paper wide holding it up in front of him. She sauntered past, obviously not in any hurry to get to work, then seeming to change her mind, looked at her watch and hurried back towards the exit, passing him closely on her way.

Out of curiosity, he decided to follow her. She seemed to know where she was going as she hopped on a bus, and he managed to sit behind her and hear her destination. He paid his fare and rose to his feet when she did. It wasn't difficult to keep her cerise jacket in sight and he stayed well back, stopping when she did, to look in shop windows. Eventually she entered an exclusive looking boutique.

'So that's how you come to be looking prosperous,' he murmured, curiosity satisfied. 'No chance of a job for me then!'

With a wry grimace, he turned away. No point in going back to the hotel; his appointment was not too far away. He went into a coffee bar and sat near the window, thinking how lucky Amy was to have found a job where experience wasn't necessarily essential if you had good clothes sense. The job he was applying for was in advertising and his experience was nil. He didn't hold out much hope, but he had to be seen to be job seeking, after giving up the good job in Southampton where he would have been easy prey for Darren Anders.

Watching people milling along the pavement, a cerise jacket like Amy's caught his eye; then he realised it was Amy and she was carrying several large bright pink carrier bags with 'Estelle's' blazoned in purple lettering across the side.

He gaped. 'How the devil?'

Hurrying out, he was just in time to see her hail a taxi.

Arriving home at six o'clock, Peter was met by an angry William. He had been at the hospital most of the afternoon and Lindsey was upset that Peter had not turned up.

"I left a text for you, saying go straight to the hospital. Why have you come home first?"

"My phone needs charging. I didn't get it; and just in case you're interested I didn't get the job either."

"Why am I not surprised?" William sneered.

"If you must know I didn't keep the appointment."

"Why on earth not; how do you expect to get a job if you can't even be bothered to attend the interviews; and where the devil have you been then? You could have been home hours ago. Don't you want to see your son? What's the matter with you boy?" William was beside himself with impatience, but Peter's next words made him go pale and sit down.

"I've been talking to Amy Bishop." William's reaction gave him great satisfaction.

"How, where, when?" he managed to say at last.

"She is staying at my hotel. I followed her thinking it might lead to a job because she looked pretty well set up. I followed her back and we had lunch together; that was when she told me her aunt had died and left her a lot of money. Uncle – Uncle, are you alright?"

William was now red in the face, breathing hard and seemed to be having trouble in getting his words out, but Peter gradually understood him to be saying, "That's my money; she stole it; no wonder she doesn't need to work."

"Calm down Uncle, you'll give yourself a heart attack. What do you mean, it's your money?"

William explained everything, glad to get it off his chest at last, and Peter couldn't help quietly applauding Amy for putting one over on him. He obviously never intended sharing anything with her, no matter how much she helped him.

"She is almost certainly responsible for taking the eleven million as well, stay away from her," William warned.

"I thought you said Monica took it."

"I said she could have, not that she did; and the more I think about it, Monica would have settled for less."

"What about the house in Tenerife? That wasn't bought with loose change."

"You know Monica has money of her own. Lindsey says her mother only left me because she found out about Amy; that is why she won't come home and clear me."

Peter looked dubious. "And you believe that?"

"I don't know what to believe any more, but the Anders family will soon sort Amy out."

"I can't think why they would even suspect her – unless – what have you done, Uncle?"

William was agitatedly, arranging and rearranging the salt and pepper pots on the kitchen table with trembling fingers.

"I trusted her and she stole my money; I wasn't going to let her get away with it."

"You never trusted her, or you wouldn't have hidden it in the first place," Peter accused him. "You weren't ever going to take her with you, admit it."

"How could I? Monica was waiting for me."

"If you still believe that, you need to see a psychiatrist." Peter gave a disgusted snort. "I'm going to see Lindsey."

At the hospital, he bought flowers and a blue teddy bear and all dewy eyed, Lindsey forgave him his lateness, when he explained he had been to three interviews that day, before racing home to see his new son.

"I haven't even eaten yet," he lied, neglecting to mention the huge, late lunch he had shared with Amy at the hotel.

"You poor thing; take Uncle William to the village pub when you get home; he won't have eaten either. He has been absolutely amazing."

She went on to tell him of William's help, adding, "I don't know what I would have done without him."

"Quite the flavour of the month, isn't he? I could have done all that."

Peter looked resentful.

"Of course you could but you weren't here – he was." She gave him a consoling kiss on his cheek. "Perhaps, next time."

"You don't want another one?" Peter gazed in horror.

"No."

He relaxed a little, until she added:

"I want another three. I don't want our baby to be lonely like I was."

He left the hospital, feeling weak at the knees, comforting himself with the thought that she could take as long to conceive the next time.

214

CHAPTER TWENTY-NINE

Fran finished setting the table and took the meat out of the oven. Felicity and Charles were joining them for lunch and she planned on looking after Felicity for the afternoon to give Charles a break. He was tireless in his efforts to hold his and Felicity's life together but it was obviously taking its toll on him. They had always been like grandparents to her and she wished her home was large enough to accommodate them, but there was hardly a spare corner. The obvious solution was for them to move back to Anders Folly, where there would be plenty of help to look after Felicity. That was why she had invited Samantha and Meg to Sunday lunch as well. She had to do something because she knew Charles would never allow strangers in their home. Tears filled her eyes as she thought of their plight. After a lifetime together, their last years were to be fraught with sadness.

The sound of happy voices came from the hallway and she quickly brushed her hands over her eyes, turning to greet them as the twins rushed in and threw their arms around her waist. William followed, eager to tell how he had swum a full length of the swimming pool and James and Robert made straight for the fridge. Adam kissed the top of her head and peeked at the large joint of pork, resting on the stove.

"Which army are we feeding today, then?" He smiled fondly as she reached up to touch his wet hair.

"Apart from us you mean? Uncle Charles and Aunt Felicity will be here soon, and Samantha and Meg are bringing the babies. Will you carve the meat, when you are ready?"

He nodded and took a peep at the roast potatoes, finishing off in the oven.

"Mmm," he said appreciatively.

Robert handed him a can of beer from the fridge, his mouth full of sausage roll.

"You won't eat your dinner," Adam warned.

"That will be the day." Fran gave a resigned look at both Robert and James. It was impossible to fill them.

A car pulled into the drive and Charles got out and went round to open the door for Felicity; they stood for a moment while she got her balance, smiling into each other's eyes and Fran felt tears prick again as she watched from the window.

"Don't be sad, they have had a wonderful life," Adam comforted, coming and resting his arm along her shoulders.

She nodded wordlessly and went to greet them.

Over dinner, Felicity was very quiet, looking as if she didn't quite know where she was, until suddenly she looked at the head of the table and spoke to Adam, calling him Gerald, asking where Marie and David were.

"Uncle Charles needs help," Fran told Samantha as she and Meg were helping to clear the dishes.

"They should come to Anders Folly, but without Granddad there it upsets them too much."

"Circumstances have changed; wouldn't it be worth asking?" Fran asked hopefully.

To their surprise, anxious not to give up their home together, Charles agreed to spend weekdays at Anders Folly. Fran had to agree the compromise was better than nothing and to her relief the arrangement went well. Lorna would pack up a hamper and everyone helped, so between them they made it possible for Charles and Felicity to spend each weekend in their own home.

Anders Folly felt better with Charles there, even though he refused to sit at the head of the table; and although Gerald's chair remained empty, a place was always set.

Samantha still had times when grief threatened to overwhelm her, but an early morning ride on Nocturn with the dogs running alongside, and arriving home in time for breakfast with Meg and the children, helped to ease the dreadful gap in her life.

Entering the stable yard on one such morning she saw Sol talking to a stranger; as she watched they disappeared into the shed that Sol used as his office, and she went to get Nocturn from his stable. By the time she returned an hour later, there was no sign of the stranger and Sol was feeding the dogs.

Ella came out when she heard Samantha return and the three of them talked about a new horse arriving the following day.

"Was that the owner I saw you with this morning, Sol?" Samantha asked.

"Yes, Luke Hathaway; he's from America; doesn't waste words, but he seems okay."

"Does he live around here?"

"He's looking for somewhere," Sol replied slowly, eyeing Ella curiously, as she smiled happily.

Early the following day, a horsebox, driven by Luke Hathaway crunched onto the drive and Samantha, just back from her ride, watched from a distance as he led a beautiful pale grey mare into the stable yard where Sol was waiting to greet him.

"She will take a day to settle; she didn't like the plane ride," Samantha heard him say.

As always, Sol made gentle noises and the horse stood quietly.

"She's taken to you; good."

"We will be fine sir."

Samantha rode forward and slipped off Nocturn's back, eager to see her up close.

"She is absolutely beautiful, what do you call her?" Never taking her eyes off the mare, Samantha glided towards her, missing the startled look of her owner.

"Sapphire," he said briefly.

"Nice!" By now, she was stroking her long neck and whispering, "Hello Sapphire, you're beautiful. Nocturn is going to love you."

Sol gave a discreet cough.

"Excuse me Miss Samantha, this is Mr Hathaway. Miss Anders is the owner of Anders Folly, sir."

Samantha turned and looked at the stranger for the first time.

"I'm really sorry; that was rude of me. How do you do?" She held out her hand and smothered a gasp as it was caught in a strong grip.

"I know your father. He thinks we can do business. Has he spoken to you?"

"Not for several weeks actually, I think he is very busy." She smiled ruefully.

"Can we talk? I'm free anytime."

"When you have settled Sapphire in, perhaps?" she suggested hoping it didn't sound too keen; but she had a good feeling about him; probably because Daddy sent him she thought, hastily dismissing the fact that his broad shoulders, very short light brown hair and brown eyes, aroused feelings best ignored.

"Come to the house when you're ready." She turned away to hide her confusion.

"Will do," he called as she left the stable yard and made her way to the house.

Meg was already in the dining room. Lucy had started her breakfast but Jacob was waiting for his and letting them know in a very noisy way that he was hungry. Samantha sat down quickly and started to feed him his cereal.

"Sorry, Mummy got caught up by the new arrival," she soothed, practically shovelling the food in his mouth when he made it clear she was too slow.

"Don't fluster yourself; it doesn't hurt him to wait two minutes," Meg laughed. "I would have fed him but I know you like to."

She smiled happily, obviously loving the life and routine of Anders Folly and Samantha reminded herself of their pact that men were off the agenda, for the foreseeable future. Anyway what was she thinking? Hadn't her fingers been burnt enough? Why was she even considering listening to his business proposition? George could tell him to go away. Yes, that would be best.

The babies finished their breakfast and Maisie came and took them upstairs, just as George announced, "There's a gentleman ta see ya, Miss Samantha; shall I ask 'im ta wait in the mornin' room?"

"Oh. Show him in please, George," she heard herself saying.

Luke Hathaway entered and apologised. "Sorry I've come too soon; I'll come back." He turned to leave and her attention was drawn again to broad shoulders, perfectly cut, figure hugging 'Gucci' jeans and white T-shirt.

"No problem; have you had breakfast?" She couldn't believe she was saying this.

"Set another place please, George. Come and sit down Mr Hathaway, this is my friend Megan. She is also my personal assistant, so feel free to speak."

George brought coffee and while they waited for breakfast to arrive, he explained that he wanted to rent the airfield. It was just what he was looking for, to start a flying school and other small ventures.

Samantha tried her best not to look eager, but the look on her face, when she realised how many problems it could solve spoke volumes and he said, "So that looks like a yes?"

Samantha took a deep breath, flecks of gold shining in her green eyes as she nodded enthusiastically.

Breakfast arrived and they helped themselves from the dishes on the sideboard.

"One other thing," Luke said between mouthfuls. "Your Dad also said you might be willing to rent a cottage to me, until I find somewhere to buy; but he wasn't sure of your plans for it."

Samantha looked resigned. "That sounds as if he doesn't intend to live there any more."

"He does seem very happy with life at the moment," Luke said philosophically.

"Well then, you are welcome to the cottage for as long as it takes. I'll show you round and you can have the key today, if you like."

Luke held his hand out as he was leaving. "Good doing business with you, Miss Anders."

"Call me Samantha."

"Samantha." He shook her hand, briefly, but their eyes met and held a little longer.

Watching them, Meg had qualms; the attraction between them was obvious, but she hoped with all her heart that Samantha wasn't going to let him take advantage of her.

They always spent the day with Jacob and Lucy on Sunday but to Meg's disappointment, after they returned from a walk on the beach, Samantha asked her to keep an eye on Jacob while she showed Luke the cottage. Could it not have waited until tomorrow she fretted, peeved when Luke turned up for the second time that day and Samantha left the house with him.

She watched until they disappeared from sight, before turning her attention to the children.

Memories came flooding back as Samantha unlocked the cottage door. It seemed like forever since Bryn had spent that afternoon with her. She quickly brushed the thought away and showed Luke around, reliving the touch of Bryn's hand in hers as Luke followed her up the stairs.

He was impressed and delighted to have the offer of living in such a charming place and said so immediately.

"I'll move in tomorrow if that is okay." Regarding her sad face, he wondered if she really wanted to rent the cottage out, but she quickly assured him it would help, having it occupied, and then appeared to be in a hurry to leave.

"I've taken up enough of your day," he apologised on the way back down the path.

"Not at all, in fact I was wondering, if you felt like taking Sapphire and Nocturn for a quiet ride along the cove. It might help to settle her for the first night."

He stopped and turned to face her. "That would be perfect; if you are sure you are happy to."

"I'm always happy when I'm with Nocturn," she said, catching him unawares with a brilliant smile; leaving him slightly mesmerised.

The two horses kept pace with each other and Luke was obviously an experienced rider. He was impressed that she liked to ride bare back and agreed it was his favourite way. They parted after a very relaxed afternoon; Samantha felt she had known him for years and returned starry eyed, to find Meg playing with Lucy, and Jacob fast asleep in the big old-fashioned pram on the terrace.

Meg was feeling left out, but bathing the little ones together in the big bath, soon brought back her sunny smile and if Samantha's attention wandered as they sat together watching television that evening, the faraway look in her green eyes and the smile playing about her lips, went unnoticed.

First thing the following morning, she telephoned her father and told him of the successful arrangements they had made. Darren sounded enthusiastic and asked what she thought of Luke.

"He seems okay," she said cautiously.

"Only okay? Mamma thought you would really like him." He sounded disappointed.

"I hardly know him, but he does love horses, so I suppose he can't be all bad." She purposely sounded offhand.

Melly's voice came over the line. "Are you teasing your father, Sam?" she asked.

"Kind of; are you two matchmaking?" Samantha rejoined.

"Kind of," Melly said hearing the smile in her voice and giving Darren the thumbs up.

Darren's voice came back. "I'm really glad he is taking over the airfield Princess; shame to let it go to waste. By the way, I put in a good word for Jonathan Sugden and Mark. I said you would have their home addresses."

"That was thoughtful Daddy; they will appreciate that, coming from you."

"Nice to know I can do the right thing some times."

Although the words were familiar, he didn't sound as sorry for himself any more, Samantha thought with relief.

"I think you have made the right move Daddy; you both sound really happy."

"Couldn't be better – unless you were here with us," he added hastily.

"How is Jack? Tell him his big sister misses him and hopes he misses her."

There was a slight catch in her voice as she said it and Darren said, "Are, you alright Sam?"

"I'm fine; just make sure you all come home for Christmas."

"That's a promise, Princess."

Meg came into the study when she heard the call finish and Samantha asked her to look up the addresses of Jonathan and Mark; thinking that later on she would walk up and give them to Luke, even help him to settle in.

It was after lunch before she was free to go to the cottage and looking up from reading emails, Meg sighed, hoping as she saw her hurrying up the path that she wasn't heading for a fall again.

The horse box stood in the drive, with its doors wide open, displaying an array of packing cases. Luke was inside, moving smaller boxes onto the tailboard and she called out to him.

"Hi there, need any help?"

"Hi; they are too heavy for you; Sol said he would come up later and help with the big boxes, if you don't mind that is."

"I can help with the small ones." She went to lift one but found it was as he said.

"Books," he explained. "The office equipment is lighter." He pointed to briefcases and empty filing cabinets.

"Where do you want them?" she asked, picking up two large briefcases.

"I thought I might turn the small bedroom into an office."

"That seems a good idea." It suddenly occurred to her that he might be married and her heart gave a painful jolt, but remembering that Melly wouldn't have considered him suitable, if that was the case, she happily carried the cases up the stairs and returned for more. When the lighter things were cleared, Luke dealt with the heavier ones while she went to make a cup of tea.

"There's milk in the fridge and tea bags in the box on the breakfast bar," Luke called from upstairs.

They sat on garden chairs, looking out over the sea, companionably dipping biscuits in their tea and Luke commented:

"What a wonderful place this is; you don't want to sell the cottage, I suppose?"

"I can't deny it would help me out of a spot, but it's not an option; Grandfather would never forgive me, if I split the estate."

"Even if it helped your financial problem?" Luke asked, not trying to change her mind; just curious as to why her grandfather would burden her with such expectations. He had heard her father's reasons for not taking on his inheritance, but after seeing the place, he thought Darren Anders was mad. He studied her, admiring not just her beauty but her deep sense of loyalty. A woman to trust.

CHAPTER THIRTY

Peter changed gear and put his foot down on the accelerator, quickly gathering speed and passing the other traffic on the motorway. His spirits rose with anticipation as London signs appeared. He was free, free from Uncle William's nagging and best of all free from smelly nappies and the awful smell of breast milk on Lindsey's clothing.

What a disgusting performance that was. How could he ever feel the same about making love to her again?

Booking into his hotel, he took a deep breath and looked about with a sense of relieved anticipation. Just that morning he had learnt about Darren Anders move to America, so he could scrap the idea of selling the house to move up here, because this arrangement suited him much better. He would have to find a job of course: nothing too demanding, just enough to pay his way. Lindsey was paying the bills, doubtless with Monica's help, because Uncle William actually didn't have a bean; Monica had made a real job of clearing him out. He couldn't help smiling; talk about a woman scorned. He had given a lot of thought to William's accusation. Had Amy stolen the money from Anders? It didn't seem likely, but on the other hand, it would be worth investigating. She had obviously had no qualms about taking William's three hundred thousand.

He came out of his reverie as the desk clerk turned the register towards him and handed him a key.

"If you would just sign, sir."

Peter signed his name with a flourish; bent to pick up his case, started to walk away, then turned back. "By the way, is Miss Bishop still staying here?"

The clerk looked at the register. "No one of that name is booked in, sir."

About to contradict, Peter changed his mind. "Sorry, must have got my wires crossed."

He walked away and stood waiting for the lift, visualising in his mind's eye, the hotel key that Amy had been carrying on the afternoon they lunched together. The numbers 112 danced in his mind and without further hesitation he decided to investigate.

A cleaner was leaving the room as he approached and he gave her a friendly smile.

"I thought a friend, who I only met last week, said she was in 112, but I could be wrong. I only know her as Amy; do you happen to know the surname of the person occupying this room?"

The girl ran her finger down a list. "Amy Brentwood."

"Thanks a lot. I'll catch her later."

Going up to his room on the next floor, he realised she would hardly use her own name if she didn't want to be traced, but she had kept her initials. It all pointed to guilt. An idea began to form.

Taking up a position in the lobby, with a good view of the entrance, he glanced over his paper each time the swing doors opened. The restaurant closed at two thirty and at quarter to two, he was about to give up and go into lunch, when Amy made an entrance. He classed it as that because she looked quite stunning, in a black silk, open neck, shirt, under a winter white trouser suit, a black trilby hat with a white band and black patent, Prada shoes with four inch heels.

He stared in spite of his previous opinion of her. Who would have thought she would scrub up that well? He caught up as she walked towards the restaurant and fell into step.

"Hi, I was just going into lunch; shall we share a table?"

"Might as well; it looks pretty full." She strode ahead and claimed the last table, stepping in front of an elderly couple, who were heading in that direction.

"Some people," the woman said indignantly.

"Did you say something?" Amy challenged, sitting down and giving her a hostile look.

"Come away dear," the man said.

Peter hung back, not wanting to be involved and Amy picked up the menu to choose a wine.

"Are you drinking wine, or have you got an interview to go to?" she asked in her direct manner.

"Yes to the first question, no to the second." Sounding equally direct he smiled disarmingly. "Relax, we could do something if you like; my time is my own, for today."

She hesitated, liking his change of attitude towards her, but not altogether trusting him. He had snubbed her when Samantha Anders was around. She scowled at the mere thought of that stupid girl.

"What would you like to do?" Peter asked in a persuasive tone.

"What would *you* like to do?" she asked staring at him over the menu.

"I'm sure we will think of something," he stared back.

"We could go for a walk in the park, or you could take me shopping," she suggested innocently.

"That wasn't quite what I had in mind." He was flirting openly with her now, allowing his light grey eyes to drop to her cleavage, noticing her breasts swell as her imagination soared. Her eyes grew sultry and for a moment she looked ready to leap across the table; obviously fighting the urge, she calmly picked up her wine glass, which the waiter had just filled.

They eyed each other, aware of the other's racing hormones; and when the food arrived had quite lost their appetites. Finishing off the wine, they gave the sweet trolley a miss and left the restaurant with as much speed as decorum would allow, because by now Amy could hardly contain herself.

"My room is the nearest," she said in a clipped voice, while they waited for the lift.

"Your room it is then," he said calmly, staring at her heaving breasts.

Once inside the room, she threw her hat and coat off, then her trousers and last of all her blouse, revealing scarlet pants and bra. He stared, whilst quickly undressing, his practised eye telling him that she needed him as much as he needed her. Two athletic hours later left him wondering at Uncle William's stamina.

Sitting up in bed, she looked down at him. "I'm starving, let's order room service; I want sandwiches and champagne. They make the most divine crab sandwiches." She picked up the phone.

"It will have to be charged to your room, my receipts are scrutinised at home."

"No problem." Speaking into the phone, she pressed herself against him and it was almost a relief when the food arrived. They sat at a small, round table to eat and the sandwiches were indeed excellent. Amy obviously knew how to live up to her stolen money.

Picking his moment, he said, "There is something I think I should tell you."

"What's that?" she asked with a triumphant little smile, expecting a compliment; shocked into silence, when he said, "William has sent an anonymous letter, saying you took the money."

"Whaaat?" she said finally. "Who to?"

"The police I imagine," he lied, watching her turning it over in her mind.

"What money?" she asked giving a loud, false laugh.

224

"Does three hundred thousand pounds ring any bells?" He quirked his eyebrow at her and she shook her head.

"Hidden in a briefcase, in your flat?" he tried again."

"First I've heard of it." She sipped her champagne and stared him straight in the eyes.

He returned the stare with a sardonic smile. "You don't have to pretend with me; everything points to you; it couldn't be anyone else. It will be so easy for the police to check your story about inheriting money from your aunt."

For a second, she looked uncertain. "Well as a matter of a fact, that was a lie. I actually won it on the lottery and asked to stay anonymous."

"That's better, that's much better; I should stick to that story. Best of luck to you I say; he never did intend taking you away – it was always going to be his wife. All that aside though, it isn't that paltry sum he is accusing you of taking, it is the eleven million, transferred from Anders Motors, by computer; that is what I thought you should know." He paused for effect. "That is why they are looking for you; you would do well to stop drawing attention to yourself, Miss Brentwood. Changing your name doesn't change your appearance and I imagine your picture is being circulated as we speak."

She looked at him sharply. "You've been snooping."

"Aren't you glad I have? Forewarned is forearmed."

"I haven't the faintest idea what you are talking about," she said coldly, jumping up and nervously adjusting the tie belt on her lace negligee. "I think it's time you went; you are becoming tiresome."

"I'm not kidding. William told me the whole story on the weekend and he will stop at nothing to clear Monica, even to blaming you. Taking the briefcase was a mistake. Why did you do that? It was just greedy and silly; you left him with nothing; that's why he is getting his own back."

Amy sneered. "He must be out of his mind. How could I have transferred that money?"

"You know how to use a computer; you were privy to all the passwords. In fact, I'm already half convinced you did it, just on William's story alone, so the police are sure to investigate; and I doubt he will content himself with just the one anonymous letter; he was pretty hopping mad, when he told me."

Amy looked ready to cry. "I don't believe he would do that."

"He didn't believe you would steal his money."

"So why did he hide it? Anyway it wasn't his money; it came from the apartments."

Peter hid a satisfied smile. "We know that, but will the police believe anything you say, if it comes out? Lindsey is absolutely convinced her mother is innocent, she has told them Monica only ran away because William was having an affair with you, and you did stay in the building on the night of the robbery. Passwords and keys to the accounts department were all at hand and available. It doesn't look good, does it?"

She was pacing up and down, looking extremely agitated now.

"So what do you want?" She stopped pacing and glowered at him.

"Just a good life; let's go abroad and live."

Amy looked wary. "Are you saying you will leave your wife?"

His demeanour changed. "Things aren't working out for me, so yes, that is exactly what I'm saying."

She still looked wary. "I heard a rumour that you got the Anders girl pregnant; is it true?"

"Of course not; do you think I'm insane? Her father would have my guts for garters."

"It would serve the stuck-up madam right if somebody has."

Peter laughed. "How right you are, but forget her, let's talk about us."

Amy relaxed slightly, considering the idea of having someone to share her life with.

"When?" she asked.

"Next week? I'll go home on the weekend as usual and leave Monday morning, as normal."

Amy gave an excited giggle at the reawakened opportunity of a new life, plus a far younger partner.

"Where shall we go?"

"Tenerife," Peter said without hesitation. "It's the only place I'm absolutely sure Monica won't be."

Amy gave a puzzled frown then laughed as he described Monica's hasty exit, leaving him stranded.

"Lucky she did leave when she did; I don't know who tipped them off but they were really hot on her heels and she only just got away in time. That was why they arrested me when I came back; they thought I was in cahoots with her." He finished with a grin and emptied the rest of the champagne into their glasses, having thoroughly enjoyed his embellishment of the situation.

On the Friday evening, he wavered. Liam, as they had decided to call the baby, was in bed and Lindsey had cooked a special dinner to celebrate his homecoming. William was not expected back until late and everything was as it used to be. They ate by candlelight then sat on the settee together watching television. Lindsey disappeared every half an hour to check on the baby and returned with a gentle smile on her face, assuring him that, "Your son looks even more beautiful when he is sleeping. You should go and check next time."

Peter poured himself more wine.

"Don't babies usually have bottles," he asked irritably, viewing her large swollen breasts with disgust.

After a full lecture on breast milk and bonding, he regretted asking. Then William returned home and Lindsey disappeared to give Liam his ten o'clock feed. Thankfully, William was full of his golf club dinner and bedtime came, without any awkward questions or frayed tempers. All was calm and peaceful and they slept until five o'clock, when, without warning, Liam let out a lusty yell.

"What the devil?" Peter exploded, nearly shooting out of bed, as Lindsey switched the bedside lamp on, explaining cheerfully that Liam was hungry.

"Not again. Not in the middle of the night," he groaned.

"He has done really well to go this long," she said, still in the same cheerful, unbothered voice bringing Liam into bed with them. Peter turned away; the mere sight of Lindsey's enlarged nipples made him feel sick. Twenty minutes later there was a strong smell and he sat bolt upright again.

"Oo that's better," Lindsey was cooing as Peter screwed up his face.

"No it isn't, it's obscene," he said leaping out of bed.

Lindsey calmly took Liam into the nursery to change his nappy, leaving Peter spraying the room with perfume.

"There, that's better, now you can go to Daddy while I clean myself up," she cooed, returning a few minutes later, with a smiling baby.

Placing a cotton nappy over Peter's shoulder, she laid Liam on it showing Peter how to burp him.

"Just in case," she smiled gazing at them both proudly.

"Just in case what?" he asked with an alarmed expression as she went into the bathroom and called. "He might bring a little milk back up."

As she said it, Liam gave a huge burp and sprayed, missing the nappy because Peter jerked him away.

"Aargh, take it," he shouted as Liam began to cry and Lindsey came rushing back to rescue him.

"That's it." Peter wrenched his pyjama top off and threw it on the floor. "Now I'll have to shower; then I'm sleeping in the other room."

Lindsey looked dismayed but calmly set about cleaning Liam up.

"Perhaps that would be best, until he starts sleeping right through," she agreed understandingly, watching Peter disappear into the bathroom.

By Sunday lunchtime, he couldn't wait to get away and under the pretext of sorting his wardrobe he packed several cases and took them out to the car while Lindsey was cooking lunch. He didn't notice William, on his knees weeding the flower bed, until he looked up to see him staring at the three large cases as he stowed them in the boot of his car.

"What's with all the luggage? William asked curiously.

"Just some stuff I thought I would get rid of. A shop in London will give me a fair price for the designer bits." To hide his confusion he reached in the boot, brought out a chamois leather and started wiping the windows.

"Things must be bad," William joked, turning back to the weeding.

"They are. In fact, I've changed my mind; I intend travelling back tonight; I have an interview first thing in the morning and can't risk being late for it."

"That makes sense," William answered losing interest. He couldn't pull strings, as he had in the past and he was tired of hearing about his nephew's failed interviews, especially when Peter never let him forget that he couldn't get another job in this part of the world because of the Anders scandal.

Neither of them said much at the dinner table but Lindsey was too busy thinking about Liam's two o'clock feed to notice, and as soon as the meal was over, she disappeared upstairs to the nursery.

"Do you want to wash or wipe?" William raised his eyebrows and Peter stared back as if he was mad.

"I don't do either," he said loftily.

"Then you should; Lindsey needs help."

Peter gave him a withering look and went upstairs. Fifteen minutes later, he came down and the front door slammed behind him. William went into the hall in time to see him drive away without a backward glance and in that moment knew they wouldn't see his nephew again. His only concern he realised with a slight shock was how Lindsey would take it.

The following weekend though, when Peter failed to come home after no word all week, she didn't even comment, and they lived this strange life, where she never mentioned him ever again. Liam was her world now.

To William's relief she asked him if he would like to live with them permanently and to his intense pleasure, started to call him Dad.

William treasured the relationship that had developed between them, since the night Liam was born, and unexpectedly found that being a dad to her and granddad to Liam completely fulfilled his sense of belonging.

Lindsey's confident attitude in the following weeks also put his mind at rest. Losing Peter had always been her worst fear and would have destroyed her at one time, but motherhood had given her a new strength.

CHAPTER THIRTY-ONE

Samantha reached the stable yard as Sol was opening up the doors, and Luke arrived a minute or two later. As they slipped reins over Nocturn and Sapphire's necks, they exchanged views on a project that Luke had suggested. Their ride this morning was to plan an adventure trail, leading through the woods, across meadows to the outskirts of Anders Folly and back to the stables.

"Hopefully it will drum up more business and create an element of fun," Luke confided to Sol as he sat astride Sapphire and watched Samantha swing effortlessly up on to Nocturn's back.

It was a fine morning, with a slight sea mist hanging over the ground promising a hot day. Starting from the long cove, they rode up and over bare cliff tops, making their way inland to where trees and hedges merged into almost untrodden woodland. Rabbits scuttled at the intrusion of their domain and the horses snorted, startled by the swift flash of brown or grey darting through the undergrowth.

"There's a green woodpecker," Luke whispered, pointing to a large oak tree.

Following his gaze Samantha saw a largish green bird, clinging to the trunk, hardly visible except for its bright red head.

As they went deeper, also disturbed by the invasion, squirrels leapt from branch to branch and a fox slunk away to its den, in a grassy bank; only his disappearing brush giving away the well-hidden lair. The atmosphere was hushed and the horses' hooves made little sound on the leaf-covered ground as they rounded a bend and came upon a small, fallow deer; ears pricked, standing stock still in the middle of the path, it stared straight at them with huge Bambi eyes. They reined the horses in, watching entranced as the beautiful creature stretched its neck, and with one silent bound, slipped away, disappearing like a shadow back into a leafy glade of overhanging trees. Samantha and Luke smiled softly at each other, sharing the magical moment.

"Have you never come here before?" Luke whispered.

"A long time ago, Bob our groom brought me, but I had forgotten how beautiful it was," she whispered back.

At one with their surroundings, they both felt the need to whisper in this serene, dreamlike place.

"I want to remember this always." He gazed at her with longing and she was, helplessly captivated as he slid to the ground and held his arms up. Slipping down into a tender embrace, she felt her senses swimming as his gentle, demanding ardour enveloped them. Not even the sound of Sol's horse aroused them until he came upon them suddenly and was only yards away.

"I'm sorry sir, but George says there is a lady at the house, insisting she won't leave until she has spoken to you."

Sol had turned Bucephalus around and was keeping his eyes averted, as embarrassed at having interrupted the intimate moment, as they were at being discovered.

"I'll get back and let her know you will be along shortly." Sol hastily retreated, as Luke found his voice at last.

"Thank you Sol; I will be right behind you."

Still half-dazed, Samantha looked at him questioningly.

"I think I'm in love with you, Sam. There are things I should have told you, before allowing myself to get carried away. I hope you can forgive me."

Filled with wonder, she answered, "I think I loved you the moment I saw you. Nothing can come between us, unless we let it."

He kissed her gently on the lips. "Hold that thought."

They rode back, blissfully happy, aware that the purpose of their ride had not been accomplished, but certain that a wide detour would be taken to avoid that one particular area of the woods when planning the adventure trail.

"She says she's is wife." George paced up and down the kitchen, while Lorna tried to calm him and Dora growing more and more excited, rolled the pastry until it was paper-thin.

"D'you think ther'll be a fight?" she asked, her eyes shining.

"What I think is that you should get on with ye work and keep a still tongue in ye head," Lorna reprimanded sternly, annoyed that George had spoken in front of her niece. Unlike Maisie, Dora was a gossip and hadn't been at Anders Folly long enough to learn respect. Lorna frowned heavily. "What goes on behind these walls, stays behind these walls, and don't you forget it Miss or you'll have me to deal with."

Suitably chastened, Dora got on with her work. Aunt Lorna seldom got really angry, but she wasn't one to be taken lightly when she did.

Voices in the hall made George hurry to tell Samantha the visitor was in the morning room, but on reaching the hall, he saw the woman already walking towards them, having seen them arrive through the window over-looking the drive, no doubt.

"Luke darling," she hurried forward and attempted to greet him, but he caught her arms and held her firmly away. "No silly games, Kelly. What are you doing here?"

"I came to bring Kimberley."

Luke turned to Samantha. "Samantha, this is Kelly, my ex-wife. I'm sorry for the intrusion. Kelly, you are in Samantha's home; we will talk, but not here."

Her eyes flashed suspiciously in Samantha's direction, before she turned to Luke with a challenging look. "I told Kimberley we would be staying with you."

"Kimberley will stay with me; you will find a hotel."

Samantha saw the look turn hostile.

Luke turned to Samantha. "I'll call later if I may."

He took Kelly's arm and guided her to the door and Samantha heard her sneering voice mimicking, "I'll call later if I may."

Luke strode towards her parked car, only the set of his shoulders showing how angry he was. Peering in the rear window, he turned towards Kelly, saying something that Samantha couldn't hear, but his expression had softened.

She watched as they exchanged words, then Kelly got into the driving seat, and Luke opened the rear door allowing a small child to clamber out and run to him. Picking her up he perched her on his shoulders and strode towards the cliff path, disappearing quickly towards the cottage.

Samantha bit her lip as she caught sight of the child's delighted face, knowing with a sinking heart that she was Kimberley. She made her way slowly to the terrace where Meg, unaware of what had just taken place, was playing with Lucy and Jacob.

"That didn't take long, did you decide on a trail?"

"No, we had to come back."

Meg raised her eyebrows.

"Visitors," Samantha said absently.

"Not altogether welcome ones, by the look on your face." Meg had an uncanny knack of hitting the nail on the head.

"No not altogether." A faraway look came into Samantha's eyes as she relived the moment in the woods.

"Oh dear, I've seen that look before; you're falling for him aren't you?"

"Just a bit."

Meg's face fell. "You hardly know him, please take care," she begged

"I will, I promise." Samantha smiled softly and Meg tutted, tossing her eyes. "Some hope. Who were the visitors anyway? Must have been important, to make him rush back like that."

"His wife and little girl," Samantha answered dreamily, then seeing Meg tense, corrected herself. "I should have said his ex-wife," as Meg scowled.

"Why has she turned up; are they getting back together?" she asked hopefully.

"You know as much as I do," Samantha answered calmly.

"So where are they now?" Meg asked, hating the thought of her being hurt again.

"Don't worry; everything will be alright."

"Huh. Where have I heard that before?"

Jacob started to cry and Samantha went to him.

"Why don't we go for a walk on the beach?" she suggested, too restless to stay indoors. She was worried about what was happening up at the cottage, but Luke had said he loved her and she badly wanted to believe him; this time it was different. Bryn would always have a place in her heart and the memory of Peter's lovemaking still excited her; but when she looked at Luke she could imagine spending her whole life with him at Anders Folly. His wife was extremely pretty though. Oh please let him stay with me, she begged.

"What's she like, then?" Meg asked as if reading her thoughts.

"Hard to say; he is obviously very angry with her."

"I mean, what – does – she – look – like?" Meg stressed.

"Mmm. Small, blonde and very pretty," Samantha admitted reluctantly.

The tide was right out and they wheeled Jacob and Lucy to the next cove in their small pushchairs, the wheels making tyre marks in the sand. In spite of her determination not to, Samantha looked up at the cottage. Only the chimney pots were visible above the windbreak of trees and knowing the cottage as well as she did she tried to picture where they would be sitting. The sitting room, the breakfast bar, sharing a glass of wine, or were they in the bedroom? If so was it the master bedroom, with the lovely lace trimmed, silk hangings; or the bedroom overlooking the ocean – the one that Tamara had occupied before her?

Luke's sincere brown eyes danced in front of her and she became aware of Meg touching her arm and asking, "Are you alright, Sam?"

She nodded, forcing her thoughts away from the pictures in her head.

"You looked as if you had seen a ghost, for a minute."

With one last glance in the direction of the cottage, she made an effort to make the walk interesting for Meg.

Since coming to Anders Folly, Meg had been more than content to work and be able to spend time with Lucy, always conscious of how different her life was and grateful to Samantha for the safe home she was providing for them.

When Samantha saw her looking too grateful, she would point out what a difference it made having another baby and company of her own age in the house.

Now as they walked companionably together, Samantha talked about the plan to create a trail through the surrounding acres, and the part Meg could play by making a plan on the computer and dealing with the bookings.

"Only if you want to, of course," Samantha said seeing Meg's doubt.

"I assumed Luke would be taking over." She sounded peeved.

"Good heavens, no. He will be too busy at the airfield when it opens in three weeks' time. The trail was his idea and he is helping to plan it because he took part in that sort of thing in America, but we will be left to make the idea work."

Meg was consoled but still looked doubtful.

"You only have to say if you don't want to," Samantha said sounding disappointed.

"I would love to, on one condition," Meg hastened to assure her.

"And that is?"

"I won't have to go near the horses."

Samantha gave a relieved laugh. "I promise. Not until you ask."

"Don't hold your breath."

"Time we went back; the tide is on the turn. Lunch will be ready soon. Just time to get changed." Samantha looked regretfully down at her jodhpurs. "We obviously won't continue the trail today."

"Wasn't Luke supposed to be coming to lunch?"

"I can't imagine that will happen either; I expect they will eat at the cottage."

She sounded miserable and Meg asked what happened to the girl who said everything would be all right.

Samantha pictured a pair of sincere brown eyes and smiled. "Thanks," she said simply.

It was late evening when Luke finally telephoned. Samantha was in her bedroom getting ready for bed. He apologised for leaving it so late and explained that six-year-old Kimberley had only just settled down. He also asked if she would mind his daughter staying with him, offering to move into a hotel if she wasn't happy with the idea.

Samantha assured him she had no objection, realising with a sinking heart that their feelings for one another were going to have to wait and afraid he was going to be snatched away from her.

"I meant what I said this morning," Luke said sincerely.

"Me too," she said tremulously.

They said goodnight and Samantha sat at the Chippendale dressing table she had inherited from great grandmother Pamela, brushing her waist length, auburn hair, picturing his face just before he kissed her that morning.

"Please don't leave me," she whispered.

Two more days went by, with only a brief telephone call each night and although Luke insisted everything would be settled very soon, he sounded worried and angry and she agonized over why he and his wife had parted and whether they would get back together for Kimberley's sake, because he obviously adored his daughter.

She caught sight of them from the study window on the second morning. Luke was riding Sapphire and Kimberley was obviously at home on Bonnie, one of the ponies from the stable. She rode well Samantha noticed, admiring her straight back and relaxed hands on the reins. Being mid-morning, he would know there was no chance of them bumping into each other she thought sadly, missing their six o'clock ride together. Oh, why didn't they just leave, so that she and Luke could be together again? She threw a pencil across the desk in frustration, drawing Meg's attention away from the computer, to follow Samantha's gaze and give a helpless little sigh.

When he left Anders Folly, Luke reached the top of the cliff path at the same time as Kelly pulled onto the cottage drive. She had slammed the car door giving him a mutinous look as he lowered Kimberley to the ground, telling her to go and play on the big swing hanging from the tree.

Once she was out of hearing he asked, "Why are you here and how did you find me? We agreed I would collect Kimberley in two weeks' time, to spend the summer holidays with me."

"Things have changed."

Luke looked suspicious. "What things?"

"Chas and I have split up."

"Why?"

Kelly shrugged. "He met someone else."

"That doesn't sound like Chas."

235

"He's changed since you knew him," she sneered avoiding his searching gaze.

"I hear he has financial problems. Is that why you are splitting up?"

"Why should you care?" Her baby blue eyes flashed icily.

"Exactly, why should I?" He shrugged, realising he should have seen this coming.

"He expected me to start roughing it in some downtown little house," she said, tossing her head.

"Why should that worry you? You were with the man you loved," he reminded her.

She blushed furiously and snapped back. "Why else do you think I married you, if not to get away from there?"

It was Luke's turn to go red and he turned away, but Kelly wasn't finished.

"You and I didn't stand a chance, with that mean father of yours and your sickening, schoolboy friendship." She stood hands on hips, with a gloating smile playing about her rosebud mouth. "I put paid to that though. It was the only way to break the two of you up."

"Why?" Luke asked incredulously.

"Just to know I could; what a pair of simpletons you were,"

"Yes, we were." His voice was filled with irony. "We were both in love with you all through our school and college days."

"That was what gave me the idea," she gloated.

"That was as much as he meant to you?"

"A wealthy lifestyle was all you both meant to me; that is why I'm here now. I know how much you want her, so you can have your daughter."

Luke looked wary. "What are you saying?"

"You can have sole custody in exchange for two million pounds."

Luke gave a surprised gasp. "You would really do that?"

"Yes." She was watching his face, holding her breath.

His eyes narrowed, taking in her perfect, petite figure, long, natural blonde hair and wide, pale blue eyes; visualising how he had been captivated by that helpless little girl look for as long as he could remember. Then the vision changed to a tall, slim girl with long chestnut hair and trusting eyes. Mistaking his faraway look for shock Kelly asked:

"Not worried about a measly two million are you? I deserve more."

Seeing him glance fondly in her direction as Kimberley waved to him laughing happily, she was confident he would agree.

"You know? I feel sorry for you," he said seriously.

236

"Save your pity for someone who needs it. Just give me the money and you won't see me again."

Luke gave a mirthless laugh. "Well strangely I don't keep that amount on me, but don't worry, it will be signed into the agreement."

She looked startled. "We don't need an agreement; we can settle between ourselves, like grownups. It will take months to go through the courts."

He held his arms out and Kimberley ran to him.

"I will get things moving straight away. There is a hotel four miles down the road. I will be in touch."

He went to her car and opened the boot. "Which is Kimberley's case?"

"All of them."

He raised his eyebrows and lifted out the five cases. "So you planned to leave her, anyway?"

"I assumed you would want to just write a cheque if it meant her staying permanently."

"Curious, after all of your previous protests, that you are suddenly in such a hurry to unload your only daughter," he said in an aside, so that Kimberley didn't hear.

"Do you want her or not?" Kelly challenged sharply.

For answer, he picked up two of the large suitcases. "Come on Poppit I'll show you to your bedroom."

Kelly left without saying goodbye and Kimberley skipped into the cottage, following Luke upstairs to Samantha's old room.

That evening he called his solicitor, in America, then sent a text to Kelly asking her to meet him in three days' time at the hotel where she was staying. When they arrived, she was very agitated to see he wasn't alone, but was prepared to sign any paper then and there, if Luke dispensed with the formality of going through an American court. She tried to insist on it being finalised that day because she was taking an early flight out the next morning to keep a very important appointment, but the solicitor politely pointed out that nothing could be done until official papers were drawn-up. She became very angry and said that unless it was settled right then the agreement was off.

"It will take time to release such a large sum, anyway," Luke reasoned.

The solicitor frowned; money hadn't been mentioned until then.

"What are we talking about here?" he asked.

"It's a private agreement between the two of us," Kelly snapped.

"I would still like it written into the sole custody agreement; I did say I wanted this drawn up properly," Luke said quietly.

"So as I understand it then, you have agreed to give sole rights of your daughter to her father, on condition that he pays you a large sum of money?" The solicitor spoke in a quiet voice, regarding her steadily.

Kelly gave a light laugh. "More like, he bribed me." She shot Luke a black look.

"Is that so, Mr Hathaway?"

Luke hesitated. "I'm willing to pay for my daughter."

It was left that she would receive papers to sign through her solicitor; then and only then would any settlement be paid and with that she had to be satisfied. She was beside herself with anger at the length of time it was taking and Luke became suspicious.

Out of curiosity he telephoned Chas, later that evening. They hadn't spoken since the divorce and at first things were stilted, but gradually it came out that Kelly had moved out of his house more than nine months ago when she had taken up with a professional tennis player.

Chas sounded embarrassed and Luke felt sorry for him.

"I need a good pilot Chas and I think you would like it here."

"You could really forgive and forget?" Chas sounded desperate.

"She didn't love either of us. Let us at least salvage our friendship. Come over and have a look for yourself; we can talk things over. I hope to start business shortly."

"Would next week be too soon?"

"The sooner the better." Luke replaced his receiver with a contented sigh. He had missed Chas.

It was a warm evening and the breeze coming off the sea invited him to take great breaths and fill his lungs with pure, salty air, stretching his arms with exuberance born of pure joy. Kimberley was going to live with him and Chas and he were to be reunited. Suddenly his world was righting itself, for the first time since the death of his father a year ago. His mind drifted to the evening when Samantha had sat here with him and he longed to go to her right then. Only the thought of Kimberley waking and finding herself alone in a strange room sobered him. He went indoors and crept upstairs, to make sure she was sleeping and found her lying peacefully on her back, arms sprawled above her head. He returned to the garden, retrieving a glass and a can of lager from the kitchen on his way. From this point, he could see the lights of Anders Folly. He glanced at his watch; it was late, but no doubt, she would still be attending to Jacob.

He rang her mobile number and she answered, sounding unsure.

"Sorry it's late. Kimberley only settled down a little while ago. I desperately need to talk to you."

"Me too." They talked for quite a while then said goodnight and she sat at her dressing table, feeling desolate again. The room was quiet, dimly lit by a single bedside lamp so as not to wake Jacob. His breathing was the only small sound, until Meg appeared in the doorway of the bathroom adjoining the two rooms.

"Need to talk?" she asked, seeing Samantha's downcast expression.

"No, I'm fine; get some sleep; thanks all the same. See you in the morning."

Meg shuffled back, mules plopping softly on the carpet.

Peace descended over the house and Samantha lay awake for a long time. Had Luke really sent his wife away, or had she flashed those big baby blue eyes at him? Sleep came at last, but she was heavy-eyed when Jacob woke her at six o'clock demanding his bottle. He was nearly five months old and his smiles always restored her spirits if she was feeling low; this morning was no exception and she managed to put her worries of the previous night behind her as Meg appeared carrying Lucy.

"Are you okay?" Meg asked anxiously.

Samantha nodded.

"I'll put the kettle on."

Samantha nodded again.

Meg went into the bathroom, where a small table with early morning tea-making facilities had been set out at Samantha's suggestion when George was planning to bring them tea at six o'clock every morning.

"I won't hear of it, there is no need for you to be up at that time," she had insisted, mindful of his advancing years. She dreaded the day when he and Lorna would have to retire and was always thinking of ways to lighten their workload. It had to be said that Dora was doing an excellent job with the cooking, under Lorna's strict guidance. In fact, it was hard to tell sometimes who had cooked what, and Lorna always praised her niece generously – as long as she was not within hearing. Having full time help in the kitchen had considerably eased Lorna's day and given her time to spend with Felicity, who although getting more forgetful about recent happenings, still loved to talk about the old days.

They always sat at the big kitchen table when she arrived on Monday morning and Abigail would join them for a cup of coffee. Once again, she had taken it on herself to be carer, when Felicity was staying in the house.

It saddened Samantha to see them all getting older. Losing her grandfather had brought home that the day would come when they too would no longer be there.

Still deep in thought, she left Jacob playing happily in Meg's charge and went for an early morning ride. In spite of knowing that Luke was unlikely to meet her in the stable yard, she kept looking for him, hoping he would appear as she set out over the headland. After exercising Nocturn, she retraced the hoof prints in the sand, searching the skyline as she reached the top of the headland. Her pulse leapt at sight of Luke waving, she waved back just as a small figure appeared beside him, and felt hurt as he turned away abruptly.

Entering the house, she followed the sound of voices to the dining room. Charles, Felicity, Abigail, Meg and the children were already waiting for breakfast and everyone seemed to be talking at once. Charles and Felicity had returned and as usual Abigail joined them; she preferred the sanctuary of her own little world upstairs on the weekends and excused herself by saying it gave the girls time on their own.

The day passed without word from Luke, and Samantha went about her tasks mechanically, stopping frequently to look over at the cottage, hoping to catch sight of him as Kimberley's high-pitched squeals of delight reached her when he pushed her on Jack's swing.

The following afternoon, George was out and Dora knocked at the study door to say there was a caller, and hurrying through to the hall hoping to see Luke, she was taken completely unawares by a familiar figure standing in the hall.

CHAPTER THIRTY-TWO

Peter and Amy were put ashore with their luggage, in a remote cove on the north end of the island. The skipper of the yacht, pointed to a car parked on the road above then cast off wishing them good luck and giving a brief salute. The driver of the car, a young Spanish man possibly in his early twenties, scrambled down the rough path, calling "Ola," picked up the two largest cases, leaving Peter to bring another two, smaller ones and Amy to bring up the rear with her make-up case and several small bags.

He shouted back encouragingly as they struggled up the uneven surface, saying something in Spanish, which neither of them fully understood but guessed it meant the hacienda was not far.

They drove at breakneck speed along a single-track road, which took them through lush green hills where small isolated dwellings could be seen perched precariously on the slopes. They clung to the back seat, with Amy staring petrified at the sheer drop, so perilously close to the wheels of the battered car.

She clutched Peter's hand and he put an arm around her, telling her not to look, averting his own eyes from possible consequences, in the event of the slightest fault on the driver's part.

Completely unconcerned, the driver nonchalantly removed first one hand and then the other from the steering wheel, giving a running commentary and waving to the marvellous views of blue sea on one side and the peak of Mount Teide in the distance.

The ride took fifteen minutes and their dismay when they finally arrived at the, to quote the advert, *'Desirable, quiet area. Wonderful views, no close neighbours. Property in need of some renovation',* was to say the least a mind-blowing understatement.

Peter had expected something along the lines of an area where Monica used to live, only a much smaller house.

The driver, who they now knew as Pablo, unloaded their cases, took them into the shack, handed Peter a key and ran back to the car.

Standing in the middle of the tiny living room they stared at each other with growing horror.

"I think we've been had?" Peter said at last.

"I thought you said all of the houses here were beautiful," Amy whispered tragically.

He nodded. "I must have missed this one."

They stared around at cheap wooden furniture and viewed the grubby wooden floor, with its equally grubby, single rug. There was a doorway, minus a door with only rusty hinges to say there had ever been one, and this led into a cupboard-sized kitchen.

"I can't believe this is happening; no one has lived here for years," Amy said incredulously. "We should have known it was too good to be true; a detached, furnished villa for thirty thousand."

"I suppose we will just have to put it down to experience and buy somewhere else," Peter said jocularly as a fresh thought occurred to Amy. The car had gone and they were in the middle of nowhere without food or transport, facts that seemed to be escaping Peter altogether.

He was so impractical in many ways, but being without him now, was her biggest dread. She realised he wasn't in love with her and had only joined forces thinking she had the Anders' money; and that was why he wasn't concerned about their present situation, she supposed.

The sound of a car exhaust back firing interrupted her thoughts and a minute later Pablo returned. He was wearing a big smile and seemed to have miraculously, learnt to speak reasonable English in his short absence.

"Por favour Señor, Señora. Manuel say you need food. I take you to shop in village. Yes?"

A small ray of hope lightened the gloom. Manuel was the vendor of the property.

"Yes," Amy answered promptly. "I definitely need a word with Manuel. Put the luggage back in the car," she instructed Pablo, before turning to Peter. "We'll have to find somewhere to stay; we can't possibly live in this."

"Si Señora, Manuel will fit you up." Pablo was apparently expecting this.

"I would say he's already done that," Peter joked.

"This is no laughing matter Peter," Amy said sharply before checking herself.

Arriving in the village, she was relieved to see a reasonable looking small hotel, where, Pablo assured them there would be a room available when they had spoken to Manuel, who they would find in the village store at this time of day.

Another shock awaited them there. Manuel turned out to be tall, olive skinned and very distinguished looking. He was immaculately dressed in a cream suit over a black shirt and his cream tie bore the initials, M.L. Dark, penetrating eyes acknowledged them from under a large, coloured umbrella, where he was sitting at a small, round table in the paved area surrounding a large shop. When challenged by Amy, his demeanour changed from watchful to disdainful as he informed them that the advert had clearly stated renovation was needed.

"Renovation? The place needs pulling down and rebuilding," Amy stormed at him, eyes flashing, beside herself with anger at his calm assertion that there was nothing they could hold him responsible for.

"You will be hearing from my solicitor." It was an empty threat and he obviously knew, because they had not used a solicitor for the transaction.

"My brother-in-law is my solicitor." Manuel pointed to an office across the narrow road, lit a cigar and drew deeply before adding, "I assure you I am within the law; you bought sight unseen; your choice."

He lounged back, crossing his long legs, indicating that there was nothing more to say and drew deeply again on his cigar as Pablo placed a glass of something red in front of him, while Amy and Peter just gaped in shocked silence.

A Spanish woman brought him a plate of delicacies and he introduced her. "My wife Luisa."

The woman smiled and bowed her head. "Ola."

"Luisa doesn't speak English," he informed them, catching her hand and kissing the tips of her fingers, while she melted at his touch.

"Oh, p-lease," Amy rolled her eyes, never at a loss for words for long.

"Is that all you've got to say?" she demanded.

"What else do you want me to say?" His piercing gaze was arrogant, only a hard glitter betrayed his anger at being challenged by a mere woman, but Amy was too angry to be intimidated. Peter on the other hand was and tried to pull her away.

"I want my money back, you cheap fraudster," she said refusing to move.

"That is slander, Mrs Chambers; I would advise you not to repeat it. My son has driven you; I am willing to accommodate you in my hotel and my shop is at your convenience. If you have further problems, I suggest you take them up with the authorities."

"No doubt you own them as well," she retorted with a withering look.

He looked offended. "I am proud to say that my eldest son is the local magistrate, yes, and I can assure you we have a high regard for the law, in my village."

There was a small silence, while he allowed them to digest the extent of his authority, before adding, "However, as you seem dissatisfied, I am prepared to be fair. I will buy the property back from you."

"That sounds good; let's take it and get out of here," Peter urged, acutely aware of what they were up against, as curious faces watched from inside the shop.

Amy was pleasantly surprised and started to agree until he offered half of what she had paid.

"That isn't fair; it's outright extortion," she stormed.

"Let's just take it and get out of here," Peter implored.

She debated with herself, glaring at him for a full minute, and had just decided it was better than nothing when a loud cackling laugh came from inside the shop and she understood enough Spanish to get the gist of what was being said.

"That Manuel has done it again; this will be the seventh time he has bought the shack back. There will be drinks all round tonight."

Further loud laughter followed as others joined in; Amy lowered her head to hide her anger.

"I need to think. I will let you know in the morning." She turned on her heel.

Manuel looked annoyed; other buyers had snatched his hand off.

"You won't get a better offer," he called after her.

"I'll sleep on it."

"What are you thinking of?" Peter asked desperately, on their way back to the car.

"It's a scam. He has bought it back six times and we are supposed to be the seventh; well he's not getting away with it, slimy creature."

"He doesn't look used to being crossed," Peter warned, glancing back nervously. "In fact he seems to own everything in sight."

As if to prove the point, they passed a colourful gift shop, with a sign saying welcome to Manuel's, and a café with 'Manuel's' printed at the top of the menus, propped up on the tables.

"Why don't we just accept his offer? Please," Peter urged anxiously.

"I'll die first," Amy said savagely.

"I wish you hadn't said that." It was exactly what he was afraid of.

244

They reached the car and Pablo came sauntering up to them.

"You want I take cases in hotel?" He opened the boot as if it was a foregone conclusion. His father always got his way.

"Not right now. We need to look at houses. Will you drive us? I will pay you." Pablo returned her friendly smile with a cheerful hunch of his broad shoulders. "Okay."

At this stage, Peter was prepared to go along with anything to get out of the village.

The roads became slightly less hair-raising after a while and they started to see tourist coaches filled with sightseers. Amy's eyes grew shrewd. She started to enthuse about the cascading bougainvillea, pointing excitedly to houses displaying, 'For Sale' boards, before suddenly leaning forward and tapping Pablo's shoulder. "Stop at that café over there. I need a cup of tea."

They pulled onto the car park of a large old house, where tourists were spilling out of coaches and making their way across the cinder like surface, towards tables and chairs. Pablo said he would be back in half an hour and went to join other drivers, gathered together on the far side of the building. Waiting until he was out of sight, Amy went up to a coach driver, who was helping the last elderly passenger down the steep steps of a coach, and money changed hands as she pointed to the car. He touched his cap and she hurried towards the café entrance. Peter had meanwhile gone in search of the toilets and joined her in the queue when she was ordering a pot of tea.

She kept an eye on the coaches and as soon as the driver she had spoken to returned, she got up casually and told Peter to follow her. To all intents and purposes they were making for the car, but the driver opened the coach door and let them in on the far side. She had chosen that particular one, because the car was parked behind it. They sat at the very back and drew the curtain across. Peter had followed blindly, glad of any plan to get away from Manuel and his family. He had already summed up that Pablo was not the happy go lucky character he portrayed to be. The apple didn't fall far from the tree with that one he decided, having watched Pablo flex his broad shoulders.

The coach took them to Puerto del a Cruz, and Peter was full of admiration for Amy's quick thinking, especially when their luggage was placed on the pavement beside them.

"You are a miracle worker; how and when did you manage all of that?" he asked with a delighted grin, his mood changing instantly now he felt safe.

They booked into the hotel where the other passengers were staying, congratulating themselves on finding a room in high season, at such short notice; blissfully unaware of what lay behind their amazing good fortune.

They had been travelling since early that morning and until now had been too worried to think of food. Dinner was at seven o'clock.

"Not sure I can last that long," Amy called from the bathroom.

Peter appeared in the doorway with a towel wrapped around his waist.

"There's one way to take our minds off food,"

"Now this is how I imagined Tenerife," she said some time later as they lay on their backs, looking up at the whirring fan creating welcome little currents of cooling air.

"Where shall we start looking for a house?" She looked at him expectantly.

"The only place I have stayed is Icos; that was wonderful."

"So remind me why you chose Tenerife."

"It was the one place I knew Monica wouldn't be. We don't want to go bumping into her do we? She would tip the police off."

Amy was silent.

"We can take our time; there's no rush." He stretched his arms, luxuriating.

"Icos it is; I want to get settled." The truth being, she knew even three hundred thousand pounds wouldn't last forever, living in expensive hotels.

"What are we going to do about Manuel?"

"Nothing; I'm damned if I'm selling it back to him half price, just so that he can make more thousands out of other poor suckers."

Peter pushed himself off the bed. He had serious doubts about crossing this Manuel person. "Why don't we just take the money and forget it?"

"Because that is what he expects; and I refuse to be bullied."

"But we are in his territory, who knows what he can get away with. I've heard about these Godfather types."

Amy slid off the bed. "You've been watching too much television, let's get ready and go and find something to eat." She laughed, suddenly feeling very light hearted.

The dining room was busy, but the waiter showed them to a table and brought a bottle of champagne and two glasses with the compliments of the hotel.

"How nice," Amy said picking up her glass. "Cheers." They chinked glasses, smiling at one another and perused the menus.

After studying the menu for a few minutes, Amy looked up smiling. "I think I'm going to have—" she froze, staring over Peter's shoulder; he glanced up, smiling with anticipation, until he saw her shocked expression and turned following her gaze.

No more than twenty feet away, raising his glass to them, was Manuel.

He rose and made his way over to them, never taking his eyes from Amy.

When he was standing beside their table, he raised his glass. "Let us drink to your continued good health, Señora, Señor." He bowed courteously, his eyes taunting her as he leant forward.

Not to be out done, Amy returned his look. "I'm glad we have bumped into you. I might decide to hold on to the property and renovate it."

He transferred his gaze to Peter. "Is the decision of your spirited wife, also yours, Señor?"

"I'm, I'm not sure." Peter's voice cracked hoarsely and he cleared his throat before continuing, "I think we may need more time."

Manuel smiled and bowed; to all outward appearances having a pleasant conversation to welcome two newcomers.

"Until manyana, then." He returned to his table and Peter took a nervous slurp from his glass.

Amy picked up her glass and waiting for Manuel to sit down, held it out with a defiant tilt of her head.

"Please don't goad him any more," Peter pleaded, catching the gesture.

"Well, you would think he owned the place," she said loudly, just as the waiter returned.

"Son of the owner Artemis Lorenzo," he corrected her. "They are powerful people in Tenerife."

"So now we know how he found us so quickly," she said sulkily, after the waiter had left with their order.

"So give him the damn property?" Peter whispered fiercely.

"Why are they playing about with two bit scams, when they have so much?"

"I don't know and I don't care. I just want to get away from here in one piece."

Amy was silent for some time, puzzling over the question. "I bet they have a lot of these, so called, hillside properties," she said at last. "That will be how they got rich in the first place and it's too good to give up."

"Now who's been watching too much television? Just forget about it. We'll find somewhere else to live."

They ate their dinner in silence, each with their own thoughts, then went for a stroll along the promenade afterwards. As darkness fell, restaurants came to life. Singers vied with each other, accompanied by guitarists strumming softly one minute, furiously the next; each establishment competing for customers to sit at their candle-lit tables, where staff, wearing immaculate white shirts and black trousers, waited to serve delicious looking food.

"Wish we had come here to eat now," Peter remarked. They came to a lido, on the edge of the sea and stood looking down, admiring the soft lights shimmering in the still waters of the two swimming pools; empty now but through the day, filled with happy, laughing holidaymakers. As the moon rose higher and the music became more mellow, they had no way of knowing that their first traumatic day on Tenerife, was to be the first of many.

In the morning, the delicious smell of cooked bacon and eggs filled the restaurant, where they served themselves from food islands groaning under the weight of dishes, designed to please every nationality.

"It would be nice to stay a little longer," Amy suggested after breakfast as they sat on a wide, round wooden seat overlooking the bay where early surfers were already preparing to ride the rough waves.

"Always supposing we could find somewhere the Lorenzos don't own?"

Peter gave a hopeless look. "I think I would rather move on. What about Manuel?"

"I haven't the slightest doubt he will find us when he is ready," Amy said bitterly. "Pity we can't hack into *his* computer." She stared out to sea and Peter glanced sharply at her. Where had that come from? It sounded like an actual admission. He smiled to himself, thinking things couldn't be better; he was actually enjoying Amy's company now. She had changed; she was much softer and looked a million dollars in her brief, but not too brief, dresses, skirts and tops; revealing just enough without being common. Unbelievably, he felt quite fond of her. She was certainly spirited, as Manuel had pointed out, but there was also something quite vulnerable about the way she so desperately wanted the good life; much like himself he supposed. Deep in thought, he was unaware of Manuel bearing down on them until Amy said, "Speak of the devil."

"Buenos dias Señor, Señora." He raised his panama hat. "I hope you slept well."

Peter remained silent but Amy replied, "Forget the false pleasantries. Give me all of the money back or I will keep the property and ruin your little scam."

"The choice is yours Señora. The property will revert to me anyway if you don't take up residence within one year. Did you not read the small print on your contract?" His mocking smile shocked her into silence.

"Take the damned offer," Peter insisted.

"Ah! Your husband is wise, but there is a small alteration to my offer; it is five thousand less today; tomorrow it will be five thousand less than today and so on."

Amy's dark eyes flashed, disdainfully. "You are despicable. You can't get away with it."

"But I can." His voice was quietly menacing as he raised his hat again. "Adios."

He sauntered away, raising his hat to passers-by, greeting them with a courteous smile.

"Well say something!" Amy ranted, beside herself with frustration.

"You can't win; you may as well give in and cut your losses."

She followed Manuel's disappearing figure with hate-filled eyes. "All right; but you tell him, I can't trust myself not to scratch his eyes out."

Peter gave a relieved sigh and hurried after him, catching up as Manuel's tall figure reached a broad set of steps with railings, where Pablo, leaning against the iron railing wearing an amused smile, was moving forward protectively, until Manuel waved him away with a sly smile.

"This is not the one to worry about, my son." His eyes twinkled at Peter, who stared back in surprise at his change of character.

"Your wife is much woman," he said with obvious admiration.

"So why are you cheating us?" Peter demanded, incredulously.

Manuel gave a careless shrug. "That is business, Señor."

"We have no choice but to accept your offer," Peter said, briefly wishing he had the courage to challenge the smug smile.

The smile faded and Manuel became businesslike. "I will come to your hotel room at one o'clock sharp; don't be late or I will return again tomorrow, when the offer will be five thousand less, as I explained earlier. Adios Señor." He turned to Pablo. "I am finished for now."

He strolled on as if for all the world they had just passed the time of day and Pablo waited for Peter to walk away, before disappearing into one of the many cafés along the promenade.

Peter told Amy about the one o'clock appointment and her first reaction was that he could jolly well take a running jump, until she was ready.

Realising Manuel had anticipated and out manoeuvred them yet again, Peter waited for the explosion when he told her the penalty of being late; but Amy was silent, knowing she was beaten.

On the dot of one o'clock, he arrived with Pablo, who stood outside the door whilst the transaction took place. They gazed dumbly as he handed over

English bank notes, held out his hand for the contract, dropped it into the metal waste bin and swiftly set light to it, with a gold cigarette lighter.

"Now it never happened," he said quietly.

"Except that I am down twenty thousand," Amy pointed out indignantly.

He walked over to her, handed her an envelope and catching her outstretched fingers, kissed them before she realised what he was going to do. "Valuable lessons never come cheaply, my dear; one day you will thank me."

She gazed, incapable of movement, as he stared deeply into her eyes, before transferring the hypnotic look in Peter's direction.

They stood, silent and incapable of movement for several moments after he left.

"What just happened?" she asked blankly.

"I'm not sure. What's in the envelope?"

She handed it to him, still in a daze.

Looking white and surprised, he held up two tickets. "We're booked on a flight home, tomorrow afternoon."

About to object, Amy gave a small shiver; her fingers tingled where the touch of his kiss still lingered and she felt suddenly breathless with desire. Closing her eyes, she turned to Peter. "Make love to me."

"Why don't we just go out for a while?" he said weakly, desperate to get away from the claustrophobia threatening to suffocate him.

"Perhaps you're right," she agreed, taking a deep breath.

Once out in the fresh air her thoughts cleared but the desire stayed with her; then across the promenade she caught sight of Manuel's tall figure, leaning against the sea wall near the lido; head tilted back, he was peering at her from under his wide brimmed, Panama hat. Their eyes met and locked; then Peter spoke, breaking her reverie.

"Let's get away from here; I feel as if we are being watched."

"Where shall we go?" She was suddenly aware of a strange kind of excitement filling her whole body, banishing worrying thoughts, creating an expectant aura.

"I'd like to see Icos again; I think you would love it." Peter gave her an anxious look. "Are you alright? You look a bit strange."

"I'm fine; where did you say you wanted to go?"

He tutted. "I knew you weren't listening. I said I would like to go to Icos."

"Whatever you say," she said amiably.

"Let's go by car and have dinner there. It will be better than bumping into Manuel Lorenzo again."

"Mm," she murmured, sensing an inexplicable disappointment at the thought of never seeing him again.

At Peter's request the car dropped them beside tall, wrought iron gates, and he pointed to the room where he and Lindsey had stayed, just visible between tall trees. They stood gazing up at the luxurious villa, resplendent in the afternoon sun with its façade of blue and cream tiles, set in intricate Hispanic symbols. Wide, Moorish arches led to highly polished double doors and huge windows behind wrought iron balconies were closely curtained to keep out the heat of the day.

They moved on, walking down into a sleepy looking plaza where tables and chairs were set out under the arched forecourt of a bodega. They ordered wine and sat watching tourists wandering about in the heat of the day. Sensible locals would be taking a siesta in readiness for the evening, when they would open their shops and the whole village would come to life. Only a few shop owners optimistically kept their businesses open during siesta.

Sipping lazily at their wine, they hardly noticed the tall figure that came and sat at a nearby table. The figure drew a book from the folds of a long, loose fitting black garment and became instantly engrossed. Shoulders hunched, head down, a cowl like hood covering face and hair, not even the black toecaps, peeping from beneath the floor length garment gave any clue as to whether the wearer was man or woman. The waiter came, read a piece of paper handed to him in silence, then fetched a glass of red wine and placed it on the table before retiring to the back of the bar again.

"One of those silent religious orders," Peter observed as if knowledgeable about such things.

Amy shrugged, looking away indifferently.

"This is a perfect place to settle down; no wonder Monica chose it. I wonder where she's moved on to? Lucky old her to have a choice; if we aren't at the airport on time, I get the distinct impression we will be bodily transported."

"Really?" Peter looked nervous; worried by the hint of excitement mixed with her anger; if he didn't know better he could swear she was enjoying their situation.

"You do realise these men could be dangerous?" He looked at her intently.

"I think you're right," she answered seriously, but there was that hint of excitement again.

They stayed, ordered dinner, then the car came back for them as the sun was setting.

"Did you ask him to come back?"

251

Peter nodded and she was surprised; his forward thinking hadn't been much in evidence thus far.

"You've had too much wine," he accused.

"Only the same as you." She leant against him in the taxi and he couldn't understand why she wasn't more worried. It made him feel insecure.

Monica gave a savage tug and threw her shoe on the floor, followed quickly by the other one, which went hurtling across the room.

"Her of all people."

There was the tearing sound of Velcro as she clawed at the black cloth and stepped out of the enveloping, nun like garment. Kicking it aside, she stood for a moment in her pale apricot bra and cami-knickers, taking deep, calming breaths, until she was thinking rationally.

They had mentioned Manuel Lorenzo, the man who unofficially, practically governed the island. She heard of him when she first arrived and had made sure to keep her distance. He had the reputation of being a good family man, ruthless businessman, a brilliant host and a consummate womaniser, not necessarily in that order.

She sat on the foot of the bed, sullenly regarding the black disguise strewn carelessly on the floor, contrasting sharply with the pale gold carpet; reliving the moment when a taxi had pulled up at the tall, wrought iron gates and a couple got out. She watched while the man paid the driver; thinking there was something vaguely familiar about him. Her heart had leapt as she recognised Peter and turned her eager gaze on the woman, expecting by some miracle that Lindsey had come to see her. One glance told her that the well-dressed, dark haired, slim woman was not her daughter and her curiosity grew. Peter had pointed to the house and they stood momentarily, before moving on arm in arm.

Under the pretext of reading, she had listened to their conversation in the plaza, growing ridged with anger as she recognised the transformed Amy.

Now, as she relived the scene, an idea began to form and without hesitating, she dressed and left the house. She drove down to Puerto de la Cruz and walked into the hotel, where she knew Manuel Lorenzo would be. It was well known that he dined there every evening, and she had already sent a note asking to see him on a matter of finance; consequently, he had invited her to join him for dinner. Going by his reputation it wasn't an acquaintance she would have chosen, but tonight she had a purpose in seeking him out, and her determination strengthened as she caught sight of Peter and Amy. She stood in the middle of the foyer as they passed within feet of her, Amy clinging to his arm, confident that neither of them would recognise her in the guise of Barbara Hayle, the rich American, who had bought the extortionately overpriced villa in Icos.

Manuel Lorenzo's expression was thoughtful as he listened to why Peter Chambers and the woman he called his wife were in Tenerife. The stolen eleven million pounds not only caught his interest but explained why they had not used a solicitor and had come ashore in a privately hired boat, avoiding customs; it was also a very large carrot she was dangling. Meeting for the first time he was intrigued. She was older than his usual conquests, but he was drawn to her mystery; why would such a desirable woman choose to be a recluse? They finished the meal and concluded their talk, with him assuring her that she could leave the matter safely in his hands. He rose to his feet and taking her hand, kissed her fingertips; then hugging her pale cream cashmere shawl closely round her, she swayed elegantly out of the dining room and along the terrace, looking back when she reached the ornamental stonewall overlooking the sea. Manuel raised a hand and she bowed her head before making her way down a flight of stone steps to the grounds where she had parked her car.

Back at the villa, she slipped into an ivory, silk kaftan, opened a bottle of her favourite red wine and relaxed in the conservatory. Some might have found the perfume of the orchids overwhelming, but to her the heady perfume was relaxing and she would often fall asleep in one of the long comfortable recliners and sleep until morning. Seldom lonely, she did miss the social life of home, and there were even times when she missed William. She had paid a heavy price for her impulsive action, but worst of all was not seeing her daughter and grandson.

She tapped the arm of the chair with long, red fingernails, going back over her talk with Manuel. There was no doubt in her mind that he would act quickly with such a large sum of money involved. The Anders' money was safely tucked away in a numbered account; she had thought many times of returning it to them, but couldn't be sure it would buy her freedom. By giving Manuel half a million, it might kill two birds with one stone, by clearing her own name and paying Amy back for breaking up her marriage. Another thing that was bothering her was that Lindsey wouldn't know what Peter was up to. "Well she would soon."

Monica's temper flared and she picked up her mobile phone. Lindsey's phone was switched off, so she rang the landline and was briefly caught off guard by William's voice, no more than he was to hear hers though. Recovering first, she brusquely demanded to speak to Lindsey.

"I'll have to fetch her, she is in bed. Hold on a minute."

"What's the matter with her?" Monica screeched down the phone, panicking.

"Nothing. It's twelve thirty and she went up two hours ago; she has to be up very early for Liam. I was just going up myself as a matter of a fact."

William sounded quite different to the man always preoccupied with his own needs. Monica automatically checked his word by looking at her wristwatch.

"Yes you are right. I didn't realise the time."

"You sound worried; can I help?"

Monica hesitated, then reminding herself that Peter was after all William's nephew, blurted out, "Peter has turned up with that Bishop woman; they are staying in a hotel together as man and wife."

She expected him to be shocked or angry but he said quietly, "So that's where he disappeared to; I have wondered." He gave a sudden laugh. "I must have convinced him that she took the money. Hope the police are convinced as well." He told her not to worry about Lindsey. "Nothing else matters to her now that she has the baby; I've never seen her so happy."

"She is better off without Peter." Monica spoke sharply and expected him to defend Peter, but all he said was, "I think we are all agreed on that; even Lindsey."

They talked for nearly an hour and ended with an amicable good night with Monica promising to phone at a more reasonable hour the next day.

Switching her phone off, she finished her glass of wine and went to bed, feeling more at peace than she had done for a long while; knowing Amy's comeuppance was on its way.

CHAPTER THIRTY-THREE

Samantha's shock at seeing Bryn standing in the hall left her speechless, and while she was recovering, he said expectantly, "Hello Sam," but the welcome he had been anticipating was missing.

Heart pounding, she stared blankly at him; robbed of any feeling other than disappointment, because it wasn't Luke.

"Aren't you pleased to see me?" he asked, also disappointed.

Her answer sounded uncertain. "Well yes, of course; but why have you come?"

"We need to talk; things have changed that affect us both."

She looked at him questioningly. "What sort of things?"

"Can we go somewhere private and talk, the cottage maybe?" He gave a reminiscent smile.

"Someone is living there." She looked about to cry when he mentioned the cottage, and thinking she still cherished memories, he hurried over to her. "I'm sorry I shouldn't have arrived out of the blue like this; I've upset you."

They went into the sitting room and sat opposite each other while she listened without comment until he had finished.

Two weeks ago Jocelyn had confessed he wasn't the father of her baby; Apparently, she fell in love with someone her wealthy parents would not consider suitable, and picked Bryn because she was afraid of losing their support if she told the truth.

Samantha felt no sympathy for Jocelyn, remembering how heartbroken she had been herself. "So what has changed?"

"She wants to marry the baby's father now and doesn't care if her parents do disown her." His voice softened. "She has always known how I felt about you, and wants to put it right."

"Huh! So you have served your purpose and now have her permission to come back to me," Samantha said haughtily.

"Well I wouldn't put it quite like that," Bryn said, reddening.

Samantha jumped to her feet. "Wouldn't you, wouldn't you really? She didn't care how we felt about each other when it suited her but now she can manage without her parents; she doesn't care about them either, because out of the blue she can suddenly marry the father of her child! And I'm supposed to be grateful because she is giving you back to me! I mustn't complain of course because that would be unreasonable of me and Jo is never unreasonable – as long as she gets her own way!" She stamped her foot. "Aargh!"

Bryn looked at her in amazement, taken aback by her uncharacteristic outburst and Samantha glared back defiantly; not realising herself, just how bitter she felt about first Bryn and then Peter abandoning her, until hearing him practically praising Jocelyn for her generosity.

"I'm sorry, I came thinking I was doing the right thing."

"And Jocelyn is making sure it is the right thing for her again but I suppose she has convinced you she wants a divorce for your sake."

"Is there any way I can make it up to you?"

His eyes pleaded with her and she relented a little.

"Our friendship will always mean a lot to me."

"We can have so much more when my divorce comes through. I still love you, Sam."

The words that she had wanted to hear more than anything in the world, hung in the air between them and she wished she could feel as she had all those months ago. Bryn moved towards her, arms outstretched expecting her to fling herself into them, as she would have not so long ago; instead, she stood up and walked through the open French doors, out onto the terrace. He followed, spreading his hands.

"Just tell me what I've got to do. I'll do anything to go back to the way we were."

She turned to face him. "You talk about changes in your life; has it never occurred to you that some might have happened in mine, as well?"

She waved to Meg, coming back from the cove with the children. Meg saw and waved back. Bryn glanced, assuming they were friends, but five minutes later, Meg arrived carrying Jacob, followed by Lucy, who was walking quite sturdily by now. Samantha took Jacob and introduced Bryn and Meg to each other before saying quietly:

"And this is my son, Jacob."

Bryn gaped as Meg excused herself and left with Lucy. Samantha raised her chin proudly, as a startled questioning look crossed Bryn's face, before he said hesitantly, "So I have a son, after all."

"No," she said firmly.

He jerked back as if she had slapped him. "But I must be his father," he said faintly.

"Why must you?"

"Well, you couldn't, you wouldn't..." He broke off embarrassed as Maisie came to take Jacob. "Meg says you may need me to give him his dinner, Miss Samantha." Samantha kissed Jacob and handed him over.

When they were alone again, she said, "Let's walk down to the cove; I would rather not talk in the house."

They walked side by side without touching, without speaking. Samantha wondering what his reaction to the truth would be; Bryn, telling himself she was denying he was Jacob's father because she was hurt and angry.

They sat well back from the water where the sand was dry; the same spot they had sat in many times before, when they were still at college and Samantha didn't want to be touched. She felt the same now and pulled away as Bryn tried to put his arm round her. It seemed to be her destiny to love men who were not free to love her.

Seeing her tragic face, Bryn tried reasoning. "Come on Sam, this isn't like you. You can't have stopped loving me just like that."

She looked at him. He was still the same Bryn from college days, who had helped her through the teasing and criticism she had suffered because of the newspaper article. Now, because he was such a good friend she had to tell him the truth.

He listened ruefully, while she reminded him of the afternoon in the cottage; how distraught she had been after her grandfather's funeral; how she had run away to Southampton; impressing on him how heartbroken and lost she was at the thought of him marrying Jocelyn. She reminded him of her reason for dropping out of university, and how she only became aware of loving him so much when she missed him so desperately.

"So it was all because you wanted to be with me. I would never have looked at Jo if you had been there; but we can be together now."

Bryn was hopeful, until she came to where she had been close to a breakdown when Peter Chambers came to her rescue. She left nothing out and he blanched, listening to how this man had driven away her fears and awakened her.

"So Peter Chambers is the father." He spoke with difficulty, confident until that moment that he had been the only one she trusted.

She noted how still he had gone. Suddenly they were strangers. He rose, brushing sand from his suit, asking offhandedly:

"I assume he is going to marry you, then?"

"He is already married."

Bryn closed his eyes in despair. "Sam, what have you done?"

"I made the same mistake again of thinking someone loved me."

"Get rid of that chip on your shoulder! It isn't the problems that shape our lives it's the way we deal with them!" He spoke harshly and strode off along the sand, stopping to look back as he reached the path. She raised her hand through a haze of tears, but there was no answering wave.

Some while later, Meg wandered along and sat down. She had seen Bryn return alone and had watched him leave, looking angry.

"So that was the love of your life; very dishy, if you don't mind me saying."

Samantha smiled. Her tears had dried and she was feeling resigned.

"In another life," she said ruefully.

They sat talking until Samantha looking at her watch realised it was the children's bath time; they hurried in to find Maisie, already bathing both Jacob and Lucy in the big bath together.

Luke took a glass of beer out into the garden and settled where he had a good view of Anders Folly. He had spent the day with Kimberley, preparing her for the following week when he would be at the airfield. Looking forward to seeing Chas and the thought of renewing their friendship filled him with emotion.

After losing his father he had practically isolated himself, breaking away from the flying club, where they had been members together (because it held too many painful memories), and making lonely trips into the hills, with only Sapphire for company. Not only to come to terms with the huge gap in his life but to get away from Kelly's violent reaction to his father's early death so soon after their divorce.

His entire life had become utter turmoil. Kimberley's regular visits were cancelled and it became a problem to see her at all because any attempt on his part always ended in upsetting Kimberley. Meeting Darren Anders and hearing about the airfield had come as a heaven sent escape, to make a new life for himself.

Moving so far away had been a difficult decision but knowing Kelly would continue looking for more ways to cause trouble and besmirch his father's good name, he decided to look into Darren's suggestion, knowing that Kimberley would eventually come to him of her own accord, when she was older.

With his father being a prominent figure, Kelly's accusations, followed by the divorce, attracted a great deal of unpleasant publicity; which at the time stopped him from subjecting Kimberley to the further trauma of a custody case. He gave a satisfied grimace. But now he could protect her.

He had taken to sitting in the garden in the evenings when Kimberley, worn out by the sea air and exercise, slept soundly in the room next to his. There had been no chance of seeing Samantha in the last two days, which was why he was sitting gazing down at Anders Folly, waiting impatiently for the light to go on in her bedroom. He couldn't risk destroying Kimberley's new-found confidence, by not being there if she woke. Her young life had been turned upside down quite enough by the constant changes.

Samantha had been in her room for some time before she turned the light on; the long sunny day had stayed light until gone ten o'clock. The instant she switched on the bedside light her mobile phone rang and she answered it in a breathless little voice. Luke said he had been waiting to ring for half an hour, which upset her, because she had been lying on the bed, waiting for his call.

"How was I supposed to know?" she accused tearfully.

"Never mind, we're talking now," he said to pacify her but she could hear the anxiety in his voice.

"But I *do* mind," she persisted. "You haven't phoned and I haven't known why." She closed her eyes, waiting for his answer.

"Things have changed," he said hesitantly. "We need to talk."

She felt devastated. There was that 'things have changed' again. She couldn't bear to listen any longer; she just knew that yet another dream was about to be shattered.

"There's no need. I understand. You have other commitments." The phone went dead, but not before he heard her unhappy sob.

He tried to call back but her phone was switched off and although the light stayed on until gone twelve o'clock, he was forced to give up, promising himself that he would take Kimberley to the stables in the morning when he knew Samantha would be there. There was no point in waiting, he must introduce them straightaway and hope that Kelly didn't get to hear and cause trouble.

*

Meg squinted at the clock, murmured eight o'clock then opened her eyes wide. Eight o'clock! How come Jacob hadn't woken her? Throwing back the bedclothes, she pattered through to Samantha's room. Both the bed and Jacob's cot were empty. Smiling to herself, she remembered Samantha vowing to take Jacob for an early ride one morning. She pattered back to her room, dressed herself and Lucy then went down to breakfast, expecting Samantha to appear with Jacob, full of how they had enjoyed the ride. Half an hour later there was still no sign of them. Maisie came and took Lucy and George hovered uncertainly, eventually clearing the table when Meg said she thought Samantha had taken Jacob riding. Abigail always made her own breakfast in her room on the weekend and Charles and Felicity had gone to their own home, so although her absence was unusual, there was no undue concern. By mid morning, when George brought coffee, Meg decided to go over to the stables. It wasn't like Samantha to just go off without a word to anyone; perhaps she was with Sol and Ella.

The stables were swarming with young riders rubbing down their ponies and Meg eyed them nervously, keeping her distance. Sol was too busy to stop but said he hadn't seen Samantha all morning; not even for her early ride.

"Mr Hathaway was looking for her earlier," Ella called over from where she was showing a five-year-old boy how to mount a placid looking Shetland pony.

"Okay, thanks." Meg made a hasty retreat, convinced that Samantha must be up at the cottage.

Lunchtime came and Meg and Lucy sat alone again. "I believe Mr Hathaway called for her early this morning," she replied to George's enquiry.

At Lucy's bedtime it felt strange bathing her alone in the big bath and putting her to bed on her own; and lonely, eating dinner opposite Samantha's empty chair. She felt more curious than hurt. Babies needed so many things. If Samantha had gone off on the spur of the moment, how was she managing? She wanted to phone the cottage, but was afraid of intruding. On impulse, when she went upstairs to check on Lucy she looked in Jacob's cupboard; it was empty except for a neat pile of new clothing, (presents too large for him, still in their plastic bags).

Going quickly to Samantha's wardrobe, she realised it would be difficult to know if clothes were missing. The rails were full; each garment carefully protected in a see through cover, except for everyday jeans and piles of T-shirts, stacked on shelves. Looking more carefully, she noticed things like her hairbrush and comb were missing as well as her toothbrush from the bathroom.

She rang Samantha's number but it was switched off and feeling slightly anxious she went downstairs to ask Maisie to listen for Lucy, while she popped up to the cottage.

On the way up the path, she worried in case she was interfering and was about to turn back, when Luke appeared at the head of the path.

"Meg? Is anything the matter?"

"I'm probably just being silly."

She started to turn away but his voice stopped her.

"Ask Samantha to switch her phone on, will you? I really need to talk to her."

She turned slowly. "I haven't seen her all day; I thought she was with you."

"I haven't seen her all day. When did you see her last?"

"About nine thirty last night; just before I had a bath."

"I spoke to her after that." He gave a guilty frown.

"Sol said you were looking for her this morning."

"She was upset and switched her phone off last night. I went to join her for the early ride and put things right; when she didn't show up, I assumed she was busy."

Taking long strides, he came towards her.

"Is her car in the garage?"

She grimaced. "I didn't look."

"You had no reason to think she was actually missing. I'll have a look; stay with Kim, will you?" he called, heading down the path.

Returning ten minutes later, he said the car wasn't in the garage and he had told George and Sol.

"There's no way of knowing when she left, but they think she will have gone to Bob and Marcia's in the New Forest? Sol tried telephoning, but there's no reply."

"She has stayed with them before."

"I blame myself; if only I had explained over the phone, instead of waiting." Luke looked upset.

"Don't blame yourself entirely. Bryn called yesterday and she was pretty upset when he left."

They were standing in the garden and before he had a chance to ask about Bryn, a child's voice called, "Who are you talking to, Daddy?" And they looked up to see a small face peeping over the balcony.

*

Samantha drove into a motorway car park and picked a space away from the bright lights of the restaurant. At this hour, it was quiet and she planned to sleep for a couple of hours before continuing her journey. She had been travelling for nearly four hours and Jacob was sleeping peacefully as she fully reclined the driving seat and lay back. Looking up at the big arc lights, lonely, tormented thoughts filled her mind, but within minutes her eyes drooped and sleep came to her rescue.

It seemed like only minutes that she slept, but sunlight streaming through the windscreen had woken Jacob and he was gurgling happily at his unfamiliar surroundings. She blinked, squinting at the dashboard as six twenty-nine, jumped to six thirty on the digital clock. She had slept for three hours.

Jacob started to demand his breakfast and she roused herself to take him over to the mother and baby room, where she quickly washed and changed him before freshening herself up. In the restaurant, an obliging young assistant heated one of the bottles of milk she had packed in a cool bag and Jacob looked around happily, while she settled his car chair on a bench seat and poured some of the warmed milk over a bowl of baby cereal, also produced from her cool bag. Preoccupied with troubled thoughts she was unaware of passers-by staring curiously at the beautiful, sad looking young mother, feeding her happy baby.

Back on the road, she changed her mind about going to Bob and Marcia's; picturing their reproachful faces, accusing her of running away again, knowing they would be right; but sometimes it seemed the only way to deal with an unbearable situation. She didn't want to hear Luke say that he was going to try again with his wife; she didn't want to remember Bryn's shocked expression as he walked away.

Blinded by tears she had to pull over as a lay-by came into view, with a parked caravan selling food. She should have eaten when she fed Jacob. Grandfather always said 'You can deal with anything after a good breakfast', she reminded herself. Thinking of him steadied her mind and while sitting munching a baguette filled with spicy sausages, a possible solution came to her. By the time, she had finished a huge mug of coffee, convinced it was the right solution, she continued her journey with confidence.

CHAPTER THIRTY-FOUR

Amy half opened her eyes, closed them then opened them wide. An ornate, golden chandelier came into view, somewhere high up, beyond her feet. Her gaze travelled blearily upwards, to be met by a canopy of fine, white muslin, gathered cloudlike above her; the material falling in soft folds, was caught back by gold brackets, one either side of what looked like a deep headboard covered in lustrous, gold and royal blue material. Gingerly she raised her head, letting it fall again as the room spun.

What was happening? Where was she? She fought the blackness threatening to engulf her; closing her eyes as she vaguely remembered sitting in a taxi on her way to – where? She opened her eyes again as memory flooded back. They were on their way to the airport. Where was Peter?

A slight movement from the corner of the room drew her attention and she leant up on her elbows to find a pair of dark eyes fixed watchfully on her. Unnerved, she tried to haul herself into a sitting position, but collapsed dizzily back against plump, satin pillows.

"Where am I? Who are you?"

The owner of the dark eyes, rose, shuffled to a door set in the wall beyond the big chandelier; and Amy just glimpsed a slim figure, in a jade green sari and gold sandals before it disappeared.

Less than five minutes later the door opened and a familiar figure entered.

"You slept well I trust?" Manuel asked politely.

"Huh," she managed to say through dry lips that refused to obey. Struggling to sit up, she fought hard to focus.

"You will soon feel better," he said calmly, beginning slowly and deliberately, to remove his loose fitting garments, while she struggled helplessly against waves of dizziness.

She watched mesmerised as he drew back the satin coverlet, unaware until that moment that she was only wearing a short, silk nightdress that wasn't hers. "Peter," she called desperately.

"Forget about Peter; you have me now." His voice was soothing, even comforting. Was she dreaming? His lips were on hers demandingly and incapable of resisting, she was being drawn towards him.

She woke to find herself alone and lay several minutes collecting her thoughts, relieved to find when she moved her head that the room was not spinning any longer. She had just managed to sit up when the door opened and a figure entered carrying a tray, laden with fruit and croissants and a pot of coffee.

"Good morning Miss Bishop; your breakfast." The perfect English took her by surprise, coming from a very pretty, dark haired young woman with huge dark brown eyes. She was wearing a rose pink sari edged with elaborate embroidery. The realization that she was in India came as a shock but the immediate question was why?

"Your English is very good," she said, hoping to find out for sure.

"My name is Yana and I was educated in England." Yana handed Amy a hot towel and Amy accepted it gratefully. She really liked that Indian custom.

"You must be glad to be back home," Amy said casually, pouring herself a cup of coffee as she spoke.

"Yes, I am very happy." Yana turned away smiling and Amy gave a satisfied grunt. Well, at least she knew where she was now.

"Where is Peter? I would like to speak to him."

"I do not understand; you arrived alone." Yana put her hands together, gave a small bow and left.

Amy viewed the tray of food and realised she was starving. One thing at a time she thought, liberally spooning apricot preserve on to a fresh croissant. Having eaten she decided to look for her clothes, but there was no sign of her own things, only beautiful saris with sandals of every colour to match and dressing table drawers full of expensive silk underwear. Everything she could wish for and more, but how did she get here and why? She wandered into a luxurious, black tiled bathroom, complete with gold fittings, fluffy white towelling robes and towels, and long mirrors reflecting shelves filled with exotic bath oils in beautifully shaped bottles and huge powder puffs in bowls of sweet smelling talcum powder.

"No time like the present," Amy murmured turning the bath taps on full and stripping her nightdress off before dancing back into the bedroom, leaving the bath to fill to the top. Just before going back to the bathroom, she went to lock the door; there was no sign of a key so she lodged a chair under the handle.

"No more surprises! Señor Lorenzo." She bridled at the thought of the liberty he had already taken, but a traitorous sense of excitement stirred within her as she recalled his dark, mesmerising gaze.

Completely immersed in the oil-scented water, she soaped her legs, holding each one up to admire, but then suddenly she was very tired and the next thing she became aware of, was sitting on a chair in front of the dressing table with Yana putting final touches to her hair. The image staring back was wearing a pale apricot sari, edged with seed pearls sewn into elaborate cream embroidery, and a large tear shaped pearl, suspended by a gold chain, hung in the centre of her forehead. She remembered nothing after being in the bath. Yana placed the comb on the dressing table, indicated to her to follow and they left the room together. Amy hoped Peter would be wherever they were going and would know what was happening; but there was no sign of him and her questions were ignored.

Manuel sat at the head of the table, with Yana on one side and herself on the other. The highly polished table had elaborately carved legs and was laid with silver cutlery and serving dishes, delicate porcelain plates, engraved silver wine goblets and snowy white napkins. Everything was opulent, immaculate and very strangely perfect, reminding her of when she was a child and the Sunday best had been brought out for a special occasion – except that this was far grander than pottery plates and stainless steel cutlery, of course.

Yana said nothing but stared at Manuel from time to time, alert to his every need.

Manuel himself was preoccupied. He had searched Amy's suitcase with a fine toothcomb, but there was nothing relating to the money and her laptop had proved beyond him; but there was no hurry, the bath oils had done their work and he had enjoyed watching her.

After dinner, they adjourned to a sumptuous sitting room where Persian carpet covered the floor, carved furniture and priceless works of art lined the walls and dozens of tiny bulbs in a huge crystal chandelier, sent sparkling rays of light around the whole room. Riches beyond imagination; in fact every single comfort including subservient women at his beck and call; so what did he want with her, Amy wondered.

After pouring her a glass of liqueur and making her comfortable on one of the long settees, Manuel said:

"Yana will keep you company. I won't be long."

"Do you live here Yana?" Amy asked when they were alone.

Yana looked surprised. "No," she answered guardedly.

"Do you live nearby?"

"Yes," she answered briefly her face expressionless

After that, the silence grew and they sat in silence until Manuel returned.

"It is time you went home, little sister." Yana rose, bowed slightly over her hands and left.

Amy felt apprehensive as the door closed. So Yana was his sister; no wonder she was so tight lipped; this man was obviously related to, or owned everything in sight, even where they were now, wherever that was. She urgently wanted to find out why she had been brought here – and where Peter was.

Manuel relaxed onto another long settee facing her; a glass topped, carved wooden coffee table separating them. "As my guest you must become accustomed to our ways."

Alarm bells rang in Amy's head.

"It would help to know what I'm doing here and where Peter is."

"Peter Chambers only wants you as a prop. I have the luxury you crave and together we will be immensely rich."

His eyes bored into hers sapping her will power; she shook her head hard, sensing the danger in meeting his eyes and her thoughts cleared.

For a brief moment his jaw hardened but he quickly relaxed, pulled a gold pocket watch from his pocket and opened the lid; it played a vaguely familiar French tune that she couldn't put a name to.

"Ten thirty already. Pretty little object isn't it?" He held it out, across the table for her to see, allowing the chain to slip through his fingers. She gazed, fascinated by the twirling reflection created by the chandelier as his soporific voice, slowly and surely invaded her senses.

"Your eyes are very heavy. I want you to raise your right hand, Amy."

Amy didn't respond and his eyes narrowed; she was fighting him.

"Raise your right hand Amy," he repeated. This time, after a moment's hesitation she obeyed and he relaxed giving a satisfied sigh.

"Forget your anger. We are friends. I want to help you, but first I need you to help me. Will you do that?"

Amy didn't respond.

"Take your time. Did anybody help you to take the money?"

She smiled. "No."

"Where do you keep it?"

"In a safe place."

He gave a satisfied nod. "You are a very clever girl, can you remember your computer password?"

Her face relaxed and she said dreamily, "I always wanted to be called Miranda. It's such a lovely name."

He gave another satisfied nod and said, "When I snap my fingers you will wake and not remember this conversation."

When Amy came round, he was refilling her glass.

"So why have you brought me here?"

Manuel was pleased to hear her pick up their conversation where they left off and pretended to think for a moment before answering.

"You challenged me to control you." He sat down beside her and she turned her head away. "Why are you afraid to look at me?"

"I did no such thing and I'm certainly not afraid of you."

He took her hand and pressed it to his lips and for a moment she could hardly breathe; she could feel herself drifting but anger came to her rescue and she snatched her hand away, answering scathingly, "In fact I can assure you I have no feelings towards you, whatsoever."

"Don't you?" He was smiling confidently and she wanted to hurl something at his self-satisfied face.

"Unless hate counts."

He continued to smile. "That will do for the time being. Hate is akin to love." His voice became business like. "Come, it is bedtime."

She looked at him haughtily. "Don't think you are coming to my room again, I'm quite able to defend myself tonight."

He ignored the remark and led the way along a thickly carpeted hallway to the bedrooms. "Sleep well," he said disappearing into his own bedroom across the hall. Amy stood for a moment in her doorway, disconcerted at being robbed of the satisfaction of fighting him off and as she lodged a chair under the handle of the door, she asked herself how Yana had entered, in spite of the precaution. The whole place appeared to be on one level. On her way to dinner, she had noticed there were no outer doors and the few windows were securely locked, but there wasn't even a window in this room. Escape was going to be tricky.

She slept badly and woke bad tempered. Yana brought her early morning tea and said breakfast would be ready in one hour.

"But I won't; I will be there in two," Amy snapped.

"Breakfast will be in one hour," Yana repeated, closing the door behind her.

Two hours later, Amy sauntered along to the dining room to find it empty; the table was cleared and the delicious smell of cooking pervading the house earlier, was being smothered by the sweet perfume of cinnamon joss sticks burning in brass holders.

Sitting in his study, Manuel watched her expression change from smug to indignant and amused himself by watching her search, until she eventually found the kitchen.

Yana turned from putting dishes away, to answer her demand for breakfast.

"My brother will return at twelve o'clock. Lunch will be at twelve thirty."

She disappeared through a beaded archway, leaving Amy with pursed lips.

"I'll help myself then." She tossed her head, strode to a small fridge, threw back the door and stood in silence, contemplating empty shelves. She stamped her foot. "This has gone far enough." The beaded curtain over the archway was still swinging as she pushed her way through; and her eyes lit up as she saw a door leading to a small courtyard; beyond which was a narrow strip of lawn surrounded by shrubs and trees. She was actually out of the house; there had to be a way out of the grounds. Picking up her long skirt, she broke into a sprint, reached the edge of the lawn and barged into the shrubs, pushing her way towards a high stone wall. In her haste, she ran into a large white sign with black lettering and after reading it fled back to the safety of the house, where she slammed the courtyard door behind her and leant against it gasping for breath.

From the study, Manuel and Yana gave confident nods and Manuel switched the screen off. "She won't try again. See you at twelve."

He left by a flight of stone steps leading to his underground garage and drove off, satisfied that the warning about snakes had been effective.

At lunchtime, Amy accused Yana of starving her, but he calmly asked, "Were you not told when breakfast would be served?"

"I wasn't ready," she argued.

"You must learn obedience. I trust you will be on time tomorrow." He calmly unfolded his napkin and picked up his fork.

"And if I'm not?" she continued.

"Then you will shed a few pounds."

Amy's eyes flashed angrily and she made the mistake of saying, "I don't need to lose weight!"

Manuel looked her up and down and even leant back a fraction, studying her critically before raising his eyebrows and continuing his meal.

"How dare you?" Outraged by his insolence she picked up his glass of wine, threw it down the front of his immaculate, pearl grey suit and sat back still defiant, but slightly aghast at what she had done.

His dark eyes glittered dangerously for a single second, before the smile returned and he stood up.

"If you will excuse me, I seem to have spilt my wine."

Some of the wine had splashed on to his plate and without a word, Yana replaced it and sat waiting for Manuel to return before continuing her meal, while Amy ignored her and nonchalantly helped herself to more curried fish. Manuel returned having changed into a fresh suit and the rest of the meal was eaten in silence.

Later when she went up to her room, her own clothes were hanging in the wardrobe and the saris had been taken away. She found the action curious but was glad to have her own clothes back, and deliberately chose a revealing, long white dress from 'Estell's' Boutique, well aware that showing her shoulders was offensive in India. Reminded of London, she felt homesick; more important though what had become of Peter?

She ate alone that evening, and Yana vanished after clearing away. Wondering what to do, she wandered through the house opening doors; puzzling over how pristine and opulent everything was. He obviously didn't live here so it was probably just a store for his tremendous collection of art and riches. That would explain the empty fridge, no doors and shuttered windows. More than likely there was a highly sensitive alarm, as well. Then there was the question of how they just seemed to appear and disappear. So what was it all about? Why had she been brought here? It made no sense.

The air conditioning kept the house at a very even temperature and was probably set to perfection for the antiques. Working on the theory that it was some kind of Aladdin's cave, she asked herself what would happen if she altered the thermostat; would an alarm sound, would Manuel come running to save his precious antiques and what would happen if she broke something? She picked up a valuable looking vase and put it down again carefully. On second thoughts she would save that one for later; no point in pushing him too far yet. She decided her clothes had been returned, as a warning that her dress would get the same treatment as his suit, if it happened again. He was holding all the cards – for now. "But fortunes can change and I know you wouldn't leave me completely unguarded for this long," she murmured to herself.

She had reached the kitchen and felt the need for fresh air. If she stayed well back from the shrubbery, it should be safe enough.

The warm evening closed around her as she let herself out through the door beyond the bead curtain, but unprepared for how dark it would be she instantly stepped back inside, just as Yana appeared from nowhere looking anxious; her relief was obvious when she saw Amy coming back through the curtain…

"Can I get you something?" she asked, bowing over her long, slim hands. Amy asked for a glass of wine and went back to the sitting room. Waiting for

Yana to bring the wine, her eyes glowed triumphantly. Without moving her head, she allowed her eyes to travel round the room searching for a camera, her smile fading as she realized with a shock that her bedroom was almost certainly monitored. What else was this man capable of? Bored with nothing to do, she decided to take her wine to her bedroom and have a Jacuzzi, but instead of stripping off as usual and going to the bathroom, she undressed carefully, wrapped herself in a big towel and held it in front of her until she was under the water.

Watching the screen in his bedroom and suspecting she had guessed, Manuel strolled across the hallway and let himself in by a concealed door. Smiling with amusement at the chair lodged under the handle he sauntered into the bathroom where, surrounded by candles, Amy was luxuriating in the foaming Jacuzzi; trying to work out how to escape the ludicrous situation she was in.

Eyes half closed she reached for the glass of wine on the side of the bath and felt it placed in her hand; her eyes shot open with fright and she slipped under the water, taking the glass with her. Manuel laughed loudly and sauntered out again.

"That wasn't funny," Amy spluttered, pulling a towelling robe on and storming into the bedroom.

Sprawling elegantly on the bed, he gave a disarming smile and patted the space beside him. "Come; why not relieve our boredom together for a while."

Incensed beyond endurance, Amy picked up a delicate china vase and hurled it, narrowly missing him as it hit the padded headboard. He shot to his feet in alarm, inspecting the vase.

Jubilant at seeing the confident smile wiped off his face, Amy picked up the matching one.

"You think you are lord and master and women will come running to do your bidding; well strange though it may seem to you, this one finds you revolting."

He deftly caught the second vase and clutching them both, was making hastily for the door when an elegant, enamel hairbrush, went whizzing past his head, hit the door forcibly and broke into several pieces at his feet, where he stared at it in silent horror before slowly turning to face her. Arm raised, ready to throw a Wedgwood powder bowl, Amy froze, noting his look of utter disbelief before she let fly again, knowing with triumphant satisfaction that she had found his Achilles heel. He watched in helpless dismay as the blue bowl also hit the door, smashing into a hundred pieces, spreading a cloud of fine powder around him. One more item hit the door as he closed it behind him and Amy wiped her hands together, with glee.

Half an hour later Yana brought her a bedtime drink and left without her usual bow.

Late the following morning, Amy awoke with a terrible headache, to find her room bare of ornaments; even the beautiful bottles filled with oils and jars of expensive creams had been removed during the night. When she left her room, she discovered more evidence of how busy they had been while she slept; everything breakable had been removed, including the vast number of ornamental mirrors.

There was no sign of Manuel, during the day and that evening she ate dinner alone again. When Yana disappeared, she made another fruitless search of every possible nook and cranny and decided eventually that a different approach was necessary if she was to escape. Calm and complacent might make them relax and get careless.

She waited up until twelve o'clock, but when there was no sign of Manuel, went to bed, convinced she had won and he was sulking.

Three days went by without any sign of him and she was getting more frustrated with each one that passed.

*

Monica had only just sat down when Manuel walked briskly towards their table. She could tell immediately that he was not his usual composed self, just by the way he moved. That would be why he had suggested meeting in this out of the way place she thought apprehensively. Two angry spots of colour showed on his cheeks as he greeted her unsmilingly and she wondered what could have upset him to the degree that his message had said: *'Be at 'Tonnanini's at eight o'clock';* no, would you, or please; just be there.

He sat down, ordered wine and waved the waiter away saying they would order later.

"She has got to go," he said without preamble. "I'm almost certain she doesn't have millions, or she would have tried to bargain her way out before now."

"What has happened? I thought you were amusing yourself."

"Not any more; she started breaking things; beautiful, things." His face lost its colour as he spoke and she reminded herself of his reputation for worshipping and going to any lengths to acquire, rare and beautiful things.

271

"They can be replaced when you persuade her to part with all that money. If anybody can do it you can." She gave a flirty little smile, desperate to persuade him to keep Amy and Peter, just until her plan to incriminate them was complete; then and only then would she be free to visit her grandson.

"You have given me a very tedious challenge and as I say I don't think she has the money. Her laptop only responds to certain things with the password she gave me."

"You have her laptop – and the password?" Monica looked surprised. "How did you manage that?"

"I— persuaded her to tell me. I have spent days trying, but it only comes up with a bank account with a relatively small amount in it. She says she has a safe. Pah!"

As much as he hated the idea, he wondered briefly if Amy could have been fooling him; but no it wasn't possible, not with his skill; he was certain she had been under. "She has no womanly attributes, no appreciation of my prowess as a lover and benefactor," he said arrogantly.

"I'll take a look at the laptop tomorrow." Monica couldn't believe her luck; now she would be able to set up a real account.

"We could go tonight," he suggested with a hopeful gleam in his eyes, still reluctant to let Amy go if there was the slightest chance.

Later as they left the hosteria, a high wind got up and heavy rain began to fall. Summer storms were frequent and sometimes caused a lot of damage but more often than not, they blew themselves out and life was only briefly disrupted. The powerful beam of the headlights pierced the darkness, eerily exposing an almost invisible track through the dense undergrowth, as the car turned off the road and approached the underground garage. When they got within thirty feet, Manuel pressed a switch and an automatic door swung inwards, revealing a dimly lit tunnel carved in the rock, before the door closed after them and inky darkness enveloped the outside area once again.

Manuel led the way up a long flight of stone steps, ducking his head as he stepped into a small room. Monica followed, gripped with an intense sense of curiosity, anxious to see how Manuel operated; knowing few people were privileged to do so. Yana was sitting writing and keeping an eye on several screens. She looked up to greet them as an opulent looking bedroom came into view on one screen. They all watched Amy emerge from the adjoining bathroom wearing a white towelling robe and carefully slip her nightdress over her head before discarding it.

Manuel gave a disgruntled frown. "She is a very astute. It took no time at all for her to realize she was being watched and she has tried every possible way to escape. I thought she would appreciate the luxurious lifestyle and be prepared to share her life and fortune with me, but she has no womanly discipline or respect."

Monica smiled to herself, realising that Amy had severely bruised his immense ego. He pressed a button and Peter appeared, stretched out on a king sized bed, looking worried and jumpy.

"Chambers on the other hand is no challenge; has no idea of being watched, nervous of what is going to happen to him and even more nervous of trying to escape. He does however suspect she has money tucked away, but doesn't know where."

Monica gave a satisfied nod.

Manuel produced the laptop and Monica logged on flamboyantly, making it look as complicated as she could. Amy's two bank accounts appeared, plus one for Estelle's.

"That could be something." Monica knew very well that it wasn't but she needed Manuel to hold on to Amy and Peter for at least another week.

"Why don't I take this home? I'm sure I can come up with something."

Manuel shrugged. "You may as well; it is of no use to me. Yana my dear, get Barbara a drink; I think she is about to make us all extremely rich."

A conspiratorial smile passed between him and Monica and she relaxed back in a chair, satisfied that she had won the essential time.

They sat talking over a glass of wine and it was late when Manuel said it was time he took her home, dashing her hopes of staying for the night. It galled her to realize she found him tremendously exciting, because his reputation for liking young women put her at a disadvantage and fear of rejection made her wary. Tonight of all nights, she had anticipated he would take her to his bed.

"Don't forget this," he said breaking into her thoughts as they were preparing to leave. Handing her the laptop, he read her disappointment and as they descended to the car he whispered, "Our lovemaking is less likely to be interrupted, in your home."

*

Yana placed the tea on the bedside table; her agitation, although obvious, completely escaped Amy in her half-awake state as Yana hurried from the room.

Amy hauled herself into a sitting position, looking forward to the tea, which at first she had found unpalatable without milk. The date on her digital watch reminded her she had been a prisoner for over a week and she glowered balefully at the chair standing back in its rightful place again.

She poured herself more tea from the plain white teapot that had replaced the dainty bone china one, and compared the white pottery mug with the Royal Albert teacup. "As if I'm bothered," she said aloud. "Just let me out or tell me why I'm here," she screamed, just before oblivion claimed her.

*

The whirr of a ceiling fan penetrated Amy's subconscious and she became aware of a body lying next to her. Slowly turning her head she saw Peter. His eyes were closed and for one terrible moment she thought he was dead, but as she watched with eyes like saucers, he stirred, turned his back to her and settled again. Her head was aching and there was that funny smell she recognised as one of Manuel's potions. She fought the nausea rising in her throat and shook Peter.

"Peter, Peter, wake up."

He made no response so she shook him harder, saying sharply, "Peter, Pee-terr, for heaven's sake, wake up and tell me what's going on."

He murmured something unintelligible and went back to sleep.

"Aargh." She pushed herself out of bed, staggered into the bathroom, filled a glass with water and staggered back, slopping it over the tiled floor. Tipping it over his head, didn't seem to have any effect and she realised most of it had spilt before she got to him. Sliding on the wet floor, she returned to the bathroom and splashed her own face with cold water, before trying to wake him again.

Instead of filling a glass she soaked a towel, rung it out as far as she could and dripped it back to the bed; this time he woke with a start when the cold towel landed on his chest and Amy collapsed beside him.

"How did we get here?" he managed to ask after a few minutes, realising they were back in Manuel's father's hotel.

"I don't know. Manuel has been keeping me prisoner."

"Me too; in this really elaborate room. I only saw Manuel once, the rest of the time an Indian woman just came and went with food. He kept asking about you and playing with this gold pocket watch. He put the fear of god into me."

Amy looked at the time and date on her watch. "That's curious; how did we get to here from India so quickly?"

274

"Not possible; we obviously never left Tenerife and were brought here in a great hurry," he emphasised, in a great hurry, by fingering the blue silk nightdress she was still wearing. They stared at each other and she crept into bed beside him, where they lay hugging each other like frightened, confused children, until excited voices in the hall, followed by a loud banging on their door, made them sit bolt upright. Too befuddled to move, they heard the door open and an annoyed exclamation, as a maintenance man strode into the bathroom and turned the basin tap off. For the first time they noticed water seeping all over the floor. Amy had left the tap running when she had soaked the towel.

The man was joined by two maids, and all three of them speaking rapid Spanish, stared curiously at Peter and Amy sitting up in bed looking half-dazed. The manager appeared and advised Peter and Amy to go and sit on the balcony while the water was mopped up. Still feeling the effects of the sleeping draught, they stumbled to the doors, trying to explain that they had been kidnapped. The maintenance man and the maids exchanged amused glances and the girls started to giggle, while the manager giving a long suffering look, muttered, "Anglaise mucho vino." Amy, realising they were saying the English couple had drunk too much wine, tried to protest as Peter flopped into a chair looking haggard and she shielded her eyes from the bright sun; both giving every appearance of a hangover.

The water was quickly mopped up and shortly afterwards, the maids could be heard giggling in the room below, where the alarm had first been raised when water started to trickle though the bathroom ceiling.

"So much for not wanting to draw attention," Amy observed, kicking herself for leaving the tap on. As the effects began to wear off, they managed to shower and dress. Their clothes were hanging in the wardrobe and they were too relieved to find them intact to wonder how they got there.

"Everything except my laptop and handbag," Amy said after searching the wardrobe franticly.

"Try the lid of that case." Peter pointed to a bulge in the zipped compartment and Amy pounced on it, with a sigh of relief and extracted her handbag.

"Don't worry about the laptop; they would need the password. Let's go and get something to eat." Peter gave her a worried look. "You wouldn't have let slip the password would you?"

"No way," she said, relieved that she hadn't entrusted it to Peter.

"I thought not. Come on; I'm starving."

Amy opened her handbag to check for her purse and the first thing she saw made her go cold.

Peter was waiting impatiently outside the open door and looked back to see her staring at a piece of paper in her hand.

"Ever had a feeling of déjà vu?" she said faintly. "We are to be at the airport in one hour; our flight leaves at seven o'clock."

He strode back in, slammed the door behind him and snatched the paper from her. "What is he playing at now? We aren't going anywhere on his say so, again."

He looked at her nervously and she nodded agreement, just as a tap came on the door.

Neither of them moved and after several seconds the tap came again; this time louder. Amy strode to the door and wrenched it open.

"Yes, what is it now?" she just had time to demand angrily before she was pushed roughly aside by Pablo, who then stood back to allow a figure to enter. Dressed in the hotel's beige uniform, of pencil slim skirt, fitted jacket and pillbox hat, neither of them recognised Yana, as she swayed in with her usual calm grace. Amy was the first to recognise her and ask in puzzled disbelief, "What is it you want with us?" as Pablo closed the door and stood with his back to it.

"It is very simple. We wish you to leave the island and not return."

She held up her hand as Amy was about to speak and out of curiosity Amy obeyed.

"First of all you should know that my brother is dead." Her words faltered very slightly and there was silence as Amy and Peter's faces stretched with shock.

"How?" Amy managed to ask.

"The mountain road collapsed and the car went off the edge; they were killed instantly."

Amy pictured the hair-raising ride they had taken with Pablo at the wheel and had to sit down.

"You said they; who else?" Peter wasn't quite sure why he asked, except that it might explain in some way what they were involved in.

"A woman friend he was conducting business with."

"What kind of business; anything to do with us?" Peter asked shrewdly, as an unbelievable suspicion leapt to his mind.

"How could it possibly have anything to do with us?" Amy asked impatiently. "The point is she is letting us go, because she doesn't want it to come out that he kidnapped us."

"You are partially right Miss Bishop, but an accusation like that would only be laughed at. The staff will be witness to your drunken state, this afternoon. You were very helpful."

Amy glared with helpless indignation, but a thought suddenly occurred to Peter.

"Hang on; how do you know her name is Miss Bishop?"

"The Hotel Register of course," Yana said quickly, realising she had let slip again, as she had once before in Amy's bedroom, but fortunately Amy hadn't picked up on it.

"No, we booked in as Mr and Mrs Chambers. Was 'this friend' by any chance, the owner of a big house in Icos?"

For the first time, Yana lost her composure and Peter pressed his point.

"And was she also responsible for having us kidnapped? And just out of interest, what would have happened to us if they hadn't been killed?"

Amy's eyes were wide with admiration as she waited for Yana to answer.

Pablo grunted. "Tell them."

"Mrs Hayle paid my brother a large sum of money to keep you away from her family. I understand you were her son-in-law, Mr Chambers. I have no idea what my brother's plans for you were. I don't think he knew for sure himself." She turned to Amy. "You, I understand, stole her husband. He planned that you would eventually become a willing – shall we say – houseguest and cater to his needs. Your life would have had many advantages, but you would have had to learn – obedience, of course."

Amy looked at her coldly. "Isn't the word slave?"

Peter interrupted. "I knew it. Monica Spencer fooled us all again. She never left Tenerife; she just changed her name and sold the house to herself, as Barbara Hayle. *That* was why it was extortionately overpriced; it stopped anyone from viewing. She didn't even have to remove her things." He gave an admiring chortle.

Yana listened, enlightened by the fact that the fabulously rich woman she had known as Barbara Hayle from America, was actually the English woman the police had been searching for; Miguel had never mentioned that, and she would never know now, whether he knew or not.

"You are right in thinking I don't want my brother's name besmirched and that I am unsure of what to do with you, other than provide private passage back to Britain. I seriously advise you to be on the plane, because you wouldn't like the alternative of Pablo taking you out in his boat."

They regarded her uncertainly until the look in her dark eyes, so like her brother's, assured them it wasn't an idle threat.

"The apples don't fall far from the tree, do they?" Peter joked nervously.

"Don't worry; we are going; why don't you go and let us get packed?"

Yana halted at the door, to say, "Just one last warning."

"And that is?" Amy drew herself up, waiting.

My brother gave his word that you two would never be allowed near Barbara's daughter or husband again; custom has it, his family must keep that word."

The silence that followed her departure was reminiscent of the one when Manuel left this very room.

"Creepy lot aren't they?" Peter said with a nervous catch in his throat.

Amy threw a case on to the bed. "Let's just get back home; and whatever you do don't eat or drink anything until we land in Britain."

CHAPTER THIRTY-FIVE

The cul-de-sac came in sight and Samantha breathed a deep sigh of relief. The drive had been long and tiring, because she had only stopped briefly to feed and change Jacob.

Bill was standing at his front door watching for the car, and seeing him she knew she had made the right decision. His delight when she called to say she was only half an hour away had been touching. She had expected to see Ann as well, but she would appear any moment, full of welcoming hugs.

Bill greeted her with a kiss on each cheek and couldn't wait to be introduced to Jacob, who as always smiled happily at a new face.

"Come in, come in," he said relieving her of Jacob in his car seat.

Samantha collected her handbag and Jacob's large holdall and followed him into the house, where the welcome sight of a ready laid tea tray greeted her.

"The kettle's boiling," Bill, said disappearing to make the tea.

"Where is Ann?" she called through to the kitchen, while rummaging in Jacob's bag for a box of tissues.

Not receiving an immediate answer, she was about to call again when he appeared in the archway. His face was serious.

"A little bit of bad news I'm afraid. Roy passed away two weeks ago and Ann had a heart attack. She is in the clinic and I'm expecting her home soon. We can visit her tomorrow, but in the meantime we will settle you in here and I will sleep in Ann's house for however long you can stay."

Samantha was devastated. "Oh no, poor Ann, but please don't go to all that trouble; I was going to stay at 'Riverview', like I did before."

"I won't hear of it." Bill shook his head and returned to the kitchen to fetch the tea.

"I really must," Samantha insisted, acutely conscious that it was a bad time to burden him with her problems.

His face creased. "Please stay. It would mean so much to me. I can't imagine my life, without Ann."

Knowing that feeling, her heart went out to him.

Later when they had eaten and Jacob was sleeping upstairs, in a travel cot borrowed from the hotel, Bill broached the reason for her visit.

"I could tell something was bothering you, even before I told you about Ann."

His perception surprised her and he explained before she had a chance to ask.

"Little ways you have of using your hands or tilting your head. You can't possibly know how many of Pamela's ways you have."

It seemed so natural to be talking to him about her mistakes and misfortunes, and he listened without comment until she said:

"And now it is happening all over again, but this time my eyes are wide open and I just know Luke is the one who could turn my life back to the way things were before Grandfather died."

Bill gave a worried frown and shook his head. "No one can turn the clock back for us; sometimes they can make a new beginning though. First you need to face what he intends to do. I don't imagine running away has helped."

Watching her struggling with her emotions, reminded him of a time when Pamela mistakenly thought he didn't want her, and the relief when they were reunited in this very room.

"From what you say, Luke is in the middle of making big decisions and you haven't given him a chance to explain."

"I'm too afraid of the answer."

Unsure of how to advise her, he said, "I think we both need sleep. Ann is sure to have some good advice." He smiled confidently. "She always has. Good night, little one."

Ann's pleasure at their arrival the following day was heart-warming; she brightened immediately when Jacob was put on the bed beside her. Samantha was saddened to see her looking thinner and older, but typically, Ann's main concern was that she wasn't at home to look after them.

"I really should have taken your cooking in hand," she scolded Bill affectionately.

"Yes dear," he answered, overjoyed to see some semblance of her old self.

When Jacob began to get restless, he picked him up, saying, "Come and meet the staff young man; mummy needs a chat."

"Do I gather from that rather obvious exit that you have a problem?"

"You don't need my problems," Samantha assured her.

"Indeed I do; they will be a welcome distraction; let me help if I can."

By the time Bill returned with Jacob, visiting was over. Ann said a fond goodbye to Samantha and Jacob, and called after Bill as he was leaving.

"There are plenty of meals in the freezer; make sure you feed them properly." He responded with a salute and a click of his heels.

On the way home, he asked if the chat had helped and looked pleased when Samantha said Ann had told her the story of when Pamela mistook the situation.

"She said to make sure I'm not jumping to wrong conclusions and to stop running away from the truth, even if it does hurt."

Through the evening, he noticed her picking her phone up and putting it back down; debating whether to phone, or willing it to ring? He couldn't tell which. Unusually, Jacob took a long time to go down.

"Teething," Samantha explained, returning downstairs for the third time.

Glancing at his watch, Bill declared, "Time for a nice cup of tea, I think."

At that moment, Jacob cried out again. "You see to Jacob; I'll make the tea."

By this time the crying was in earnest and she hurried back upstairs while Bill eased himself out of his chair. As he was half way to the kitchen, Samantha's mobile phone vibrated on the arm of her chair; he called up the stairs but his voice was drowned by Jacob's sobs and he decided to leave it until she came down.

When Samantha did return she was carrying Jacob and the next hour was taken up with soothing cuddles and tooth gel, until eventually, she said wearily that she would take him back to bed and stay with him. As he saw the landing light go out, Bill took the cups to the kitchen. He returned to the sitting room, planning on an early night himself, but a slight sound, coming from down the side of Samantha's armchair, caught his attention as he turned the television off and he retrieved her mobile phone, remembering then that he had forgotten to mention the earlier text. He started towards the stairs, but changed his mind, on hearing no sound.

"Sleep is more important at the moment," he murmured, recalling her tiredness. Intending to switch the phone off, to avoid it disturbing her again, he pressed option by mistake and feeling guilty read the message:

'Please speak to me. Everything is being sorted.'

On impulse, he sent his address before he could change his mind, praying that he was doing the right thing, then switched it off and put it on the bookcase for Samantha to find in the morning

*

Luke paced up and down, waiting for Chas's plane to land, hardly noticing how damp he was getting. It was barely light and the mist coming from the sea wasn't helping visibility, but the runway lights blazed a clear path and the jet plane made a perfect landing, earning Luke's admiration, even in his state of agitation.

They greeted each other as they always had before events had turned them into strangers for nearly two years, and without more ado, they hurried towards Luke's car.

"Thanks for coming so quickly." He had contacted Chas barely twelve hours ago.

"You know you only have to say," Chas replied, humbled by the fact that Luke still trusted him.

They reached the cottage and Luke got breakfast underway, aware that Chas had travelled all night and needed sleep as well as food.

"We'll talk after you've slept. I've made a bed up for you in Kimberley's room for the time being; she is staying at the big house for a couple of nights while I put things right with Sam. I'll leave tomorrow if it's okay with you."

"Is Kimberley alright with that?" Chas looked anxious, knowing how the constant changes had upset her.

"Absolutely." He gave a rueful shrug then grinned. "I quote: 'They have this ginormous rocking horse and they let me sleep in a house in the roof with an old lady, who talks funny and isn't much bigger than me'."

Chas raised his eyebrows and Luke shook his head. "Don't ask."

"It all sounds a bit wacky, but as long as she is happy," Chas said yawning widely.

While Chas caught up with some sleep, Luke slipped down the path to make sure Kimberley was all right. George showed him to the study where Meg was working and he told her that Chas would be staying at the cottage.

"I've made a note of phone numbers you might need." She handed him a piece of card with neatly written names and numbers.

"Thanks a lot and thanks for looking after Kimberley."

"She doesn't take much looking after. When she isn't with Abigail she is with Ella and Sol in the stables. She's there now if you need to speak to her."

Meg looked downcast and on the spur of the moment, knowing how much she would be missing Sam, he said, "Why don't you come and eat with us tonight?"

Meg accepted, welcoming the unexpected break from sharing the evening meal, with Charles, Felicity and Abigail.

"We'll eat about seven thirty then. Come early, you can chat to Chas over a glass of something while I cook."

Making his way to the stables, he was greeted by a squeal of delight from Kimberley and excited barking from the dogs as they all ran to him. Children of different ages watched curiously and Kimberley pointed to one saying, "That's Nadine; she's my friend. Can she come to tea?"

Luke smiled indulgently and picked her up. "Of course, but first I have to go away honey; it will only be for a couple of days and I promise to phone each night."

She clung to him. "Am I staying here?"

"Meg says you can, but you can come with me, if you would rather."

She let go, kissed his cheek and wriggled to be put down. "I'll stay."

He gave a small sigh of relief, but at the same time felt slightly rejected as without a backward glance she ran to Nadine. Sol caught his look and they exchanged good-humoured shrugs.

A frisson of nervous excitement gripped Meg as she climbed the path that evening. Unused to the luxurious life style, she worried that it showed. If only Sam were here, to say if the yellow cotton dress dotted with small white daisies was right.

She hesitated shyly at the top of the grassy slope, as Luke called to her to come and meet Chas. He was heading for a shiny, new BBQ, set up a short distance from the cottage, closely followed by a dark-haired, slightly built figure carrying a tray of food. Her nerves disappeared immediately. She guessed by how relaxed and organized they were, that it was nothing new to them, but alfresco living was new to her and she thoroughly enjoyed helping to carry freshly made salad dishes out to the table, where crusty rolls and a bottle of wine were already set out on a pale blue tablecloth. Thick steaks had been marinating all day, in a delicious smelling concoction of garlic and herbs, and Luke settled his guests down with a glass of wine each, before wandering off to place them over the glowing embers.

It was a perfect August evening with a calm sea, looking like a big blue blanket with a white crocheted edge where it whispered onto the shore. A light, warm breeze drifted in as they sat enjoying the panoramic view and Luke was standing very still with his back to them. Meg thought he was watching the food until she saw him slip his phone into his pocket.

He grew quieter as the evening progressed, but Chas was easy company, and good food and wine kept them talking until the candles burned themselves out and Meg reluctantly said it was time for her to go home.

"You walk Meg home, I'll get ready for tomorrow," Luke said.

"Send out a search party if I'm not back soon," Chas called from the path.

Luke heard Meg's light laugh and smiled to himself as he picked up the glasses and took them to the kitchen. His holdall was packed and he left it beside the front door, placing his mobile phone on top so that he wouldn't forget it. Waiting for Chas to come back, he wrote down a few last minute details and left the pad on the kitchen breakfast bar. Chas was going to make himself known to Jonathan Sugden and set up the office at the airfield while he was away; which would free the small bedroom until more space could be arranged for him.

Chas returned looking thoughtful. "Now that is a lovely girl; why aren't you interested in her?"

"Wait until you see Sam," Luke answered soberly, dashing to the front door as his phone buzzed.

He came back clutching the phone. "Sam is in London; not Southampton."

"And that makes a difference because?" Chas waited.

"No one even mentioned London."

"So?"

"Whose address is this?"

"Only one way to find out."

"Supposing it's Jacob's father?"

Chas looked flummoxed. "Who's Jacob? Maybe you had better tell me exactly what you have gotten yourself into here."

They settled in the sitting room with a pot of coffee and Luke brought Chas up to date with events, including how Kelly had turned up unexpectedly, demanding money in exchange for sole custody of Kimberley. He hadn't actually intended telling anybody about that, but the old habit of confiding in Chas had quickly returned.

"I can only assume she hired a private detective to find me. I gave my solicitor strict instructions not to give her my address."

"I'm sure you're right, knowing how desperate she must have been to find you. Apparently this tennis player is quoted as saying: 'Lose the baggage. I don't do brats; cute or otherwise'."

Luke looked startled. "Thank goodness she did find me. He sounds a right ***. I dread to think what Kimberley has been subjected to."

"Apparently Kelly is absolutely crazy about him and needs money to follow him on the circuit. I wanted her to leave Kimberley with me, but she was afraid of losing her hold over you. She squeezed every last penny she could get out of me."

"Is that how your business failed?"

"That was mostly due to bad publicity. When people rely on you for security systems, they have to feel they can trust you, so business dropped off. My name was mud and I could see the writing on the wall, so I decided to sell up rather than go bankrupt. She told everyone from the day she moved into my house that you had run off with someone, your father had thrown her out and we were planning to get married as soon as she could divorce you. We played right into her hands one way or another. Thank goodness I told her my dad hadn't left me a huge fortune and she changed her mind pretty quick. Don't know where she got that idea from in the first place, but it is my guess this guy was on the scene, even before you broke up."

Luke was silent with shock.

"You don't have to pay her; the last thing she wants is to take Kimberley back with her. It's my guess she and the tennis player are in this together."

"What makes you say that?" Luke asked curiously.

"I met him at a couple of the parties, before it became obvious they were having an affair. He was always on about starting his own training centre when he had enough money but once he is set up he could leave her."

Luke's jaw set hard. "My solicitor is coming over from the States, next week."

Knowing that look from old, Chas gave a satisfied nod; it said Kelly's fun at their expense was over. Luke, like his father, was a good man but having been taken for a fool once, he wasn't about to let it happen again.

They talked long into the night, piecing together exactly what happened.

Brian Hathaway had been a robust, energetic Scotsman who married an American girl and through sheer hard work became successful. Being a wily Scot, he summed Kelly up on their first meeting, when she was nearly nineteen and four months pregnant with Luke's baby. It was clear to him that she planned to marry his son and leave with a large settlement, as soon as possible. Convinced of this he took steps to ensure there was very little money in his son's name, and without voicing his suspicions, watched and waited, hoping he was wrong.

Fresh from college, Luke shared none of his father's misgivings, and after one attempt to dissuade him, Brian knew any objection on his part would only estrange his son, because he was absolutely besotted with his beguiling young wife. When Kimberley was born, Luke's only thought was to create a home and raise a big family and hardly daring to hope that he was wrong, Brian moved into a smaller property, saying he would sign his large, six-bedroom house over to them, as it was much too big for him anyway. Somehow or another though he never did get round to actually signing the papers, so when the split came less than two years later, the house Kelly thought would be part of her settlement, still lawfully belonged to Brian.

Luke was devastated and tried to hold the marriage together; convinced that more children would rekindle the love he thought they had shared. Kelly laughed and said the last thing she wanted was more children with him. Luke finally gave up when, on learning how little she would be entitled to, she flew into a rage and told him Chas was the one she should have married; he was the one she had always loved.

He packed a bag and rode off into the hills, on Sapphire. In boyhood pacts they had always agreed that, whichever one of them Kelly chose, the other would accept it without any hard feelings.

He stayed away for three months; going over how he could have been so blind and by the time he got back, Kelly was already living with Chas.

Luke learnt now that she had gone to his house late one evening, saying Luke had run off with someone else and that Brian had turned her out. Carrying Kimberley and appearing to be on the verge of collapse she had begged Chas to let them stay, insisting they had nowhere to live. Bewildered and unable to make sense of her story, Chas had taken them in and overnight it became gossip that they were living together although that was never the case. In Luke's absence, Brian assumed his son had taken off, after discovering Chas and Kelly had been having an affair behind his back and refused to see Chas or listen to any explanation from him.

Rumours abounded, and any denials from Chas were greeted with derision. It had always been common knowledge in their small community, that both boys were besotted with her and the last straw came when doubts were cast on which one of them was Kimberley's father.

As influential as he was, Brian Hathaway was helpless to quash the scandal and with his good name under fire, his health began to suffer. Often outspoken towards the newshounds, they in turn spared him no mercy. Luke got a speedy divorce to put an end to the gossip but nine months later, Brian, who everyone thought would live until his nineties, died of a massive heart attack.

Kelly neither denied or confirmed any rumours. Playing the injured party she tearfully brushed aside awkward questions and gained local popularity by throwing impromptu parties at the tennis club. That was when she supposedly met Jason Leopold the local tennis ace, or Leo, as he liked to be called. Tall and athletic, he was easily recognised by his wavy golden hair, deep blue eyes and ruggedly handsome features. A lazy smile, practised to perfection to display perfect white teeth, made him the idol of every woman, on and off the tennis-courts and his magic worked instantly on Kelly, when he first bestowed one of those famous, well rehearsed, come to bed smiles on her and murmured sweet nothings in her ear.

Piecing the individual bits together, made Luke and Chas recall the strain Brian must have been under, dealing with Kelly's lies, missing his adored granddaughter and watching Luke go to pieces over, not only losing his daughter, wife and best friend, but having his private life spread in all the papers.

"Perhaps Dad would still be alive, if he had just given her the money," Luke said miserably.

"There was no way your dad was going to let her get the better of him; and that is all the more reason not to give in now."

"She could still make a horrible mess of our lives here if she spreads the same lies."

Chas gave him a worried look, cursing Kelly for her vengeful vendetta against Luke, when he had just found this idyllic place, to start life again. A vendetta he himself had unwittingly been a part of.

"Let's get tomorrow over with first; you will feel better when you have sorted things out with Samantha."

CHAPTER THIRTY-SIX

'4am. Have gone to the clinic. Ann needed me. You were both sleeping soundly so wouldn't wake you. Will be in touch later.'

Heart thumping wildly, Samantha reread the note from Bill, before quickly dressing Jacob, putting his breakfast in a cool bag and calling a taxi. By six thirty, she was standing beside Ann's bed.

Looking grave, Bill explained that matron had sent for him saying Ann was in pain and having difficulty in breathing.

"But she seemed fine yesterday," Samantha whispered, tears rolling down her cheeks.

Bill gave a resigned nod. "Complications set in and we are waiting to see if she is strong enough to be operated on."

"Please don't let her die."

Bill shook his head sadly. "It's out of my hands. I'm not allowed to operate; but even if I were, I'm not capable any more." He sat down, clutched Ann's hand in both of his and buried his head on the bed beside her still form.

At that moment, the door opened to admit a white-coated figure.

"Sorry Bill, I came as soon as I could."

Bill raised his head. "I knew you would," was all he said.

Samantha went in search of Jacob. Matron had taken him off and at that moment, having been fed he was sitting playing happily in his pushchair, while Matron dealt with paperwork in her office. Waiting for the result of Ann's examination seemed to take forever, but eventually Bill arrived with news that an operation would be performed later that morning and he was going to stay with her whilst she was prepared. By this time, Jacob was getting restless and Matron had her rounds to do so Samantha put him in his pushchair and went for a walk along the embankment. It was a grey morning, with darkening clouds forecasting rain later; the river looked murky, reflecting the dull grey of the sky, reminding her of the sea, when the sand tossed about by giant waves, muddied the crystal clear sea of sunnier days. Suddenly homesick, she stopped and reached down in the well of the pushchair for her handbag. Doubts and fears were not important now. She just wanted to hear Luke's voice. Ann and Bill's encouraging words rang in her head as she searched for her phone, before realising she had left it at the house. Disappointment brought a sob to her throat, but missing the soothing movement of the pushchair Jacob cried out and she had to continue walking. By the time, she returned to the clinic, he was sleeping soundly and Matron invited her to wait in her office.

One of the kitchen staff brought them a tray with a pot of tea and fresh croissants, and she ate hungrily.

"I rather guessed you forgot to feed yourself this morning," Matron said briskly, tutting at Samantha's white face, adding more kindly, "Mrs Murry will be going down in about an hour. Why don't you have a nap while baby is sleeping?"

Samantha assured her she wouldn't be able to sleep, but gratefully sat in the armchair rather than the upright one. Matron left and returned ten minutes later; as expected they were both sleeping soundly, and before leaving she put a, 'Do not Disturb' notice on the outside of the door.

By mid afternoon, Ann was through the operation and in the recovery room. Jacob became fretful again and Bill advised Samantha to go home and wait for his call, which could still be several hours away.

Hating to leave but realising it made sense she decided to walk part of the way, to get some fresh air. So much of her day was spent outside at Anders Folly that she couldn't imagine being cooped up on a daily basis.

She strode out; as always, the movement of the pushchair comforted Jacob and although it had started to drizzle with rain, the plastic cover enveloping the whole chair kept him completely dry. Confident there was no need to worry about him, she put the hood of her anorak up and briskly wended her way between hurrying pedestrians.

About halfway to Bill's house the rain grew heavier and within seconds the storm clouds that had threatened all day burst in a torrential downpour. Awnings bent under the weight and drainpipe hoppers, inadequate to cope with the torrents of rainwater, overflowed on to the pavements, drenching passers-by before they had time to dodge the cascades. One extra strong gust of wind all but took the pushchair out of Samantha's hands and she looked about in panic for somewhere to shelter.

Seeing a doorway not far away, she used every ounce of strength she could muster and practically carrying the chair, edged her way along, keeping as close to the wall as possible until she was able to step inside a doorway, which turned out to be the small lobby to a slightly dark looking wine bar beyond. Thankful to have found shelter, she decided to wait out the storm in the small lobby and then hail a taxi, but at that moment, a man came through the inner door and held it open, urging her to hurry so that he could close the outer door. She hesitated, but the man was already helping with the pushchair by guiding it into the dimly lit interior.

Forced to follow she quickly caught up with the chair and started to release Jacob from his straps. He was crying loudly, frightened by the sudden rough handling and noise of the storm.

The man returned from fastening the doors and pointed to a chair. She picked Jacob up, trying to soothe him, and as her eyes got used to the dimness, noted couples frowning at her for disturbing their peace; most likely unaware of the violent summer storm, that had forced her to seek shelter in what appeared to be a huge cellar, stretching into dimly lit corners. She looked around warily, observing uplighters in wrought iron cradles, illuminating the arched, stone ceiling and bare stonewalls. High-backed, red velvet seating formed secluded alcoves, each dimly lit by gold shaded lamps on round tables covered with red linen cloths. The only thing clearly visible was the drinks bar with its fluorescent lights. This stood against one wall to her right.

She became aware of raised voices, and a man's figure appeared from that direction. "Children are not allowed and you are disturbing other patrons; I must ask you to leave."

Samantha removed her dripping wet hood and gazed at Peter. He gazed back and they both froze.

Jacob was still crying and another figure appeared, demanding, "What on earth is going on?" They all three stared speechlessly at one another until Amy recovered and hissed, "What the devil are you doing here? Get out!"

"Why are you here?" Peter asked faintly, mesmerised by the sight of Samantha jogging Jacob in her arms.

"I'm sheltering from the storm, in case you hadn't noticed. You can't imagine I came here on purpose?" Her voice was scornful and Amy looked first at Jacob, who had finally stopped crying and then at Peter.

"He isn't Peter's, if that's what you are thinking," Samantha said, clutching Jacob to her.

Peter slumped onto a nearby chair.

"I know there were rumours; but Peter assures me it's impossible – and I believe him." Amy went and stood behind Peter and put a possessive hand on his shoulder.

Peter's pale grey eyes fixed beseechingly on Samantha and she looked away, saying indignantly, "I should think so!" She put Jacob back in his pushchair. "I believe the storm has passed. I will be on my way."

Out on the rain soaked pavement again, she sighed with relief, murmuring, "I could almost feel sorry for her – but perhaps not."

The storm had blown over as quickly as it came and although the wind remained quite strong, she decided to walk the rest of the way, smiling to herself when she thought of the old line. Of all the bars in all the world.

Heart pounding, Peter closed the door firmly behind her, relief making him keenly aware that although life wasn't to his liking, without Amy it would be even more intolerable; afraid as he was to go back to Lindsey, even though he was sure she would have him in a heartbeat.

On arriving back in Britain, they had spent miserable weeks, hiding out in a cheap bed sitting room, until they heard on the news about Monica's death and a diary discovered in her house in Icos. Meant for her eyes only, it disclosed that she and she alone had succeeded in pulling off the big robbery, and how cleverly she had evaded the police ever since. It also told of her plan to blame Amy for the robbery, as punishment for her affair with William. The newspaper had gone on to say that the stolen money had been restored to the Anders family and Peter's last remaining hope was crushed.

Free from the fear of being arrested and aware of Peter's disappointment, Amy was now tormented by thoughts of him leaving her. With that in mind she had invested the remainder of William's money in a wine bar and told Peter that his name would be added to the deeds on their wedding day, as her wedding gift to him.

"Promise me again that you definitely aren't the father," Amy called from the bedroom, as they retired that night.

Peter paused in the act of towelling himself down and glanced towards the shower, with a yearning expression.

"You heard her; you don't have to take my word for it."

"What are you staring at?" Coming up behind him, she snuggled against his damp back and he said the only thing on his mind:

"Just thinking about having a shower together."

*

A taxi drew out as Sam reached the cul-de-sac, but head bent, she hurried on as Luke turned to ask the driver to take him to a nearby hotel. Then Bill telephoned as she was getting Jacob ready for bed, to say that although Ann wasn't completely out of the woods it was alright for a short visit and quickly putting Jacob into a warm sleeping bag, she drove to the clinic.

Having been driven the short distance to 'Riverview', Luke settled in his room and went down to an early dinner. Mulling over his wasted day he considered the possibility of someone playing a practical joke on him. Why send the address and then not be there? He had spent the day sitting on a bench in the small park opposite the house, except for when the heavens opened and he had sheltered under a huge tree to keep dry. Samantha's car was parked beside the railings, so he had rung the doorbell several times through the day and rung Sam's mobile, but each time it was switched off. He placed his phone on the table beside him, and waiting for his meal to arrive debated whether to ring Chas, before deciding it was unlikely he would be able to help anyway. After eating, he decided to walk the short distance the taxi had driven him and check the house again; in fact, covering the exact same route Samantha had walked earlier. Deep in thought, he passed within thirty feet of her parked car, in the driveway of the clinic.

Thoroughly frustrated at finding the car missing when he got back to the cul-de-sac, he went and sat on the park bench that he had vacated earlier in the day; two hours later, cold and weary he gave up and took a taxi back to the hotel.

Breakfast time was busy at 'Riverview' and by the time he returned to his room to collect his few belongings it was nearly eight thirty. Sitting outside the house again seemed his only option, unless Samantha answered her phone. A piece of card fluttered to the carpet as he withdrew his phone from his pocket and he automatically bent to pick it up whilst ringing Samantha's number. Receiving the message that her phone was switched off, he absently read the list of numbers that Meg had written down.

There was no point in worrying Meg, but he thought he remembered Sam mentioning an Aunt Fran, who had a horde of children. He rang the number and when a woman's voice answered, accompanied by a background of children's voices, he guessed it could be her.

"Hello, my name is Luke Hathaway. You won't know me but I am a friend of Samantha's. I'm in London, but can't contact her at the address I was given. I wondered if you would know of anywhere else I could look? I'm pretty desperate or I wouldn't have bothered you."

"Oh hello; No bother; I didn't know Samantha was in London. What is she doing there?"

"Probably better that she tells you herself."

Luke heard a sigh, before Fran answered.

"Right, well I don't know him, or even if he still does, but the only person I have heard of in London is a William Jessop, who owned the clinic near to a Riverview Hotel."

"I'm staying at 'Riverview'."

"Worth a try then."

"Definitely is. Thanks. Hope we get to meet soon."

"Me too. Bye."

Feeling in better spirits, with something definite to do, he strode out of 'Riverview', his steps quickening eagerly as he neared the tall Victorian mansion set at the end of a row of other tall Victorian houses overlooking the South Bank of the River Thames.

His enquiry to speak to William Jessop was at first met with a polite, "Mr Jessop is not to be disturbed today, but if you call back in the morning I will see he gets a message." Matron gave him one of her looks that usually brooked no argument, but not easily daunted Luke persisted.

"It is really important that I speak with him, concerning Samantha Anders."

Matron held her hand up. "Wait here Mr?"

"Hathaway. Luke Hathaway."

Matron disappeared and returned a few minutes later, followed by Bill, who came towards him, hand extended.

"I'm really pleased to meet you and terribly sorry for messing you about."

Bill explained quickly why they weren't at the house when he arrived, and Luke relaxed, relieved that the tall, distinguished, grey-haired man obviously wasn't Jacob's father.

"But she hasn't been answering her phone either."

"I fear that is my fault as well; after sending you the address I switched it off, put it on the bookcase and unfortunately forgot to tell Sam. I can't tell you how sorry I am."

"You had too much on your mind. I'll go straight to the house now." Luke made to leave but Bill's next words stopped him.

"I think you may have missed her again. She had no idea you were here and left early to travel back to Cornwall."

"How early?" Luke asked, his face a picture of dismay.

"Seven thirty?" Bill said reluctantly giving a helpless gesture of apology.

"Not your fault. Glad to hear your sister is recovering. I can be home before Sam; my plane is at the airfield."

"Let me give you a lift there; it is the least I can do."

Luke accepted and when Bill had dropped him off and was driving back to the clinic, he said softly, "He will do very nicely for your lovely great granddaughter. Take care of them both on their journeys home, Pamela."

After spending the evening with Ann and being assured that she was out of danger, Samantha had slept for a few hours, before making an early start for Cornwall. She found her mobile phone where Bill had left it, only to discover that it needed recharging; and threw it into her handbag in disgust.

On the way home, she had plenty of time to think things over. Everyone said the same thing; running away wasn't the answer; so what was?

Jacob started to fret so she pulled into the next service station. Changing him in the car wasn't easy but she didn't want to stop for long; he would need feeding soon. She settled him with a bottle of boiled water and before long he was sleeping soundly, lulled by the movement of the car.

Unhappy thoughts returned of what she would do if Luke went back to America to be with his wife and daughter. What did the future hold for her and Jacob? She pictured herself and Meg as two single mothers, growing old together in the small world of Anders Folly, which seemed to be getting even smaller as everyone left or died.

She stopped at a Little Chef for an early lunch and, watching people going happily about their daily lives, envied their carefree light heartedness.

By the time she reached the more familiar countryside of Devon, she was impatient to get home and hear what fate had in store. Being August, the roads were busy, although not quite as busy as they would have been on a Saturday. The usual bottlenecks held her in queues of caravans, mobile homes and cars weighed down with children and luggage, and something of their holiday mood rubbed off on her, as admiring enthusiasts tooted their horns and hung out of car windows to get a better view of the ice blue, Mercedes Cabriolet, with the stunning looking girl behind the wheel.

One young man even got out of his car and walked along to speak to her while the queue was at a standstill, but cut the conversation short when he saw Jacob in the passenger seat. Feeling more light-hearted, she reached Anders Folly in the late afternoon and was surprised when no one came out to greet her. George was nowhere in sight, the kitchen was empty; in fact the whole house was empty. Carrying Jacob, she went in search of Sol and Ella; they were sure to be in the stables.

Ella greeted her with a serious smile but Sol disappeared into the stables.

"He has been worried about you; I told him there was no need." Ella held her arms out to Jacob, smiling brightly.

Taken aback by Sol's reaction, Samantha passed Jacob to her, murmuring, "Sorry; just had to get away. Where is everyone?"

"Mrs Charles had a fall about an hour ago. George has driven Lorna and Abigail to help and Meg went out early with Lucy."

Samantha was dismayed. "Is Aunt Felicity all right?"

"Why don't you go and see; they would be pleased to know you are home."

"Of course, but didn't Meg say where she was going?"

She sounded cross and Ella just raised her eyebrows with a sideways look.

"Maybe not," Samantha said quickly, taking Jacob and hurrying off.

Overcome with anxiety, Charles hardly gave her a glance when she arrived, and after a swift greeting, Lorna and Abigail turned their attention back to Felicity who was propped up in bed looking pale and dazed. Fran was sitting with her arm about her and Samantha couldn't hold back the tears when Felicity mumbled, "Ah, there you are Pamela, where are Robert and Sophie? It's their bedtime."

Samantha clasped her hand. "They will be here soon."

The doctor came and said that, although nothing was actually broken she needed to rest before being moved and he gave her painkillers to ease the extensive bruising sustained to her shoulder and head, in falling against a concrete sundial in the garden.

After the doctor left, Charles blamed himself. "I should never have left her, but I thought she was safe, sitting on the bench while I made us a pot of tea."

"You can't possibly watch her every second, Uncle Charles," Fran said pouring a large whisky and handing it to him. He nursed the glass, looking miserably defeated and her heart ached for him. The last months had been a tremendous strain, but she knew they were as nothing, compared to the thought of losing his beloved Felicity.

It was decided that Abigail and Lorna would both stay and look after them until Felicity could be moved to Anders Folly.

As they were getting into their cars, Samantha gave Fran a hug.

"I'm so sorry for adding to your troubles again, Auntie Fran."

"Not now Sam, maybe tomorrow. We need to talk seriously." Her eyes were clouded with unhappiness and Samantha wanted to throw herself in her arms as she used to as a child, but there was no answering gesture from Fran, only a look of resigned weariness.

Returning to Anders Folly Samantha found it deserted again. It was strange to walk into the empty kitchen and even stranger having to get Jacob's dinner herself. She was tired after the long drive and had looked forward to coming home to a cooked meal and Maisie to look after Jacob.

A freshly cooked chicken was sitting in the fridge, along with prepared vegetables; Lorna was obviously making evening dinner when she was called away.

Although she hadn't eaten since lunchtime, she couldn't be bothered with food for herself and just took out enough to make Jacob's meal. He sat happily in a highchair whilst she fed him; and played on the floor while she cleared away the few dishes, before taking him upstairs for his bath. As she was undressing him, Meg hurried in with Lucy; she was smiling broadly.

"Saw your car. I'm so glad you are back." She tickled Jacob's bare tummy and he laughed, obviously pleased to see her, and Lucy hugged him so hard he struggled to escape.

"Nice to know someone is pleased to see us." Samantha pulled a face.

"What do you mean? We were all worried about you; but never mind, you are here now."

Meg's eyes were shining and it was obvious she could hardly contain herself.

"You look as if your day has been good."

"It's been wonderful. I can't wait to tell you my amazing news." She swallowed hard.

"Chas has asked me to marry him," she blurted, waiting for Samantha's reaction.

Samantha finally found her voice to ask, "Who is Chas?"

"Of course, you don't know; he arrived the day after you disappeared. He is Luke's best friend, and came over to help while Luke was looking for you; isn't it marvellous? He is absolutely wonderful." She pirouetted around the room.

"But you can hardly know him." Samantha stared in disbelief.

"Isn't that just what I said to you? But I know now that it is possible to know from the first minute." She fell backwards on the bed, arms outstretched. "I am so o happy."

Samantha knew she should share in her excitement, but that little bit of inherited, controlling gene stopped her.

"I hope you aren't going to rush into anything."

Meg sat up, eyes still shining; nothing could dampen her mood."

"He is wonderful with Lucy and Kimberley adores him."

"Kimberley? You mean Luke's daughter?"

"Yes, she stayed with us while Luke was away; she is absolutely in love with Abigail's accent and her little house in the roof, as she calls it." Meg giggled. "And she loves Felicity, because she keeps calling her Sophie and asking where Robert is. Kimberley thinks it is a game and says he is hiding behind the settee."

Meg's bubbly excitement was making Samantha more and more resentful about what had gone on in her absence, especially as her homecoming had been so cold.

"It would seem a lot has gone on in my absence."

Meg heard the offended note in Samantha's voice and tried to make amends.

"It was—"

Samantha interrupted her. "You won't know then that Aunt Felicity had a fall while you were out and is seriously ill."

Meg was immediately sympathetic. "Poor woman; I am so sorry; is there anything I can do?"

"Everything is in hand thank you." Samantha still sounded offended, but encouraged by a slightly softer tone Meg said, "I was going to say, this all happened because Luke went looking for you. Chas flew over straight away to handle the airfield and Kim wanted to stay here, rather than go with Luke. She is a lovely child and really loves it here. And Luke wouldn't even let her stop him from coming to look for you."

She had been undressing Lucy while she spoke and now lifted her into the big bath, before taking Jacob from Samantha's lap and placing him at the other end. "This could all work out so well for you," Meg finished softly.

Samantha nodded dumbly, ashamed of her jealousy.

"So where did Luke find you?" Meg changed the subject, up to her elbows in soapsuds.

"He didn't. I didn't even know he was looking."

"I think you need to speak to him. He arrived home this morning and said someone called Bill had helped? Apparently he was relieved to find that Bill wasn't Jacob's father."

Samantha gave a glimmer of a smile. "I have been such a fool. I will never run away again."

"I am going to hold you to that." Meg laughed and lifted Jacob out of the bath. "Go and phone him; I can't bear being this happy on my own."

Luke answered his phone straight away.

"I phoned the house when I saw your car in the drive but there was no reply and then you drove off again. Your mobile has been switched off for days and I thought you didn't want to speak to me; but I had to keep trying until you actually said so." He sounded as distraught as she felt.

"I'm sorry. I couldn't face the thought that you were leaving me."

"That will never happen. Come to the window so that I can see you."

She leaned out and he waved. "Just keep talking to me," she said tearfully, slipping into the bathroom and miming to Meg to look after Jacob.

Luke's voice carried on soothingly and she murmured "Mm" every now and then, until he caught sight of her climbing the path, still holding her mobile to her ear. He ran to meet her and pulled her into his arms, kissing her as if he never wanted to stop, sweeping away any lingering doubts.

It was a perfect night; big bright stars filled the heavens, looking as if you could almost touch them, while a big yellow moon hung low over a calm sea. Luke spread a sleeping bag on the lawn and they clung together until dawn crept over the horizon.

CHAPTER THIRTY-SEVEN

Lorna was preparing breakfast when she heard the doorbell ring, and then Charles' delighted cry as Sophie said, "Hello Daddy," throwing her arms around him.

"I'm so glad you are here," he mumbled into her hair. Looking past her he saw Darren standing beside an unfamiliar car, talking to a stranger. "Darren, too?"

"Yes he is waiting to see if you would rather not have too many people right now," Sophie explained emotionally.

Charles waved Darren in. "Come in dear boy, come in."

"Two more for breakfast Lorna," Abigail said giving a relieved nod.

"Yes, Mr Charles will be alright now." Lorna returned the nod.

"They both will, now their girl is here." Abigail continued to nod.

"Don't build up hopes; that was a nasty fall," Lorna cautioned.

"Once we get her back to Anders Folly," Abigail nodded confidently.

Lorna gave her a worried look, knowing that, like herself she saw Felicity and Charles as their last link with the past; and Abigail had nothing but memories these days, whereas she had George to keep her company on lonely nights. Thinking about that she wondered how he was coping. They had never been apart overnight since they married sixteen years ago. How those years had flown, she thought softly to herself.

With breakfast over and cleared away, Sophie said she would manage and Lorna and Abigail should go home. Darren said he must go as well, to see Samantha and Jacob and catch up with Fran.

Left alone, Sophie sat with her parents for what turned out to be one of their last few precious days together. Fran called in on her way up to Anders Folly and left, knowing that things were as happy as they could be.

"They are just sitting peacefully. Sophie is telling them all about her grandchildren and her plan to bring the whole family over for Christmas. They look so happy and peaceful together. All the years apart must have been a terrible wrench for them." Her face creased but she forced a smile. "Hope you are prepared for a house full at Christmas, Sam."

Darren put a comforting arm around her. They were standing on the terrace looking out over the sea and he had just explained to Samantha that he flew Sophie over, after Fran's phone call the previous day.

"Uncle Charles told me this morning how reluctant he has been to tell Sophie about her mother's memory loss problem because of how upset she would be. I can understand that; and apparently, Sophie still has no clear idea, because Felicity is sleepy from the painkillers. He says he managed to cover up a lot, when they spoke on the phone, by suggesting Grandma should talk to the great grandchildren, who are too young to understand much, anyway. Knowing she had Matt to worry about, you can't blame Uncle Charles," Darren said.

Fran agreed wistfully. "Uncle Charles did what he thought was right at the time; who are we to say otherwise?"

Samantha stood, silently watching them. Her father had changed; he looked confident and in control. With a flash of understanding, she realised it was because for the first time since leaving the air force, he had self-respect. She suddenly realised they were both looking at her.

"You young lady, have got to stop this running off without telling anyone; you are neglecting your duties and worrying us all to death," Fran said sternly.

"You have my solemn promise I will never do it again."

She looked penitent but happy.

"And we should believe that because?"

"I think I can answer that." Darren gave a teasing smile. "Top guy, isn't he?"

Samantha blushed and Fran said, "I gather that will be the one who chased half way across London and would still be looking now, if Meg hadn't given him my number?"

"He didn't mention that." Samantha's green eyes shone.

"So what did you talk about until dawn this morning?" Darren gave her an enquiring look.

"How did you know that?" Fran asked as Samantha's jaw dropped.

"A certain young man drove us from the airfield this morning. I believe he went by the name of Chas Cartwright? I got the distinct impression that he has also just found the love of his life." Darren inspected his fingernails intently.

"We certainly don't need text messages or emails, with our own personal pigeon post," Fran exploded. "So what else did he say?"

"Nothing much; he might just have hinted at two New Year weddings."

"Meg didn't tell me that," Samantha said indignantly.

"I gather you were rather busy," Fran said with heavy sarcasm.

The conversation ended abruptly when Maisie brought Jacob down to lunch, and Meg joined them with Lucy, just as Luke turned up with Kimberley. Although unprepared for so many, Lorna and Dora managed homemade soup and crusty bread with a cheese board for everyone. Darren and Luke were delighted to see each other again and Fran got to meet the voice on the phone. Kimberley pleased Samantha by shyly asking to sit next to her, with Jacob in his highchair on the corner between them. Luke was highly amused by his daughter's efforts to help feed Jacob, and Kim confided to Samantha afterwards that she didn't really like potato in her hair.

Samantha suggested they should teach him better manners, between them.

"That went well." Luke gave a grin and kissed Samantha's cheek as they went out on the terrace.

Fran said she wouldn't stay for coffee because she wanted to pop in on Sophie on her way home, and it was as she was saying goodbye that Luke asked if they would all like to come to the cottage for a meal that evening. "We could have a BBQ and I can get to meet your family, Fran."

"There's a lot of us," Fran warned with a laugh.

Darren came up with the idea that they should make it a combined effort on the beach, rather than leave it all to Luke. Luke objected, saying he wanted to thank everyone for their help. After a lot of discussion it was eventually settled that Luke would be in charge of the cooking, he and Darren would shop for meat and set the BBQ up in the cove; and Fran would go home, fetch the children and tell Adam where they would be, so that he could join them.

"Make sure to tell Chas, Meg and we must ask Abigail, Lorna and George, and Sol and Ella – if that's alright with everybody. I don't know what I would have done without them."

Samantha was impressed by the speed and organizing skill Luke showed and his outgoing and passionate nature excited her; most of all though she loved his generous-hearted spirit in including absolutely everyone. The more certain she became of her love for him though, the more anxious she became about losing him.

They gathered in the cove that evening, for one of those incredibly balmy evenings that lasted until dark, with a wonderful sunset promising a good day to follow.

Uncertain of the newcomer, the twins stood close together and hung back, but William and Kimberley were having such fun in the water that Philipa, the leader, decided she and Celine would join in and William being William made sure that Kimberley was not left out.

"Twins take time to make friends, because they have each other," Fran pointed out to Luke. "Sam and Tim were the same."

Luke nodded, watching Kimberley swimming strongly, effortlessly keeping up with William, who was nearly three years older, as they simultaneously touched the Lilo, held by Philipa and Celine.

"Kimberley swims well for her age," Adam commented.

"We had our own swimming pool and she could swim before she could walk," Luke said in a matter of a fact way, adding, "She also rides very well; skills I suppose I took for granted because they were always available. Sol and Ella are doing a great job in teaching youngsters without that advantage."

Leaning back, Fran scrutinized him. Had he come to Britain because Darren had made him an offer he couldn't resist? Darren had said nothing – apart from the Americanism, 'Top Guy'. He could be a fortune hunter using the flying school as an excuse to get to Sam and she would be heartbroken again, when he left and went back to America. Darren was sure to have told him the family background. Once her journalistic imagination took flight, there was no end to the possibilities.

As the light faded, they started to pack up and she took the opportunity to share her fears with Darren.

"You have absolutely nothing to worry about," Darren assured her, laughing aloud at the idea that Luke was a fortune hunter.

"How can you be so sure? He says all the right things, in fact he is almost too good to be true but that is what con men do. How well do you know him?" She frowned at Darren, exasperated by his easy dismissal of her fears.

"Well enough to know he isn't a con man; there are just some things you will have to take on trust for now; his business is his business."

He returned her questioning gaze, openly. "You can trust him; believe me. Let it go Fran," he insisted.

Darren walked away and joined Samantha, relieving her of Jacob as she carried him up to the house. Luke and Chas were on their way back to the cottage carrying the BBQ between them; and watching them talking earnestly, Fran would have given anything to hear what they were saying. Darren, of course, should have known that leaving his sister with titbits was an invitation to probe.

CHAPTER THIRTY-EIGHT

Felicity and Charles never did return to Anders Folly. Felicity was too ill to be moved and between them, Charles and Sophie stayed with her constantly, refusing to rest even when Abigail and Lorna offered to sit with her. At night, Charles slept beside her on their large double bed, her hand in his, their heads close together, and that was how Sophie found them on the third morning. Her first thought was that her grief-stricken father had taken his own life, but the doctor pronounced death by natural causes.

"His heart just stopped." Sophie told Fran, as they stood together by the bedside. Fran put her arm about Sophie's shoulders.

"They would have wanted to end their days together and they wouldn't want you to be sad about it. Remember how happy you made them when you traced Grandma Charlotte? It was the most wonderful present you could have ever given them."

Sophie nodded her eyes shining brightly through her tears.

"It was the only time I ever saw them really annoyed with me."

"They forgave you a hundred times over," Fran chuckled softly. "Right now, though, I want you to come and stay with us. Darren is going to attend to everything here."

At that moment, Darren called up the stairs to say Matt was on the phone, and with a sob, Sophie rushed to take the call.

"The family are coming over in the next few days and Mellie is coming with them," she announced emotionally on putting the receiver down.

Fran breathed a sigh of relief. Sophie badly needed Matt right now.

The funeral was arranged and Sophie's children, their partners, and four grandchildren all arrived to stay at Anders Folly. After the first two days the weather changed and the house rang with the sound of 'coming ready or not', as the four American children joined with Fran's three youngest and Kimberley in a rowdy game of hide and seek all over the house. George locked the study door and any unused bedrooms, to save extra work, which would mean extra time spent in the house for two women he had reluctantly hired.

"Lorna is very sorry but she 'as run out o' nieces," he had said seriously when confessing apologetically, that more help was needed.

"It's only for one week," Samantha had consoled him, understanding how upset they were at having strangers in the house; knowing that it was a matter of family pride to Lorna that her sister's girls, were the only ones to 'do' for 'her family'.

Two days before the funeral, when Fran was getting ready to take her children home, she said firmly, "As lovely as it is to see you all, if the weather is like this tomorrow we will stay at home." There followed a chorus of objections from the children, who were all having a lovely time.

"They could all come and play in the wigwam. That would be good wouldn't it kids; tea in a real Indian wigwam?" James raised his eyebrows innocently and Fran narrowed her eyes at him, knowing it was a ploy to keep her too busy to keep an eye on him.

She had grounded him on the day of the BBQ in Anders Cove, after going home to collect the bathing costumes and finding him with a girl in the wigwam. Linda had taken the smaller children, when Charles phoned to say Felicity had had a fall, and James said he and Robert were going to meet their friends in town.

Reliving the scene now, she shuddered at what could have happened if she hadn't arrived in time to see James hurrying down to the wigwam, carrying a bottle of wine and two glasses. She had parked the car on the grass verge, to save opening the gates, so James was unaware of her until she appeared in the doorway of the wigwam. He had jumped guiltily, stepped quickly outside and pulled the flap down.

"You said you were going to meet your friends. Where is Robert?"

"He stayed in town; I wanted to come home and chill out."

"And of course you needed a bottle of wine to do that."

It was then that a girl's voice came from inside, "I thought you said your Mum wouldn't mind," and a leggy teenager appeared.

Adam had a serious talk with him. And she grounded him for the last week of the school holidays; but now there was the added worry of keeping an eye on him. It seemed the battle of wits that had always raged between them had suddenly escalated into a full-scale war, and she asked herself on a daily basis where she was going wrong with James. The other children weren't impossible like him. Right now, he was regarding her with a taunting grin.

"Okay, we will do that," she agreed when she could make herself heard above whoops of delight from the children.

Still grinning, James turned away and sauntered out to the car.

"Are you sure Fran?" Matt asked. He and Sophie were sitting quietly on the long settee, watching their lively grandchildren with sad expressions. Coming back to Anders Folly was never going to be the same for them again.

Fran went and knelt beside them.

"Yes; it will give you all a day to prepare for the funerals." Her heart ached for them, sharing the ordeal to come.

The following morning at breakfast, Adam looked up from buttering his toast to say, "By the way James, that was nice of you to invite the children here for a wigwam tea; of course you should have consulted your mother first, but she doesn't mind you looking after them for the day. When you have cleared up after them, if you do it well enough, she may even reduce your grounding; other than that, well done!"

James nearly choked on his cereal and glared at Fran.

William looked earnestly at James. "I told Dad how kind you had been and he was really, really pleased with you." He hated it when his brother was in trouble.

"I certainly was; and thank you William."

William gave a happy sigh and carried on eating his breakfast.

Adam regarded James with a look that belied his words. "As I was saying, it was a kind gesture. Your mother, like everyone else, is very sad just now and you offering to look after the children showed real kindness. I know you will entertain them and help with the food etcetera, and I shall look forward to hearing all about it when I come home."

Adam looked at Fran and she looked at James. This battle of wits between them was wearing, and not the relationship she wanted with her son. James stared back sulkily as she said:

"That means no silly pranks and no winding the children up." Her look told him not to think he was going to be let off lightly and for the rest of the day, he behaved, albeit reluctantly. Samantha and Meg joined them in the afternoon to let Lucy and Jacob share tea in the wigwam and Darren brought Luke and Chas, when they finished work.

Darren had spent the day at the airfield, interested to see what was going on: impressed by what they had already achieved; pleased that he had found someone who would make use of the facilities. Away from Anders Folly, he could see more clearly how it had become such a large part of his grandfather's life; glad and proud at the same time, that although he didn't want the responsibility himself, Anders Folly would remain his family home.

Samantha touched his arm. "Penny for them."

"I was just thinking what a good man Grandfather was."

"He would be pleased you said that." Samantha turned away to pick up Jacob and he saw a tear in her eye.

"I'm sorry Princess."

"For what?"

"Burdening you with my responsibility. Thank you."

"Let me get you a beer, Daddy." She wandered away and he could see her on her mobile. Five minutes later, looking extremely pleased, she handed him a glass.

"Mamma and Jack have arrived; they are coming over shortly."

Fran was in the kitchen when Mellie and Jack arrived and much to her surprise, Mike was driving the car. She waved, and filled bowls of nibbles whilst waiting for him.

"Had to come and say my goodbyes to a lovely couple," he said solemnly greeting her with a hug.

James trundled in carrying a tray of dirty plates, his miserable expression brightening briefly when he saw Mike.

"Mum's got you roped in then," Mike teased.

"She's in meltdown because the twins start school next week, she goes off the deep end at the least excuse," James retorted balefully.

Fran gave him a warning look and he banged the tray down on the draining board.

"You can wash them later," Fran said as he scuffed back to the garden.

"Trouble?" Mike asked.

"The beginning of yet another more worrying phase, I fear."

"Ah. Girls," Mike guessed with a sympathetic grimace.

"He is only just fourteen."

"And you are thinking, same age as Sam, when trouble started? You can't compare the two; he hasn't been wrapped in cotton wool like she was. Cut him some slack. Make it clear he can bring girls home, but only when you are here."

"You don't understand; I'm comparing him to Alexander, not Sam; apparently James is the living image of him at that age."

"Mm; heard a lot about that one; pretty bad lot by all accounts."

"And that is from people who don't know the half of it; only a very few know his worst misdemeanours, but to James he is a hero."

306

"Perhaps you should tell him of Alexander's worst misdemeanours; it sounds as if you are one of those few."

"Fran blushed violently. "I couldn't."

Mike gave her a puzzled look but didn't pursue the matter. It was obviously something she couldn't share, even with him.

"Come on, let's join the others." Can you put me up or shall I ask mine host at 'The Smugglers'? Anders Folly is full to the rafters." He laughed and picked up two bowls of nibbles.

"We will always make room for Uncle Mike," she said, following him into the garden, glad to change the subject.

Much later, when everyone had gone home and Mike was sitting with her and Adam, Mike commented that Darren looked well and seemed to have found his feet in America.

"He's certainly helped Sam financially, in finding that tenant for the airfield and the cottage," Adam agreed.

"Except that we don't know anything about him," said Fran, with a reproachful look at her husband.

"Seems alright to me; what's the problem?"

"Fran's got a bee in her bonnet about Luke being a fortune hunter." Adam went to refill their glasses, glad to get away from the subject. Fran had been on about it for days and despite Darren's assurance that Luke was genuine, she obviously wasn't going to let it drop until she was satisfied about him.

Left alone, Mike gave Fran a quizzical look. "Out with it then; what's got your nose twitching?"

"I blame myself for some of the dreadful things that have happened to Sam and I don't intend to stand by and do nothing again."

"I can understand you want to protect her from fortune hunters but in no way can you blame yourself for the other things that have befallen her." Mike looked sympathetic, remembering how it had fallen to her to look after the twins, when their mother died.

"All I want to know is his background; that's not too much to ask is it?"

Fran had put on her stubborn face and Mike knew better than to argue.

"I'll see what I can do, but mum's the word, or I'll be in trouble," he said quickly, hearing Adam returning with the drinks.

Fran gave a satisfied nod, confident that Mike would get results.

Two days later, with the funerals over, Sophie and her family returned to America and Darren, promising to return for Jacob's first Christmas, flew Mike back with them. Infuriatingly, just as he was leaving, Mike whispered, "Forget about Luke, absolutely no worries."

"Well, I know he is hiding something and now you obviously know what it is," Fran had whispered back fiercely, glaring at him suspiciously.

"Ark," said George, sitting in his chair by the Aga after lunch.

"I can't hear anything." Lorna, opposite, sat forward, cocking her head on one side.

"No, marvlous innit?" he sighed.

Lorna tutted and relaxed back with a sympathetic look, knowing how hard the past week had been. It was at times like these she wondered how long he could go on working, never thinking for a moment that she should be retired herself. Well into her seventies, she still put in full days; although it had to be said, she looked forward to forty winks after lunch now.

CHAPTER THIRTY-NINE

It was a wet Saturday morning and Meg was helping Samantha to turn out her wardrobe.

"I have far too many clothes; some of them haven't even been worn. There might be something you like; we're much the same size, except in height."

Meg glanced gratefully. Samantha was so generous to her and she wished she could return the favours.

"Anything for charity can go on that chair."

Samantha reached an armful down off the rail and laid them on the bed. Meg followed her example and soon, wanted or unwanted outfits had been sorted into various piles, with a separate one Samantha kept adding to for Meg to try on, pleased to see her face light up when a particular garment caught her eye.

At last, the long wardrobe was empty, except for ten designer labelled boxes stacked in the very left hand corner.

"Those are from the shortest modelling career ever, I should think. They definitely stay."

"Can we look?" Meg asked eagerly.

Samantha laughed, pleased by her curiosity.

Meg gasped as one by one the beautifully made suits and gowns were lifted from masses of tissue paper.

"Try them on," Samantha encouraged. "You never know when you may go somewhere really posh and want to borrow one."

Meg shook her head. "It's enough just to see them."

As the last box was opened Samantha fell silent as hurtful memories stirred. Staring at its contents she could hear Peter's voice telling her to wear the little black number and vivid pictures of that fateful evening flashed through her mind. Filled with deep regret, words of long ago came back to her. Caitlin had said she loved David so much that she wished he had been the first and only one in her life. Samantha hadn't fully understood at the time, but she did now and wished with every part of her being that Luke could have been that first one in her life.

Meg's voice broke into her thoughts. "What's the matter?"

"Nothing, nothing," she repeated in a sad voice.

"It obviously isn't; let it out." Meg drew her down on to the bed and they sat cross-legged, facing one another as Samantha, painfully confided her regrets; even down to when she had sheltered from the storm and lied about Jacob.

The room was very silent. Meg asked, "Why didn't you want him to know? and why keep the dress? You will never want to wear it again."

Samantha pulled herself together. "Jacob belongs to me; and I didn't know I still had the dress. Mamma or Abigail must have packed it away when I came home. It can go to charity."

Meg put the lid on the box and dumped it on the floor beside the chair.

"Why is it these awful people like Peter and Luke's wife get away with everything? They deserve some come back." She spoke angrily and kicked the box with her foot.

She badly wanted to tell Sam things that she knew. Chas had told her, because there was nothing Kelly could do to hurt them, but Luke didn't want Sam involved until things were sorted. The thought of Kim being exchanged for money made Meg's own blood boil, so she could well imagine how Samantha would react and why Luke was keeping the situation to himself.

Samantha was thinking about what Meg had just said.

"What about if I…" she watched Meg's face break into a mischievous smile and then a broad grin as she suggested playing a not very nice joke on Peter.

"How can I help?"

*

September brought cool breezes and frequent rain. Summer seemed to have come to an abrupt end. Samantha and Meg very often walked up the path to be with Luke and Chas, leaving Lucy and Jacob with Maisie, but on Saturdays, Abigail would put Kimberley to bed in the nursery at Anders Folly, leaving the four of them free to spend the evening relaxing.

It was one such Saturday, when Luke and Chas decided to cook at home that Kelly arrived at the cottage, unannounced.

"Who in tarnation is that, get it, will you Chas?" Luke called from the kitchen when the doorbell rang.

Chas went to answer it, with a bottle of wine and a corkscrew in his hand. His face dropped and it was hard to know who was most shocked. Recovering first, Kelly gave him a hostile glare and demanded to know what he was doing there.

"I might ask you the same," Chas said in a fierce whisper. "Go away; you've done enough damage!" He went to close the door but Kelly pushed it hard, catching him unawares and causing him to drop the bottle of wine, which hit the wooden floor with a loud report and smashed, bringing Luke, Samantha and Meg shooting out to see if he was alright.

Kelly stared at the four of them; then face twisted with rage, she turned on Luke.

"Where is Kim? You haven't kept to your side of the agreement, so I'm taking her back with me."

"She is staying with a friend," Luke said coldly.

"I don't believe you." She started towards the stairs but Meg barred her way.

"Get out of my way; I want my daughter,"

"Really? That isn't what I heard." Meg stood her ground, her gaze steady and accusing.

"It's none of your business," Kelly shouted. "I suppose I've got you to thank for all this," she rounded on Chas.

"Oh don't thank me; it was a pleasure," Chas said witheringly.

Luke intervened. "Kim isn't here, so please go. You will hear when my solicitor has looked into this whole thing thoroughly."

Kelly gave a sharp glare. "What is there to look in to? It was supposed to be a simple, straightforward arrangement until you involved your solicitor and so called friend."

"Be that as it may, it is the way I want to do things. Now please go."

"You surely won't trust *him* again?" Kelly sneered stepping over the broken bottle and striding out of the door.

"With my life."

"More fool you. The newspapers will love this story," was her parting shot.

Dismayed by the heated conversation and the realisation that Meg was up to date with the situation and she wasn't, Samantha asked Luke, "What arrangement?"

He told her briefly and Samantha's answer was, "Give it to her; Kim is more important than money. We can raise it. Anders' stolen money was returned recently."

"You would do that for Kim?" Luke asked softly.

"For you and Kim," Samantha corrected, returning his gaze unflinchingly.

Luke hesitated for a long moment.

"Tell her everything," Chas urged quietly.

They were still standing in the hallway, with broken glass around them and wine staining the polished wooden boards.

"Dinner will keep; you go and talk, we will clear this mess up," Meg offered. Luke took Samantha's hand and they went into the sitting room. Chas and Meg joined them a little while later with a freshly opened bottle of wine. Sitting on the settee, her hand in both of his, Samantha was saying, unhappily, "You will never get rid of her completely."

"She says we won't see her again if I give her the money, but I don't trust her; I want it in writing; so it has to go to court, I'm afraid," Luke apologised.

"But the last thing I want is for you to get tangled up in her trouble making; the truth of the matter is I can easily afford it; my father left me a hotel group and Kelly feels entitled to a share. That is why she is over here threatening to tell the newspapers where I am, if I don't agree to her terms."

"Two million pounds and he can have sole custody of Kim," Chas sneered, "who I happen to know is excess to requirements, to the new boyfriend."

"Well Kim is certainly not going back, but what will happen if you don't pay her?" Samantha asked.

"We will get newshounds pestering us. Chas and I will be front-page news again and the name Anders will be dragged in to make an even better story. I can just see the headlines both here and in the States:

"*'Hathaway's Cornish hideaway. Hathaway and Cartwright's Folly'.*"

"And they would be the least embarrassing ones; they would have a field day," Chas added with a knowing look.

There was silence while they dwelt miserably on the situation.

"The publicity obviously doesn't worry her, but this tennis player might not want to be plastered over the front page in a scandal. Why don't you play them at their own game?"

They all looked at Meg and then at each other.

"Go on," Samantha said slowly.

"Well – tell her you will go to the papers and say he was the cause of the marriage break up – or something to make him look bad."

"Why not just threaten to tell the truth? He wouldn't want to be accused of blackmail," Chas added.

Luke looked thoughtful. "It might work; supposing he just drops her though; then we would really have a harridan on our hands."

"Would he do that?" Samantha and Meg chorused.

"I think he might, if he thinks she can't get the money to start this tennis coaching centre. I think that is his main interest; she is the one who is besotted. Once he gets his centre he could drop her and she will be back for more," said Chas glancing at Luke who suddenly had a gleam of hope in his eyes. Thinking aloud, he said slowly:

"If I buy the property and give him full control of the business, with an option for them to buy it jointly when he is up and running, it would give them a reason to work together and stay together."

He gave a big smile and Chas said, "Will Kelly have enough sense to see it is in her best interests though?"

"The solicitor can point that out to her." Luke leaned back, clasping his hands behind his head, thoughts racing at the possibility of settling the problem without more unpleasantness.

"It could all be over by Christmas," he said almost to himself, "and we could make a fresh start in the New Year. Thank goodness she came this evening."

Chas poured the wine and they chinked glasses.

"To us and Kim, and Jacob and Lucy," Samantha said softly.

CHAPTER FORTY

Peter was having a bad day. Divorce papers had arrived in the post that morning, dashing any hope he had of returning when the baby had grown up, to resume his carefree life of luxury with Lindsey. He had never imagined for a minute she would, or even could bring herself to divorce him.

He tucked the envelope out of sight, hearing Amy approaching the office and opened the petty cash book to look busy, unaware that his day was about to get worse.

He had been sitting for two hours, reading and rereading the words that had such a final ring to them; dwelling on the fact that the choice was going to be taken away from him unless he did something about it, pretty quick. He had dismissed the idea that Manuel Lorenzo's family were any threat. Things like that just didn't happen in England.

Amy burst in, not noticing his stricken look, in her excitement to tell him there was a deliveryman at the door with strict instructions to personally hand a parcel over to Mr Peter Chambers and no one else.

"Be quick." Amy was beside herself with excitement over the large box. It was her birthday in two weeks' time.

Peter rose without enthusiasm, wondering what could be so important; then hastened his step, in case it was something from Lindsey saying she couldn't go through with the divorce.

Standing beside the bar, a burley figure in black leather motor cycle gear was holding a large, brown paper parcel and looking impatient. "Sign 'ere, guv."

Peter signed a glass panel; the man handed the parcel over then left.

"What is it?" Amy said her eyes shining expectantly.

"No idea," Peter shrugged.

"Can I open it now? Or is it for my birthday?" She was already carrying it through to the office. Peter stretched his face and followed; he had no idea when her birthday was, but she had obviously mentioned it.

"Go ahead," he said with distracted indifference, still thinking about the envelope, burning a hole in his pocket.

Watching her tear the paper off, he felt sorry for her, but wasn't sure why. When the paper was strewn on the floor, Amy opened a box, which at first appeared to contain nothing but tissue paper, then watched her draw something black and flimsy out and stare in amazement, before turning and flinging her arms around his neck, tears of happiness streaming down her face.

"I have never had anything so beautiful. Thank you, thank you, thank you!"

Quite bewildered, he thought the deliveryman must have made a mistake in the address, but Amy was already discarding her skirt and blouse and slipping the dress over her head.

His mind still on Lindsey, he went and sat behind his desk, preparing himself for breaking the news that it would have to go back, until he looked up and nearly fainted with shock. The black, Givenchy creation was unforgettable as were the memories it evoked. So, it was no mistake; he knew exactly where it had come from. Panic seized him; a note was sure to be enclosed. He shot out of his chair and snatched at the tissue paper, sending it in every direction, but the box was empty.

"What are you looking for?" Amy asked, twirling around, fascinated by how the skirt swung and caressed her legs; missing his panic-stricken expression, as he tried to think of an excuse to avoid endless unanswerable questions; he would have to let her go on thinking it was her birthday present.

"Er – er – I didn't want you to see the bill."

"It must have cost a bomb. How did you afford it?"

"Oh, er, I've been saving up," he gulped, closing his eyes in relief as she accepted his explanation.

"You really are the sweetest and most generous man I have ever known," she purred, putting her arms around him again and resting her head on his shoulder. As she did so, a faint but unmistakable whiff of 'Clive Christian' perfume assailed his nostrils and he breathed it in deeply. Even after all this time the perfume clung to the delicate fabric of the dress, causing his senses to swim with a burst of desire. Lost in reverie he was jerked back to reality by Amy murmuring:

"When are you going to get a divorce, so that we can get married?"

His nerves snapped and he responded with, "Lindsey won't hear of it. Just forget the idea; we're fine as we are."

"Ohh, but I want to be your wife," she wheedled, twisting his tie round her bright red fingernails.

"Well you can't; it is as simple as that." He took her by the shoulders and stood her firmly away, conscious of the envelope in his jacket pocket. The last thing he wanted was for Amy to find out about the divorce papers. With abrupt decision, he said, "I have to go out."

Amy pouted full red lips. "It's your turn to open the bar."

"I have to go out," he repeated. "Now go upstairs and look at the dress in the mirror; you look stunning." He kissed her briefly, pulling away as she would have clung to him again. "I won't be long."

"Where are you going?" Seeing that she was more absorbed in fingering and admiring the dress again, he made good his escape.

Once in the car, he sped towards Southampton as if his life depended on it, convinced he could stop Lindsey from divorcing him. He made record time and stopping opposite the familiar driveway, he asked himself why he had ever left, forgetting the disgust he had felt at the time; only remembering the comfort and freedom he had enjoyed married to Lindsey. Both were missing from his life now, and living in that dreadful wine bar, at the beck and call of its so called jet set customers, was driving him mad; even worse, his designer clothes were being ruined. Replacing his entire wardrobe every year had always been a top priority to his appearance, as the private gym was to his fitness; he missed the convenience and abhorred the extortionate fees charged by London clubs. "I only want to join, not buy the place," he had said, amongst other derogatory things to the well-toned young man behind the desk, just before he was asked to leave.

Waiting impatiently, while traffic from the other direction passed, a maroon Lexus, slowed down; he assumed the driver was giving way, but at the last minute a left indicator came on and the car turned in. More traffic was following and whilst waiting, he saw Lindsey come out and greet the vaguely familiar driver. They embraced and entered the house, arms linked about each other.

Unable to believe his eyes, Peter sat transfixed until a horn tooting from behind, reminded him the road was clear and he turned into the drive.

Striding to the front door, he tried unsuccessfully to insert his key in the lock and in a state of consternation, rang the doorbell. He heard Lindsey's footsteps, as she called happily, "Make yourself comfortable; won't be a minute," before the door opened and her smile disappeared.

"Why are you here?" she demanded.

He took a step back, wondering at the transformation, noting the cream linen dress, tailored to her nicely-rounded figure. Gone was the timid, retiring creature, clutching a cashmere cardigan protectively around her. In her place was a smartly dressed, confident looking woman ready to stand her ground. He put on his most disarming smile, prepared for her immediate forgiveness.

"I've come back. I want to start again."

Lindsey's face broke into a smile and he moved towards her, before realising her amusement as William's voice called, "Who is it Lindsey?" and she answered. "Only a salesman, Dad."

"Not another one. What's he selling this time?"

"Nothing of interest to me."

The driver of the Lexus strolled into the hallway and stopped as he saw Peter.

It was then that Peter recognised the family solicitor and knew why Lindsey was confident enough to sue for divorce. Making one last desperate attempt, he turned to her. "One last try; I promise things will be different."

"Not this time thank you, Peter." Lindsey closed the door.

"I won't give up," he called through the letterbox.

The door opened again. "You might as well," William advised, looking at his nephew seriously. "Lindsey is happy at last; don't stand in her way."

Peter stared back. "I suppose, calling you Dad, gives you the right to speak for her; well, talk to her and make her see sense. You should be on my side. Blood is thicker than water," he accused, before turning on his heel and striding to his car. Passing the brand new Lexus, he was tempted to drive into the side of the immaculate, maroon paintwork, but fearing the consequences, resisted.

William watched him drive away with a heavy heart. Peter was his dead sister's only boy and he had looked after him since he was eight years old. If he thought for a moment he would even try to make Lindsey and Liam happy, he would speak up for him, but Peter didn't have it in him to make a considerate husband, let alone a loyal one. Lindsey had found her soulmate in Jeremy, and as soon as the divorce came through, they were to be married.

Peter put his foot down hard on the accelerator asking himself what he was doing driving this second hand wreck. He had never driven a cheap car in his life and certainly never a second hand one, but it was all they could afford since Amy bought the wine bar.

Amy would be wondering where he was. If Lindsey had been reasonable he wouldn't be going back at all, he thought morosely. As it was, he had nowhere else to go. Thinking of Amy, reminded him of the Givenchy dress and from there his thoughts turned to Samantha. She obviously still had feelings for him or she wouldn't have wanted to remind him of their time together; and was it really by accident that she had come to the bar that day?

Nearing London he dreaded going back to the wine bar and decided to park the car and walk along the embankment; there was a boat moored there, where he could sit on deck and think. He had missed lunch and they sold food and drinks.

He had been sitting for more than an hour, with the remains of a Cornish pasty and an empty glass, when a couple arrived and sat at the far end of the deck. Deep in thought, he was only half-aware, as they sat with their backs to him, obviously in love, sitting close together, talking and smiling intimately into each other's eyes; the girl's animated profile seemed somehow familiar as the man listened intently.

Losing interest he rose, paid his bill and went to lean on the bridge; watching the busy life on the river until he caught sight of the same couple leaving by the gangplank. This time he recognized the girl.

No prizes for guessing who got the dress delivered then, he thought bitterly, reminded of the visit Meg made to the hospital, when he fractured his shoulder.

Unaware of being observed, Meg and Chas sauntered in the autumn sunshine, stopping now and then to look at something of interest and Peter followed because his car was parked in that direction. They reached the Tate Gallery and Meg obviously wanted to go in but the man looked at his watch and shook his head regretfully. They walked on, pointing every now and then at interesting sights on the river and then suddenly waved to someone ahead.

Looking beyond them, Peter saw Samantha. She was standing alone and waved back, smiling broadly. He wanted her desperately, longed to feel the softness of her body and smell that wonderful perfume. She must still want him and they could be together now. He hurried forward and reached her at the same time as Meg and Chas. Pushing past them, he grabbed her.

Samantha let out a startled cry and tried to pull away, as Chas caught his arms and Meg recognised him "Peter! What on earth do you think you are doing?" Samantha recovered. "Peter? For goodness sake, you frightened the life out of me."

Luke suddenly appeared, having seen the incident from where he was queuing at an ice cream kiosk. "Hey man, move away." He faced Peter, feet apart, fists clenched ready for any further trouble. Peter calmed down and looked from one to the other of them. Fighting wasn't his style and he didn't fancy his chances anyway. He looked at Samantha.

"I needed to tell you we could start again. I know you must want to, because of the dress."

Luke and Chas looked puzzled as Meg and Samantha started laughing.

"I know you are a master of excuses, but how did you explain *that* away?" Meg managed to gasp, between laughing.

Peter looked offended and started backing away, looking at Samantha. "Just thought we could try again."

"Go back to your wife, Peter." Samantha suddenly felt sorry for him and stopped laughing.

"We are getting divorced," he said looking at her hopefully.

"I'm very sorry to hear that."

He watched them turn and walk away; laughing at Luke who was complaining that he had lost his place in the ice cream queue, now!"

Later that evening, when Kimberley was in bed and they were sitting together on the settee, Luke asked if Peter was Jacob's father.

"I have to confess I knew your story before I came over. Mellie told me; but don't be upset with her; your Dad was hopping mad and she needed a listening ear, as I did at the time. She is a great listener and we exchanged stories. Neither of us knew I would come to live here then, or that you and I would meet and fall in love."

"Don't be too sure of that. If I know Mamma, she handpicked you; she always knows best." Samantha patted his hand. "And the answer to your question is: I'm honestly not sure. I just hope not."

"Ann was glad to be home," he said changing the subject.

"Bill was glad as well. I hope he won't find it too much looking after her."

"You don't need to worry; a nurse who used to work in the clinic has offered to go in daily."

Samantha snuggled against him. It had been a long day. They had flown up to see Ann and Bill and Chas and Meg had taken the opportunity to go with them to see some of London.

"I'm going to have to go over to the States. Several suitable properties have come up, and I want to get things moving. Kelly raised objections, but seems to be going along with the idea now she has had time to consider, so it is just a case of finding the right location; it shouldn't take long."

"Kimberley can stay with us, if you like?" She turned her face up to be kissed, hating the thought of him not being around.

"She will like that," he murmured kissing her hungrily and releasing her hair, from its restraining clips. Deeply absorbed, neither of them heard Kimberley, until a sleepy voice from the doorway made them draw apart.

"Can I have a glass of water, Daddy?"

They looked at each other with good-humoured resignation.

"Coming honey; what woke you?"

"I had a bad dream."

Samantha held her arms out. "Come and cuddle."

Chas arrived shortly afterwards and found all three of them, nearly asleep and playing I Spy.

"Race you to bed," Chas challenged Kimberley, catching Samantha by the hand and helping her up.

"What do I get if I win?" Kimberley was already off the settee, knowing what the answer was.

"One story," Chas called, chasing her.

Luke walked Samantha home. The darker nights had brought a chill, but October had turned out to be an Indian summer, and they saw it as a good omen for a bright new future together. The adventure trail was already a success with local children and Sol and Ella were fully booked for a good many weekends ahead. Anders Folly would provide not only fun but knowledge for less fortunate children, who, in turn would bring the real world to Jacob, Kim and Lucy.

*

Peter arrived back at the wine bar, when the evening was nearly over.

"Where have you been?" Amy greeted him with an annoyed frown and the first thing he noticed was that she was wearing the black dress. Catching a whiff of the perfume was the last straw.

"Out," he snapped, pushing past her and heading towards their private accommodation upstairs.

She followed him. "I need some help in the bar; I have been serving all day by myself."

He walked unsteadily to a side table.

"It's what you wanted, why are you grumbling? I hate the very sight of this place."

There was a shocked silence, before Amy whispered, "You wanted to be your own boss as much as I did."

"Not of some tatty wine bar."

Amy looked ready to cry. "You never said it was tatty before."

"Well I am now," Peter said savagely, slopping whisky from a bottle into a tumbler.

"Why are you being like this?"

"Like what?" he said weakly. His heart was suddenly thumping and he sat down trying to loosen his tie with fingers that refused to work. Seeing him fumbling, Amy undid the knot and helped him remove his jacket when she saw how hot he was. Relieved of his jacket, he slumped.

"Peter, are you drunk or ill, what have you been doing to yourself?" Amy shrieked, already dialling for an ambulance. Memories of when her mother died flashed before her eyes. One minute she was cooking dinner for them and the next... Peter mustn't die; please don't let him die, I couldn't bear it.

The medics said her prompt action saved his life as she accompanied him to the hospital, where he was diagnosed as having had a stroke and would more than likely be a patient for several weeks.

Returning to the wine bar well after midnight, Amy found the head waitress asleep on one of the alcove seats, because the keys were in her handbag and she had taken them with her. The following morning the other staff offered their sympathy and support and told her they would cope until she felt ready to come back to work. Their support was unexpected and heart warming and she felt confident of being able to carry on without Peter, for a while. Mooching miserably about the flat, whiling away time until she could go and visit him, she picked his jacket up from the floor where it had dropped the previous evening, intending to hang it in his wardrobe; knowing how particular he was about his clothes. She buried her face in it, trying to hold back the tears and felt something bulky. Peter never put his clothes away with anything in the pockets, so she automatically withdrew the brown envelope and seeing that it looked official, assumed it was to do with the business. Laying it on the dressing table, she went through the rest of the pockets, unearthing his wallet, a car park ticket, a receipt, a small pack of tissues and the inevitable comb. She laid it all beside the envelope, hung the jacket up neatly and closed the wardrobe door before putting the wallet and comb in his chest of drawers and picking up the remaining items. She glanced idly at the car park ticket, noting yesterday's date and also the receipt for a Cornish pasty and a glass of lager. Why hadn't he just come home? She felt annoyed that he had been sitting doing nothing while she was rushing about, but quickly reminded herself he must have been feeling unwell, even then. Walking through to the small kitchen, she made a cup of coffee and sat at the breakfast bar. The postmark on the envelope was the day before yesterday, so it must have arrived yesterday. It was unlike Peter to spoil the line of his suit, by putting anything that bulky in the inside breast pocket. He obviously wasn't feeling himself at all; it must have been to do with the contents of the envelope she decided, opening it and withdrawing the stiff, folded sheets of paper.

On reading the letter, accompanying the legal forms, her senses leapt with joy. This was what he was doing, all day; trying to surprise her; but he came over ill and things went wrong. Heart singing, she forgave him all the horrible things he had said; he hadn't meant them, he just hadn't been himself. When they were married, she assured herself, he would make it up to her generously. He loved her and the dress proved it. There was nothing to worry about, except getting him well again and if he didn't like this bar, she would buy one in Spain where the weather was better. She was going to look after him and be the best wife a man ever had: never letting him out of her sight.

CHAPTER FORTY-ONE

Plans had been underway for several weeks in the big kitchen, with Lorna supervising the making of the Christmas puddings and helping Dora make a large fruitcake, ready to be iced nearer the day. Nothing was to be left until the last minute, she insisted. Anxious about not being able to do the heavy work herself now, she had to be content with organising. Dora was kept extremely busy and Maisie helped when she wasn't looking after the children, but very often, Mary, who worked for Fran every weekday now, was called in as well at the weekends.

"How did you manage on your own?" Dora gasped, struggling to stir the huge pot of ingredients for the puddings, certain her arms were going to drop off any minute.

Sitting at the big kitchen table peeling vegetables, Lorna rested her chin in her hand and thought for a moment.

"Truth was, I didn't."

George, popped his head out of the big pantry, where he was busy clearing the top shelf ready to store the puddings when they were ready. "Mrs Charles always 'elped, so did Abigail, and everyone 'ad a stir of the puddin' – fer luck."

"And before your time George, there was my lady; she cooked for them all; wonderful cook she was; and all the men used to help bring in the logs and keep the fires going. Everyone mucked in, in them days; must have been the war. Ah, that would be it."

"Happen we could suggest they all had a stir for luck now," Dora said hopefully.

"Don't see why not." George emerged from the pantry with a big smile. "Bring back an old custom."

"I reckon you're right." Lorna was thinking of the simple fun, when the whole family, grownups and children alike, had queued up to give three stirs each and make a wish. It had certainly helped to get the pudding well mixed. Was it really an old custom or was it just a clever idea to get help with the arduous task? she asked herself now.

November brought sea mists and cold days. Fires were kept burning with logs stacked by Jake, under the walkway leading to the stables, and one of George's jobs was to keep the rooms well supplied. Luke saw him struggling with a heavy basket one day and without a word took a load to the nursery in the west wing. Lorna nodded with approval as he gave a cheery good morning on his way through the kitchen.

At first, she hadn't liked the idea of a foreigner taking Mr Gerald's place and being in charge of Anders Folly, but seeing how he cared for Samantha and the children, she was slowly coming round to the idea; in fact he had a lot of Mr Gerald's ways, she reluctantly conceded. A fact that was confirmed later that day, when to Dora's delight, her young man was given the job of George's assistant. Daveth, had recently lost his job due to cutbacks in a local food store, and seeing him call for Dora when the dark nights set in, Luke liked the look of him. It was patently obvious to him that both George and Lorna were doing too much, but realised the situation needed delicate handling. Samantha would be devastated at the slightest suggestion of them retiring or leaving Anders Folly, and in all honesty he couldn't picture anybody else doing such an excellent job of keeping the house running like clockwork, with its comings and goings and last minute changes. Such loyal retainers would be impossible to replace these days; without them, things would have fallen apart when Sir Anders died, and probably even before that with his bad health. They, Abigail, Sol and Ella, had ensured the family home was still there for them all to come to. The time was coming though when all that would change.

Daveth joined the household that same day and at Luke's suggestion Samantha had an informal chat with all the staff to say what his duties would be. Luke sat beside her as they gathered around the big kitchen table and Lorna gave him another approving nod, knowing that she had him to thank for the additional help. After Samantha had spoken, Luke said that, with Daveth's help he hoped George would have time for more important jobs he had lined up for after Christmas.

"You only 'ave ta say, sir." George sat up straight. It was constantly on his and Lorna's mind these days, of where they would go when they had to retire. It had to come eventually and then their rooms would be needed for new staff.

Daveth brought new energy and strength to the house and the bonus was that he liked cooking. He was a natural clown and frequently had them all laughing. Only when Lorna turned her nose up at a modern concoction, did they disagree.

"What are the jobs you intend for George?" Samantha asked curiously, as they companionably groomed Nocturn and Sapphire.

"I'll think of something; in the meantime he's got help over Christmas. I have quietly informed everyone that from now on George and Lorna are on light duties."

Samantha looked at him and smiled. "I love you."

He grinned. "Mm, love you too."

They finished the grooming and swung up on the horses' backs, calling, "Won't be long," to Sol and Ella who stopped what they were doing to watch them ride out of the stable yard. Ella gave a contented sigh. Her visions had come true.

"Top Guy," Sol observed, copying Darren's Americanism. "I think even Sir Anders would approve?"

"Oh he does."

"Please tell me you're not in touch with him," Sol begged. His wife had ceased her far away looks and predictions these days, or had she? he wondered as Ella just smiled.

With Christmas only two weeks away there was great activity in the house. The decorations were brought down from the attic, George was polishing the best silver cutlery and space had been made for the huge Christmas tree in the sitting room. Luke and Chas had been volunteered to help hang the decorations under Abigail's supervision, and everyone was thoroughly tired of hearing how Pamela had done this and where Pamela had hung a certain garland or created a flower arrangement. Everyone except Samantha.

"Where would you like it though?" Luke asked Samantha more than once, and each time her answer was, "Abigail says it always goes there, so that's fine," not remembering exactly where everything had gone, only that it had to be the same.

She ended up feeling very tearful about the whole thing, so Luke and Chas just followed Abigail's instructions to the letter and Luke made a mental note to deal with the sticking to the past phobia, at another time.

Darren, Mellie and Jack arrived ten days before Christmas and were in time to help put the tree up. Jake and Jed brought it to the front door and all five men helped to carry it through and erect it in the alcove by the fireplace – where it had always stood.

An emotional surprise came two days later, when Sophie and Matt asked if they could spend Christmas with them. The 'Windsors' were booked until the

New Year with special concerts and Caitlin was taking all four grandchildren to spend the festive season with Mike and Nicole, at the stud farm.

"They will have a wonderful time, ice skating and going on sleigh trips. We are invited but they won't miss us, and Matt would just love to come and spend a Christmas at Anders Folly again. Do hope you can put up with us, coming back so soon."

Samantha burst into tears and Mellie took the phone from her.

"I think we can safely say that was a yes," she answered with tears in her own eyes.

They arrived two days before Christmas and everything was just as they remembered it, even to the huge turkey cooking overnight in the Aga.

Then at the very last minute, on Christmas Eve, Timothy kept his promise to spend Jacob's first Christmas with him and walked in, carrying a huge teddy bear. Twenty-one of them sat down at the big table, beautifully laid by Abigail and Ella, just as it always had been in Pamela's day, with gleaming silver cutlery, sparkling crystal glasses, snowy white table linen and a huge bowl of dark red chrysanthemums in the middle. Everyone had a homemade, blue or red cracker with a place name on it, made by Ella; and Pamela's portrait appeared to be looking down benevolently. She would be well pleased Abigail thought contentedly.

Luke and Chas were impressed and at last understood why things had to be the same. Meg spent the day staring in awe; she had never in her whole life even imagined a Christmas like it. It was like a fairy wonderland with the holly and mistletoe and fairy lights everywhere, and the mountains of presents under the huge, bauble and tinsel covered tree. It had to be seen to be believed.

Best of all for Fran, her doubts were finally dismissed. After supper when all of the small children were in bed and Robert and James were playing computer games on the nursery television, Luke told them he was the owner of 'Hathaways': one of the largest hotel groups in the States.

"So why didn't you just say?" Fran asked, embarrassed by her previous suspicions.

"I wanted to be treated normally and liked for myself; some people find that difficult when they know you are wealthy. I came here to get away from being front page news."

"Much like my case when I first met the family and didn't want to say I had a famous mother," Matt intervened quietly.

"Exactly," Sophie agreed.

"Samantha wouldn't have told anyone," Fran insisted, stubbornly.

"Samantha was the last person I wanted to tell; from the moment I met her, it was important that she of all people wanted me for myself. I have already told you I had just lost my father, my wife, and to all intents and purposes Kim; plus my good name was being plastered all over the front pages at home. I needed anonymity because I didn't want it to follow me here."

"So what happens now?" Fran persisted.

"I have come to an arrangement with Kim's mother and her partner, in return for complete custody of my daughter," Luke answered patiently.

"And that is quite enough questions and answers for this evening," Adam interrupted, pursing his lips at Fran.

"Yes, Luke does have a right to *some* privacy," Tim defended lazily.

"Sorry, I was just looking out for Sam." Fran sat back and stared into the fire. There was another matter she wanted to have out with Sam, but that was between the two of them.

"So when am I going to be summoned home again, for this wedding?" Tim changed the subject adroitly.

Samantha and Luke looked at each other and replied together. "We thought the beginning of March."

"And when do you hope to get married?" Sophie asked kindly, thinking Meg and Chas might be feeling left out. They were sitting quietly at the end of the long settee holding hands and Chas was in fact feeling uncertain about Luke keeping his part in everything from the family, but Luke said that in his opinion, it was of no consequence to anybody but the four of them and therefore should be forgotten.

"Soon, but we aren't sure yet," Meg said shyly.

Mellie laughed. "I think we are embarrassing these young people and just to change the subject, when are you going to make this your home, Samantha? Everywhere I look, I see Marcia or Pamela."

"I can't change anything, what would Granddad say?"

"I think he would say well done," Tim volunteered, giving Samantha a reassuring look. "Those curtains have definitely seen better days and the colour is far too old for you. You need something to reflect your own personality." Everyone looked at Timothy in amazement, while Luke offering up thanks to his future brother-in-law, squeezed her hand comfortingly.

Samantha looked uncertain.

"Just what's needed, I would say," Sophie gave Timothy an admiring look. They hadn't expected help from his direction at all and such sensitive help, at the very right moment. They understood Sam wanting things to stay the same, but she was young; a new generation was taking over, and with Luke her life could move forward if she allowed it to.

"No good will come from living in the past, Princess; make a clean sweep and start again. It works, I promise you," Darren smiled encouragingly.

"Good job the Egyptians didn't think like that. I would be out of a vocation," Timothy joked, afraid that things were getting too serious.

George entered with bedtime drinks and they saw with some surprise that it was eleven o'clock.

"I think I might ask Samantha if she will have my piano at Anders Folly; I feel it belongs here and they are going to need a good piano, in the future. William is going to keep them entertained; he will have Daddy's gift of hearing a tune and being able to play it. Kim is interested in learning as well; those two make nice companions."

Matthew nodded agreement. "Much better than letting her stay unloved in an empty house." Sophie smiled fondly, always amused by Matthew referring to musical instruments as living things.

They were in Laurie's old room, laying on their backs in the wide four-poster bed they always shared on visits to Anders Folly. His dream of living in his dream home had lasted so briefly and she knew he would always regret having to take her away from her parents again, but for her, his recovery was all that mattered. Looking at him now it saddened her to see the toll his treatment had taken. He still played brilliantly at home but concerts were out of the question, and his heartbreak showed when the children were up on stage without him; but he seldom missed one of their concerts.

"Do you remember that Christmas when we all did a turn? Laurie was so good at Old Macdonald, wasn't he?" Matthew was reminiscing and she could hear the happy nostalgia in his voice.

"Yes, we had a very talented family." Neither of them ever thought of Laurie as anything other than family. It had been hard for her to return so soon, but Matt had wanted to come so much, and she lived in dread that each Christmas could be his last.

Gazing up at the worn, gold Tester, recalling the evening's conversation, she commented absently, "Mellie is right, things do need updating."

"Do they?" He followed her gaze. "All part of the charm surely?"

"In Uncle Gerald's day maybe, not any more."

"Mm, don't worry; Mellie is onto it; it's as good as done."

He rolled on his side and kissed her lightly. "Time we went to sleep."

"Are you saying Mellie is bossy?" Sophie said turning the bedside lamp off.

"Only in the nicest possible way; you know, a bit like you."

Sophie turned the bedside lamp back on. "I'm not bossy."

"No dear; anything you say dear."

Sophie kissed his forehead and turned the bedside lamp off again. "That's better," she said to the sound of stifled mirth.

A few minutes later, Matthew switched the bedside lamp on.

"What's the matter?" Sophie turned to look at him anxiously. He was looking serious.

"I hope I didn't put my foot in it by advising Chas to be independent. I just thought it would be a shame if they found themselves in your parents' situation in a few years' time."

"Mm, hope Sam won't think we are harbouring an old grudge, for Mummy and Daddy. What did Chas say?"

"It's all organized; they plan to live in the cottage until the flying school is established; and then Chas hopes to build their own place. Luke wanted to give them a house, but Chas won't hear of it. Can't say I blame him."

Matthew gave a grunt and switched the lamp off. Within minutes, soft snoring left her to dwell peacefully on the future of Anders Folly, alone.

CHAPTER FORTY-TWO

It was the second week in January. The decorations had been taken down and returned to the attic, relentless pine needles and tinsel still turned up in odd places and the weather was foul, so much so, that riding had been abandoned and the horses were turned out daily into the big paddock to exercise themselves. It was a dreary time of year, and having what was normally regarded, as its 'Old World Charm', referred to as shabby and dated, had made Samantha see the house in a less favourable light. It was definitely overhearing Mellie and Sophie, speculating that the carpets and curtains were donkey years older than Samantha herself though, that made her look closer and see how the furniture was strategically placed to hide bare patches in the once beautiful Persian carpets. But when Jake proudly informed her that he and Jed had unpacked and laid them in nineteen forty-seven, that finally decided her. Luke had swatches of carpets, curtains and wall coverings delivered for her to choose from, but she was totally out of her depth and too much choice resulted in confusion; an interior designer was brought in and eventually, between them they created an elegant, restful sitting room.

Fresh cream paintwork surrounded delicate, pale green, embossed wallpaper, and leaf green curtains, reached a patterned carpet of soft, autumn colours. Two plump, cream sofas with three matching chairs, replaced the two, long settees and Luke decided that a cream fur rug was needed for in front of the wide hearth, except that it wasn't real fur. The small, Rosewood table, harbouring Laurie's chess set was returned to its place in front of the middle set of doors and just two of the glass cases holding family heirlooms were allowed to stay; the other three were put in the hall and on the landing, where they looked much more in keeping. Although the huge chandelier having been taken down and cleaned, now sparkled brilliantly with every light bulb working, Luke confessed to preferring softer lights to sit by in the evenings and a number of lamps, with Apricot silk shades, now gave a warm glow. The huge gilt framed mirror that had always hung over the fireplace somehow seemed out of place now and Luke suggested the Stubbs painting of the beautiful black mare and her foal, at present hanging in the study, would be perfect there.

Samantha had misgivings about removing it from where it had always hung in Gerald's time, but had to admit, once it was in place, that it was shown to advantage and far more pleasing to the eye.

It took four weeks to complete and having made a good start, Samantha was keen to begin another room, but there was no time before the wedding. Meg and Chas, although flattered by the offer of a double wedding, felt it was inappropriate for them and they arranged their own small affair, with just Samantha and Luke as witnesses and Lucy and Kimberley as flower girls. Their service was held in the local church, with Meg in a simple dress of the palest pink, carrying deep pink roses and the two girls in rose pink with daisy garlands in their hair. Dora and Daveth prepared a lunch and Abigail, Lorna and George were invited to sit down with them. Luke provided champagne and the staff joined in to toast the bride and groom.

Samantha said it was so simple and intimate; she quite envied them the lack of fuss.

They were deliriously happy when Luke moved into Anders Folly, to give them the cottage to themselves and Lucy was more than content to stay with Kim and Jacob for the honeymoon week. Meg returned looking radiant and ready to concentrate on Samantha's big day. With family alone, the guest list reached fifty and Luke suggested inviting Bill and Ann, if she was well enough to travel. Samantha wanted Simon Hall and his wife and Wendy to come, as they had been such staunch supporters during the closure of Anders Motors.

The family gathered this time for a happy occasion. Timothy rang to say he was bringing a friend and surprised everyone by arriving with a pretty, half-Chinese, half-English girl, whose name was Mae. Although shy, she spoke perfect English, obviously came from a good family and never left Timothy's side.

Meg was Samantha's maid of honour, Kimberley, Philipa and Celine were bridesmaids and Lucy was a flower girl. All of the dresses were long, pearly cream chiffon with a very pale green bow at the back of the skirt and Samantha was simply elegant, in a long fitted dress of cream lace and a short veil with lover's knots in each corner. A diamante clip attached to the veil securely held her waist length hair, caught back loosely in soft curls and she carried a bouquet of green orchids, Lily of the Valley and cream freesias.

The simplicity was stunning and gasps of admiration were heard as she walked down the aisle on her proud father's arm. It was a magical day, ending in a flight to Paris, where they spent three nights in a bridal suite overlooking the Seine. Luke had plans for a proper honeymoon later in the year, while central heating was installed in the upstairs of Anders Folly and all eight bedrooms were refurbished. It was to be a six-week cruise in the Caribbean, with a nurse to take care of Kimberley and Jacob.

When everything was back to normal, Samantha was ready to start revamping the dining room. She debated for two days, on whether the gold edged, brown and cream Regency style wallpaper suggested by the interior designer, was too dull to go with the lustrous, gold velvet curtains, reaching to a slightly darker, plain carpet, until Luke said:

"It's absolutely you; I like it."

They all worked well together. Chas wanted no favours and seemed determined from the start to keep things on a boss, employee relationship at work. On Saturdays, routine changed and after taking Kimberley for an early morning ride together, Luke would go to work at ten o'clock, and William and Kimberley at Sophie's suggestion, began taking music lessons together. Her grand piano had already been delivered and now took pride of place in the music room, where a teacher came each Saturday morning for an hour.

With workmen everywhere, Samantha sought peace in the study, anticipating that Meg would be there. George arrived with morning coffee and said that Meg was helping upstairs; adding that Abigail needed help these days with the heavy bed linen and Meg was learning how to organise and rotate the big, warm cupboards.

Sitting at the desk, she nursed her coffee and took in the shabbiness that until now had entirely escaped her. Abigail said that the plum coloured velvet curtains had been there ever since she could remember and had originally hung in 'Forest End' before it was turned into a rest home during the Second World War.

Reminded of 'The Vintage', she was reminded of Marcia, not allowing Alexander's name to be mentioned, and wondered how many other secrets were left untold; she would never know now because the few remaining people who remembered Alexander had tightly sealed lips, or bad memories of him.

A knock came at the door and before she could say come in, Ella appeared; she said one word: "Curtains?"

Samantha shrugged. "Yes, help me choose a colour for the new ones; these are only fit for burning."

"You must not destroy these curtains." Ella was looking intense, and Samantha began to get the familiar shivery feeling, that came when Ella's eyes went that amber colour.

"I think time has done that." Samantha gave a nervous laugh.

Ella walked to the curtain beside Samantha's chair and ran her hands down the edge; then did the same to the one on the other side of the tall, patio doors. She appeared to be listening to an invisible voice and shaking her head. She went to the set of doors on the other side of the desk and felt them, all the time shaking her head. Then she ran back to the first curtain and bent down. Picking it up, she slid her hand into the deep hem and after a second or two, withdrew something black, holding it up for Samantha to see. It was a book and full of wonder, Samantha took it as Ella collapsed into one of the big wing chairs in front of the fire.

"Are you alright?" Samantha asked anxiously and received a quiet triumphant nod.

The leather cover was soft and well worn and the pages inside were covered with handwriting, instantly recognisable as Gerald's fluent copperplate. She started to read and on seeing her rapt expression, Ella crept out; the voice reaching out to her had been stilled.

Luke arrived home at teatime to find Samantha in the stables, sitting in the straw surrounded by dogs, reading. Sol kept giving anxious glances but Ella, looking confident advised Luke that it was something Samantha needed to get out of her system and best to leave her to it.

She eventually joined them halfway through dinner, looking thoughtful, saying nothing, having made up her mind to show the journal to Luke but no one else. She felt she owed that to Marcia for keeping her word to Grandfather.

The book was a journal of Gerald's innermost thoughts; beginning with the grief when his twin brother died so tragically, going on to tell of the comfort it brought him and his parents having Charles to live with them during the war years, and their double wedding. He wrote of his bitter disappointment when his eldest son Robert, not only failed to follow in his footsteps but married a girl pregnant with another man's child, his agony when his wife and father were killed in a road accident and his beloved mother dying a year later.

Then his writing became scrawled and practically illegible, when he discovered that Pamela had been having an affair before she died. This was followed by months of almost demented effort, to wipe out all memory of Pamela. After that, a very long gap was explained, when he commenced writing the journal again; telling of the horrific accident and being confined to a wheelchair for the rest of his life. His second marriage brought fresh hope for a time, but quickly deteriorated when he couldn't give Marcia the life she wanted. George became his rock then. He blamed himself for the bitter quarrel that eventually led to Charles and Felicity leaving Anders Folly, when his dear friend

Laurie passed away and made it possible, by leaving them his property. Anger and pride had prevented him from confiding in Charles that one and only time, but he always referred to him as his brother, and the loss of his company and support brought deep unhappiness. He became convinced that the family was cursed.

Not being able to love Alexander as much as Robert obviously played on his mind a lot, and at times he sounded almost regretful for having refused him an acting career; but much later, his disgust at discovering his son was gay, gave him the absolution he needed. His satisfaction on discovering great grandchildren, and the joy they brought to his life, brought tears to Samantha's eyes, and after Alexander's death, when Abigail revealed he was Fran's father, Samantha felt nothing but hatred for Alexander. After that, there was only one more entry before the journal came to an abrupt end. It told of his decision, even though he didn't believe in divorce, to give Marcia a chance to be happy with Bob, after the injustice his son had done to her and their daughter Tamara; the granddaughter Gerald himself only learnt about after her death. The sad events spoke of wilfulness, deceit, stubborn pride, misunderstandings and secrets, but above all, Gerald's passion for Pamela and his abiding love for his family shone through.

She stowed the journal in a safety compartment of the big desk until she could decide what to do with it and returned her attention to refurbishing the study. Knowing she would never be able to disassociate the study with her grandfather, she chose cherry red, velvet curtains and matching carpet to go with the oak panelled walls, and looking around with admiring tears, Lorna understood. "Mr Gerald would like that."

Luke arrived home each evening, delighted to see the transformations. All thought of sticking to the old fashioned, formal décor had been forgotten when Samantha saw the up-to-date materials and ideas. Things were changing rapidly and he felt able to make suggestions, without fear of offending her or the rest of the family any more. He thought, for instance, Pamela's portrait would look better on the upper landing, and instead of just Lady Anders, why not create a portrait gallery by adding Sir Gerald and his parents, Charles and Felicity; and if Samantha didn't mind, one of his own mother and father.

"There are many good local artists, who would paint from a photograph," he said watching her glow with pleasure. She also liked his idea of hanging the large, ornate mirror from the sitting room, over the dining room fireplace, where it reflected the long table.

When the main rooms and the hall were finished, they invited Fran, Adam, and the children over for Sunday lunch. Fran was very quiet and Adam watched her anxiously, but the children were in fine fettle. James especially was full of himself during lunch, boasting about getting a yacht when he was eighteen.

"Yachts cost a lot of money," Robert said, bored with James' endless obsession with Alexander.

"If Alexander can do it, so can I; and there will be a yacht in Anders Cove again; you see."

"I think not," Samantha said quietly.

James jerked round sharply, looking at her indignantly. "You can't stop me!"

"I can and will." Samantha looked him straight in the eyes. "Alexander was a thoroughly bad person and I don't intend helping you follow in his footsteps, by allowing you to anchor in the cove."

Fran and Adam slowly turned their heads to look at her, realizing from her tone that she had somehow uncovered Fran's secret.

"I shall do it anyway," James said rudely, as Adam ordered, "That will be enough James."

James glared. "Well, she isn't the boss of me and she's not going to tell me what I can and can't do!"

Abigail, sitting opposite, was reminded of Alexander; the same slate grey eyes, auburn hair and even at fourteen, the same well-built frame and flare for clothes. It was good that there were strong, young people around to keep him in check, she admitted to herself.

"You will find that in this particular instance, I can and will." Samantha calmly carried on eating.

"Just wait and see when I'm eighteen," James jeered.

"Yes, why don't we? Now eat your dinner like a good little boy and let us enjoy ours," Samantha snapped.

James opened his mouth to retort, but Luke, seeing that things were about to get out of hand, intervened.

"Why don't you try flying lessons when you are old enough instead?"

James closed his mouth and shot Luke a speculative look. "Are you offering to give me lessons?"

"If your parents agree."

"When?"

"Three or four years yet, but in the meantime you could come to the airfield on Saturday mornings and get the feel of things; maybe earn yourself some pocket money by helping with any jobs Mr Sugden can find you; you come too if you want to, Robert."

"Thanks, but I help Dad in the office. It sounds great for James, though. What do you think Dad, Mum?"

Adam and Fran looked at each other hopefully, as an unexpected solution to their biggest problem was offered.

"I only hope James appreciates your offer and doesn't make you live to regret it." Fran gave James a stern look, at the end of her tether with her troublesome son.

"I'm sure he does," Adam said quickly.

"Working with expert mechanics makes you realise pranks have dangerous results." Chas had been sitting quietly up until then. "I remember our first Saturday job was similar; we started together, didn't we, Luke?"

Luke laughed and looked at James. "We swept floors, ran errands and made tea for three months before we were allowed to even look inside a plane – and we were sixteen."

James responded with, "I don't care if I can learn to fly."

Luke and Chas gave satisfied nods and Chas told James to report next Saturday morning at eight thirty.

Samantha admired the way they had handled James and was glad to see Fran's relief at the thought of having her wayward son usefully occupied, but as they were leaving the dining room, Fran whispered seriously, "We need to talk."

"Now or shall I come to your house in the morning?"

"Better in the morning."

"Are you feeling alright? You don't seem yourself."

"Just getting old, I expect."

"Just need a holiday, more like."

They sauntered down to the cove, where the men were organising a game of rounders and sat on the sand with Jacob, while Lucy played in a rock pool. Samantha noticed Fran watching Jacob with an odd expression and wondered if she was feeling broody.

"Don't tell me you want another baby."

Fran gave a sad smile. "I'm too old."

"You are not old."

"I think I'm going through the change."

Samantha shrugged, reluctant to air her ignorance about that particular subject. "So?"

"It's the end of your childbearing years; just knowing that you can't is depressing."

"This isn't like you, Aunt Fran. I think you should see a doctor."

"That's what Adam says, but I think I'm just missing the twins now they have started school. You will come tomorrow morning, won't you? There is something really worrying me that we need to discuss."

"I will definitely be there; ten o'clock."

Samantha went against her original decision and put the journal in her handbag; confident she knew the reason for her aunt's anxiety.

She found Fran in the laundry sorting clothes into piles ready to wash and Mary was upstairs hoovering the bedrooms; in fact everything was normal for a Monday morning in the Wesley household – except for Fran's behaviour. Leaving her task unfinished, she gave Samantha an agitated look; went through to the kitchen, where she made coffee then led the way to the sitting room, closing the door firmly behind them.

Samantha broke the long moment of silence, as Fran fought to find the right words.

"I have got something to show you. It will explain how I suddenly know a great many things." Reaching into her bag she withdrew the journal.

Fran took it and the silence stretched while she started to speed read Gerald's well kept secrets. Samantha sat watching pain cross her aunt's face as she was reminded of or learnt something new.

They sat for nearly an hour, and it wasn't until she reached the end that Fran looked up sadly.

"I was sad I didn't know Tamara was my half-sister until after she was dead – and poor Tamara never knew she actually belonged to the Anders family. It could have made such a difference to the way she led her life."

"I wasn't going to show you the journal, but it's time to stop all the secrets, don't you think?"

"I certainly do, which brings me to what I want to speak to you about."

"I thought we had covered everything." Samantha gave a happy smile and spread her arms along the back of the settee. "No more secrets."

"Just one," Fran corrected.

Samantha's smile faded as Fran said, "I'm concerned about what you are going to tell Jacob about his father."

"Jacob is mine. Luke will be his father." Her head went up stubbornly.

"And when Jacob finds out the truth?"

"He won't. I've decided," Samantha said crossly.

Fran got to her feet, pacing the floor. "I thought you said no more secrets; haven't you learnt anything from Grandfather's journal? Jacob will inevitably find out and his world will fall apart." She burst into tears and Samantha finally realizing what was troubling her, jumped up and flung her arms around her. "I'm sorry Aunt Fran. I promise to tell him when the time is right."

"*No more secrets,*" Fran agonized and slipped to the floor in a dead faint.

Samantha phoned for an ambulance then called frantically to Mary. Less than an hour later, looking happy but sheepish, Fran was discharged by a smiling nurse. On the way home in Samantha's car, she announced she wasn't going through the change; she was pregnant. Samantha had telephoned Adam as they were leaving the hospital and he was waiting for them when they arrived home. He smiled with relief when Fran said she was only pregnant; he had been seriously worried by her depression; and this was without doubt the one thing that would put her world to rights.

Samantha felt their need to be alone and left. She went straight to the study when she got home. The new red curtains and carpet created a warm welcome and Grandfathers' desk with her own blue chair behind it gave comfort beyond words. She sat thinking about Fran's plea for no more secrets, before reaching for her handbag and taking the journal out. Steepling her fingers she contemplated the black leather book then started to write in the remaining few pages, realising that her grandfather had actually been trying to clear his mind by writing down things he wanted to forget. She filled four, closely written pages of painful memories. The last page she left untouched for when she knew for certain who Jacob's father actually was; seeing his brown eyes and lopsided grin had raised a doubt in her mind and one day she would confirm it for Jacob's sake. After that, perhaps there would be no more secrets at Anders Folly. Luke said she should stop worrying about past generations because they were going to create a new beginning for Anders Folly. She laid her pen down and leant back with a peaceful smile.

On the wide stone mantelpiece the ormolu clock ticked sonorously, giving almost hypnotic reassurance of continuity, with its timeless antiquity; and above it where the Stubbs painting had hung, Luke had placed the water colour of her riding Nocturn, with Tamar, Tavy and Mischief running along the waters' edge beside her.

Still daydreaming she pictured the Wedgwood blue bedroom she was planning for them. The blissful nights she spent in Luke's arms had banished her fears and phobias. He had stopped her from living in Pamela's shadow; at last, she was her own person.

She rose slowly and picked up the journal, then going to the curtain behind her chair, she slid the black book deep into the hem.

The end.

ANDERS FOLLY

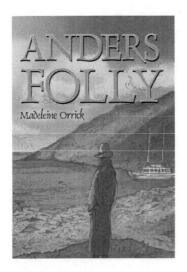

Part one in a trilogy of the Anders family.

The saga begins in 1992, when having disowned his eldest son, Robert, many years ago, Gerald is desperately unhappy about leaving his beloved home to his middle-aged, pleasure-seeking son Alexander. He has specifically forbidden his wife's and eldest son's names to be mentioned and inexplicably had his wife's portrait removed from its place over the fireplace.

Fran is left alone in London with his three-year-old twins, when her brother's plane goes missing, until a stranger turns up on her doorstep and takes them all to Anders Folly, where another shocking revelation awaits her.

We then go back in time to 1939 when Marie and David Anders, their son Gerald and his friend Charles are living in Southampton. Gerald and Charles get married to Pamela and Felicity, and to escape the aftermath when the war ends, they all move to Anders Folly, the ancestral home that has been in the Anders family for generations. They breathe new life into the rambling, stone built house, which because of its strategic position beside the sea was commandeered by the Ministry of Defence for RAF Headquarters. It is very much the worse for wear, although nothing compared to the blitzed cities they left behind them.

Life is good; halcyon days follow and serendipity is a word Felicity often uses to account for their good fortune over the next two decades. Felicity gives birth to Sophie, and Pamela has two sons, Robert and Alexander. Alexander, the youngest, is trouble from the day he is born.

Charles joins Lawrence Harcott, in his law firm and Uncle Laurie, as he is fondly called, becomes a great friend to the family and a grandfather figure to the children. He has great bearing on all of their lives

When Gerald contracts tuberculosis Pamela accompanies him to a London clinic. There she meets William Jessop, the owner of the clinic; unbeknown to Gerald, Bill shows her around London and she realizes how much she is missing, tucked away in Cornwall.

Robert unwillingly joins the family business, but at nineteen, says he is going to marry Celine, who is pregnant with another man's baby. Gerald has set his heart on Robert following in his footsteps and won't hear of it, but Robert is adamant and Gerald disowns him. Pamela tries to intervene but it ends in disaster when she and David Anders are killed in a car crash.

Gerald has a sailing accident, which leaves him in a wheelchair for the rest of his life, certain that the family is cursed. His salvation comes when Marcia arrives to nurse him. In spite of him being an invalid and thirty years her senior, they get married. Marcia resents Gerald's close relationship with Charles and Felicity and plans to drive them out; she then tells Gerald about her seven-year-old daughter Tamara, who is at boarding school.

Laurie comes to Charles and Felicity's rescue by leaving them his house and business and the unthinkable happens. Gerald and the friend he has always called brother, go their separate ways. Only when he needs help to find his eldest son does Gerald ask Charles for help, and they are reunited.

Alexander finally gets his just deserts for his treachery and two great grandchildren bring new hope to Gerald's visions for the future of Anders Folly.

ANDERS HERITAGE

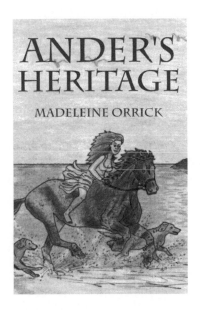

Part two in the trilogy of the Anders family

Anders Heritage continues the saga of the Anders family. Gerald is content that the future of his beloved home is safe and he is enjoying having his grandson and two great-grandchildren dependant on him. He likes to keep them close and provide for their every need.

It would seem like a perfect existence and Gerald is confident that they want for nothing, but should he be?

Samantha is now fourteen and beginning to feel the effects of the stifling life.

Consequently, when a young man, Dean Masters, shows an interest in her she is flattered and slips away to be with him, unaware of his manipulative character and the humiliating consequences to follow when he doesn't get what he wants. Unwittingly she puts the orderly respectable life of the Anders family in jeopardy and creates a long lasting, emotional problem for herself.

Traumatised and unable to name the person who has assaulted her, suspicion falls on others.

To avoid publicity Samantha and Timothy are removed from school and tutored privately at home, but life becomes even more confined and Samantha turns to horses and dogs for company as doubts to her truthfulness are voiced.

At the same time, Sophie comes home from America and unaccountably disappears, leaving her parents, Charles and Felicity, stressed and unaware of her mission to search for her past. A chance encounter with a stranger brings unexpected and extraordinary changes for them, as guided by a hand from the past, Ella leads them along a mystical path, where intriguing questions are answered; bringing them self-belief and irrevocable changes, when they meet a one hundred-year-old woman, living in a house haunted by evil memories.

Dean Masters is eventually apprehended, with the help of Mischief the white German Shepherd, but not before he brings the Anders family name into disrepute and destroys the family's peace of mind and privacy.

If the family aren't safe in the confines of private beaches and an estate of a hundred acres, where can they be? Fran asks Adam, fearful for their own fast growing family.

Samantha comes to terms with some of her demons even though it will be another six years before she is completely set free – but that is another story in the lives of the Anders family.